‘‘I’ve …
murmured, his voice husky.

Alexa’s lips parted. ‘‘And I you.’’

‘‘Would you care to make a wager?’’

Alexa allowed her eyes a bold raking of his splendid form, as if she were assessing him. ‘‘And what would I win, were I to place my confidence in a novice?’’

One dark brow lifted wickedly as he tested the tip of the machete with his finger. ‘‘Me.’’

‘‘To do with as I wish this night?’’

The flames leapt in his eyes as they moved with brazen intent over her. ‘‘Anything you wish, my lady.’’

‘‘And if I lose?’’

His teeth flashed in a smile that set Alexa’s blood churning and he reached out to capture a curl nestled upon her breast. ‘‘If you lose, beauty, you will be mine, to do with as *I* please until dawn. And it will be a very long night, I promise you . . . !’’

Dear Reader,

April brings us another great batch of titles!

Readers of contemporary romance will surely recognize Judith McWilliams. In her first historical, *Suspicion*, she pens a tale of intrigue and danger in which young Lucy Langford must team up with Colonel Robert Standen in order to find a would-be killer.

Popular historical author Elizabeth Lane brings us *MacKenna's Promise.* Meg MacKenna travels to East Africa to get a divorce from her estranged husband, Cameron. But when tragedy strikes, they must band together to save their family and their love.

When ruthless businessman Oliver Keane inherits part of a Barbados plantation, he learns how to love from Alexa Fairfield—a woman he's been raised to despise. *Island Star* is by Kit Gardner, one of the 1992 March Madness authors.

In *The River Sprite* by Kate Kingsley, Serena Caswell is determined to take over as pilot of her father's steamboat. But handsome riverboat gambler—and half owner of the boat—Nathan Trent has other plans.

We hope you enjoy these titles. Next month look for four brand-new releases from your favorite Harlequin Historical authors!

Sincerely,

Tracy Farrell
Senior Editor

KIT GARDNER

Island Star

Harlequin Books

TORONTO • NEW YORK • LONDON
AMSTERDAM • PARIS • SYDNEY • HAMBURG
STOCKHOLM • ATHENS • TOKYO • MILAN
MADRID • WARSAW • BUDAPEST • AUCKLAND

ISBN 0-373-28817-4

ISLAND STAR

This edition published by arrangement with Harlequin Enterprises B. V.

Printed in U.S.A.

Books by Kit Gardner

Harlequin Historicals

Arabesque #117
The Dream #138
The Stolen Heart #160
The Gilded Lion #193
Island Star #217

KIT GARDNER

is a former C.P.A. who lives outside Chicago with her husband and two young sons. When her busy schedule allows, she enjoys skiing, golf, travel and reading anything from romance to the latest in sensationalistic thrillers.

Every writer needs someone in their life who
fosters in them the sheer delight of storytelling.
Thanks, Dad, for being such a good listener.

Chapter One

Chicago, May 1890

"So the bastard finally had the good sense to die."

His words echoed stark and bleak against the wall of windows, as devoid of warmth as the slate gray of murky dusk beyond those panes. Those hollow tones rose over the clatter of the rail yard some ten stories below, even above the incessant *tap-tap-tap* of his solid gold quill upon the exquisitely turned slope of the chair's arm.

Tap-tap-tap.

Fingers flexed, he crushed the telegram with far more force than he would ever have wished to display, prompting a vise-like twisting deep in his abdomen. To force his thoughts elsewhere, anywhere but upon the contents of that telegram, he shifted his gaze to Lake Michigan looming somewhere out there through the gray muck...an unimpeded view from this vantage, on a clear day, of course. He'd paid a fortune for it, after all.

Tap-tap-tap.

"Fog," he snarled to no one in particular, for the panes reflected but one broad-shouldered frame amidst all the honey-smooth splendor of his office. No doubt beside that fog-enshrouded pier sat a veritable legion of his ships, stern to bow in a monotonous row, their bellies full of iron ore, grain and copper, all bound for other ports, but idle since the fog lumbered in two days past. The breath hissed between his teeth when through the mist he spied one midnight blue sail emblazoned with the White Star Line insignia. All a gross testament to the fortune certain to be lost due to a mere fluke of Mother Nature.

Tap-tap-tap. Force his thoughts elsewhere....

Would that he could turn a blind eye to the fog, as did many of his fellow merchantmen whose fleets plied the Great Lakes, men who judged their ship captains solely on maintaining tonnage statistics, no matter the damned weather. Efficiency-minded businessmen whose offices were rarely visited by fog. To them, the weather was an occasional inconvenience, something the captains of those vessels should be able to do something about, by God. Haze, they typically called it, a term which when inscribed in a captain's log legally allowed a vessel to steam full ahead into impenetrable murk, a perilous pursuit at best and one which he deemed far too great a risk. Charging stem on into another vessel virtually guaranteed loss of an entire cargo and crew, lawsuits...

Tap-tap-tap.

No, his ships sat, dutifully shackled to shore, awaiting his command, which he steadfastly refused to grant until the fog lifted. The figures clicked in his mind as monotonously as did his quill against polished wood, as did the rail cars below. Overhead, idle crew, lost profit...

The telegram suddenly seemed to burn into his palm, and his stomach constricted beneath the finely tailored, black worsted wool vest, beneath the most precisely starched, smoothly combed white cotton shirt money could buy. The contemptuous sneer returned, no matter that he willed it and the myriad emotions roused by that telegram from his mind, from his soul. No matter that with every tick of his gold pocket watch his shipping empire wallowed in fog upon an idle pier. No matter that he hadn't given thought to anything but his business empire, to the attainment of power, to the proving of his worth from the moment he'd left Barbados over fifteen years prior...vowing never to return.

"A damned inconvenient time to die," he growled at the crumpled telegram before tossing it upon his desk, where it found rest next to a mound of wheat futures. He spun from the windows and snatched the wheat futures in hand. His eye moved with practiced skill over the figures...then strayed, momentarily, before swiftly sweeping back to anticipated profits . . . then again, straying to the telegram.

He arched a disdainful brow and gave momentary vent to all that checked emotion. "Why must your death concern me after all this time? Why, now, must I be subjected to all that became of you, to all that you had done, and mostly, to all that you would never accomplish?" He snorted and shook his head. "And why the hell am I talking to myself?"

The office door burst open as if beneath the force of a cataclysmic wind, a shrill female voice interrupting his thoughts. "Oliver, *dear heavens,* what on earth is the matter with you? Summoning poor Daphne, *here,* to your place of toil, and so very late in the day! Dear God in heaven, *cease* your work for one blessed moment, if you possibly can, and just *look* at your poor fiancé!"

He regarded the two women for a moment. How the very air compressed and congealed beneath the presence of overly fluffed and feathered females. How their amply perfumed and powdered mien made a man suddenly yearn to leave their presence and breathe deeply of fresh air as if it were his very last gulp. Resisting just such an urge, Oliver Keane dutifully rose from his desk and moved toward the pair, wondering idly whose dainty, gloved hand propriety dictated he gently clasp first. His gaze shifted between the two women, one overblown middle-aged elegance and fanfare, the other all plump, soft white curves and youthful dimples somewhere beneath a feathered pink monstrosity women dared call a hat. Business instinct prevailed and he clasped both extended hands at once, noting immediately that the softer of the two, his fiancés, trembled like a fragile bird. His grip upon it tightened.

"Mother, Miss MacAdoo." He returned his mother's trussed up nod and released her hand. His attention, however, as well as his mouth, lingered just a hint overlong upon the quivering fingers still within his grasp. His gaze drifted upward, over a stiff, high-necked dress of the palest pink satin imaginable, a dress so snugly encasing those ample curves he had to wonder if perhaps her blush had more to do with a torturously cinched corset than with his mild attempt at flirtation. Like any well-tutored debutante, Daphne MacAdoo allowed her thick lashes to sweep downward the moment their eyes met, presenting him with the rounded curve of her cheek, exquisitely framed by her upswept chestnut locks. His gaze locked upon her mouth, so tiny, blooming like the reddest of cherries amidst a sea of the whitest cream. Like a confection she was, all but oozing sugar. A cream puff. His for the taking.

Something carnal stirred suddenly within him, like a roused ember...so very rare, that emotion, especially with Daphne...prompting him to fix his gaze upon her bosom. Her gloved fingers wavered beneath his mouth, as if she direly yearned to snatch them free, as if she direly yearned as well to flee from *him*.... One glance at those wide brown eyes, at the softly parted mouth, at the suddenly heaving bosom made him offer a gallant smile before he relinquished her hand. Her fingers fluttered at her neck and she murmured something that brought the color higher into her cheeks and prompted the requisite scathing look from his mother. He merely raised innocent brows before hooding his gaze upon sweet Daphne.

Odd, but amidst all Daphne's comely twittering and fussing he still couldn't help but contemplate the impending union...of his White Star Line with Theodore MacAdoo's International Shipping Line, of course. MacAdoo's company enjoyed a virtual stranglehold upon the transatlantic shipping lanes, and Theodore MacAdoo was a man intent upon controlling Great Lakes traffic, as well. For years, Oliver had relentlessly pursued just such a merger from every angle, certain that such a union of shipping greats would all but guarantee worldwide success for his White Star Line. Never once did he consider such a proposition unattainable. After all, Oliver Keane was supremely used to getting whatever he wanted. Yet, never once did he envision that his mother, Eleanor Keane, awash in her Chicago high-society pomp and circumstance, would manage to help him in his plan.

Consumed with the idea of snatching the reigning debutante of the year into her fold, Eleanor had dangled Theodore MacAdoo's daughter Daphne before her son, only to gasp with glee when Oliver had snatched at the opportunity. What man wouldn't? He'd long since abandoned thoughts of a wife and children as fitting only for men who weren't married to their life's pursuit, men who could devote some measure of themselves to such a precarious proposition. Certainly not fitting for him... *unless,* of course, the arrangement happened to be one that brought tremendous opportunity in the form of a shipping monopoly, and duty-bound him to a sweet, retiring little virgin like Daphne. No matter that she all but trembled upon the brink of womanhood at a mere sixteen years of age, eager to find her place beside the Potter Palmers and the Marshall Fields within the social elite, even more eager to marry *well.*

Almost as eager as Theodore MacAdoo was to marry her off. Thus, Oliver's whirlwind courtship of Daphne and their imminent marriage served to seal the business pact. Tidy. Efficient.

What he had to tell them would surely send both into a swoon. Despite his mother's carefully tended facade of genteel elegance, he was quite certain she hadn't an inkling of the contents of that telegram. He could only guess at Theodore MacAdoo's response, and thus had given much thought to precisely how he would allay the man's blustering. Oliver considered himself a risk taker, to be sure, but he was no fool. No matter what transpired as a result of the telegram, he felt quite certain that if MacAdoo's daughter kept smiling her dimpled little smiles, the merger, as well as the wedding, would go forth... one way or another.

"Would you care to sit?" Oliver offered, drawing forth a cushy leather chair for Daphne.

Oh, but the hours he could envision waiting for this creature to determine the entirely proper thing to do. Having to date endured a total of four chaperoned meetings with her, Oliver could precisely anticipate her every move when posed with a question. The slight chewing at her lip. The covert slanting of her eyes at Eleanor beneath her hat brim. The almost imperceptible wavering of her fingertips upon her reticule.

He shifted his weight and forced a patient smile, which dissolved into a lengthy dispelling of his breath when Daphne murmured something, then executed a magnificent glide into the proffered chair. On impulse, he lingered behind her chair, leaning closer to her until he could just spy the curve of her dimpled chin beneath her hat. A fraction closer and she swayed ever so slightly away from him, as she was wont to do whenever he happened within a good two-foot radius of her. A keen eye could detect the stiffening of her spine, could imagine the crawling of her skin beneath all that satin, as if his very presence repulsed her.

"Very well, Oliver," Eleanor said, casting him an appropriately agitated look. She perched upon the very edge of her chair, looking as if she all but itched to fiddle with the wilted feather dangling from her hat. "What is it that necessitated such a visit? Dear heavens, asking dear Daphne to *endure* this foul weather was preposterous enough, let alone expecting her to navigate that lifting contraption."

"We call it an elevator," Oliver informed her, easing his bulk into his chair. With some annoyance he found his fingers wrapped about the crumpled telegram.

Eleanor waved a dismissing hand. "Call it what you will, but the poor thing shouldn't even be *out* much less *seen* a scant four days before your wedding! And in the *rain?* Women have their hair to think about, Oliver, and milky complexions, and rheumatism and incipient consumption—"

"Miss MacAdoo seems to be faring remarkably well." Oliver settled back in his chair, the better to peruse the furiously blushing Miss MacAdoo from beneath shadowed brows. Those doe eyes had yet to meet his, focused as they were somewhere upon the thick Persian carpet beneath her dainty feet. He was given to wondering what sort of heinous tales her society sisters had whispered into her delicate little ear regarding her future husband to warrant such an obvious fear of him. Or perhaps repression had found too comfortable a home with the girl, a circumstance many a man would find very much to his liking. Oliver, however, found himself contemplating a lifetime spent with such a creature stirring nothing within him but a decided coolness. Bedding the girl could prove his most arduous task to date.

Tempering his scowl, he contemplated the telegram balled in his fist and lifted his gaze to his mother. She wore her lofty society-hostess station like the most luxurious of fur capes, visibly, ostentatiously, without reserve and with a studied precision as to render it nearly an art form. Some said it was all in the breeding. Oliver knew better. With his mother, it had always been the desperate, hell-bent *want* of status from the moment she could breathe. Perhaps because she had been born the ninth of ten children to a Chicago rail worker. Perhaps because she knew well her path in life had not been an easy one. The social position she craved he had provided for her in the form of a monthly allowance since that fateful day fifteen years prior when it had become his responsibility to do so. He also knew she would do anything to protect herself now that she'd attained that status, even against the inevitable dredging up of the past.

"I received a telegram earlier this afternoon," he began. "That's why I summoned you so hastily." He paused. "It's from Bridgetown."

The blood drained from Eleanor's face and her fingers gripped her parasol as if to wrench the very life from it. "From Barbados?" she said sharply, her upper lip twitching slightly. "Not from Bellefontaine?"

He nodded. "My father died not two days past." Odd how saying it stoked all that suppressed anger like a torch to tinder such that the burn of bile rose menacingly to his throat.

"And why should that concern any of us, especially Daphne and me?" Eleanor's pointy chin resumed its regal perch, her words their clipped, precise articulation, all emotion swiftly concealed beneath that powdered veneer.

"I've been requested by the British governor of Barbados to attend the reading of the will," Oliver replied, his gaze shifting momentarily to Daphne, whose mouth had formed a tiny, silent "Oh." "I leave not two hours hence for Boston to secure passage."

Eleanor visibly shook upon her perch. "You cannot. The wedding—"

"Postpone it," Oliver returned smoothly. Eleanor paled and Daphne made a gurgling noise one could imagine sounded something akin to a strangling baby bunny.

"Postpone it?" Eleanor croaked.

"Indefinitely."

Daphne looked as if she'd just received a death sentence.

"Indefinitely?" Eleanor's parasol met with the floor in a great *thump.* "The *idea!* A preposterous notion! An unmitigated disaster, I tell you! Why, whatever shall we do about the nightingales we hired to sing from the very trees? And what of the liqueurs we had shipped directly from France . . . those expensive ones bottled before the French Revolution? Have you considered the true nature of this calamity, Oliver?"

Oliver tempered his disbelief. "Postpone it."

Eleanor blinked at him, then snapped her mouth shut. "Then you must wed this very afternoon, *before* your departure."

Daphne had but a moment to attempt to shake her head, or perhaps it was just Oliver's imagination that she even tried, so surprised was he by his mother's response. Never had he expected one so completely attuned to the social graces regarding this sort of thing to even suggest a hasty marriage.

"No." Oliver shook his head with finality and indicated a nearly apoplectic Daphne. "Miss MacAdoo obviously needs more time to accustom herself to the notion."

Eleanor seemed curiously stricken, her gaze flickering heatedly over Daphne as if to rouse some sense in the girl. "But—no—dear God, child, *think.* The talk shall be horrid. Why, imagine the papers . . . the society columns! Debutante of the year abandoned at the altar."

Oliver leaned back in his chair. "Simply postpone it for a few months."

"Months?" Eleanor shrieked, rising in a rustle of starched taffeta. "Oliver, you've chosen a grossly inappropriate moment to begin shirking your responsibilities."

Oliver issued a caustic grunt, wondering as he did so if perhaps he should reach a comforting hand to his distressed fiancé. "This was hardly my doing. I would like nothing more than to wed Miss MacAdoo this Saturday, but I've a feeling the governor of Barbados would find some disfavor with that."

"Bother the governor!" Eleanor railed, casting a swift glance toward a swooning Daphne and rushing to pat the girl's limp hand. "Dear heavens, look what you've done to the poor child, Oliver. She'll never recover from such a blow. The gossip will be nothing short of *heinous.*"

"For a time, perhaps," he replied. "Until I return, and I've every intention of doing so as soon as possible. The Association of Great Lakes Merchants convenes in less than two months and I must be there to charter my cargoes and make tonnage commitments for the coming year."

"How very gallant of you, Oliver, to think of tonnage commitments at a time like this." Eleanor pursed her lips and commenced with a frantic waving of her gloved hands over Daphne's prostrate form. "Oh, good heavens, the poor child has swooned dead away. Summon someone...for God's sake, *do* something!"

Swiftly navigating his way around his desk, Oliver pressed his fingers to Daphne's throat, and scowled as a fleeting disquiet swept over him when his fingertips met with her cool, translucent skin. "She'll recover momentarily. Perhaps her stays have been laced a notch too tight."

Eleanor's lips compressed and she swung upon him. "Spoken just like a man. Dear God, Oliver, why would the governor himself summon you to that godforsaken, rat-infested hovel of a plantation? Surely Gabriel didn't *bequeath* something to you after all these years?"

"If he was fool enough to do so, I intend to rid myself of it as expeditiously as possible." His memory filled with the letters he had returned to his father, letters still unopened, year upon year. His voice thickened. "I want nothing from him."

"Then why go, dear God? Send someone in your stead. You've at least two score lawyers under your employ to conduct your business. Send one of them."

Oliver shook his head. "I've inquired into that already. Barbadian law is quite specific regarding these matters. I have to go."

"The bastard." The words hissed through the air like venom dripping from Eleanor's tongue, catching Oliver momentarily off guard. "The cheating, lying bastard. Forsaking *me,* his very wife, *you,* his only son. Squandering an entire fortune... and for what?" Her lips spread thin over bared teeth, her dark eyes suddenly aglitter with something savage, her fury as if unleashed for the very first time. "That English whore killed him," she raged. "Did the telegram say anything about the whore?"

Oliver shook his head, his eyes narrowing upon his mother. Where had refinement and elegance flown in the face of a woman scorned? Or perhaps Eleanor's memories, even those fifteen years old, haunted her far more than Oliver ever would allow his own. A fleeting vision of a flaxen-haired woman and a young blond child all in white suddenly swept through his mind and was as suddenly gone. "He was an intolerably weak man," he said, half to himself.

"First she lured him away from me and possessed him with her witchcraft, then she killed him." Eleanor shook her head with vehemence. "But I didn't surrender, did I? I never allowed him to divorce me, did I? After fifteen years, I won, *didn't I?*"

"It was never a game."

"Ah, but it is, Oliver . . . it always is." A feral gleam shone in her eyes. "And I intend to prove myself the victor." She lifted her chin, drawing herself to her full height as if to assure herself of who she was, of the lofty perch she'd scratched and clawed her way to occupying. "I'm going with you to Barbados."

Oliver clenched his teeth. "That wouldn't be wise."

"And why not? I was the man's wife until the day he died. Certainly I've a place there. Perhaps I, too, shall inherit something entirely worthless."

Oliver rubbed the ache mounting between his eyebrows. His gaze found the windows, seeking his ships somewhere in that fog. This journey would prove twice as burdensome with a vengeful woman in tow. "You've nothing to gain by coming along," he ventured, knowing full well there was no stopping her now. She was like a locomotive steaming out of control.

Her touch upon his arm was anything but soothing, for the menace dripping from her tongue was palpable. "We've our pride to recoup, Oliver. Remember that."

"You're wrong, Mother." Something in his expression caused her to shrink back a pace from him. "Pride was the one thing *I* never lost. *You* would do well to remember that."

Chapter Two

Bridgetown, Barbados
June 1890

There was really no sense in delaying the inevitable a moment longer. Absolutely *no* sense in lingering simply for the sake of avoiding something unpleasant. No sense in pretending to ignore it in the hopes that it would conveniently go away... perhaps in yet another laudanum-induced haze. No matter the heartache certain to be roused, the tears to be shed, the grief to be endured. It simply wasn't her nature to fear confrontation.

At first she thought the droplet came from the heavens. But then another followed and still the sun dappled upon the freshwater pond, heating her bare shoulders, and the sky loomed cloudless and brilliant above her. Only then, when she tilted her face upward and closed her eyes did the tears spill slowly to her cheeks instead of into the pond. Only then did she realize she'd been weeping... again.

A great lump lodged itself in her throat, refusing to be swallowed. Her breath released in a whispered groan only to be snatched back when she splashed her heated cheeks with cool water, again and again, before turning and wading for shore before the tears could return.

She paused but a moment upon the grassy bank, once more lifting her face skyward, allowing her fingers to thread mindlessly through the tangle of her hair.

"You're dallying again," she said after a moment, the sound of her voice somewhat startling in so enchanted and deserted a spot. Deserted enough for a woman to dally entirely nude upon the shores of this pond without reservation.

Breathing deeply of the heady scents of frangipani, hyacinth and gardenia hanging heavy in the thick air, she willed a peace to her soul. She cast the sun a sideways glance, quickly assessing its position. At this very moment, they were waiting for her, she was certain, and Bellefontaine was still a good walk from here along that single dirt road tamped smooth by bare feet . . . a path that led directly past her own cottage. At this time of day, her mother would have been serving afternoon tea in the front parlor. The white lace curtains would waft in the fragrant breeze, and Gabriel Keane's voice would rumble pleasantly, all afternoon and oftentimes late into the evenings. A peaceful time it had once been.

She thrust the thought aside and cast a clouding glance about for her clothes. On especially hot days such as this, she found native dress far more suitable than whalebone corsets and the starched linen day dresses filling her mother's closet. White dresses they were, to the very last, not a one bearing a hint of color. All still hung neatly in a mahogany armoire, precisely where Lily had left them on her last fateful night...the night she had wandered into the jungle and never returned.

The lump in her throat welled up again and she snatched blindly at the tumbled pile left carelessly upon the sand. Finely woven white batiste spilled over her head, brushed her bare breasts, and her belly fluttered slightly when her nipples tightened against the cotton. She'd grown rather heedless of this reaction over time, as she had to the feel of tropical breezes caressing her semibared shoulders, and to those drifting over her exposed ankles and up her bare legs whenever she walked. With a practiced skill, she knotted her narrow linen skirt tightly at her waist and adjusted her neckline just at her shoulders, her fingers lingering upon the tie between her breasts, her thoughts drifting to a time of lazy afternoon teas.

Absently she plucked a white gardenia from its bush and tucked it into the banded brim of her straw hat. She'd nearly reached Bellefontaine's wrought-iron gates when she realized she'd forgotten her kid slippers upon the shores of the pond.

The circular cobblestone driveway was cool beneath her bare feet as she approached the house nestled amongst towering cabbage trees, which shaded it from the tropical sun. Only once, before her mother had henceforth forbidden it, had she visited Gabriel Keane's Bellefontaine, and that had been some fifteen years prior. She had been but a girl of six, a mere child whose one lasting impression had been the sheer grandeur of the place, and of course the heady scent of beeswax, which permeated the luxurious furnishings. Amongst it all, Gabriel Keane had loomed, a towering, black-haired giant of a man . . . at first imposing, yet infinitely gentle, warmhearted, ever so kind, ever so patient, with such wonderful eyes. Smiling eyes, her mother had called them, her tone wistful in its breathiness, haunting.

She paused directly before the enormous double portal, her eyes straying over the weed-choked profusion of hibiscus and bougainvillea that climbed the mansion's stucco walls. A roofed open gallery flanked the second story on all sides. A macaw's crow broke the silence, a sultry breeze stirred her hair, and her mind filled with the still-vivid memory of Gabriel Keane poised upon that open loggia directly above her, his chiseled features devoid of expression as he watched their carriage roll slowly down the curved cobblestone driveway, never to return.

"Miss Alexandra Fairfield, I presume?"

Reality washed over her and she blinked at the gentleman poised in the open doorway. He was a servant, judging by his dress, but certainly not his skin, for nearly all plantation workers were black. Gabriel Keane, however, had imported an English servant, Cyril, appropriately pale, pinched, serious, a man who had been in Gabriel's employ for more than twenty years. His colorless brows rose over a look that was at once bored yet brutally assessing, a look that made her lift her chin as she'd so often observed her mother do when faced with some nasty tidbit of gossip.

She returned his stare from beneath the wide brim of her hat and squared her shoulders. "Indeed, 'tis I," she replied in a voice still hoarse with unspent emotion.

Cyril receded into the shadows of the house and swept a white-gloved hand before him, his tone and manner unmistakably admonishing her late arrival. "You're awaited rather anxiously in the parlor. If you would kindly follow me."

Kindly, so overemphasized she knew at once he'd judged her so irresponsible a chit that her simply following in his wake would be a feat accomplished. As they passed through the dark, cool foyer into a wide hall, she stared at the precisely combed strands of colorless hair along the back of Cyril's head and wondered why a man like Gabriel Keane would employ a servant so obviously attuned to the rumors, a man eager to pass the harshest of judgments upon her, so very unlike his employer. Fifteen years had passed since she'd last seen Cyril, but she couldn't quite place his stiffness of movement; it was due to age, she supposed, or a bad back, perhaps. Or a nagging rheumatism.

He paused before an imposing set of closed double doors, rapped twice upon the polished wood, then, without the benefit of a response, pushed the doors wide. Perhaps she should have hesitated a moment, as her mother might have done, before entering the room. She was flagrantly late, after all, inappropriately dressed and shoeless, an indiscretion for which her mother would have taken her to task forthwith.

She'd been all but banned from the house for fifteen years. Yet something prompted her to breeze past that prunish Cyril with head held high, straight into the middle of a room so elegantly furnished, her bare feet seemed to sink entirely into the carpet. Three steps, four, and she paused as the very air seemed to condense around her, as if in warning, and then a familiar voice and face captured her attention.

"I say, Alexa!" From behind an enormous desk, directly before a wall of windows, Stuart Jeffcoat all but leaped from his chair and momentarily did battle with his sheathed sword as he attempted to scurry around the desk. His grin was boyish and unrestrained beneath a much-tamed sweep of reddish gold hair as he encased her bare hands in his white gloves. "How positively enchanting to see you again so soon. You're looking well."

For the briefest moment, Alexa detected the slightest dip of his gaze as it rested upon her, as if his rank and station as general commander of the British forces occupying Barbados allowed him nothing more by way of an assessment. His chest visibly expanded within his snug red, white-and-gold uniform, perhaps for want of air, the brass buttons gleaming as if polished with the utmost care. His grip upon her fingers tightened, even as his voice dropped to nearly a whisper. "I say, I've longed to see you again under...er...well, under better circumstances, of course. But the governor himself bade us officers to see to these nasty tasks. And in this case, the circumstances couldn't be nastier. Perhaps after the reading of the will, I could, you know, escort you home...all very proper, of course."

"Enough." Like a finely honed blade, a deeply masculine voice sliced through the air, banishing Stuart's next words and Alexa's smile with deadly precision. For some reason, Alexa's breathing quickened. She glanced curiously about in search of the cause for such disquiet. She found him immediately...so immediately that she had to wonder how she'd managed *not* to spy him upon entering.

He stood before the unlit hearth, poised as if preparing to strike, cloaked in an air of supreme agitation. That, she noticed first, and his stature, immense and forebodingly black in formal trousers and topcoat, his high white collar stark and unforgiving of tropical heat. Eyes the color of a turbulent ocean assailed her, and in an instant, swept her from head to toe and back again, never once registering anything but that profound annoyance, as if he had far more pressing matters to attend to. As if he had stood before that hearth for a good part of the afternoon, tapping his gold fountain pen upon the mantel, waiting...for her. Something rebellious roused deep within her and she narrowed her own gaze upon *him,* as if *she* found something supremely irritating about the squareness of his jaw or the harsh planes of his beard-roughened cheeks, the unresisting slash of dark eyebrows, the predatory hook to his nose, or the untamed mane of blue-black hair worn so long in back it nearly rested upon his massive shoulders.

Her breath caught deep in her lungs, forcing a brief gasp from her lips. This man, this annoyed, aloof, entirely unlikable man was Gabriel Keane...the facial structure, the stature, the arrogantly regal bearing all Gabriel, yet a harsh, cynical, much younger version of Gabriel. Even the manner in which he dismissed Stuart Jeffcoat with one flicker of his eyes brought a renewed ache to her soul, so much did this man stoke memories of Gabriel Keane. That ache tempered beneath a growing suspicion. No... it couldn't be... not after all this time... not the son... What was his name? Oh, yes, Oliver.

"On with it, Jeffcoat." Those cobalt eyes swept over Alexa once again, his generous mouth twisting sardonically. "I haven't the time nor the inclination for your romancing of your peasant wench, here. Save it for the proper time and place. I've a ship to catch for Boston."

"I say, Keane!" Stuart sputtered, his sword clanking against his black boots as he swiveled about, red-faced with indignation. "I will have you know I harbor only the most honorable of intentions toward this young woman, who is by no means a mere peasant. Indeed, she was summoned here by the governor himself for the reading of your father's will. Why, Miss Fairfield—"

It was then, not a moment after her name rang clearly through the room, that Alexa became acutely aware of yet another presence in the room. From somewhere at her back, nestled in a darkened corner, came a furious rustling of taffeta skirts accompanied by a shrill, "*Fairfield?* In *this* house? *Out!* Out, I say! Remove the *tramp* at once!"

Perhaps a lifetime of enduring many a covert glance that screamed with innuendo prompted but a mere stiffening of Alexa's spine in response, an almost imperceptible lifting of her chin, the purposeful ignoring of the woman screeching at her back. Then again, perhaps she would have responded in an altogether different, more obvious manner had she not been held captive by the sudden ferocity of Oliver Keane's stare.

An accusatory stare it was, so coldly assessing a shiver chased through her when his eyes drifted almost insolently over her, his lids lowered. By God, she hated him in that moment for reasons having nothing to do with who they were, but for the sudden stirring deep in her belly, the heat coiling between her thighs, the swelling and tightening of her nipples against cotton... drawing his gaze.

She returned his stare, wondering if he realized she had as many reasons to despise him as he had to scorn her. And then he moved so quickly, so unexpectedly, yet she remained as if frozen in a block of ice, with nerves taut, her every fiber tingling for some unexplainable reason . . . as if in anticipation.

Agile as a cat, three smooth strides, and he was upon her, one warm hand sliding in a most familiar manner over her belly, snaking about her waist and shoving her none too gently behind him. Her breasts rubbed against the fine wool of his coat, against a back that seemed to emanate heat, like that of the hand still lingering upon the curve where her waist met her hip. She was vaguely aware of the clanking of Stuart's sword behind her, but then the room reverberated with an anguished female cry when Oliver Keane's fingers wrapped about a closed parasol, stilling its flight midair.

"Out of my way, damn you, Oliver! Let me at her, tramp's daughter!" the woman railed, her taffeta skirts impeding thrashing legs, her arm wavering above her head to better aim her parasol this time. Broad shoulders blocked all of Alexa's view of the woman save for the wild bob of her feathered hat, but she grew all too aware that the woman struggled with all her might when Oliver muttered an oath and the parasol clattered to the floor.

"You're embarrassing yourself," Oliver rasped between clenched teeth, but the woman merely intensified her struggle, her voice shrill.

"Let go of my arm, Oliver! How *dare* you forcibly restrain your own mother to protect this—this—! By God, how can you *allow* such a travesty? The woman's very *daughter*—in this house! Was it not I who banned them both from ever stepping foot upon this property?"

But Eleanor Keane was given no further opportunities to plead her case or wield her parasol, for that matter, for the servant Cyril materialized at her side as if at Oliver's silent command. The servant murmured something indecipherable to the older woman in his nasal, ever-so-British manner, something that seemed to calm Eleanor Keane momentarily.

"Fine, fine," she said almost distractedly, pulling and tucking at her coiffure and mindlessly fussing with the high neck of her gown. Yet the look she leveled at Alexa before she turned to exit the room was one which dripped with savage hatred. It was a look Alexa still remembered well from fifteen years before, the last time she had laid eyes upon Eleanor Keane. Alexa stared at the closed door for several moments until the earth beneath her feet seemed to rumble with Oliver's voice.

"On with it, Jeffcoat," he intoned from close above her, and she found herself staring at the mother-of-pearl buttons adorning the front of his shirt not a hand's breadth from her nose. "Miss *Fairfield*—"

Oh, how the mocking and contempt oozed from his tongue, despite the chair he held for her. Her gaze crept up, past the knotted black cravat at his throat, and her lips parted with unspoken retorts.

"Allow me," Stuart piped up a trifle too boisterously, clanking and clamoring his way to offering yet another chair directly before the desk. Ignoring Keane entirely, Alexa nodded fleetingly at Stuart and slid into the chair he offered, all too aware that Oliver settled his bulk in the chair next to hers. Far too close he was, looming like some predatory bird. A hawk. Eyes hooded, upon her. She could *feel* it. That heat, seeping from him, wrapping about her chair, engulfing her so that she felt suddenly breathless.

"Now then, I say, but that was a rather extraordinary display of female temper, was it not?" Stuart began, scooting behind the desk and casting Oliver a dubious look.

"A matter of unsettled histories," Oliver replied, his tone brimming with impatience, dismissing any further inquiries on the subject. "Shall we proceed?"

With a dissatisfied grunt, Stuart shuffled through a mound of paper upon the desk. "Of course, but before I commence with the actual reading, there is this rather nasty matter of the deaths, which I assume we shall all do our very *best* to keep quiet. Governor's orders." His gaze lifted to Oliver. "You are aware of the...er...the rather untidy circumstances surrounding the deaths, are you not, Keane?"

Oliver's jaw took up a rhythmic tick. "I was not."

Stuart cast Alexa an apologetic look, which only served to baffle her further. "Miss Fairfield, I more than anyone realize the delicacy of such a matter, particularly when one's own mother is involved and the circumstances were somewhat less than, shall we say, *suitable* for a young woman's ears."

"Spit it out, Jeffcoat," Oliver said with crisp impatience.

Stuart flushed clear to the roots of his hair. "I say, Keane!"

"Dammit, man, then *say it!*" Oliver barked, looming in his chair. "You speak, Jeffcoat, but you *say* nothing."

Stuart pursed his lips, and paused to moderate his words, one red eyebrow arching. "I'll have you know I've Miss Fairfield's best intentions at heart, Keane. A young woman's constitution cannot withstand hearing such things."

"I haven't a notion what you're talking about, Stuart," Alexa interrupted, her voice echoing husky and deep, her flush sweeping her cheeks beneath both men's intense regard. "I was told my mother was found...alone...in the jungle, close to our cottage."

Stuart Jeffcoat paled, and his Adam's apple bobbed wildly for a moment. "Who told you—well, I suppose that doesn't matter, but you didn't know that your mother and...uh, were found—oh, dear."

Despite the fevered hammering of her heart, Alexa willed a steadiness to her voice. "Anything you have to say to Mr. Keane regarding my mother's death you can say to me."

For a moment, Stuart simply gaped at her. "I say! A peculiar notion, what. Are you quite certain, Miss Fairfield? Well, then, Keane, what with the impending visit of the Princes Albert Victor and George of Wales, and, of course, being that your father was a prominent and highly regarded member of the plantation community, and Lily Fairfield, the widow of one of Her Majesty's most celebrated naval captains, you can understand the governor's desire to keep the lid on the pot, so to speak, regarding the precise nature of the deaths."

"Which was?"

Stuart's gaze darted to Alexa for a fleeting moment. "The bodies of your father, Keane, and Lily Fairfield were found together."

Alexa suddenly had to struggle for breath, her mind swimming with the implications, the reasons that she had never been told anything other than that her mother had been found dead in the jungle, supposedly by her own hand. That was all that had been said before they'd administered the laudanum to sedate her, to keep her mind foggy, her soul from sinking into the depths of despair. No, this couldn't be....

Oliver's voice penetrated the fog. "Found by whom?"

"Your father's servant Cyril."

Alexa gripped the curved mahogany arms of the chair, her vision clouding, her ears straining for Oliver's next query, her voice trapped somewhere in her throat. "Where?"

"The...er...your father's private chamber, in the...well, to be entirely precise, in the...uh...the bed."

"No..." The breath whispered through Alexa's lips, barely audible even to her own ears. "No, she wouldn't..."

"The cause of death, Jeffcoat?"

"I believe they both died of knife wounds. Your father in the back...rather odd, that...oh, and also to the chest, and Lily Fairfield, one can only assume self-inflicted, directly to the heart."

"No—" Her lungs would burst...with her very next breath....

"She killed him." Those words, so callously spoken, so entirely full of conviction, plunged like a blade into Alexa's soul.

"No—" she gasped, lunging to her feet directly in front of the detestable Oliver Keane even before the echo of his words had died. She clutched the thin cotton of her linen skirt in a death grip, if only to keep herself from clawing the smirk from the man's face. "She didn't kill him. She couldn't. She loved him."

Keane simply stared at her, his expression entirely unreadable, though something smoldered in the depths of those cold eyes, something that stoked Alexa's fury. "Never—" she breathed, her chest expanding until it seemed incapable of containing enough breath. "Never would she have come here after being thrown from the place. *Never* would she have turned a knife on herself."

"My dear Miss Fairfield," Stuart crooned in his patronizing tone. "She *was* here. What you believe she might have done is really of no importance." His sympathetic smile dissolved beneath the look she swung upon him.

"Of no importance?" she whispered with disbelief. "Then what is, may I ask, if not two wrongful deaths? Your governor's desire to see that this awful matter be swiftly and efficiently swept under a royal rug, solely for the sake of a pair of worthless aristocrats who happen to be visiting?"

Stuart visibly winced, then forced what seemed his best attempt at a patient smile. "My dear Miss Fairfield, the governor makes it his business to, shall we say, *cover up* those indiscretions the British populace would rather not come to light lest it reflect poorly upon them. One would think you would be more than grateful."

"Grateful?" Alexa gripped the edge of the fine mahogany desk. "Grateful that the British government believes my mother a murderess?"

Oliver muffled a cough. "I believe your mother's reputation was rather a moot point even fifteen years ago."

Alexa swung upon him so fiercely, her hat tumbled from her head. "*You,* more than anyone, have no right to judge a woman you never knew."

A dark brow lifted slightly. "My generally disreputable character has scant to do with this, Miss Fairfield. I believe the facts speak for themselves."

Alexa all but trembled with frustration. "I don't care if she was found with a bloody knife in her hand. She didn't kill him."

"She was in love with a married man," Oliver countered.

"Ah, yes!" Stuart interrupted from behind her. "The unrequited love motive. A tragedy, I tell you. And, as a matter of fact, she was indeed clutching the murder weapon."

Alexa shook her head, her eyes closed, futilely trying to banish this nightmare from her muddled mind. But she could no more do that than she could banish Oliver Keane's image. "Of course," she said wryly. "I see the logic quite clearly now. She loved him but he was married, so after fifteen years, she killed him. Loving a man does, after all, make a woman capable of murder." Her laugh erupted short, harsh, husky. "Am I to understand you won't be conducting any further investigation into the matter, even if I believe it's more than warranted?"

Stuart stared at her. "Why ever for, Miss Fairfield? As Mr. Keane stated quite simply, the facts speak for themselves, and the governor wholeheartedly concurs. And might I add, the stirring up of this matter will only infuriate the governor, if not the queen herself, and will bring you nothing but further heartache. Imagine the talk, my dear, if the populace had even an inkling that your mother and Gabriel Keane were found *together?* As it is, they believe the deaths separate tragedies, though there is some talk, nevertheless, that Lily was unable to cope with Gabriel's death and thus took her own life out there in the jungle. Let them believe what they will, Miss Fairfield. It will save your mother's reputation. Now, I understand the difficulty you women sometimes have in coping, but a small dosage of laudanum from time to time and adequate rest—"

Alexa shuddered and pressed trembling fingers to her temples, blotting out the drone of Stuart's voice. The reality of it all settled like a burdensome weight upon her shoulders. "I'll never believe it," she whispered, unaware that she had spoken aloud until Oliver's voice rumbled about her.

"You have no choice." He leaned forward to sweep her hat from the floor. As such, when he paused to hand her the hat—an odd gesture indeed for so despicable a man—she grew uncomfortably aware of the alarming lack of distance between his brooding countenance and her bosom. Perhaps it was the sudden stifling heat. Or perhaps something in his manner made her entirely certain that he had purposefully positioned himself at the very edge of his chair.

She snatched the hat close to her breasts and managed to find her chair once again, despite the flicker of something in his eyes, the fluttering in her belly and the brand of a flame upon her bosom. Despite the fact that the man believed her mother a murderess.

"This will all, of course, be kept very quiet," Stuart explained. "The deaths as separate matters, and all that. Cyril intends to comply, and I assume both of you have no objections. The truth need never leave this room. So, Miss Fairfield, you needn't fret over the stain of the matter upon your own reputation."

"I hadn't given that much thought," Alexa replied softly. She wondered if Stuart detected the bitterness in her tone.

Stuart's upper lip twitched slightly, his tone losing its formerly patronizing quality. "Ah, yes, I don't suppose that surprises me. Your Bim friends don't care much for gossip and the like, do they, Miss Fairfield?"

Alexa arched a brow, the words tripping unheeded from her tongue. "No, they're far more concerned with educating their children and achieving some sort of liberty for themselves." Ah, the touchy subject, one which she would never have dreamed of broaching with a fellow like Stuart Jeffcoat, of all people. A British commander, no less, instilled from birth with the notion that the Creoles and Bims populating the island were a restless people, perched daily upon the brink of revolt. He may be a man of high standing, but he had somehow managed to disgust her this afternoon even more than Oliver Keane. If such a thing were possible.

That resonant voice pierced the foreboding silence. "The will, Jeffcoat."

Stuart started, his gaze shifting about, his gloved fingers probing the piles upon the desk. "Of course, the will. Ah, here it is." From somewhere amidst the jumble, Stuart drew forth a rolled parchment, bound by a red ribbon and sealed. He loosened the ribbon, broke the seal and cleared his throat before speaking. "I, Gabriel Keane, being of sound mind and—"

Oliver's hand sliced through the air. "Dammit, Jeffcoat, dispense with the formalities. I've a damned ship waiting for me, man. What the hell does it say?"

Stuart pursed his lips. "In essence?"

Oliver nodded brusquely and consulted his gold pocket watch.

Stuart flipped through several pages of parchment, his eyes scanning the scroll. "Mind you, I haven't read it yet, of course, and know not where I might find the particulars and... Ah, here it is, he bequeaths..." He paused, his eyes darting between Alexa and Oliver, his jaw sagging in a most undignified manner. For several moments, he seemed to have some difficulty finding his voice and the silence lingered, foreboding, heavy. "H-he bequeaths his entire estate—the house, lands, servants, all his holdings—in equal parts to one Oliver Westbrook Keane and one Alexandra Victoria Fairfield."

Chapter Three

Oliver could only stare at the signature at the bottom of the will, a sprawling, heavy script one would expect from the likes of Gabriel Keane. He should have known his father capable of something so ludicrous, so entirely irrational, so supremely irritating and untimely.

One last dying attempt to ruin his life, and an ineffectual one, at that, as far as Oliver was concerned.

Dismissively, Oliver thrust the will at Jeffcoat and found himself wondering why the red-haired British officer annoyed him so much. Perhaps it was the fellow's air of self-importance, the whole damned uniform to the very tip of his sword underscored his infuriating attitude. Perhaps it was Jeffcoat's relative youth, not that Oliver's age entitled him to arrogance any more than it did Jeffcoat, but a man had to *earn* his character, dammit, not simply *assume* it with the donning of his uniform every day. Oliver could well imagine the man bestrode only the most ostentatious stallion, and with sword unsheathed, brandished his mock authority up and down the streets of Bridgetown.

Then again, perhaps his dislike for Jeffcoat stemmed from something to do with Miss Alexandra Fairfield.

Alexa, Jeffcoat had called her.

Oliver relented to instinct and allowed his gaze to drift toward her, as had been its wont since the girl had entered the room. Of course, being Lily Fairfield's daughter, she bore close scrutiny. It didn't help matters that she was inarguably the most beautiful creature Oliver had ever seen.

She sat in a state of stunned disbelief, her lips parted slightly, her gaze focused somewhere beyond the windows, beyond the flowering trees and shrubs, beyond all that had transpired in this room. He knew those averted eyes were the most astonishing shade of emerald, a vibrancy of color one wasn't likely to find anywhere near Chicago. And her hair... he could well imagine a fellow like Jeffcoat all but itched to sink his fingers into that tumbling mane. Silken curls in every imaginable shade of blond fell in a torrent about her shoulders, nearly to her waist, flaxen wisps curling against her forehead and cheeks. Skin the color of warm honey could assail a man's senses...if a man were so inclined; the slit in that lame excuse for a skirt that only emphasized the narrowness of her waist, her hips, her thighs, bared a length of leg from the tips of her toes nearly to midthigh. Yes, he could well imagine lesser men than he waiting hours with bated breath for that slit to part or her peasant's blouse to slip from her shoulders where it seemed to perch rather precariously. And if a man were so predisposed, his eyes could probe that thin batiste blouse, seeking the generous swell of upthrust breasts, the impertinent nipples straining against soft cloth...

Like a sudden tempest, desire raged through him. He gripped the arms of his chair if only to keep himself from lunging from it to crush her against him. He longed to touch this woman looming just beyond his reach. He would drown himself in her scent, which had invaded his senses and taken over his mind. She moved, and his world seemed to tilt with her. She spoke to Jeffcoat, and the officer spoke, as well; of what, Oliver was uncaring. And then she rose and left the room, and he found himself on his feet glaring at Jeffcoat.

"Where the hell is she going?" Oliver's scowl only deepened when Jeffcoat gave him a disbelieving look.

"I say, Keane, no need for theatrics, is there? The lady is simply leaving. And you've a ship to catch, if I remember correctly."

Oliver stared at the other man. "A ship. Yes, of course." He snatched his watch from his pocket, glanced at it without seeing it and stuffed it back into his coat. "Leaving." Shoving a hand through his hair, he thrust the chairs from his path and strode from the room. "See yourself out, Jeffcoat," he muttered over one shoulder.

He found her in a garden to one side of the house, standing amongst a profusion of rosebushes, all white to the very last bloom. And she, as well, in her peasant's garb, as if she, too, had been born of this garden—yet another of nature's treasures waiting to be plucked.

He sucked in his breath, startlingly aware of the thickness of the air as he forced it into his lungs, of the fragrances, heavy in the still air. Almost like a narcotic, they were, the profusion of blossoms, the scents, the torrid, almost imperceptible shifting of the air, this woman. Everything conspired to lull a man into a kind of tropical stupor such that for a fleeting moment he'd forgotten entirely his purpose there, his ship awaiting departure in Bridgetown's harbor, the fiancé awaiting him in cold, foggy Chicago, the merger with Theodore MacAdoo's company.

With renewed purpose amidst a certain self-disgust, he stepped into the garden. His rather abrupt movement startled a pair of doves nesting in a nearby tree; their furious flapping drew a curious emerald gaze so magnificent in its innocence, he felt a sudden tightness in his chest. And then their eyes met and hers clouded, the look increasingly guarded the nearer he came. Her fingertips trembled upon a rose, rousing something in him, something deep and entirely foreign, and grossly unsuitable for a man with supposedly nothing but business on his mind. She started, her lips parting with a silent gasp, and she snatched her fingers to her mouth.

Gallantry had never been something to which Oliver had even remotely aspired. He preferred, rather, to employ the gentlemanly graces sparingly, only when necessary...as a means of protecting himself, of course. He had learned long ago that society women possessed a most remarkable talent for turning the more eager of gentlemen into mere lackeys, demanding and demanding of them with but the lift of an eyebrow, all for the sake of impressing one's peers or buoying one's self-image. In Oliver, however, their tireless and inane demands had stirred only a fleeting disgust and a renewed purpose to avoid the typical gentleman's fate. Thus, his reputation as a bit of a scoundrel had flourished. Society women, however, were exceptionally forgiving of this, particularly when the subject of his fortune was near at hand.

Odd, but even Daphne MacAdoo's effortless swoon had failed to evoke even a fraction of the protective surge now welling up in him at the sight of Alexandra Fairfield's pricked fingertips. He found himself with handkerchief in hand, murmuring a gallant, "Allow me." What she expected of him, he'd never know. Judging by the belligerent flash of emerald fire in her eyes, she must have thought him capable of many a dastardly act with that handkerchief. Yet, as if some part of him were bent upon affirming her every suspicion, he found his fingers wrapped about her wrist, drawing her resisting hand closer... closer... and a sudden, mindless desire to kiss her pricked fingertips swept over him.

He gritted his teeth and pressed his handkerchief to the wound, willing some return of rational thought. "I've a business proposition for you, Miss Fairfield. Given the circumstances, I trust you'll be more than willing to cooperate."

Her fingers slipped like a whisper of air from his grasp. She glared at him. "You're rather presumptuous, Mr. Keane, assuming that I would even speak to you, much less agree to one of your business schemes," she said, her singsong voice husky with vehemence. Then she tossed his handkerchief at him and stalked past him, intent upon leaving the garden.

Muttering under his breath, he retrieved the handkerchief from the flagstone path and started after her, his gaze immediately drawn to the smooth undulation of her hips and backside in that skirt. He advanced upon her, feeling very much like a lion stalking its prey, then blocked her path and summoned his best smile, given the circumstances. The heat, he assured himself, nothing else, had sucked his lungs of air such that he felt as if someone punched him in the stomach every time she looked at him. The heat... not her... *never* a woman, most especially not *this* woman. He'd learned long ago that a man could have no weaknesses. His father had indeed taught him well.

"You misunderstand, Miss Fairfield. I simply wish to alleviate some of the burden."

"Then leave me alone." Again, that glare, as if *he* were somehow to blame for all this. She seemed about to slip past him, but he blocked her path yet again, leaving her no means of escape save for plunging through densely grown rosebushes—something she seemed less than inclined to do. "Your reputation precedes you, Mr. Keane, but hardly does you justice."

Oliver couldn't temper the wry twist of his lips. "I wouldn't think Lily Fairfield's daughter could afford to lend idle gossip a kind ear."

She visibly trembled, her temper quite in keeping with so vibrant a woman. "When a father speaks of his son, one can hardly label that gossip, Mr. Keane."

"The ramblings of a stubborn fool. He knew nothing of me."

"Believe what you will, but your father made it his business to know as much as he could about you, and corresponded regularly with friends in the States who kept themselves abreast of your—" her full lips curved snidely "*—accomplishments.* And of course, you're quite an enigma to the merchants who regularly ply their trade in Bridgetown's harbor. Yes, Mr. Keane, he employed every means of knowing his only son. You left him with little choice, refusing his letters, his every attempt to contact you. Indeed, I would wager he knew *you* far better than you ever knew *him.*"

"I know enough. The man sacrificed everything of any worth in his life for a woman who wasn't his wife." Suddenly, the air grew too stifling, his starched celluloid collar far too tight, his coat far too constricting of a chest expanding with rage. "He gave my mother and me little choice but to leave fifteen years ago, and what little I'd wager you truly know of it was unforgivable. He squandered his family's fortune at gambling parlors, made a mockery of his plantation, a laughingstock of his wife, himself..." The last words hissed through his teeth, and for a moment all but the red haze of rage filled his vision . . . and then that husky voice penetrated that fog.

"How cynically you twist the truth to suit your purpose, Mr. Keane. But even if all you say was indeed true, is that why you care so very little that he died, and in my estimation, most probably by underhanded means? Is that why you can stand before me and speak so casually of business arrangements and alleviating burdens?" Her words trembled upon her lips. "*That,* Mr. Keane, is unforgivable. Now, if you would kindly let me pass—"

"The hell I will," Oliver muttered, his fingers wrapping entirely about her upper arm, just below the sleeve, stilling her feet beneath her. Her arm was startlingly fragile, birdlike, far too vulnerable for a woman capable of rousing all that emotion, all that rage. "Listen," he rasped. "Whatever happened between my father and your mother doesn't matter much at the moment. Just ask your noble government. What does matter is the settling of this damned estate. Now, I'm prepared to offer you a fair price for your share of Bellefontaine."

She stared at him as though she thought him half-mad, the color flaming high in her cheeks. "And I suppose you intend to conveniently peddle it off to one of your fellow New Englanders whose boats began choking our docks not three months past. One of those pompous buffoons who thinks nothing of stripping the workers of their livelihood, the land of its resources, this island of its history, solely for the sake of generating tourist revenues. Are you in league perhaps with those New Englanders who wish to callously buy up every plantation solely to turn them into tourist hotels?"

Never had a woman been so magnificently enraged. Oliver could only stare at her, this odd creature. A paradox, she was, fiery and passionate amidst all that naïveté and virginal white linen. He couldn't have contained a wry smile if he'd tried. "Miss Fairfield, think of me what you will, but I am no New Englander. I'm from Chicago."

This somehow seemed to frustrate her further. "I know what you are, Keane! Even after all these years, Bellefontaine's workers still speak of your bitter betrayal of your father, and rightly so. You're a despicable, cynical businessman. You're a man obsessed with money, with power, with gaining influence and market share, no matter the cost…even the loss of a father." She wrenched her arm free and stumbled back a pace, her chest heaving. "You've not an ounce of compassion—"

"I said I'd offer you a fair price," he said pointedly.

"You're a beast," she breathed, her fingers crushing her hat against her belly. Gardenia petals scattered over the path at her feet, their scent permeating the thick air. "Never—*never* would I lay Bellefontaine in the hands of so ruthless a monster as you. *Never.*"

"My father obviously thought me deserving," he observed calmly.

"Your father loved you enough to forgive, Mr. Keane, and presented you with one last opportunity to carry on his dream for Bellefontaine. Perhaps this was his dying attempt at reconciliation. I, however, am not foolish enough to believe you deserving of forgiveness *or* trust."

"I don't think you realize the inherent difficulties in joint ownership," he said, appealing to her rationality.

"Then sell your share to me," she said. "That sounds fair."

His eyes narrowed upon her, this island nymph who dared to bait him. She had no idea with whom she was dealing, of the business pacts he'd negotiated, the legions of high-powered financiers with whom he'd shared a table. "My price is far too high. Besides, you couldn't possibly manage the place."

Those emerald eyes glittered dangerously. "Stuart Jeffcoat is quite able-bodied."

God knows why, but something ominous surged through him, prompting him to advance a step closer to her, and another. She simply stood her ground, hat crushed in hand, her chin inching ever upward in proud defiance. Even though the top of her head didn't reach past his shoulder, she seemed oddly confident of her ability to do battle with him, verbally or otherwise, something few men had ever been able to display so profoundly. Or perhaps one of those confounded female instincts was to blame. Perhaps she understood far better than he the reasons for his sudden overwhelming urge to bellow and bark like a man possessed. All he knew or understood, for that matter, was that he and he alone would control Bellefontaine's fate. Not some bumbling lummox like Jeffcoat.

The oaf had called her *Alexa.* Oliver looked into those fathomless emerald pools where weak men like Jeffcoat could indeed lose themselves, forsaking years of toil, of sacrifice...

"No," he managed to say, his fists balling against his thighs.

"Then it would seem we're at an impasse, Mr. Keane." Her lips curved bewitchingly, a self-satisfied smirk on any other woman but she, and fleeting, the look of a woman who had far more important matters on her mind. "Excuse me, but I've dallied long enough. And you've a ship to catch, if I remember correctly."

"It can wait." He blocked her path with a shift of his shoulders. "I'm asking you to reconsider my offer."

She merely lifted an eyebrow, her voice deceptively soft. "You'd best hurry, you know. The tide has never been known to wait for a woman to change her mind... or for a murder to be solved."

"You'd best leave that alone."

"I'm not afraid of anyone, Mr. Keane."

"Perhaps you should be. I've heard the British government can be quite unfriendly when crossed. And don't count on your Jeffcoat to protect you. Something tells me patriotic fervor runs far more rampant in the boy's veins than gallantry."

"Better a loyalty to one's country than no loyalties whatsoever." He caught her meaning even before she paused to allow her words to sink in. "You shan't dissuade me, Mr. Keane."

"You're asking for trouble."

Her gaze flickered dismissively over him. "I shall consider that a challenge, Mr. Keane. Bon voyage."

She slipped past him in a whisper of white linen, vanishing into the house before he could reach out to stop her. He stared at the empty, darkened doorway, then at the gardenia petals scattered at his booted feet. Then at his pocket watch. Muttering a curse, he strode into the house.

Alexa had but stepped from the front portal when a huge, gray stallion emblazoned with the formal red, white and gold dress of a British commanding officer pranced along the curved cobblestone driveway toward her. Stuart Jeffcoat sat poised atop the magnificent mount, his red-plumed helmet pulled so low over his eyes he had to peer primly down his nose in order to see her. With a clank of his sword, he pulled the horse to a halt and dismounted.

"The roads can be quite unforgiving of bare feet," he observed, mumbling something under his breath when she agilely sidestepped both him and his pompous mount and strode determinedly away from him. "I say, Alexa—er, Miss Fairfield—might I offer you a lift?"

"I'd rather walk," she replied. She settled her hat low over her eyes against the late-afternoon sun. The clamoring of Stuart's sword in her wake would have roused a smile had she not been so supremely vexed with all men in general at the moment. "Thinking he could simply name a price and Bellefontaine would be his. Arrogant beast."

"I say, what was that?" Stuart huffed, pulling alongside her with a fierce tug upon his mount's reins. She glanced over at him, which prompted his typical self-conscious smile, something she had grown all too familiar with over the last several months. It had been a good six months prior that she'd first met the British officer. The occasion had been one of those interminable military ceremonial parades upon the savannah at St. Anne's Castle, an occasion that seemed to Alexa to occur with monotonous regularity. The fluff of the British Barbadians, Lily Fairfield included, viewed any sort of military display as *the* opportunity to see and be seen, and promptly outfitted themselves as could only be viewed on swank Rotten Row.

Or so Stuart Jeffcoat had once proclaimed. Alexa knew no better. Rotten Row was a fashionable district in London, a place she'd only heard tales of from her mother, tales told in that flat tone reserved solely for those rare occasions when her mother had spoken of her life in England before she'd journeyed with her infant baby Alexa to Barbados . . . a time Lily had preferred *not* to remember.

"I say, steady!" Stuart's gloved hand clasped Alexa's elbow, veering her out of the path of a small herd of goats ambling about the wrought-iron gates marking the entrance to the plantation. "Filthy, wretched, flea-bitten—"

His next words seemed to clog in his throat when Alexa bent to stroke a tiny goat. "The young ones seem so precariously balanced upon their hooves." She rubbed a thumb over the nubs at the top of the kid's head. "So vulnerable without their mothers."

"And what of you, Alexa? Are you faring well these days?"

"Shura tends to me well enough, as she did my mother for so many years."

Twin red eyebrows rose despite the slightly distasteful twist of his lips. "Ah, yes, your Bim servant. I've heard tell around the Queen's House that she may be one of those Obeah women."

Alexa faced Stuart with a chilling glare. "Shura does not practice witchcraft. Perhaps your government would be better off channeling its efforts into solving my mother's murder rather than orchestrating witch-hunts."

Stuart's cheeks flamed. "I say! Her Majesty's forces upon this island have never once wasted a moment's time in the aimless pursuit of witches. Why, we've far more important matters on the agenda! Indeed, far more important. Black unrest being the very least of it. Yes, the very least. And as for your mother's death, this talk of murder is pure poppycock, the fabrication of a traumatized mind, perhaps?" He leaned closer to her. "A mind refusing to face the truth?"

Again, the patronizing tone; the hesitant touch upon her elbow, which only irritated her further. She forced a rigid smile, instinctively realizing the futility in arguing with this man, or any man for that matter. She all but choked on her words. "Of course."

Stuart cooed, his fingers tightening about her elbow, guiding her through Bellefontaine's gates. "Now, now, my dear Miss Fairfield, allow me to be a bit concerned for your welfare. As a friend, of course, for God knows I am not duty-bound to do so. I just find myself rather . . ." He paused beneath a low-hanging cabbage tree, his gaze suddenly imploring, his face flushed and beaded with perspiration. He seemed to grapple with his words, then fumbled for her hand and cast a hesitant glance about.

Alexa felt strangely detached, oddly out of sorts with Stuart Jeffcoat and his sudden confusion, decidedly unforgiving of whatever it was that ailed him. Some peculiar sickness, no doubt, for his grip was clammy even through his white kid gloves.

His mouth opened and closed three times before he finally spoke. "I find myself growing rather fond of you, perhaps unwisely so given the circumstances of your mother's death."

Alexa's lips twisted. "Ah, yes, one wouldn't expect the governor to endorse any sort of alliance between a commanding officer and a murderess's daughter."

Stuart seemed on the verge of wincing, his eyes momentarily sweeping closed. "Indeed, you can well imagine my quandary. But, by Jove, I cannot seem to help myself, realizing, of course, what this must make me, even in the best of lights." He licked the perspiration from his lips and laid a clammy hand atop hers. "Yet, I could never forgive myself if I didn't ask you if I could perhaps...*call* upon you from time to time...at your cottage, with Shura chaperoning, of course. All very proper, you know."

"At the cottage." Alexa's gaze drifted to Bellefontaine through the dense curtain of leaves. Only the shadowy entrance amidst its profusion of overgrown bushes was visible from her vantage. "Why not here?" she heard herself ask. "At Bellefontaine. It *is* half mine, is it not?"

Stuart stared at her. "Here? Why, yes, yes, of course it is."

Alexa summoned a whimsical smile. "Then I suppose I shall have to move in quite soon, wouldn't you think?"

"Soon, of course, yes, quite soon."

Her eyes narrowed upon the mansion. Half hers. Inside that house lay all the secrets of her mother's death. She looked back to Stuart, a man capable of aiding her in many ways. "And you shall help me, won't you?"

"Me? Why, yes, yes, help you. Of course."

"Tomorrow." Slipping her hand free of his slackening grip, she gathered her skirt in hand. "Teatime, perhaps."

Stuart blinked. "Right. Teatime."

She flashed a smile and spun about. "Goodbye, Stuart," she said over her shoulder, entirely unmindful of his response, of anything but the gnawing determination to prove her mother's innocence. No matter the cost. No matter the sacrifices to be made. No matter the risks.

No fear of confrontation. If only she could vanquish Oliver Keane from her mind as she had all fear. But it wasn't important. The man would sail out of her life by sunset.

Oliver narrowed his gaze even further, as if by so doing he could penetrate the impossibly dense, low-hanging branches shielding what he sought from view. With a grunted curse, he shoved the nearest chair beneath him and leaned closer to the window, and closer still until his breath fogged the panes, all to no avail. Only that peacock Jeffcoat and his equally pompous mount were clearly visible from this vantage. Of Alexandra Fairfield he could see only her bare feet and ankles. His gaze shifted to Jeffcoat's polished black boots, then back to those bare feet. He didn't need to see much more to know Alexa and that pompous ass were standing too damned close.

"Oliver! Dear God, *here* you are! What the devil are you doing all hunched over like that?"

Oliver rubbed his eyes, then studied the richly patterned Aubusson carpet between his booted feet. It was of an infinitely fine weave, the very best money could buy. Odd that this office seemed to comfort him in some way.

"Oliver, have you any idea of the time? Our ship—"

"Left about twenty minutes ago." Again his gaze was drawn to the windows, to those low branches, to those bare ankles and the flimsy white linen hem drifting into and out of his sight with her every movement. "What the hell are they doing . . . ?"

"Oliver, you're grumbling and mumbling and not making any sense," Eleanor snapped with marked impatience. "Quit staring out the blasted window. You're becoming addled."

Addled, indeed. With an irritated grunt, he rose, still staring through the window, his hands on his hips, and gave fleeting consideration to the smug satisfaction seeping through him when Jeffcoat mounted his horse *alone* and disappeared down the dirt road.

"Oliver, you're ignoring me."

"Have a drink, Mother." With calm deliberation, he doffed his topcoat, tossed it upon a chair and moved past his mother to the sideboard where two crystal decanters awaited his pleasure. "Rum," he said, sniffing of one of the decanters and lifting an eyebrow. "No?" He felt a mild amusement at his mother's look of stunned disbelief. "Perhaps this, then." He splashed a liberal portion of a deep burgundy liquid from the other decanter into a glass and drained it in one gulp. "Not bad."

"Sangaree," Eleanor hissed, eyeing his empty glass with disdain. "Your father inhaled the stuff. All the plantation gentlefolk did."

"But not you, I take it."

"I despised everything about this island from the moment your father brought me here from Chicago. I still do. When are we leaving?"

Oliver poured himself another sangaree. "Had enough recouping of pride already, Mother?"

"Hardly," Eleanor snorted, shifting her attention to the windows. "You left me little chance of that... all but throwing me out of that room for the sake of that tramp's daughter, that—"

"Alexa." He found himself staring into his glass.

"The twit looks just like her mother, God help her." Eleanor seemed to draw herself up, her palm flattening against the generous curve of her belly beneath burgundy taffeta, a fashionable plumpness, of course, expected of society queens who paid proper heed to fashion. She shuddered, looking thoroughly repulsed by some thought, and tucked an invisible strand of hair into her upswept coiffure. "Of course, only men with a less than discerning eye could find such a creature attractive. Too skinny and far too heathen-looking with all that hair and those rags she calls clothes. Of course her mother took great pains with her looks. I mean, wouldn't *you* if you looked like that? But all the clothes in the world cannot compensate for coarseness of breeding. Perhaps that's what your father found so irresistible about her." She sighed and cast Oliver a slightly startled look. "You men are forever finding the most common the most fascinating."

Oliver merely refilled his glass.

"You know I'll never forgive you for embarrassing me in front of her... *allowing* her to remain where *I* belonged."

"Your name wasn't mentioned once in the will, Mother."

"And so you chose to humiliate me further?"

"Hardly. Miss Fairfield was bequeathed half of Bellefontaine."

Eleanor clawed at the high, ruffled neck of her gown with one hand, the other groping blindly for the edge of the desk. "She *what?*"

Oliver dispelled a resonant sigh and strode to the windows once more, where the lengthening shadows of dusk played upon the cobblestone driveway. "I own half and Miss Alexandra Fairfield owns the other half."

"Dear God, what shall you do?"

"I'll buy it from her, of course." He tipped his glass to his lips. "She, however, seems far more concerned with proving that Father and Lily Fairfield were murdered, even though the governor believes otherwise."

"That whore Lily Fairfield killed him," Eleanor rasped from the depths of the chair into which she had sunk. "Surely you know that."

"That seems to be the prevailing opinion."

"Dear God, I don't care what it takes, Oliver, offer her a small fortune for her share—and if that doesn't work, steal it from her, but she *cannot* own even half of this plantation. I *shan't* allow it. *You* cannot. He makes a mockery of us all even in death. Of *you.* His vengeance knew no bounds."

"So it would seem."

"She's nobody, Oliver, merely a harlot's wayward offspring, unworthy of stepping one filthy foot in this house."

Oliver glanced sharply at his mother, at her dark eyes aglow in the late-afternoon light. "I'll cable Theodore MacAdoo early tomorrow," he heard himself say. "The wedding will obviously have to be postponed a few more weeks. I'm not leaving Bellefontaine until this little matter has been resolved. Perhaps another day or two."

Eleanor seemed not to have heard him. She seemed blissfully unconcerned with the wedding, with her society sisters, with sweet, retiring little Daphne. "Be ruthless with this Alexandra Fairfield, Oliver."

A cold smile crept across his lips, a smile no amount of sweet sangaree would appease. "That was my intent, Mother. How different from business can this be, after all?"

Chapter Four

Alexa lay curled upon the overstuffed chair, with half-closed lids, watching dawn creep over the island. From this vantage upon the cottage veranda, she'd lingered throughout the night as she had been wont to do every night since her mother's death, in the hopes that the distant rush of waves upon sand would kindly lull her into some sort of fitful dozing . . . anything to avoid reaching for the tiny bottle left just within her reach. Shura knew well Alexa's unholy fear of sleeping in the cottage, and thus provided the nightly doses of laudanum, though Alexa knew not when the servant had done so, so silently did she move upon the veranda's whitewashed planks. Last night had been one of the few Alexa had not gripped the bottle close and drained it. She needed her wits about her if she was to find her mother's murderer. Little good it did her to forego such a drug, however, if without it she barely slept.

Drawing her light blanket about her shoulders, she eased her cramped limbs from the chair and perched at the veranda rail, willing the morning's peace to seep into her soul like the mists slipping into the dense foliage surrounding the cottage. The sky bloomed pale pinks and apricots over the surrounding lush hills. The District of Scotland, as this region was called, was the only area of the island liberally sprinkled with gentle slopes and verdant forest glades. Dark dells and narrow ravines crossed the valley between lines of jagged hills mantled with heavy rain forest. The mansions of the former plantation aristocracy sat conspicuously upon every height, their towering cabbage trees and windmills nestled around them. Like Alleyndale Hall, just visible through the mists, perched precariously upon the very cliff's edge overlooking the ocean. Supposedly haunted, or so the British Barbadians whispered amongst themselves. Alexa was inclined to believe otherwise. Her eyes swept closed and she breathed deep of air thick with fragrance. And again, as it did every morning, the water beckoned.

The blanket slipped from her shoulders, her hair from its loose coil as she drifted down the veranda steps. The sand was cool beneath her feet along the familiar path that led through dense forest, along a narrow gorge to the cove, *her* cove, secluded upon the craggy eastern shore of the island. She knew well Shura watched stonily from behind one of the cottage's lace curtains, a hint of disapproval marring the generous curve of the servant's mouth, for the island's eastern shore was notorious for its treacherous waters, so treacherous and unpredictable even the locals kept themselves to the western coast. Everyone except Alexa...ever since she'd discovered her cove. She maintained a certain reverence for that ocean, never venturing beyond the barrier reef or the breaking surf, oftentimes content to simply sit upon the shore with her feet buried in sand, pondering the capricious ocean...that churning, unforgiving mass that had claimed her father's ship and his life so long ago.

An admiral in Her Majesty's Royal Navy her father had been, Sir Brighton Fairfield, much decorated and suitably revered by all, or so she had since gleaned. She had no memory of him save for the faded photograph upon her mother's bedside table, and the enormous oil portrait she had once seen hanging in the foyer at the President's House, directly at the entrance to the governor's quarters.

Far too awash in devotion to his country and his ships he had been. Indeed, according to her mother, he had visited his young wife, Lily, and their baby daughter, Alexa, just once in London where he'd ensconced them in a fashionable townhouse well suited to the wife of a naval great. On those rare occasions when she had spoken of that time in London, Lily had been bitter, no doubt due to her insufferable loneliness, or so Alexa surmised. Why else would she have so fervently hastened to her husband's side with her infant daughter in tow, on the eve of her learning he'd been stationed temporarily in Barbados? A tragic set of circumstances, indeed, for they'd arrived in Bridgetown, Lily weak and traumatized by the voyage, Alexa fitful and colicky, only to be swiftly ushered to the President's House where they'd received the news that Admiral Brighton Fairfield's fleet, ships and all hands, had been lost in a hurricane not three days prior.

Alexa shed her garments upon the shore and waded into the surf. For some reason, she ventured farther from shore this morn, diving into the foaming surf only to emerge to the glory of a fiery sun peeking over the murky horizon. She swam with clean strokes, farther still, relishing the power of the current, the vitalizing buoyancy of the water as it nestled her in its palm, almost lovingly. Her father must have felt this way about the sea . . . and her mother, in her own way.

With barely any effort, she floated upon her back, blinking the salt from her eyes, arching her back so that her naked breasts thrust through the water toward the sun's heated caress. A languid heat seeped into her limbs as the water lapped at her flesh, as the tide lifted, then settled her . . . and the vision loomed suddenly in that cloudless pink sky above her, the eyes a turbulent cobalt blue, hooded, insolent as they moved over her, rousing this same heat deep within her.

Her fingers pressed against her throat, then slipped lower, finding a pulse at the base of her neck, then lower, drifting through the water over flesh that tingled at the slightest shifting of the water. He'd stared at her . . . here. Her fingers brushed like a whisper over her breasts, over one taut nipple, then the other . . . and the liquid seemed inside her now, pulsing from the very peaks of her breasts, through her limbs to coil like some ache deep in her belly. No, lower . . . her palm pressed against her stomach, slid lower . . .

Something shivered through her. She submerged, and surfaced with a huge gasp of air, feeling somehow that all had been suddenly robbed of her. Her pulse pounded in her ears above the call of the surf, and her limbs momentarily refused command when she would have set out with swift, sure strokes back to shore. She blinked saltwater from her eyes and shook her head to banish all thoughts of Oliver Keane, for even the idlest speculation on the man prompted this *re-*

sponse, this unconscionable and entirely uncontrollable bodily reaction to him. She must be ill. Light-headed. Perhaps she ought to cease all this swimming about in the nude, though she knew well this heightened sensitivity, this undue awareness of herself had commenced just yesterday, the day she'd met Oliver Keane . . . the moment he'd looked at her as if he meant to have her for his midday meal. Unholy man. He'd cast some sort of spell upon her.

She waded to shore, uncomfortably aware that her thighs brushed together like seductive whispers, that her breasts felt unusually full and taut, swaying like overripe fruit awaiting a man's caress.

"Damnation," she grumbled under her breath, snatching the cotton blanket from the sand and burying her face in its softness. After a moment, she rubbed her face vigorously, then did the same over her limbs, almost painfully, so fervently did she will her thoughts elsewhere. Better to occupy her mind with another man, a man who could best aid her in her plan to ensnare a murderer. That man was Stuart Jeffcoat. Her lips compressed at the thought and the images it inspired. It wasn't that she found Stuart distasteful to any extreme. She simply wasn't an accomplished actress, and profound annoyance was something she thought she might have difficulty hiding. It invaded one's speech. It prompted one to avoid any sort of bodily contact. It made a girl entirely uncomfortable with the notion of "calling," or whatever it was Stuart had in mind for her.

Her sheer, white lawn nightgown spilled over her head, falling to just brush the tops of her feet, and her hands stilled upon her belly. Yes, she'd be far better off coercing information from a love-smitten British commanding officer than ruminating on the disturbing memory of a good seventy-six inches of masculinity smoldering and seething like a beast confined within his finely tailored black topcoat. Those eyes savagely aglow with his every lascivious thought. Those huge hands with their long fingers deftly handling that gold quill . . . Would those hands be capable of gentleness amidst all that untested strength? What would those palms feel like moving over flesh still damp from a morning's swim?

A gasp escaped her parched lips when her eyes met Shura's. The servant had all but materialized before her upon the sand, enormous brown eyes full of something peculiar, a knowing gleam, as if she knew well the turn of Alexa's newfound thoughts. With some confusion and some difficulty, Alexa swallowed and eased her fists open, releasing the bunched nightgown where she'd clutched it at her belly.

"Shura." She pushed the tangled mass of her hair from her face. "I was—"

"I know what's you was," Shura replied in her singsong Bajan tone, a tone Alexa was certain was laced with frank disapproval. The sun colored Shura's skin like lightly creamed coffee, smooth and flawless from chin to forehead where a white scarf concealed what Alexa knew to be thick, waist-length plaited black hair. Of Shura's precise age Alexa was uncertain, though the servant had been under her mother's employ since just after they'd arrived in Barbados twenty-one years prior.

Though sturdily built and capable, Shura had chosen domestic duties over countless hours beneath an unforgiving sun piling newly harvested sugar cane into the wagons for the plantations like Bellefontaine. Some time ago, Alexa had somehow grown aware that Shura nevertheless had more than a passing interest in the cane fields, particularly at Bellefontaine—an interest in the form of a mammoth black named Luke, a man known islandwide for his incomparable ability to cut five tons of cane in one day.

Alexa had seen Luke only on one or two occasions . . . at dawn, when the jungle's rousing lured Alexa from sleep and she happened to peek from her bedroom window. Through dawn's eerie gray she'd spied Shura and Luke, half-clothed, sleep-tousled, consumed with bidding each other a night's farewell upon the very edge of the jungle. Alexa's cheeks still flamed from the memory of their bodies writhing together, joined from head to toe in some mutual agony. Of Shura, quiet, domestic Shura, with her hair tumbling about her naked shoulders, and of Luke, the bunched muscles in his thighs, his arms and his huge hands grasped about Shura's hips, lifting her, rocking her against him rhythmically, ruthlessly . . .

Unable to bear more, Alexa would then seek the haven of her bed and stare at the beamed ceiling over her bed, straining for some sound that Shura had returned, trembling from what, she knew not, her sheet drawn clear to her chin. This was all she knew of men and their women, for her mother had never spoken to her of such things. Indeed, her mother, with her lily-white skin, that luminous, almost childlike breathiness of manner, couldn't possibly know of such things. Her mother was far too refined, far too noble, far too delicate. She preferred afternoon tea and cakes in a parlor brimming with white lilies, and Gabriel Keane suitably positioned *alone* on the settee opposite hers, doing his very best to balance a porcelain teacup upon his brawny knee. Lily had preferred conversation and soirees upon the savannah at St. Anne's Castle, elegant parasols and strolling about gardens. No, Lily had known nothing of writhing bodies bathed in a sheen of jungle mist, hands roughly grasping about hips, breasts, shoulders.

Odd, but for some reason, Alexa had forever found Shura that much more fascinating after witnessing such an encounter. Perhaps because some part of Alexa thought Shura unduly traumatized. But the servant would conduct herself as always, meticulously groomed, starched and coiffed, wearing a thoroughly placid expression as she embarked upon her duties, humming some deep-throated melody.

Alexa never asked why Shura and Luke never married. But she was instinctively certain, as Shura's gaze narrowed, then slid briefly over Alexa from head to toe, that Shura would know something of this heat Oliver Keane had stoked within her.

But if the servant was indeed aware of Alexa's thoughts, she didn't indicate as much, simply staring at her, then at the ocean for several long moments. "Come," Shura said, scooping Alexa's blanket from the sand and starting off with her gentle, loping strides. "Piano-boy comes soon."

Alexa closed her eyes. "Yes, of course, his lesson. I—"

"Forgot." Shura didn't need to cast her an admonishing glance.

"Yes, I know, Shura, I've been doing an awful lot of that lately."

"The coconut pie."

"Yes, well, an unfortunate set of circumstances. I *did* remember at long last to get it from the oven, you know. Only a trifle burned, it was."

"Ruined. Like the wash."

Alexa jutted out her chin. "Now, that's not quite fair. How was I to know it would rain like that? And without warning? But surely you can't blame me. I simply lost track of the time and fell asleep."

Shura pushed into the jungle, finding the path with little effort. "You should do that at night in your own bed. Not on the sand-beach." Shura paused to fix relentless dark eyes upon her. *Especially without clothes on,* her look implied. But she turned without another word and clambered up the gorge.

Alexa kept pace easily, clutching at her gown and feeling abominably guilty of something for some reason. She cast this feeling aside in favor of her newfound purpose. "Shura, did you realize that mother was found... that her body... dear God, I can barely speak of it... that she didn't die in the jungle like we were told?"

Shura's stride retained its measured pace, her soft grunt the only indication she'd heard Alexa.

Tempering a frown, Alexa chose another tactic. "Gabriel Keane's son, that... that... *Oliver*... was at Bellefontaine yesterday. He thinks mother murdered Gabriel. The governor himself thinks thus and I am determined to prove otherwise, with some help from Stuart Jeffcoat."

At the top of the gorge, Shura suddenly paused, her gaze riveted upon the Scotland hills in the distance. "Stay away from man-beast."

Alexa's stilted laughter echoed through the gorge. "Oh, Shura, Stuart may be somewhat repulsive in a fleeting sort of way but—"

A deep hum suddenly swelled about them, and for several moments Alexa didn't realize Shura was swaying back and forth, almost imperceptibly, that the drone rising eerily around them rumbled from deep in Shura's throat. "Not him," Shura rasped. "Man-beast." Those deep eyes swung upon Alexa just as Shura's palm pressed like a branding flame over Alexa's belly. "Keane," Shura said hoarsely. "Man-beast wants you, woman-child, *inside*. Will take whatever he wants. Then he will leave. Stay away from man-beast."

A tremor swept through Alexa, pulsating like a living thing beneath the heat of Shura's palm. "He's gone, Shura," she whispered, aware that her teeth were chattering. "He left last eve . . . on a boat, for Boston."

Shura's gaze swept to the distant hills and Alexa felt as if she were poised upon some yawning precipice, scant moments from a fatal plunge. "No," Shura rasped. "He stays."

Oliver drew the phaeton to a halt and for several moments squinted through the settling dust at the small cottage nestled beneath a grove of towering cabbage trees. Unimposing in its cloak of pale pink stucco trimmed in white, it slumbered cozily amongst the profusion of white, pink and lavender blooms surrounding it, and those framing the whitewashed veranda, seeming magically suspended above it. The place emitted so sleepy a tranquility Oliver had to wonder if his father had sought it and Lily Fairfield solely for that reason.

Heady fragrance choked the air, air so thick with torrid heat that Oliver cast the rising sun his tenth scowl of the morning and shifted uncomfortably within his linen shirt. He'd forgone his topcoat and cravat for the sake of comfort, and was inclined to think a less disciplined man would have abandoned the shirt as well.

Tossing the reins aside, he leaped from the vehicle and approached the cottage with a determined stride, rolling his sleeves to his elbows and unbuttoning the first few buttons of his shirt. Upon reaching the very first step, however, he paused, only to realize the annoying sound in his ears was his own grinding teeth. He shoved a hand through his hair, kneaded the base of his neck, then stood for several moments with hands on his hips, listening to a faroff melody that seemed to be coming from inside the cottage. A piano, if he wasn't mistaken, abominably out of tune, to his ear. Or perhaps it was the playing. Season tickets at the Chicago Metropolitan Opera obviously possessed one of some sort of ability to recognize such things. It was an unexpected benefit, as he'd procured the tickets solely because Theodore MacAdoo was rumored to live and breathe for the opera.

Theodore MacAdoo. The merger. Sweet, repressed Daphne.

With a grunt of irritation, he started off along a path that led around the side of the cottage to the back. He had to duck under a narrow archway choked with some sweet-smelling white flowers, then scowled and grumbled at the bees suddenly swarming about him. With far more force than was necessary, he shoved a white picket gate open, achieving no small measure of satisfaction when it thwacked against the house and banged closed behind him. Growling a curse, he swiped several bees from his arms, swatted one flat against his neck and plunged head-on into a clothesline hanging heavy with white linen. He skidded and took an abrupt step backward, his fists clenched against his thighs as if intent upon doing battle with the damned clothesline. Instead, he found himself confronted with row upon row of flimsy, feminine attire, a visual feast for any man, but for Oliver as potent as any aphrodisiac known to man.

Transparent silk stockings, rows of chemises, peasant blouses, swatches and swathes, all of the finest, sheerest white linen imaginable. Conjured by some unseen force, the first breeze he could recall of the day filtered like a whisper through the tempting array, inundating Oliver with an elusive fragrance that prompted a fierce and immediate tightening in his loins. As if it were all suddenly beyond his power to do otherwise, his eyes feasted first upon those silk stockings and he found himself imagining long, gently curved legs, slender thighs… He scowled at his imaginings and shifted his gaze, his eyes devouring oddly shaped strips of cloth he knew served as those narrow skirts she wore. Something prompted him a step closer, then another, and he found his fingers just brushing the scalloped lace edging of a delicate chemise, then venturing within those transparent folds, his fingers almost hypnotic in their rhythmic stroking. A narrow silk white ribbon brushed against the back of his hand, unbearably soft, alluring, and he crushed the linen in his fist as a suffocating heat washed over him. He buried his face in the chemise, breathing deeply of the scent of gardenia for one mindless moment. So cool the cloth was, soothing upon his skin like a woman's gentle touch, yet stoking an ardor that left him so shaken he found himself staring at his trembling hands and the chemise, crushed within his fists.

He thrust the linen aside and spun about, rubbing a hand over his damp forehead, striving for some control. His lungs threatened to burst from his chest, his manhood from his trousers, and he gritted his teeth against the bellow of rage and frustration, and yes, something far more potent, aching for release. It was then, at the precise moment that he cursed the fates for bestowing upon him this weakness, his *father's* weakness—yes, his father had bequeathed to him far more than a floundering plantation—only then, when the deep haze receded from his mind did he spy the woman watching him from the back porch. Half-secreted behind a trellis of purple flowers, she simply stared at him with huge, brown eyes devoid of expression. A black she was, there on the sun-dappled porch one moment, gone the next. In four huge strides, he reached the porch. In two bounds, navigated five steps, then skidded to a halt as if all but leveled by a blow to the stomach.

Alexandra Fairfield stood a good ten paces inside the cottage, staring at him. The open top half of a heavily whitewashed closed oak door allowed him an unimpeded view of her, though the beast inside him, the beast rising anew at the very sight of her, would have trod over anything to get to her, to lay one paw upon her, upon all that white linen.

"Oh, hullo again," she said softly, her voice as whimsical as the sunlight playing about her like a golden halo. She was dressed precisely as she had been the day before, clear to her bare feet, her hair a tumbling blond cloud falling nearly to her waist.

"I missed my boat," he heard himself say.

"I'm sure another sails today."

"Two days." He stepped nearer to the door, his gaze straying momentarily over her shoulder, when he realized the piano-playing had ceased some time ago. The whole place was a soft white, walls, furniture, floors, *her,* in varying shades, save for an enormous vase of blood-red lilies upon a square whitewashed table. His eyes found hers. "I'm not—"

"No." She waved a hand over her shoulder toward a doorway. "I'm just—that is—we were quite finished." She turned slightly and called someone's name softly, though Oliver barely heard, so intently did he feast upon the artless curls cascading down her slender back to just brush the gentle high curve of her buttocks.

A scruffy Creole lad of at least fifteen appeared behind her, dousing Oliver in reality. His eyes narrowed upon the gangly youth gazing with unabashed adoration at Alexa . . . then narrowed suspiciously when her slender fingers lingered upon the boy's arm, fleetingly, as she spoke to him in hushed tones. The whole scene made Oliver feel like a bumbling intruder, a lummox chained in his cage just beyond a half-closed door. As it was, when the lad brushed past him to leave the cottage, something prompted Oliver to puff up his chest and glower at the boy before catching the door with the toe of his boot.

"May I?" he asked, pushing the door wide and advancing into the tiny kitchen before Alexa could more than blink. He paused directly before her, feeling extraordinarily massive for some reason, or perhaps it was this woman that made him so aware of himself as a man . . . and of what he was capable of doing to a woman. *To her. Only* her. To hell with every repressed virgin he'd ever known.

"Good morning." He drank in the sight of her so close once again, her enormous eyes, the upward tilt of her lips, so full, so pink and inviting. The air crackled between them, and he might have imagined it, but she seemed to sway toward him for one breathless moment before she turned and drifted to the table.

"These are vermilion lilies," she said, glancing slightly over her shoulder at him. "Gorgeous, aren't they?"

"Gorgeous," he murmured, his voice thick with something, and God knew it wasn't logic or reason. He'd even managed to forget why the hell he'd come here.

She seemed entirely unaware of what she had done to him. "The bulbs are deadly." Her voice rose cool and distant. "From them the original Indian inhabitants of this island extracted the poison to tip their arrows for hunting game and fish. Some of the blacks still do."

"You know the blacks well."

"I've lived among them for over twenty-one years." She cupped the nearest lily and drew it to her nose. "Would you care for some tea, Mr. Keane?"

"Oliver," he muttered, adding swiftly, "Not throwing me out?"

She slanted him a glance. "No, *Mr. Keane.* I wish to discuss a murder with you." She moved past him, stirring the air with her scent, and pushed the back door open. He followed, across the porch and down the steps, not two paces behind her. She paused at a rather rusted water pump and thrust a metal bucket into his belly.

"Hold this," she said, and with both hands set about pumping so vigorously upon the handle that her feet left the grass beneath her. "Under the spout there. Just a few moments..."

He positioned the bucket beneath the spout. "No running water in your cottage yet, I take it."

"You're in Barbados, Mr. Keane," she managed to say between pumps. "Not Boston."

"Chicago," he found himself reminding her.

She seemed entirely uninterested, preferring to pump with all her might. "Now, just a few more and it will come."

"Here... let me."

"No, absolutely not, I—"

His hand closed entirely over hers upon the handle.

She pursed her lips and huffed, all but tapping a bare toe in the soft grass, frowning at his massive forearm blocking her sight. "Now you're in my way. And you're not holding the bucket properly."

"Contrary today, eh?" He slipped his arm around her back and settled his hand once more atop hers. With one flex of his arm, the handle plunged down, then drifted upward again. Water spewed into the bucket he held steady with one foot.

She swallowed, as if biting back some retort, though she didn't look at him. Somehow, amidst all her naïveté, she knew better than to purposely tempt the beast beyond his endurance. Of her innocence, he had very little doubt, or perhaps some small shred of male intuition assured him the slight trembling he felt in her against his arm, against his chest, beneath his palm, was not prompted by fear or revulsion. No matter the adversarial nature of their encounter the day before. He, more than anyone, was grimly aware that today was an altogether different set of circumstances.

The pump plunged, then retreated, again and again, but Oliver performed the task mindlessly, his focus upon the woman poised but inches from him...Alexa, her lips slightly parted and moist, all but begging to be kissed. He barely moved, yet somehow the distance between them dissolved. Golden tendrils whispered against his face, luring him ever closer, until his chin just brushed against her temple. His skin beneath his shirt was damp, yet burned from the feel of her back, the softness of her buttocks against his thighs. Fire exploded through him, raging like a beast unchained. His mind reeled with the scent of her, with the memory of the feel of her skin beneath his hand, with the thought of ravishing her... here...*now*....

His palm slid over her hip, to her belly, his fingers splaying over a softness that trembled, tightened, yielded. She seemed to dissolve against his shoulder when his mouth found her temple, his thumb the hollow between her ribs. Then, in one movement, he caught her against him, his arm slipping beneath her breasts, turning her, intent upon crushing the breath from her lungs. One hand caught in her hair, forcing her head closer until his mouth found hers in a savage kiss, a kiss meant to trounce the demon in his blood, to vanquish this weakness, to give him some surcease from this torment. If only, for that one agonizing moment, she hadn't responded.

Yes, before it all ceased suddenly, far too suddenly, she yielded him all that promised so very much beneath her white linen, clung to his shirt as if for her very life and parted her lips with but the slightest provocation. And he wanted more. So much more....

Yet as quickly as she yielded, she tensed, twisting from him with a cry.

"No," he growled, catching her wrist before she could flee. He realized that the water had overflowed the bucket, that they stood nearly ankle-deep in a puddle...that he couldn't have cared less. But she seemed to.

She reached for the bucket, attempted to lift it, despite her one hand still encased in his. "Please—"

"Forget the damned tea." He moved to take the bucket easily in hand, though for some reason she seemed intent upon doing the job herself. "Listen—"

She sidestepped his reach, then slammed against his chest when he yanked upon her arm. He held her unreasonably close, well aware that her eyes flashed that belligerent emerald fire.

"Is this what you came here for?" she asked tonelessly, her palms flat, resisting against his chest.

"No," he replied. His gaze rested upon her mouth. His arm flexed, drawing her even closer.

"I don't believe you."

"Well, you should. I'm not in the habit of seducing every virgin I meet." His eyes narrowed and he bent his mouth to her neck, despite her immediate stiffening. "Now, hush, Alexa," he murmured, tasting her skin, his hands molding her to him.

"Cease!" With a surprising show of strength, she shoved against him, achieving escape, then slipped behind the water pump. "Don't think I don't know you, Keane. Seducing virgins? Ha. You're intent upon far more."

Oliver gritted his teeth into a grim smile and advanced upon her, his boots squishing in the mire. "Come here, Alexa."

She whisked around the water pump, easily evading him, her feet far more secure in the muck than his leather-soled boots. She lifted a saucy eyebrow and hiked her skirt to her calves. "Would you not employ every means to get what you want, Keane?"

Oliver lunged for her, but his fingers grasped only air when she circled the pump yet again. "Yes," he all but hissed through his teeth. "I always get what I want. Knowing this, I would think you'd cease this game, Alexa."

Like a frightened yet agile doe, she again scooted away from him, her mouth curving winsomely when he skidded in the mud and glowered at her. "Only you think of this as a game, Keane. My very life is at stake here."

"I'm not interested in taking your life, Alexa."

"The bloody hell you're not," she railed. "You've schemed and plotted like the devil himself to achieve your business empire. Not to mention your astonishing lack of regard for

your own father, for all that he devoted his life to. Ha! For a man like you, seducing my portion of the plantation from me would be but a stroll in the park and grossly in character, would it not?"

"Perhaps, though I seem to be doing a damned poor job of it."

She lifted her chin. "Miserably poor. I wouldn't think failure would sit well with you, Keane."

"I wouldn't know." He dug his feet into the mud for leverage, his thigh muscles bunching in anticipation of another lunge. "I've yet to fail."

"A pity. I'd wager you shall have a wretched time getting used to it then, eh?" Slender legs flashed through the slit in her skirt when she slipped, yelped, then just escaped him. A genuine smile curved her lips, her blush high in her cheeks as though the thought of his enjoying a wretched time proved inordinately satisfying. "After all, I'm not some poor sod from Boston."

"Chicago," he growled, first lunging right, then instantly changing direction when she lunged to his left. She gave a squeal and attempted to spin about in a flurry of limbs and blond curls, but he had already caught her beneath both flailing arms, spun her and lifted her easily from her feet. With booted feet braced wide in mud, Oliver held her to him, nose to nose, his every fiber screaming for release, but the words rising in his throat were borne of some other demon.

"You want a fight?" he snarled, ignoring the luminous emerald gaze, the slightly trembling lower lip, the feel of supple woman squirming all over him. "I'll give you what you want. I'll fight you over anything... *anything*. Hell, I'll stay on this damned, miserable island as long as it takes to prove to you that *I never lose. Never.* I *always* get what I want. I'd suggest you choose your weapons well. Something tells me the stakes are somewhat higher for you than me."

"You're a beast," she spat, her breath fanning the flames smoldering within him.

"That I am. Get used to it." And with that, he crushed his mouth over hers, a bruising, ruthless quest, a punishment for goading and baiting him, for wiping all logical thought from his mind. For shoving his weakness at him.

Her nails dug painfully into his shoulders, her legs thrashed against his thighs, but he didn't release her. . . . He couldn't . . . he wanted more. So much more. He wanted her surrender.

It never came.

He tore his mouth from hers and found himself staring into her eyes, at her swollen lips, and was suddenly overcome by some unfathomable desire to apologize to her. He even opened his mouth, loosened his hold upon her, but the words failed to materialize upon his tongue. Not that it would have mattered. She'd slipped from his arms and run for the house.

"Ah, hell." He shoved an unsteady hand through his hair when the back door slammed closed in her wake. With a last glance at the sun-dappled porch, he set off for the phaeton, cursing every last squish of his boots.

Chapter Five

Alexa made a face at the enormous brass lion's head that served as a door knocker, and slipped her fingers through the ring hanging from the beast's jowls. Then, at the precise moment when she would have sent a sharp rap echoing through Bellefontaine's halls, she froze.

Good God, what was she doing? The air spilled from her lungs in a defeated rush and she studied her soft kid shoes with odd detachment. Yes, what indeed was she doing here upon Bellefontaine's flagstone doorstep, her belongings piled high in a buggy, and her champion, Stuart Jeffcoat, in tow simply to provide the legalities, if necessary?

Over her shoulder she cast him a quick glance, noting that he perched rather stiffly atop the curricle in the blazing afternoon sun. He stared over the horse's head, his chin tucked under, his back ramrod stiff. All polished brass even now. An asset, to be sure, willing to aid her, support her... unlike Shura.

A fleeting disquiet whispered through her and she studied the lion's head once more, her fingers cold and stiff upon the brass. Not that she had expected encouragement from Shura, since the servant had no doubt witnessed all that had occurred around the water pump earlier that morning. Shura had made no mention of it, of course. She never had to explain herself. Alexa simply *knew,* even amidst her own jumbled thoughts and scatterbrained shuffling about.

She'd wondered as she'd packed, how Shura managed to simply maneuver about after being kissed by a man. How did she, for example, keep her knees from wobbling together, or her hands from trembling uncontrollably...or those thoughts, those maddening thoughts of *him,* how did she keep them from invading her mind? And how did she keep the flush from her cheeks, that throbbing, heated, supremely guilty flush that arose whenever Shura simply glanced her way? Surely the sight of that blush was all the servant required in order to know Alexa had been ravaged in a puddle. And, God forbid, that she'd managed to enjoy it, despite her every reason not to.

Shura had spoken to her only once that afternoon and that had been when Alexa had rather breezily announced her intent to take up residence at Bellefontaine. Actually, the servant had simply stared at her, her silence oh so telling, and, as usual, prompting Alexa to chatter on, revealing so very much more than she would have, had Shura simply spoken. How *did* she manage it?

"I have to do this, Shura," Alexa had tried to explain as she arranged her clothes into her mother's traveling trunk. "The key to mother's murder lies in that house." She'd glanced at Shura, who loomed stoically in the bedroom doorway. "Don't stare at me so. The entire British government thinks Mother a murderess and I refuse to believe it." Her fingers had twisted in the folds of a linen blouse. "Shura, someone—some twisted, demonic soul—murdered Mother and Gabriel Keane. I'm certain of it. So certain, that I will risk anything to expose them. *Anything.*"

"You will risk you, woman-child."

"I'm not afraid of a tongue-lashing from the governor."

The servant had grunted and shook her head. "The governor doesn't live at plantation house. Man-beast does."

Ah, yes, Alexa's very deepest fear exposed, as if hearing it made it so much more frightening than simply thinking it. Oh, she feared him, all right...feared all that he could do to her, all that he could take from her. The plantation, yes, but so very much more. "Yes, he does. But he's leaving... soon...I...hope. In any case, he shan't dissuade me. I vow he shan't. He...he's *abominable.* Truly he is. A man with no soul. A...a—"

"He wants you, like man wants woman."

A tremor had whisked through Alexa, that blasted flush sweeping to her forehead. "I...why, yes, of course, I'm somewhat aware of that, but, Shura, not for the reasons you're thinking."

Shura had given a knowing *harrumph* and crossed her arms over her bosom, regarding Alexa with lips pursed.

Alexa had tossed the blouse into the trunk and spread her hands wide in supplication. "He...er...*wants* me—for lack of a better word—simply because he seeks control of Bellefontaine." Her lips bared, the words but a soft hiss. "So he can sell it...parcel by parcel, piece by piece, destroying Gabriel's dream. Why, he probably knows nothing of his father's quest for Bellefontaine, nor would he care even if he did know. He simply wants whatever he wants, for whatever reason—or perhaps for *no* reason other than it provides his twisted sense of purpose some challenge—and he will employ every tactic to achieve his ends. *You* know that as well as I. His reputation as a ruthless, power-seeking monster has flourished amongst Bellefontaine's workers for over fifteen years, and apparently for good reason. Can you deny it?"

Shura's eyes had narrowed. "The time will come when man-beast wants woman more than all else in life."

Alexa all but snorted and resumed her packing with fervor. "Not this man-beast."

"Yes, *this man-beast.*"

"Shura, the man is a far cry from his father. And even if what you say should somehow come to pass—which it won't—he won't get me *or* the plantation. I tell you, *he won't.*"

"He will."

Alexa had glanced up sharply but Shura had vanished like a specter, silently...reappearing sometime later when Stuart Jeffcoat had tossed Alexa's trunk into the curricle.

"Come with me," Alexa had murmured against the servant's shoulder as they embraced.

"No place for me," Shura had replied, her brown eyes solemn, her palm moving softly over Alexa's cheek. "Keep safe."

"I will. I'm not afraid."

"You will be."

Those words echoed all the more ominously now as she stood upon Bellefontaine's portal, her trembling fingers capable of sealing her fate were they to simply release that knocker. She had to do this...for her mother, for Gabriel...no matter Shura's dire predictions. No matter that she, herself, could be the ultimate sacrifice.

The knocker banged against the wood and Alexa jumped, clutching her wide-brimmed hat atop her head and stepping a pace back. She encountered Stuart Jeffcoat's sturdy chest close behind her and attempted to draw something from his proximity...something besides a fleeting annoyance when his gloved hands moved upon her waist in an attempt to steady her. At that moment, the pinch-faced Cyril appeared in the open doorway, his thin nose assuming a lofty perch after a moment's brutal perusal.

"Miss Fairfield has arrived," Stuart boomed a trifle too boisterously for Alexa's taste. "Prepare a room, man. Posthaste."

The servant remained in the doorway, entirely unfazed. "I think not."

"I say!" Stuart barked, his sword clanking as he took a step forward and gestured dramatically. "As a commanding officer in Her Majesty's forces, I *demand* you remove yourself from my path."

Arching an eyebrow, Alexa offered Cyril a smooth smile, then preceded Stuart into the house when the servant apparently thought it best to step aside. Without a word, Cyril disappeared into a darkened hallway, leaving Alexa and Stuart to linger in the foyer.

"The staggering pomposity!" Stuart hissed, pacing to and fro, his boots squeaking upon polished cream-colored marble. He paused and flung an arm in Cyril's wake. "Did you see that? He openly defied me. *Me,* a government official, no less!"

"Some harbor no great reverence for those with more power than they," Alexa said. Her gaze as well as her thoughts rested upon the hulking figure moving in his casual yet deliberate manner toward them. Oliver Keane, wild-haired and equally as wild-eyed. Closer and closer he came, forcing the air from Alexa's lungs with each step such that the room seemed to tilt beneath her feet. He glanced neither at Cyril, shuffling along behind him, nor at Stuart, poised gallantly at her side. His cobalt gaze skewered Alexa, swept shamelessly over her from head to toe and back, and he paused not a hand's breadth from her.

"Welcome, Miss Fairfield." Those impossibly deep tones seemed to shake the floor itself. Then he grasped her hand and drew her fingers to his lips, his eyes glittering dangerously. "You're late."

Alexa blinked and sought her voice. "I—"

His breath was hot upon her fingers, far more torrid than nature's blazing heat. "I was expecting you sooner."

"Well, I say," Stuart piped up. "A bloody surprise, this is! Thought we'd come to blows over this, Keane."

But Oliver's gaze didn't falter, his hold upon her fingers viselike, unrelenting. "Fetch her bags, Jeffcoat," he said without so much as glancing at the British officer. "Cyril, have him deposit them in the lady's chambers."

Stuart blustered for a moment until Alexa glanced up at him and offered a smile that seemed to tremble upon her lips.

"I shall be but a moment, my dear," Stuart said stiffly, despite the cold look he leveled at Oliver. Drawing himself to his full height, Stuart all but clicked his heels before maneuvering his way to the door.

"An obedient pet," Oliver observed. "You've trained him well."

"Gentlemen require no training, Mr. Keane, I—"

"Oliver," he interrupted, pinioning her resisting hand upon his arm and leading her down a wide hall. "You can cease with the formalities, Alexa. We're living together now."

Alexa immediately bristled at his implication, yet bit back any display of temper. Indeed, she had vowed to remain entirely unaffected by the man, at least *outwardly* so.

Despite the hint of levity in his words and his overly solicitous manner, she sensed a palpable undercurrent of suppressed tension in him, as if a beast did indeed lurk within him. Perhaps it was in his voice, so very deep and ominous...or perhaps in all that untested strength keeping her hand beneath his, forcing her along, close beside him...so close that his thigh brushed against her hip with his every step.

Alexa pondered her suddenly parched throat and cast her eyes elsewhere...anywhere but upon him, looming darkly forbidding beside her. Her eyes flickered over Gabriel Keane's treasured artwork lining the hall, pieces her own mother had helped him choose over the years, and several original works by those French Impressionist painters Monet and Degas. Indeed, Alexa had heard Gabriel speak reverently of these works so often, she knew them by sight. Would Oliver callously sell all that his father had cherished? "I would like to unpack my things," she ventured, wondering where the devil he was taking her.

"We have to talk" came the muttered reply. And then he shoved open a set of double doors and held a hand before him. "My lady," he mocked, his eyes aglitter with something that set Alexa's blood churning in her veins.

She lifted her chin and breezed past him only to pause in the center of the semicircular room, her gaze captured by the wall of windows overlooking Bellefontaine's famous gardens. From those windows, plush green lawns sloped gracefully to a brilliant profusion of blossoms encircling a marble fountain. As far as the eye could see beyond that, the gardens lay like sumptuous carpets, resplendent in their lush summer garb—all torrid pinks, fuchsias, whites. So enthralled was she, Alexa barely heard the doors close behind her, but she sensed him when he moved silently past her to pause beside a desk littered with paper. She glanced at him, noting that he paid the visual feast at his back little heed, that his brows dived into that familiar scowl as he studied the papers that lay upon the desk before him. His eyes flicked right and left quickly, efficiently, yet something told her he missed nothing in his haste. A tick began in his jaw, drawing her gaze, which then strayed to the arrogant thrust of his cleft chin...then lower still where the parted top buttons of his shirt revealed a thickly furred chest.

A faint trembling seized her in its grip, and she found herself assailed by his scent, by the manner in which the sun flamed in his tousled blue-black hair, by the memory of those long, tapering fingers forcing her mouth to his....

She shuddered and turned abruptly toward the windows, then rather self-consciously began tucking stray tendrils beneath her hat.

"Would you care to sit?" he asked suddenly.

She felt those eyes upon her. "No, I'd prefer to stand here and admire the view."

"Oh." As if he couldn't quite comprehend that. "Tea?"

"No." She glanced at him from beneath the brim of her hat, finding him seated rather casually, half on, half off the desk, arms folded, staring at her. "Thank you," she heard herself say.

"If you'd like any—"

"I'll get it myself."

"Of course. You live here now." He stared at her for several moments in silence, then indicated a finely scrolled linen parchment lying atop one of the farthest piles upon the desk. "I found this under a heap of unopened mail today. Has that pompous, important look about it. An invitation to some governmental hobnobbery for those two visiting princes from Wales. Dinner, dancing, that sort of thing. Tomorrow night. The entire plantation community is expected to attend. That means us."

"Is that so?" Alexa replied. She wondered what game the man was up to, though he offered her little insight when his attention returned to the jumble of papers.

"You do dance, do you not?"

His question caught her by surprise. "Dance? I—"

"I'll expect you in the foyer promptly at seven." He resumed his shuffling through the heap of paper upon the desk, entirely oblivious to Alexa's mounting ire.

The nerve of the man. Ordering her about as if she were one of his blasted employees!

"I've a prior engagement," she offered airily, as she moved closer to the windows, her gaze purposefully averted.

"Cancel it," he muttered distractedly, bending to rummage deep within one enormous pile.

"No," she all but sang with a breathy sigh. "I don't believe I shall."

"Do you women find some perverse pleasure in being difficult?" he snarled. He growled a curse under his breath when a stack of correspondence slid to the floor and scattered.

For some reason, the sight of him grumbling and mumbling on all fours, retrieving strewn pages, brought a curve to Alexa's lips. "I'm not being difficult, Mr. Keane, I simply don't wish to attend one of those blasted functions."

"Then you must not dance" came the muffled reply from somewhere beneath the desk.

Alexa scooped up several pages just at her feet and placed them upon the desk, pondering his logic. "That has nothing to do with it."

He materialized directly behind her, rising like Neptune himself from the depths of a turbulent ocean, his chest brushing like a whisper against her back. "Then you're going," he said, reaching around her with a fistful of papers.

She stared at the crumpled paper in his mighty fist, then at his arm, braced against the desk as if he meant to keep it there a while. He'd done the same with his other arm, entrapping her between the desk, his arms and his immovable bulk. Fleetingly, she wondered if the man had purposefully scattered the pages simply to achieve such an end.

She tried valiantly to ignore the heat emanating from his chest, penetrating thin linen, branding her entire back. Tried to ignore the wicked thoughts prompted by the corded muscle and bulging veins in his forearms, arms that looked strong enough to do just about anything to a girl. "I shan't be ordered about, Mr. Keane."

"Oliver."

"I detest those functions, *Mr. Keane.*"

"I'll be damned." His surprise seemed genuine though she didn't dare glance over her shoulder at him for that telltale mocking gleam in his eyes. "I thought you women lived and breathed for that sort of thing."

"Women like my mother, perhaps."

"Not you?"

She shook her head and wondered why air suddenly seemed so scarce. "I find them dreadfully dull, and everyone stalks about bloated with self-importance, expecting the entirely proper from you."

"Ah, yes, I suppose shoes would be required at such an event, and the appropriate dress. Do you have one, by chance?"

"A dress? Yes, several." She swallowed and wondered if she simply imagined that he loomed even closer at her back.

"Come with me tomorrow evening, Alexa." His breath fanned against the exposed nape of her neck, his voice deceptive in its softness.

Her fingers, just inches from his, gripped the edge of the desk. "Give me a good reason."

"I'll teach you to dance."

"I don't care to learn."

"Look at it as an opportunity to while away an afternoon in a bath, then spend hours putting yourself together or whatever it is you women do."

"I'd prefer a swim in the ocean."

"What about the food? Surely that interests you. Imagine a feast fit for the governor and two pompous Princes of Wales."

Alexa's lips curved slightly. "A bout with dyspepsia, to be sure."

"Good point. I don't suppose hobnobbing with British royalty interests you, either."

She shook her head, aware that some part of her relished their byplay, that some deeper part of her reveled in the rich reverberation of his voice, the simple feel of his warmth so very near.

"No interest in food, dancing, leisurely baths, nonsensical froufrou or idle aristocrats. Rather peculiar for a female." He seemed to ponder this for several moments. "That leaves only me."

"You?" Her laugh burst forth unchecked. "I don't even like you, Mr. Keane."

"Oliver," he reminded her, his voice suddenly so very close. "Consider this, Alexa—a roomful of the top echelon of Barbadian government do-goods, their bellies full of undercooked beef and too-sweet champagne, their tongues loose yet all but begging to be loosened even more by a beautiful young woman with ample reason to bend her every womanly wile upon gleaning information about her mother's death."

Alexa swallowed thickly. "I have no wiles, Mr. Keane."

"*Oliver,*" he murmured. "Trust me, you don't need them."

A shiver swept through Alexa and she gulped past a suddenly parched throat. "You're stooping to bribery and I cannot help but wonder why, Mr. Keane."

"Don't you like my name?" he asked softly. "Not many women do, you know. It's Oliver, remember? Rather clumsy on the tongue. O-li-ver. Say it."

"I have to unpack."

"I'm not letting you go until you say my name."

She glanced sideways from beneath her hat and caught a glimpse of his stubbled chin. He needed a shave...and seemed to be grinning. *Him?* Her stubborn tongue almost refused command. "Oliver."

"Not so fast." He thwarted her attempt to slip away from him with the firm pressure of his entire torso against her back. "Tomorrow evening. Seven."

She glared at that arrogant chin. "What game are you about, Mr. K—"

"*O-li-ver.* Simply going after what I want, Alexa. Surely you expected a good deal of persistence on my part."

"Actually, I anticipated your tempting me with an offer of more money, not a dance lesson."

"I would be hard-pressed to put a price on what I seek. Any idea how much a king's ransom would be worth in today's market?"

"Your father would have considered even that an insult. Now, if you'll excuse me—"

It was a small gesture, given the nature of the beast, but performed by him, it proved as potent as anything he had done in that puddle. Alexa froze, her breath compressing in her lungs, when his thumb stroked softly over her hand. Ripples of delight pulsed from his touch, danced along her arm, then spread like liquid heat through her belly. Had she not gripped the edge of the desk, she was quite certain her wobbling knees would have sent her crumpling to the floor.

"Tomorrow evening, Alexa. I'm leaving at seven, not a minute later."

Only an abominably arrogant man would release her then, without waiting for the favor of a reply, and stride from the room. Only a supremely presumptuous man would behave thus, yet manage to leave her feeling far too alone, far too *abandoned* for a woman who had every reason to loathe the very sight of him. He was indeed arrogant, presumptuous, and, yes, loathsome . . . yet she could only stare at her trembling hand, long after the door closed behind him, aware only of a mindless, incomprehensible yearning for his touch upon her once again.

Oliver blinked once, twice, rubbed his tired eyes, then squinted at the parchment, all to no avail. Even his father's bold scrawl remained blurred. With a grunt of irritation, he shoved his chair away from the desk, from all that had occupied him for well over four hours, and sought the brandy decanter. He poured himself a liberal draft, drained it, then poured another and strode to the windows. He stared unseeing into the gathering dusk, his thoughts straying as they had been wont to do over the past several hours, much to his frustration, to *that woman.* No, Alexa was like no woman he'd ever known. She was a child. A woman-child.

Little good it had done him to sequester himself in his father's study. His purpose had been to wade through all that had accumulated upon the desk since his father's death, and, as he'd discovered, over the course of several months prior to that. Typically, engrossing himself in paperwork and financial documents filled him with a sense of accomplishment and eased his tensions. On this fateful afternoon, however, his sole achievement had been a monumental headache prompted by his forever-straying thoughts, compounded tenfold by the disastrous state of his father's papers.

He shook his head and ground his teeth with annoyance. In all his rare and cynical imaginings about his father, he'd never suspected the man to be so entirely disorganized, a trait Oliver had long deemed a fatal character flaw in anyone, particularly a businessman. His father's personal files were a shambles, the plantation records all but illegible or arranged in so convoluted a manner no logical person could comprehend them. Indeed, he had to wonder how a bumbling buffoon like Stuart Jeffcoat had managed to declare the plantation financially sound. Then again, one could readily assume thus if no creditors had appeared at Bellefontaine's door upon notice of Gabriel Keane's death. Even Jeffcoat could make such an assumption. A ten-year-old child could.

He was certain no one could possibly know the plantation's actual worth. But did his father's killer?

He drained his glass in one gulp, relishing the liquor's effect as it worked its way through his stiff limbs. He felt oddly tired and old, far too old for only thirty-three years. And angry...perhaps because he had found himself abandoning the plantation records for the leather-bound journal he'd discovered in the desk's bottom drawer, stuffed behind a stack of correspondence dating back several years.

His father's daily journal. He'd realized it immediately upon opening it. He'd scowled, then tossed the thing aside when, for some damnable reason, his hands began to shake...only to reach for it moments later, prompted by some unseen force to part that worn leather binding and settle low in his chair, the journal opened to the very first page.

He pondered his empty glass and wondered how often his father had lingered thus, staring from this same window, perhaps with this very glass in hand. It was an odd feeling, one Oliver was decidedly uncomfortable with, this fleeting sense of melancholy...mixed with a certain disquiet, almost as if he were a young boy trespassing on someone else's property. Only the property was his father's thoughts, his father's home...and Oliver was no mere boy, but a man struggling with his demons.

"*Oliver.*" The door banged open and his mother's shrill voice shattered the silence.

Oliver scowled into his glass. "Do you have some aversion to knocking upon closed doors, Mother, or is the house on fire?"

"Worse." Eleanor rustled to a halt directly at his side, her face beneath the dramatic sweep of her hat flushed and flustered with obvious indignation. "Cyril just informed me we have a house guest. *That... that...*"

"Alexa is her name. She has legal claim to half the plantation, Mother, remember?"

Eleanor thrust her taffeta skirts aside to take up an agitated pacing to and fro. "Look at you, Oliver. One could almost think you comfortable with such a calamity."

Oliver strode to the brandy decanter. "An unsuccessful day of shopping, Mother?"

Eleanor glared at him with pursed lips and fists clenched. "Remarkably successful, I'll have you know. I only just returned. Bridgetown has somehow managed over the course of fifteen years to acquire an extraordinary number of French couturiers and even an exquisite milliner's shop. All very posh. One could well imagine oneself in Chicago, if it weren't for this blasted heat. And I even managed to achieve the acquaintance of several of the wives of some highly placed naval fellows."

Oliver's gaze flickered over his mother's elegant burgundy gown, replete with swags and ruffles and enormous puffed sleeves. "Hardly the grieving widow, are you?"

"*Oliver.* Women of that caliber know better than to expect a scorned wife to openly grieve for her dead husband. Trust me, none of them would swathe themselves in that horrid black for an entire year simply for the sake of propriety. They're far too proud. Just as I am far too proud to allow that vagrant Fairfield chit to sleep one night under this roof."

Oliver gulped his drink and gave fleeting thought to getting himself thoroughly soused this eve. Ignoring her tightening jaw, he strode to the windows once again. "I've the matter well in hand."

"In hand? How, pray? What the devil does she want?"

Oliver gazed at the cane fields in the distance. "I believe she thinks she's protecting her interests."

"Oliver, the brat deserves to be flung from this house."

Something foreign welled up in Oliver's chest, clear into his throat, and he clenched his teeth to achieve a measured tone. Yet the look he swung upon his mother forced her back a step. "Your grievance is not with her, Mother. You would do well to remember that."

She blinked at him in momentary confusion. "And you would do well to do everything in your power to strip the girl of her ownership in this plantation. Offer her more money, blast it."

"She won't take it."

"Then steal it from her."

"That wouldn't be quite legal, now, would it?"

"Don't give me that legal rubbish. You know as well as I, you've employed less than exemplary methods in the past to get what you want from a business deal. Do the same with her."

"The rules of business can be stretched."

Eleanor gave a harsh laugh. "Call it what you will, Oliver, but I've watched you gobble up small shipping companies without a moment's consideration or hesitation. Indeed, in some circles, your shipping conglomerate is synonymous with corporate villainy. Something you're rather proud of, I would wager. Yet you're treating this . . . this . . . *girl* like the finest porcelain."

Oliver stared at his mother, then swung back to the windows, one hand roughly massaging his neck. "She's rather . . . unusual."

"Trust me, Oliver, every woman has a price."

He considered that a moment. "There *is* this murder business, Mother."

"Dear God, surely you don't actually *believe* such nonsense?"

"*She* does. That's part of her logic behind moving in here. Perhaps if I lend her investigation a hand—"

For some reason, Eleanor's throaty laughter grated upon him like a dull knife. "Good heavens, she'll make a laughingstock of you amongst the entire plantation community. Dear God, you would be better off attempting to seduce the plantation out of the girl. Surely you've considered that."

"Any man would." Oliver drained his glass. "Indeed, it seems the best course. But what of dear Daphne, my ever-patient fiancée?"

Eleanor gaped at him as she would at a madman. "What of her? Oliver, we both know the nature of marriage these days. What the devil difference does a brief premarital liaison make, especially if engaged in solely to achieve a justifiable end?" Eleanor's eyes glittered above a smug smile. "Seduce her, Oliver. Blast it, ravish her. *Ruin her.* Then blackmail the blasted plantation out of her. Even a whore's daughter must value her reputation." Eleanor's finely plucked eyebrow lifted wickedly. "After all, she's made it all painfully easy now that she's beneath your roof. Trust me, it will make bedding your sweet flower Daphne all that much more enjoyable."

Oliver pondered his empty glass and merely grunted, but his thoughts were not on bedding sweet Daphne. No, he was far more consumed with the precise manner in which he would seduce one peculiar little island flower. And try as he might to convince himself otherwise, at the moment his reasons had nothing to do with a justifiable end. Absolutely nothing.

Chapter Six

Perhaps the whistling frogs, shrill in the garden, kept Alexa from sleep. God knew, the bed upon which she tossed fitfully was certainly not to blame. Made of choice goose down it was, with sheets of crisp white cotton. A fine mosquito netting, draped about the four-poster, offered further comfort as did the breeze floating through her open second-floor windows. But somehow, the stirring of the air seemed only to further rouse her this evening.

No, the frogs couldn't possibly be at fault for this restlessness, this need to thrust that netting aside and venture out upon the loggia, the roofed open gallery that flanked her room on two sides. She paused at the rail and inhaled deeply of the night, her gaze sweeping through the moonlit darkness. The gardens loomed below, fragrant and alive with the trills of night creatures. Upon a gentle rise in the distance, a sea of cane rippled under a foamy white moon...and still, the restlessness invaded her, prompting her toward the steep stairs that led below to the first-floor veranda.

Her bare feet moved silently along the planks, her sheer lawn nightgown drifting between her legs, just sweeping her ankles with each step she took. All the windows were dark, the house still, but not with the silence of a peacefully slumbering household. This was a household where secrets lurked.

A faint salt breeze ruffled her unbound hair and billowed through her sleeves as she hurried through damp grass, away from that house, into the gardens and beyond, where the fountain beckoned in the moonlight like a precious jewel. The water was cool beneath her fingertips, and soothed skin heated by some inner fire.

Without pausing to lift her hem, she stepped into the fountain. Her gown floating around her, she waded about, heedless of all but the water lapping at her thighs and the spray shooting from the enormous white marble Cupid in the center of the fountain. It drifted through the air like fine mist, bathing her face, sprinkling like dew into her hair, seeping into her skin. She sat upon the curved edge of the fountain, her feet and legs immersed, the spray drifting over her. And silhouetted against the sky, the house loomed. A house full of foes.

Somehow, fool's luck to be sure, she'd managed to avoid confrontation with Eleanor Keane that afternoon. Not that she'd sequestered herself in her room for that express purpose. Indeed, she'd ventured through the house undaunted both by Eleanor's imminent threat and Cyril's pinched countenance forever lurking in every shadowed doorway, making her suspect the man was following her. And when she mustered the courage to venture into what had once been Gabriel Keane's bedchamber, the very chamber where he and her mother had died, a chamber long swept clean of any hints of misdeeds, her feeling that she was being covertly watched had prompted an even swifter closing of the door to that room.

The house did, however, harbor one friendly soul. Alexa discovered this when she'd appeared at the kitchen table, eager to sample some of Cook's fare. She was a plump, kindly black woman, possessing of a ready smile and an exceptional vichyssoise, which she served to Alexa, all the while humming, melodious and deep-throated. She moved continuously about the enormous, overheated kitchen, speaking only once or twice, her speech common to the blacks throughout the island. *Rock-stone. Ram-goat. Bull-cow.* Like Shura, when she'd spoken of man-beast.

No, Alexa hadn't seen *him* either and the fleeting relief she'd experienced over that disturbed her. Immensely. For she'd determined, agonizing as it may have been, that she did indeed require some assistance from someone inside that house if she was to solve the murder. And Oliver Keane, dangerous as he might be, was that someone.

If only that wouldn't require speaking to the man.

She blinked through the fountain's spray and rose to her feet, her gaze probing the darkness, seeking a sudden flash of light that seemed to have come from the house not a moment past. Again, from one of the study windows from which she'd peered that very afternoon, came a flicker of light, shadowy, covert, suggesting that someone was moving stealthily about with a dimly lit lantern. So very late at night?

She stepped from the fountain, heedless of her dripping gown, and moved toward the house, her feet stopping when they met with damp grass. The hour had to be well past midnight. What soul would prowl about at such an hour, in a room containing Gabriel Keane's personal correspondence? Oliver Keane, no doubt. She took another step, her curiosity amply piqued.

What the devil was he doing?

Then again, he seemed the type to avoid sleep altogether, or perhaps the image of him slumbering peacefully didn't quite suit one of so notorious and beastly a reputation. Far too vulnerable he would be, asleep, his lashes resting upon his cheeks, his breathing even and deep, like a child's....

She mentally shook herself. No, she didn't imagine he'd allow himself any sort of vulnerability. Her eyes narrowed upon the flickering light and she tried her best to ignore the anticipation bubbling low in her belly. Best to avoid him and that room altogether this eve, no matter that some part of her direly wished to venture past those windows...very slowly...to discover what he was up to, of course. Nothing more. God alone knew what clues to the murders lay hidden in Gabriel's personal papers, the very reason she had decided Oliver Keane would prove a formidable ally. After all, he had ready access to any and all of his father's personal effects, whereas she, the unwelcome daughter of that murderess Lily Fairfield, would certainly be denied even the briefest glimpse.

Besides, something told her that Oliver Keane possessed at least some whit of brilliance and deductive reasoning. After all, a man didn't ascend to his lofty status of shipping tycoon on luck and ruthlessness alone.

Somehow, instinct bade her glance back toward the fountain. Perhaps it was the simple stirring of the air that prompted her, the sudden peculiar shifting of the ground beneath her feet, or the fluttering in her belly, all so very instinctive, so beyond her control. Yet still she gasped when her eyes found him, a shimmering, unmoving shadow not three paces from her. The moonlight spilled over him, casting him in a silvery sheen, his hair, a silver-blue cloud, his shirt, foamy white. His eyes . . . like diamond shards.

"Oliver," she managed to whisper, her fingers suddenly gripping her sodden nightgown.

"Are you afraid?" Like distant thunder his voice rumbled, ominous, full of warning, yet like a lion's soft purr.

"Of what?" Her knees threatened to buckle when he took yet another step nearer. "Surely not of the night."

"No, I wouldn't think you would be." He loomed but a breath from her, radiating a heated scent of brandy. Perhaps the liquor lent his voice this mellow drawl, his manner this focused, raw intensity. "But are you afraid of me?"

"No," she whispered, her eyes seeking his, *feeling* his all over her. "I'm not afraid of you, Oliver, as you might want me to be."

"A peculiar woman." He said this half to himself. And then he caught a wayward blond ringlet lying over her shoulder and slowly worked the curl between his fingers, studying it through half-closed lids. "Most women are, you know. Afraid." He let out a slow rush of air. "Repulsed, I suppose. One would think you had more reason than most."

"To detest you, perhaps. But fear? No, fear is something I reserve for the unknown."

"Then you should indeed fear me." Like a whisper, her curl slipped from his fingers to rest upon the high curve of her breast. Faint was the touch but her breath caught deep in her lungs. "Alexa, you know nothing of me."

"I would venture to say I know more than most."

"Perhaps." His chest expanded visibly, making it look even broader. "A twisted lot of lies, I'd wager."

"You've done more to prove them true in the past few days than fifteen years' worth of gossip."

Again, the air hissed through his teeth and his hands found his narrow hips. "So tell me about myself... from your perspective, of course."

Alexa swallowed. "I wouldn't think you'd care awfully much for that. Besides—" she waved a hand toward the house "—someone roams about the house."

"I don't see anyone."

She had to wonder if he'd even glanced away from her. Yet, when she hastened a look at the house, all windows were again dark. "But I saw a light—in the study. I thought it was you."

"Moonlight can play tricks on young maidens, Alexa, especially young maidens who venture into fountains and fragrant gardens at three in the morning."

Alexa bit her lip and rubbed her palms over her arms. "I saw someone."

"Are you cold?" Still closer he moved, the strong scent of brandy invading her senses.

"No." Her response was too quick, and this time she took a step back, and he, another step toward her, his eyes glittering in the moonlight.

"So the rumors paint me a despoiler of innocent females."

"Actually, rumor has you rather smitten with...er...that is... When a fellow does nothing but accumulate a fortune—"

"Money is useful only for making more."

"And then?"

"Then?" He gave a harsh, deep laugh. "There can never be enough in this world for a man to conquer, Alexa. Indeed, to be an American means to be enamored of the future, of the machine, the whirl of change. To be buoyant, optimistic, and above all, *unbeaten.* It's a time of brisk men, energetic of movement and speech. The dollar is their god. How to get it, their religion." He regarded her with cocked head and those lazy eyes. "Fine. So I'm married to my work. I already knew that."

"No, actually I wasn't referring to your work at all, although the rumors regarding that tend to be rather...harsh."

"Harsh." His tone was flat.

"Oh, and terribly scathing, as well."

"I suppose I should take that as a compliment. Have the workers nothing better to discuss?"

"You're rather a legend here at Bellefontaine," Alexa replied. "You see, your father was dearly loved by the workers . . . and you—"

"I was the worthless, thankless son."

"Of course, and more . . . You know, the cynical corporate villain. A ruthless tycoon bereft of soul, of compassion for all except your mindless and consuming passion for the accumulation of wealth, power . . . that sort of thing."

"A coldhearted beast."

"Precisely. But as to the rumors regarding your . . . er . . . *preferences,* and the fact that you're rather smitten with . . . that is . . . When a fellow hasn't married by a certain advanced age—"

"Advanced?" He frowned. "I'm but three and thirty."

"There, you see, you're well past your prime already. Rather unfit for a husband, but then again, that matters little when your preference lends itself to . . ." She bit her lip again, aware of a palpable tension emanating like the brandy from him, of her own inability to actually voice the most heinous of the rumors, and one she'd had ample opportunity to doubt. And then he threw back his head and laughed.

A bellow of a laugh it was, full and rich and hearty, lifting high into the night sky. His teeth gleamed savagely in the moonlight. His eyes twinkled like the devil's himself. And he looked years younger. "God, don't tell me you actually believe that I prefer . . . over women." He shook his head and contemplated the starlit sky, as if seeking something in those fathomless depths. "Ah, hell . . . I guess I'll have to do something to right that. I don't suppose a fiancée awaiting me in Chicago would suffice."

A sudden melancholy swept through Alexa and was as suddenly gone. "How lovely," she heard herself say. "When do you wed?"

His face took on that familiar scowl and he thrust an impatient hand through his hair. "When I return to Chicago."

He seemed entirely too disturbed by this. No doubt he yearned to complete his business in Barbados all the more expeditiously, the quicker to return to his fiancée. Suddenly, lingering in a moonlit garden with this man seemed atrociously cavalier, especially when the man stared at her as if he hadn't any loyalties whatsoever to a fiancée in Chicago.

"No." He lifted the curl from her breast. "This rumor requires my immediate attention."

Alexa felt the heat of him, and something stirred deep within her. "Do not feel . . . uh . . . compelled to do so for my sake. I . . . that is, even before you mentioned your . . . er . . . fiancée, I tended to believe otherwise."

"You should." In one swift movement, he caught her elbow and yanked her roughly against him, his brandy-laced breath harsh and rasping. "My preference, Alexa, is rather stubbornly set in one direction at the moment. *Yours.* And as for being past my prime and unfit..." His hand was hot upon the small of her back, pressing her hips brazenly close against his, against all that sinew and male muscle straining against his trousers. "*That* rumor is one I would take great pleasure in proving false to you."

"Please..." Her palms pressed against his chest, feeling the damp heat of his flesh beneath the thin linen of his shirt. Her mind screamed for escape, her body for some mysterious release from the slow burn deep inside her.

"Are you begging me?" he rasped, his hand catching in her hair and forcing her head back, her mouth to part just a whisper below his. "Do you want me to prove it to you? Or do you even know what the hell I'm talking about?"

A shudder rippled through her and she shook her head, unable to give voice to anything, suddenly incapable of coherent thought . . . as if she, too, were suffering the heady effects of the brandy. And he was so very undeniable here in a flood of moonlight with the rushing of the fountain in her ears.

"So much to learn," he muttered softly. Before she could resist, before she could even comprehend his intent, he was bending her back over his arm yet crushing her to him, his mouth, his stubbled face ravishing her neck, her jaw, her cheeks. And then his lips found hers, parted, and ravaged her with a brandied heat, drawing forth soft whimpers from the back of her throat, robbing her of all breath. In a rush of air, his mouth released hers to brand the skin along her neck and the high curves of her breasts before closing over one thrusting nipple. Her eyes flew wide, a startled gasp escaped her lips and she jerked against him. But his hold upon her only tightened. Through her nightgown, she felt the heat that was his tongue on her breast as he suckled like a man starved until she cried out from the sheer torture of it and the stars swam in the night sky above her. Only then did he bend his attentions upon her other breast, teasing and tormenting until her nails dug into his shoulders and the breath fell in swift gasps from her lips. But the torture was far from complete.

Damp lawn swept over her thighs, then heated night air, then a callused male hand. Her lack of undergarments seemed to disturb him, for he uttered a strangled sound and paused momentarily, his head buried between her breasts, his hand cupping her womanhood.

"Oliver—" she managed to utter through parched lips, her hands pushing against massive, immovable shoulders. "Yes, do stop—"

She thought perhaps he laughed, short and harsh, an odd reaction, indeed. His teeth nibbled at the row of pearl buttons adorning the front of her nightgown. "Take this off."

"I can't—*Oliver,* you can't—" A breathless, vain attempt at a rejoinder if there ever was one, yet he seemed to heed her for a moment, until his fingers moved between her thighs, delving to the very core of her womanhood with rhythmic, soft strokes that sapped her of all resistance. She sagged in his arms, clinging to his shoulders as the urgency mounted like flames deep within her. So utterly undeniable. . . .

"You're like a flower," he rasped against her mouth, his fingers slipping within, without, again and again. "Like a soft, wet island flower, waiting to be filled. Do you understand, Alexa? Do you know what I want to do to you?"

"No. . ." A groan escaped her lips. "No, please . . ." And then he grasped her buttocks and guided her pelvis against his hand in a slow, sweet rhythm. With head flung back she surrendered to the movement, and the urgency spiraled within her, higher and higher, brighter than the stars. She felt his mouth upon her, and she heard his voice, murmuring wicked, wonderful things she could never comprehend . . . things that sent a shaft of potent molten heat to her core. And then she dissolved like melted butter all over him, a torrent of spring rain amidst tremors and ripples that brought cries of near anguish to her lips.

For a brief, glorious moment, she was caught up against his powerful length, felt the trembling restraint in his arms as he held her fast.

"Oliver—" She pressed against his shoulders, seeking some whisper of distance between them. Yet he seemed oblivious to her, or perhaps she merely had no strength left in her limbs with which to fight him. And then his hands grasped beneath her hips and lifted her high against his thighs. Hadn't the man had enough? "Oliver—it was quite . . . yes . . . but we cannot, *again.*"

"Didn't you like it?" Suddenly, he was intent upon the buttons of her nightgown. "Quit squirming, Alexa. You've more to learn. Trust me, that was only the beginning."

"Oliver...no...you've a fiancée..." Her voice trailed off into a helpless whisper and her head fell back when warm hands slipped within her gown and began stroking her breasts. Delicious...the feeling was far too delicious. "Oliver—" Her fingers sunk into his windswept hair as he bent to spread impassioned kisses over her bosom. "Oliver . . . your fiancée . . ."

"Stop talking about her, Alexa."

"I can't help it. How can you manage *not* to think about the poor girl at a time like this? How could she let you leave her in Chicago? I mean . . . knowing this about you . . . what you can do with your hands and your— *Oliver.*"

"Sweet heaven, you're beautiful," he rasped against her ribs, his mouth upon her belly, then moving lower still. "I want to taste you, Alexa—"

"Oliver—" She stiffened and tried to dissuade him by crossing her legs. "Dear God, please stop. Oliver, do get up, for heaven's sake."

"I must be losing my touch." He glanced up at her, his eyebrow arched. "Anytime now, you should be incapable of speech."

"Is that what typically happens when you do this sort of thing with your fiancée?"

His hands lay still about her waist, all but spanning it, his thumbs moving slowly between her ribs. "No, dammit." With something akin to a growl, he rose to his towering height before her. "For your information, I have yet to do 'this sort of thing' with my fiancée. As a matter of fact, it's been a hell of a long time—dammit, *too* long—since I've done 'this sort of thing' with *any* woman."

Alexa drew her gown together over her breasts. "You sounded so very sure of your abilities . . . I mean, to rob a woman of her speech."

"An impossible task if there ever was one," he muttered wryly. "But, hell, we tycoons typically lack humility. Now, come here." He yanked her close, one hand slipping within her gown, capturing one breast as if it were his right to do so at his will, at his convenience, whenever he so desired. . . .

Something exploded through Alexa's mind. She shoved against him, twisting from his grasp. Her breath came in tremors and again she clutched her gown over her breasts, her gaze upon the glowering beast not three paces from her. She pointed one wavering finger at him. "Stay."

"You've no water pump to hide behind, Alexa. You know damned well I can catch you."

"And why should you? You've taken what you wanted. Despoiled yet another virgin. I was but another conquest in an endless list of conquests, an entire *world* of conquests, I believe was how you phrased it. Once was surely enough. Off to bed with you, you drunken lout."

"What the hell . . . ?" Again, his ill-timed laugh and that lazy half smile that set Alexa's knees to wobbling. "Alexa, you're still a virgin."

"I am not," she declared hotly, drawing her gown even closer about her. "You—" she waved a hand at him "—you did that . . . you know . . . and I know why. Honing your skills you were, before you do the very same with your fiancée. Or do you simply wish to seduce the plantation from me? Well, I won't have any more of this abuse, I tell you. As it is, I shall consider myself lucky if I don't bear your child nine months hence."

In his own twisted way, he seemed to find some humor in all this as he rubbed his beard-roughened jaw and studied her. "Alexa, trust me, there's little chance of that."

"Ha!" Alexa set about buttoning her gown with decided vehemence, her progress impeded by her irreparably tumbled hair. "You seem the sort that would propagate with relative ease, despite your age."

"I would like to think so, if that is indeed ever my intent."

"No doubt you've a score of illegitimate children littered throughout the world. Men like you always do, you know. Does your fiancée have any notion what she's gotten herself into?"

"Alexa . . ." He started toward her, his lips curved slightly, his eyes alight with that devilish, entirely uncharacteristic twinkle. "Innocent, foolish child, who the devil taught you about men and women?"

"Nobody," she stated proudly, thrusting her chin forward and taking several steps back, away from him.

"Not even your mother?"

Alexa gaped at him. "Good heavens, no. My mother didn't speak of such things. Dear God, she wasn't that sort. No, I learned what I could from eavesdropping upon Shura and the boys on the plantation, though they don't say much."

"Stay away from them." His sudden sharpness of tone roused her ire further, as did his unrelenting grip upon her upper arms.

"I will not! I teach them piano, I'll have you know. And ever so eager they are."

"I'll bet they're eager. Showing up daily?"

Alexa shrugged, entirely at a loss to grasp his meaning. "Sometimes twice a day."

"How old are they, Alexa, all of sixteen or so?"

"Around there. Perhaps older."

"Dammit, woman, you walk around half-dressed . . . Any man with eyes in his head, if he's a man at all, can barely function—"

Alexa grimaced. "Good heavens, Oliver, they're not ill. They function quite well, I'll have you know. They've been my friends, the only friends I've known, for years."

He shook his head, a slightly befuddled shake even for so arrogant a beast. "So entirely unknowing." Then the words hissed through his teeth. "You've a body that makes a man's hands itch to touch you...that makes a man yearn to strip your clothes from you and do things to you, with you—"

"Like what we did?"

"More," he said softly. "So very much more."

Alexa swallowed deeply and shook her head. "I don't think most men are like that, Oliver. Really. Take Stuart Jeffcoat, for example—"

"To hell with Jeffcoat," he snarled, his fingers digging into her arms. "Believe me, he's tripping all over himself to keep himself in his trousers."

"Oliver, you're making no sense...and you're hurting me."

He released his breath in a rush, his hold upon her suddenly gentle, his hands moving slowly over her arms as if to soothe any ache. "Just wear more clothes," he muttered.

"And if I don't?"

He seemed to grit his teeth into some semblance of a smile. "Then you'll have to risk the consequences of living beneath the same roof with me. You see, Alexa, I'm half-mad with wanting you in my bed. And unlike Jeffcoat, I'd have no trouble wielding my blade to its full advantage."

"Your *what?*"

His teeth flashed in a wicked grin. "Someday very soon I'll explain that to you...if I don't go out of my mind before then." His arm slipped about her waist and drew her close, so close his chin rested atop her head. "Go to bed, Alexa. Straight to bed, and don't look back."

She slipped from his arms without a word and ran toward the house, clutching her gown high in one hand. Only when she'd just reached the first-floor veranda did she pause, her breath catching, when out of the corner of her eye she detected a lantern's dim light filtering into and out of her vision as it moved through the brush, away from the side of the house, into the gardens. She hastened a glance over her shoulder, expecting to find Oliver's broad-shouldered shadow somewhere beside the fountain. But he'd disappeared into the night. And when her gaze once again probed the gardens and beyond, she found only darkness.

Without hesitation, she ran to the back of the house, deep into the gardens, following what seemed to be a path through the densely overgrown foliage. When she emerged, she was upon a gently sloping hill that overlooked sleeping cane fields...and a good half mile beyond that, a cluster of small, dark cottages, the plantation workers' cottages. All dark. Peaceful. The cane's soft swishing lulled her, prompting her to turn around and indeed seek the softness of her bed.

Chapter Seven

"Hold still, Miss Alexa. There be another one on your back. You won' be able to reach this one."

With a sigh, Alexa cast a smile of thanks at the hulking black man crouched in the garden beside her. "Good heavens, Luke, the place is as overrun with these little fellows as it is with weeds." With nary a flinch, she watched as Luke's meaty fingers plucked a rather large, spindly-legged spider from her back and tossed it into the dense foliage surrounding them.

Sweeping the back of her wrist over her damp forehead, Alexa settled back upon her heels, rubbed her grimy hands together and surveyed her work. In her lap lay a heaping tangle of weeds she had ruthlessly yanked from this relatively small portion of the gardens where a profusion of coral hibiscus and frangipani struggled for life amongst the choking grasses. She'd ventured from the house several hours earlier, intent upon filling Bellefontaine's dark and lifeless corners with vases brimming with fragrant blossoms. But Gabriel Keane's once neatly tended gardens had become hopelessly overgrown. Before she'd realized it, she was squatting amongst the blossoms, barefoot and bareheaded, up to her elbows in weeds, dirt and the occasional spider. Not long after, Luke had ambled by and offered his help. From him she had learned the reason for the plantation's state of disrepair. Since Gabriel Keane's death two months earlier, Luke had told her, the plantation had all but been shut down, its cane works abruptly halted and every servant, save Cyril and the cook, every grounds keeper, every worker from the sugarcane fields and the mill told to seek employment... and lodgings... elsewhere without notice.

"Told by whom?" Alexa had asked, only to discover that the directive had come from Stuart Jeffcoat himself, on behalf of the Barbadian government. Alexa had pondered this, knowing only too well that these blacks who had devoted their lives to Bellefontaine knew all there was to know of planting, growing and harvesting cane, of negotiating sugar from cane juice, but knew relatively little about anything else. Especially a man like Luke, a man who had been under Gabriel's employ for over twenty years. Due to his notorious strength, though, he'd been offered much to aid in the reconstruction of old Alleyndale Hall into a resort inn, a job he had stoutly refused... and not because it was rumored that the place was haunted. Alexa knew the blacks well enough to recognize the puffing up of Luke's enormous chest within its coarse muslin shirt, the glitter of pride deep in his eyes, the reason for the clenching of his massive fists against his thighs. Indeed, blacks like him would rather starve in their huts on Bellefontaine soil than lend their hand to the misuse and exploitation of the land and country they loved... solely to line the pockets of the pompous and greedy British and American businessmen who sought to convert every last plantation into a tourist attraction. Yet another playground for the bored British gentry, complete with quaint, and frightfully cheap black labor, labor with little alternative.

How often had Gabriel Keane spoken of that very situation during those long, lazy afternoons he'd spent in Lily's parlor? His eyes glazed, his lip curled savagely, he'd vowed with every thump of his beefy fist in his palm to uphold the tradition of the plantation, vowed to protect and preserve Bellefontaine for himself and the workers who had long called it home, vowed never to sell one inch of Bellefontaine's land no matter the price offered, or the tactics employed to sway him, both gentle and otherwise. No matter that with every passing year sugar prices fell, exports decreased and profits declined. No matter that each sunrise brought word of yet another of his fellow plantation owners who had sold his lands and fled to England with a small fortune in his pocket.

Gabriel's dream of the old plantation aristocracy was one which Alexa vowed to pursue relentlessly in the face of all adversity, and in spite of Oliver Keane's every intention otherwise.

Alexa closed her eyes as a gentle breeze washed over her, banishing such thoughts with the stirring of pungent fragrances around her, stirring, as well, the dusky memories of last eve spent in this very garden . . . with a brandy-enhanced Oliver Keane.

"Water, Miss Alexa?"

Alexa shook her head and pressed suddenly trembling fingers to her heated neck, feeling the sweat trickling between her breasts . . . almost like the feel of a man's tongue.

"Your cheeks is awful red, Miss Alexa."

"Is that so?" With renewed vigor, Alexa applied herself to weeding, her flaming cheeks averted. "Perhaps it's the sun."

"You plantation lady now, Miss Alexa. You should be in the plantation house."

"Good grief, Luke, I would die of boredom or suffocation. Besides, there's so very much for me to do." She heaved a tangle of weeds to the side, swept a scampering spider from her arm and regarded the man through a helpless tangle of hair. "Fine, you would have me act like a plantation boss. Go see to informing the rest of the plantation workers that they are, as of today, once again gainfully employed."

"Yes, ma'am." The twinkle in the depths of his eyes was unmistakable as he slowly rose to his feet and squinted into the horizon. "Sugar fields need to be tilled. Planting come soon. But no overseer. He with Pomeroy now, at Alleyndale Hall."

Alexa frowned, probing her memory. "Pomeroy... Ah, yes, that English businessman Gabriel despised. So much for loyalties, eh? No matter. Congratulations, Luke, you're Bellefontaine's new overseer. Hop to. Good heavens, quit gaping at me like that and help me up." She grasped Luke's extended hand and disentangled herself from the garden, pausing to brush the grime from her skirt before she smiled at Luke. "Don't look so surprised, Luke. Gabriel spoke very highly of you, even talked of making you overseer himself. Surely you knew this."

Luke stared into the distance. "Never a Bim overseer."

"On other plantations, perhaps," Alexa replied, gathering a heaping armful of hibiscus and frangipani and inhaling deeply of the heady scents. "If anyone should find cause with that, they can come to me—"

"Is that so? And what of my son?"

As if conjured from air, Eleanor Keane suddenly materialized before them, swathed in reams of high-necked, long-sleeved, heavy emerald satin, her feathered hat perched just so upon her upswept coiffure. Her fringed emerald parasol wavered slightly over her head, perhaps due to the effects of the relentless sun and the perspiration running in rivulets down her face. To this she seemed impervious, as was to be expected, her gaze cool and even, suggesting she couldn't be more comfortable, sweating or not, or more assured. Yes, that was it. The woman wallowed in self-confidence, her very bearing a constant reminder of her awareness of her elevated station in life.

Alexa endured a critical perusal with a thrust of her chin, noting well the increasingly disdainful arch of Eleanor's eyebrow, the pursing of her rouged lips, the almost imperceptible lifting of her nose, all performed swiftly yet so very thoroughly Alexa was given to wondering how a woman honed such a skill. And then Eleanor did something quite peculiar for such a woman. Quite out of the ordinary, actually. Of course, Alexa supposed she could have imagined it all, so fleeting it was. For a moment, Eleanor blushed, from the top of her starched collar to the very roots of her hair, her gaze wavering slightly, skittish even . . . but so fleeting Alexa merely thought it some premonition of sunstroke.

"Thank you, Luke." Alexa cast the man a smile, though it seemed he wished to linger for some reason. He stared at her a moment, then turned and disappeared silently into the garden.

"An odd pastime for the mistress of this plantation," Eleanor mused. "Lingering with the workers . . . in the gardens."

"I was weeding," Alexa replied, her eyes even with Eleanor's. "And Luke is my friend."

"Ah, yes, of course, nothing suitably genteel about you, is there, my dear?" Again, the distasteful sweep of her eyes, the curl of her lip. "No concern whatsoever about the use and possible disfiguring development of your muscles, eh? Not to mention the possibility of sunburn." Eleanor pasted on a sweet smile and adjusted her parasol over her head. "Try archery, my dear, if you so desire outdoor activity. It's a highly acceptable pastime, you know. Rivalry is keen to the last degree but refinement and courteous dignity prevail." Despite the beads of sweat gathering in profusion upon her upper lip, Eleanor cocked her head and proclaimed airily, "Then again, there's tennis. A tasteful game if there ever was one, refined enough to discourage the riffraff. You know, the ladylike forehand return of a well-mannered lob shot. If you're to own a plantation, you must behave as if you're deserving of it."

Alexa pasted on her own version of a sweet smile and plucked a spindly spider from her arm, dangling it before her for several moments as if she gave it thorough consideration before she tossed it into the garden. "Tennis and archery over swimming in the ocean?" she mused, noting well Eleanor's sudden pallor, the unbecoming sag of her jaw, albeit momentary. "I think not."

"Good God, but you're as crass as those blacks," Eleanor breathed, sucking in a hissing gulp of air. "I tell you, I shan't endure a daily parade of them through the house. It's blasphemy."

"You'll get used to it. They've their piano lessons, you know, and some will be coming quite often simply to practice."

"Not when Oliver hears of this, they won't. You're lucky he's been in Bridgetown since very early this morning. He would have put a stop to it, I can promise you that. I mean, dear God, to the last they somehow managed to end up in the kitchen with Cook. She actually *fed* them, if you can believe it." Eleanor shook her head with finality. "No, Oliver shan't stand for any of it...much less your assigning that man to the post of overseer."

"Oliver knows very little about running a sugar plantation."

Eleanor's lips thinned over her bared teeth. "Ah, but you're wrong, my dear. Oliver is a brilliant businessman. He knows positively everything there is to know of managing any business . . . and, of course, effectively dealing with anyone who happens to get in his way. He's made it an art form."

"He knows nothing of Bellefontaine."

Eleanor's guttural laugh rang harshly and she swept a deprecating hand about. "As if his father did? Or you?" Her eyes flickered with disdain over Alexa. "Ha! My dear, five years ago Oliver knew nothing of Great Lakes shipping. And now he's king of the White Star Line empire, gloriously wealthy, and the most sought-after man in all of Chicago by any debutante worthy of her rank." A queer light glimmered in the depths of Eleanor's dark eyes. "Odd, but I would have thought even *you* would find all that a touch irresistible."

Alexa's eyes narrowed upon the other woman. "And what might you be suggesting?"

Eleanor's eyebrows shot up. "Why, I'm merely stating the obvious, of course. There isn't a girl in all of Chicago who wouldn't *kill* to become his wife . . . or, better yet, his mistress."

"A pathetic reason for committing murder," Alexa muttered, gathering the flowers close. "Now, if you would excuse me—"

Like a snake, Eleanor's gloved fingers coiled about Alexa's arm, stilling the younger woman's feet, and bringing her startled gaze to meet with that dark and glittering stare beneath a quivering parasol. "You're playing with fire, Miss Fairfield, and you know it, don't you?"

"What the devil . . . let go of my arm!"

Eleanor's upper lip twitched. "We're both women, my dear, and it is instinctive to a certain degree, is it not? We both know what a girl like you . . ." The parasol clattered to the ground and Eleanor's fingernail hooked and twisted in the top of Alexa's linen blouse. ". . . dressed like this, you know what that does to a man like Oliver, don't you?" Eleanor's breath fanned hot against Alexa's face despite the ferocity of the sun. "Beware, my dear. He's the epitome of the male animal, chock-full of those diabolical desires. He seethes with it, even more than he does with his thirst for power. You've sensed it, surely. This power is unmatched by any man. And he won't be denied."

Alexa fought against the mounting flush in her cheeks, against the frustration welling in her breast, against the uncommonly powerful grip Eleanor had upon her arm and the clawlike fingernail twisted into her blouse. Her voice tremored. "Odd behavior, don't you think, for a man engaged to be married."

Eleanor's chest heaved within all that damp satin, her words all but spat. "Ah, so he's told you about Daphne, eh? As if one woman would ever be enough for Oliver, or any man, for that matter. The male animal in lust is far too profane to keep only a wife." Her glare flickered over the high curves of Alexa's breasts, prompting Alexa to shrink from the woman, her skin crawling from far more than the grime and heat. "No, even you could never be enough for a man. My dear, they take what they want, whenever they want it. They're ruthless, with little or no appreciation for the virtues of the gentler sex, using us solely for the pleasure they take upon us, at will. Relentless they are. Merciless in their pursuit. *And they always win.*"

"With other women, perhaps. Now, if you please—"

For a brief moment, Eleanor seemed to tremble uncontrollably, her grip upon Alexa painful, and then she released her, and drew herself up with a toss of her head. "Consider yourself lucky, Miss Fairfield. You're one of a select few that Oliver has ever taken a keen interest in. Indeed, Oliver's fiancée, Daphne, considered herself so lucky she rejected any number of suitors in favor of Oliver. *Titled lords* from England among them. The girl even fancied one of them enough to claim she was in love with him. But her intelligence prevailed, of course, though she'll merely be Oliver's wife, a brood mare if nothing more. While you, as his mistress—"

"This is preposterous," Alexa hissed, backing away from Eleanor and clutching her flowers close to her roiling belly. "Ludicrous and...and perverse. That you would even speak to me of such things—"

"Someone has to, my dear. Why, you seem so very surprised by all this. Odd, being that you're Lily Fairfield's daughter. It's all common knowledge, you know, fervently discussed in every lady's boudoir throughout Chicago. Our fate as women. What you choose to do with your power, your position..." Again, the lingering of her gaze upon Alexa's breasts. "Yes, what you choose to do with that power is up to you."

It was all too much, too complex, too dark and foreboding for Alexa to contemplate. And Eleanor...her cold black eyes held Alexa captive. Alexa took a step back, and another, and then she spun about, tripping once, twice, over her skirts, her fingers clawing at the crumbling earth in her haste to scramble up a gently sloping hill for the safety of the house. In her wake she left a trail of coral hibiscus...and the harsh echo of Eleanor Keane's laughter.

Step, *squeak,* step, *squeak.* Oliver paused, his teeth gritting against the infernal echo of his booted heels against meticulously polished marble. He shoved a hand into his breast pocket, glowered first at his gold pocket watch, then at the second-floor balcony directly above him. His ears strained for some sound, some hint that Alexa would appear at any moment upon that balcony.

He glared at the watch. Seven-twenty. With a flick of his thumb, he snapped the watch closed and thrust it into his pocket. Again, step, *squeak.* Step, *squeak.*

He paused before an enormous, gilt-framed oil painting, his jaw working against the frustration seething like boiling oil in his belly. "Damned lollygagging woman," he grumbled, his eye moving with practiced skill over the glorious artwork, noting well the flawless mastery of every stroke. Who would have guessed his father had shared his passion for art?

With a grunt, he turned about. Step, *squeak.* Step, *squeak.*

Even the candles in the enormous gold-and-crystal chandelier suspended directly above him seemed to emit a thick heat this eve, choking the air such that Oliver felt his chest would explode from the confines of his starched evening finery with every breath he took. Then again, perhaps it was simply frustration that he choked on, frustration over waiting like a damned schoolboy in the foyer for over twenty minutes, pacing to and fro, waiting for *her*—something he had vowed never to do for any woman, or man, for that matter. Punctuality was something he expected of himself and all others, and he was well-known to be ruthlessly unforgiving of those who squandered even a moment of his time. Hadn't he told Alexa he would be leaving at seven, not a minute later? His feet stopped and his eyes darted to the balcony once more, narrowing at a sudden thought.

Could it be she wasn't coming? Or perhaps she'd already left for the damned function, accompanied by her lackey Jeffcoat.

Something fierce welled up in his chest, forcing a snarl from his lips. He took to the stairs, two at a time. Three strides, four, down the wide hall and without preamble he shoved open the double doors to her chamber.

"Oh, hullo, Oliver."

He stared at her. It was really all he was capable of, suddenly—that and looming half in, half out of her room, his fists clenching and unclenching against his thighs.

She stood directly in the center of the room, her back turned partially toward him, her fingers fumbling with the clasp of her dress, high at the back of her neck. She seemed part of some other world, suspended there before him, swathed in a figure-hugging dress of creamy linen, the room about her hazy and soft with pale candlelight, the air heady with the scent of the flowers spilling from every shadowed corner of the room. Or perhaps the fragrant heat was hers alone. The light played over all her curves and hollows as she moved to a dressing table deeper in the shadows.

"I can't decide which hat," she said. He watched her slender fingers drifting over one broad-brimmed cream-colored hat duly festooned with plump white gardenias nestled along its brim.

"That's fine," he heard himself mutter, his gaze sweeping her slender back, the narrow waist and hips, the softly curved underside of her buttocks. And then she turned and walked slowly toward him, a tremulous smile curving her lips. His eye strayed, drifting over her. Pristine white, high-necked lace and linen had never looked so fetching, concealing with its poufed sleeves and intricate lacework bodice and skirt, yet revealing so very much to a practiced eye. A woman had never looked so utterly ravishable all in white.

She stopped directly before him and turned about, her shoulder brushing softly across his chest. "Could you hook me, please?"

He stared at the exposed nape of her neck, so very vulnerable, yet womanly and provocative...beckoning a man's lips just as she beckoned with her every movement. Everything about her set him afire. His fingers managed the task despite his wandering gaze, which found the artless mass of curls tumbling from atop her head curiously distracting. As with a will all their own, his fingers lingered upon her neck, his thumb resting gently on the nape. Yet she drifted away, tossing a husky thanks in her wake. She retrieved her hat and slipped past him in a warm wave of gardenia scent, and confidently proceeded down the hall, her demeanor proclaiming that she was entirely certain he would simply follow, that she was uncaring that she was, at the very least, thirty minutes late, and he and the rest of the world wouldn't find that the least bit inconvenient.

He closed her chamber door and did indeed follow her, obediently, docilely ambling along close behind her. Her step seemed a trifle unsteady, due no doubt to the two-inch heeled white slippers he observed peeking from beneath her swaying hem when she paused at the top of the stairs.

He offered her his arm, achieving a certain satisfaction when her fingers wrapped about his sleeve and clung. Her eyes she kept downcast until they'd reached the foyer and she murmured something inaudible before her hand slipped from his arm and she hurried to a gilt-framed wall mirror. Again he found himself waiting, hands clasped behind his back as she took her time about inspecting herself closely in the glass, eyebrows lifting, lips pursing, head turning from side to side, a pat to the hair, a tug at all those wayward tendrils, a huge grin and then a frown. He merely observed this womanly rite with a certain fascination, supremely aware of the passage of time, yet somehow uncaring at the moment. She settled her hat upon her head, her eyebrows knitting, then tipped the brim this way and that, obviously unsatisfied, then angled it in its original position and glanced at him. Again, that tremulous smile.

"You look beautiful," he said, offering his arm and indicating the door.

Her eyes flickered over him as if registering him for the first time and she uttered another thanks, her hand fidgeting with her skirt until he grasped her cool fingers and pressed them into the crook of his arm.

"You're nervous." He cast her a sideways glance as he pushed the front door wide and led her into the dusky evening air. With eyes still averted, she again said something he couldn't discern and allowed him to help her into the landaulet, scooting far to the side when he settled close beside her upon the tufted gold velvet seat. He nodded to the driver, a man he had hired that very afternoon expressly for this purpose, just as he'd purchased this sleek, elegant carriage in which to escort Miss Alexa Fairfield to this highbrow function. The same woman who had accused him of robbing her of her virtue last evening in the garden. A torturous memory, that, with her now poised and fidgeting in all her innocent white linen not six inches from him.

A grunt escaped the thickness in his throat and he forced his attention to the passing countryside, lush with blossoms, thick with fragrance and bathed golden by the haze of salt hovering in the early-evening air. Above the clopping of the horses' hooves he could detect the muted rush of waves upon the shore somewhere beyond the carriage. A lulling sound it was. And he cursed it all, every last blossom, every last sultry sunset, every damned assault upon his senses. He'd never thought he'd yearn for the fog and damp gray chill that was so very common to Chicago, the city huddling beneath a shroud of gloom. It was so very easy to retain one's senses, to keep one's mind upon what mattered in such a place, as easy as it was difficult to function with any sort of mental clarity here, amidst this incessant tropical inundation of sensual awareness. And the unforgiving heat . . . tightening his starched celluloid collar like a vise about his neck, dampening his skin such that his trousers clung to his thighs, making him wish he could shed them.

And there she sat beside him, silent, aloof, as cool as a tall glass of chilled lemonade on a torrid day. The wind, which would have sent any other woman into near apoplexy over the horrid state of disrepair to their coiffures, only seemed to enhance her tousled curls. She seemed to bend the very breeze as easily to her will as she did the sun, the moon, the stars . . . the tides.

His father's journal brimmed with anecdotes and musings on those Obeah women, the blacks who practiced their own version of witchcraft. At the moment, Oliver was hard-pressed not to at least consider the highly illogical notion that this woman, this child-woman Alexa, was quite possibly a witch.

His fingers gripped his knees and he clenched his jaw, casting her a sideways glance. There *was* some logic to the notion. What else could explain the mind-numbing effect she had upon him? She was like some narcotic filling his blood, clouding his reasoning, filling him with yearnings over which he had little or no control. . . .

He watched her fingers suddenly fiddling together, plucking at her skirts, fidgeting with the pointed lace at her wrists, noted, also, the heaving of her breasts as if she drew in deep gulps of air. Without thought, he grasped her hand and trapped it beneath his upon his thigh.

"Stop it," he said. "I'm going to start thinking it's me you're afraid of. And we both know you can't possibly be anymore."

"I never was," she replied softly, squirming uncomfortably against him. "Must you hold my hand so?"

"Of course I must. We men are remarkably possessive once we've ruined a girl, you know." His fingers curling around her hand brought those luminous emerald eyes to meet his. "A gentleman, Alexa, offers for a lady's hand in marriage in circumstances such as these." His gaze grew hooded when her lips parted slightly.

"Is that why you proposed to your Daphne?"

"She's not my Daphne," he rasped, that familiar scowl hovering over his face. "And, no, that's not the reason. Not every marriage results from some bumbling male overstepping his bounds."

"Ah, then you must love her deeply."

He glowered at her a moment. "You're remarkably naive, Alexa." Drawing her hand closer, he studied the delicate fingertips crushed in his palm. "You more than anyone has ample reason to doubt my affections for my fiancée. I don't love her, though many are wont to tell me that that will come, over time, of course. Some deep and abiding affection for each other. All very expected with these marriages of convenience."

"That sounds rather dreadful. Nothing at all like what I imagined."

He looked closely at her. "And what did you imagine?"

She inclined her head, a wistful look caressing her golden-hued features, emerald eyes soft and dreamy beneath a fringe of fragrant gardenias. "My mother journeyed across the ocean with an infant daughter to be with my father. She wasn't content to wait in London until he returned. She couldn't bear to be without the man she so desperately loved."

"Perhaps she simply hated London."

She pursed her lips and shot him an agitated look from beneath the brim of her hat. "So very cold you are, Oliver, to look at it that way. She loved him completely, and mourned for months after his death. To the day she died, she remained true to his memory."

Oliver's harsh laugh puckered her fair brows. "Alexa, you should consider writing one of those romantic dime novels. There's money to be had in fiction, you know."

"Money," she snapped. Her fingers wriggled for an escape he had no intention of granting. "Is that all you think about?"

"I've been thinking too damned little about it lately. In fact, I wasn't thinking at all about it last evening under all that moonlight."

"A rare occurrence to be sure," she mused, averting her flushed cheeks, her fingers going limp within his hand.

Oliver's lips curved in a wicked grin and he leaned toward her until his mouth hovered but a breath from her ear. The breeze tossed a blond ringlet against his cheek, filling his voice with a huskiness. "If you're bent upon reforming me, Alexa, I'm more than willing to try, perhaps later this evening."

She ignored him as best she could, squirming within her white linen and pressing herself against the opposite side of the landaulet. A soft rumbling laughter filled his chest and he leaned back against the seat, cradling her resisting hand in his.

"So why are you marrying her?"

He glanced at her sharply, her question surprising him. Dispelling a lengthy breath, he contemplated the distant horizon, then her once again. "Her father owns transatlantic shipping lanes."

She stared at him a moment, obviously uncomprehending. And then those full lips parted with a gasp and her eyes blazed a glorious emerald fire. "You're detestable," she hissed, struggling for her hand and shoving ineffectually at his arms. "No, *worse* than detestable. Abominable. Utterly loathsome. I cannot bear the sight of you. It's a wonder poor Daphne can."

"Because I'm not marrying her for love?" In one swift movement, he grasped both her hands in one of his. With one flex of his arm, he hauled her against him, nearly out of her seat. "Alexa," he rasped, "get your feet firmly in reality. *Nobody* marries for love."

"How dare you speak of love," she protested, her lips trembling. "*You,* a man incapable of feeling any emotion whatsoever, save for yourself and your bloody empire. If not for financial gain, why the devil do anything?"

"A valid question, Alexa. You're finally showing some sense."

"You wretch!" She struggled for release, but managed only to dislodge her hat, which slipped from her head and landed in a pool of gardenia petals upon the seat beside her. "How simpleminded you must think me to practice your...your *masculine* ways upon me for no other reason than ravishment."

"Give me a better reason."

She tucked in her chin and squinted at him as if she thought him addled. "You've never done anything without some ulterior motive. Are you alone so transparent, Oliver, or are all those businessmen in Boston as thick-headed as you?"

"Chicago." He brushed a gardenia petal from a tangle of blond curls. "When are you going to remember that I'm from Chicago?"

She gritted her teeth into a sweet smile. "When you return there on the next blasted boat."

"And what if I don't? What if I choose to stay here, in the same house with you, under the same moon, the same stars..." His arm flexed, drawing her closer until her full breasts pressed against his chest. "What if I mean to have you no matter what?"

She seemed to quiver against him. "I'm not Daphne."

"I know that. I've never wanted to devour Daphne, Alexa." His words rasped through clenched teeth, his gaze finding her lips. "I never even thought once about tasting every inch of her flesh...." His hand caught in her hair, pressed her head closer, until her breath fanned sweet and hot against his mouth. "Kiss me, Alexa."

"I'd rather not," she whispered.

"Fine. I want to enough for both of us. Open your mouth."

"If you promise to help me."

Help her? Hell, he'd teach her all she ever wanted to know. Desire flamed through him, hot, fierce, undeniable. His thumb brushed over her full, lower lip, so soft, so sweet, and a groan rumbled in his chest, his mouth seeking all that she promised... until her elbows shoved him in the chest.

"I don't need help with *that,* Oliver," she huffed.

His eyes darted to hers, glittering with some womanly intuition that roused a deep male instinct in him, some gnawing suspicion. "So what the hell *do* you need me for?"

Her tone was cool, even, despite her labored breathing. "You must promise to help me find my mother's murderer."

"Fine. Done. Now, kiss me."

Again she resisted, stiffening in his arms and twisting her head to the side, neatly avoiding him. "Absolutely not, Oliver. You've done nothing even remotely helpful yet."

He stared at her. The blood pounded in his temples, firing in his loins. "You're trying to bribe me."

"Precisely."

"You can't do that."

"And why not? Would you even consider helping me with my murder investigation if I didn't give you ample incentive? I have no money, Oliver, and I know how your mind works."

"The hell you do," he said, decidedly uncomfortable with the notion.

She raised an eyebrow full of meaning. "Shall we strike a deal, Oliver? Consider it a business proposition. That's something you're grossly familiar with."

His hand moved slowly down her spine, pausing at the gentle curve of her buttocks. Saucy and sly she was, thinking to deny him after last evening, concocting this little scheme to keep him at bay. "I always require prepayment, Alexa. Standard contractual terms, you know."

"Consider last night more than ample prepayment, Oliver. And would you kindly remove your hand from my posterior? You've done nothing to warrant such a liberty."

He smiled slyly, his hand firmly planted and unmoving. "But what of consideration? No contract is legally binding without it, Alexa. Typically, in any business transaction, I require a token payment of some sort, you know, something to signify the agreement of both parties to the contract. In this case..." He lowered his eyes to her breasts just resting against his chest, felt the fullness of her buttocks beneath his palm, pondered the lushness of her lips, the tumbling cloud of curls. "Lord, Alexa, with you, one doesn't quite know where to begin."

"A simple handshake would do very nicely," she replied in that airy tone, making it appear that their proximity did positively nothing for her, that this was all some blasted business decision. She was making a show of presenting herself as someone who had supreme control of herself, her thoughts, her yearnings.

"And what of the terms?"

"Terms?"

"I typically operate on an installment basis."

"Meaning?"

"Meaning that I periodically require payment. Meaning that I require appropriate *incentive* from time to time." He grinned, his fingers splaying over the plump curve of her derriere. "Meaning that I won't wait until the crime is solved to take my due."

"And if I refuse?"

"No contract. You lose."

"As would you."

He gave a soft laugh. "If last night was any indication of what losing might be like, I don't think I would mind in the least."

"Is that so?" How divinely confident she was. "And would you be so splendidly content if I was to tell you that last evening was merely a baiting of the line, so to speak?" Her lips curved in direct proportion to the narrowing of his eyes. "A simple taste, a lure."

"Last night was no careful orchestration on your part, Alexa. Not even on mine."

She cocked her head. "Odd, how some things just manage to happen very neatly. If you're saying you've no interest in this arrangement, Oliver, I'll—"

"You'll what?" His teeth suddenly ground in his ears. "You'll seek help from another, under the same terms? Like hell you will." He crushed his mouth over hers, a bruising, forceful ravaging of her that did nothing but fill him with an unquenchable need for more. "There," he breathed against her lips. "As of now, we've a binding agreement. But be forewarned, sweet Alexa, I *always* fulfill my part of the bargain. Be prepared to do the same."

Chapter Eight

By the time the landaulet pulled to a stop before the brilliantly lit Government House, Alexa had satisfied herself with regard to the state of her hat, her hair, her slightly wrinkled dress, and in particular, the disgruntled set of Oliver's jaw. Yes, with this she was inordinately pleased. The man smoldered like a fire requiring but a whiff of oxygen to explode. As if some part of him positively loathed being baited like a fat fish, all for the favors of a mere woman.

Ah, but smugness never felt so divine. Indeed, it brought a springiness to a girl's step, a readiness to her smile, a mischievousness heretofore lacking in her dealings with particularly bothersome men. A hint of flirtation, even, as she slanted her eyes at Oliver and allowed him to escort her up the steep marble steps leading to the entrance of the Government House. How very easy this skill became when one's escort emanated masculinity as easily as Oliver did. The simple manner in which he towered over her and moved along beside her with his powerful strides made the clinging to his biceps all that much easier to accomplish. A coquettish blush proved to be rather effortless, requiring but a glance at his brooding profile and that wild mane of blue-black hair that rested just over the back of his collar. The man conducted himself with a seething yet devil-may-care manner, an intensity of purpose that filled Alexa with a giddiness tempered only by the knowledge of the power she wielded over him, albeit temporary and untested.

A naive stroke of genius her scheme had been, being, of course, that he had agreed. Now all she had to do was keep her own wits about her. Something in his gaze as it slid over her with alarming frequency told her he'd achieve far more pleasure from foiling their contract than abiding by it. And she'd rather throw herself into boiling oil than give him that satisfaction . . . no matter how potent his effect upon her. She need only remind herself that she loathed the man, that he deserved her contempt far more than he did romantic, seductive delusions.

"No wandering off," he whispered close to her ear, his hand engulfing hers upon his arm as they passed through an enormous double-doored entrance into a three-storied foyer, bulging with fashionably elegant folk. Above the din of the crowd, an orchestra's melody drifted through the thick air, prompting them toward the arched entrance to the grand ballroom. The women in attendance had outfitted themselves in their finest taffetas, silks and brocades, complete with heaps of spectacular jewels at their ears, throats, wrists and every finger. Some seemed nearly weighed down with it all, incapable of simple movement in their fashionably narrow sheathed dresses, their rouged smiles forced beneath beaded upper lips as they stood like stone statues at their escorts' sides. Their men merely tipped their hats and offered greetings, looking equally as hot and uncomfortable in their evening finery as the women. In full regalia, British officers flanked every doorway. Some received the scrolled invitations and granted entrance, others merely cast stony-faced glances about, their swords potently at their hips. Some bore holstered pistols.

"One can't help but wonder where your friend Jeffcoat is busying himself," Oliver said, leveling her with his blasted hooded look. "Seems as good an opportunity as any to parade his pomposity before us commonfolk."

She paused beside him, in line behind those awaiting entrance to the ballroom. "Stuart is a commander, Oliver. Possessing of such a rank, he shall be duly positioned very near the princes."

"I never thought I'd pity the poor fellows. But then again, I won't have to worry about him trying to steal you on the dance floor."

"I've no intention of stepping one foot on the dance floor."

"Oh, but you will." He flashed her an uncommonly dazzling grin. "Both feet. With me. Again and again. All night long."

Alexa tucked a stray lock into her hat and busied her eyes elsewhere. "I think not. That's a favor you shall have to earn. Besides, with so much sleuthing to accomplish, there will not be much time for dancing."

"You're grossly underestimating my abilities, Alexa. And my desires." His heated breath stirred the air beside her cheek, his voice rumbling deep and sensuous. "I'll get that dance, and more, before we're through. I'll move the damned earth itself to get what I want."

She lifted her chin. "Finding my mother's killer might be a trifle easier to accomplish. You know, less strain on all those muscles." For some reason, she found it necessary to punctuate her awareness of him, her gaze drifting over his massive chest, her fingers tightening of their own will around his biceps. "So," she said a bit breathlessly, her gaze skittering wildly over the crowd, "where do you intend to begin?"

"Doubting my abilities already, Alexa?"

They moved forward several paces and Alexa spotted through a parting in the crowd ahead of her the two crown princes of Wales receiving guests at the entrance to the ballroom. "To be honest, you seem to have given very little thought to the matter."

He leaned nearer, his voice an ominous tremor. "Maybe I'm having some difficulty getting used to a woman who would dare to bait me as you have. I know of many men who would envy you your temerity."

"Why?" she asked airily. "Because I dare to challenge the almighty Oliver Keane?"

"Few rarely do."

"They ought to a little more often, from the looks of you. You've a decided gleam in your eye. Rising to the challenge, perhaps?"

"Trust me, no prize has ever been so worth having."

A flush heated her cheeks. "Perhaps, though I would venture to say no businessman ever felt as strongly as I do about my quest."

"Obviously. No man would ever sacrifice his honor for a mere business contract."

She stared at him a moment. "All the honor I require is that which I shall find when I see my mother's murderer on the gallows. The personal sacrifices to achieve that end could never be too great."

An ominous glimmer shone in his cobalt eyes. "You make your keeping of the bargain sound like some sort of torture."

"Indeed," she sniffed, casting him a dubiously arched eyebrow. "From what I can discern, Oliver, 'tis a torture I shall be spared for quite some time."

"Don't count on it," he muttered, drawing her several more paces along. "Fine. Let's talk motive."

She gaped at him, a flamboyant, overt gaping replete with a blink of her eyes and a pressing of her hand to her bosom. "Pray, could it be you wish *me* to help *you?* And make my doom that much more imminent? Surely you jest."

He seemed to grit his teeth into a savage smile. "The stakes are far too high, my dear, for game-playing, don't you agree?"

"Perhaps." She looked closely at him, her nose wrinkling. "And you don't look at all to be the sort to enjoy games."

"Not the kind you're familiar with." His eyes devouring her lips conjured forth all sorts of heathenish thoughts.

"Motive..." Averting her gaze, she peeked on tiptoe over the coiffed heads blocking her view of the princes. She heaved an impatient sigh and set a toe to tapping upon the polished marble. "What about something rather ordinary and simple like revenge?"

"Don't tell me... You've been reading mystery novels to hone your deductive skills." A hint of a smirk eased the tension in his mouth. "Okay, fine, revenge. A justifiable motive for murder if there ever was one and as good a place to start as any. So, revenge for what?" He jutted his chin toward the crowd. "Are your mother's enemies wont to lurk in shadowed doorways?"

She pursed her lips. "Other than you and your mother? Oliver, she had no enemies. She was loved by all who knew her."

"A paragon of society."

"Precisely. She was, after all, the widow of one of Britain's naval greats."

His laugh was harsh, bitter and laced with sarcastic bite. "Of course, what better reason for the British to canonize the woman? I suppose she was crushed to the very bosom of British Barbadian society for such a stroke of good fortune."

Alexa gritted her teeth. "I cannot help but wonder what horrible misdeed wrought such a cynical streak in you, Oliver. Surely you weren't simply born that way."

He stared at her a moment. "There are days when I honestly believe I *was* born this way, Alexa. Days when all my thoughts teem with suspicion, cynicism and doubt, with examining, reexamining and reexamining again every last angle of a problem, lest I overlook something."

"Perhaps because you fear failure so very much."

"Perhaps because there's so very little in this world to lay one's entire trust in. Perhaps because there *is* someone lurking behind *every* door, anticipating your slightest misstep, the merest hint of weakness or lack of control. Perhaps because success in this world means survival of the fittest, outwitting one's opponent, always, *always* thinking like your enemy while you stay one step ahead of him. And above all, knowing *who* your enemies are."

The unchecked raw intensity of his gaze robbed her of breath for a moment. "Not everyone is your enemy, Oliver," she whispered. "Not every situation a test of your worth."

"You're wrong," he rasped, his teeth bared. "I suppose your mother subscribed to the same sort of thinking and look what fate awaited her. Trust me, she had enemies, Alexa, at least one, someone cold enough to murder her or calculating enough to simply use her as bait."

Alexa swallowed deeply. "Bait?"

"For my father, of course." He drew her before the crown princes of Wales, his jaw working, his eyes flecked with shards of ice. Close to her ear his voice rumbled. "Smile sweetly for these fellows, my dear, and start thinking. A veritable roomful of suspects awaits."

* * *

"Who was that?" Oliver asked as he pressed a glass of champagne into Alexa's hand. He looked away from the tall, elegant, dark-haired woman gliding slowly through the crowd away from them, back to the gardenias upon Alexa's hat. She seemed momentarily oblivious to him, her head bent low over the heaping plate of canapés he held before her, her tongue moving slowly over her lips. His mouth curved when her fair eyebrows quivered with obvious indecision. "Hell, Alexa, try one of each."

She smiled softly and that yearning to kiss her became almost too much to bear. "Of course." Gingerly, she lifted one particularly bothersome-looking concoction, one Oliver would never consider even tasting. "Why not?"

He watched her take her sweet time about eating the thing until the images it conjured up in his mind became far too provocative and he had to force his gaze away. "So, who was that woman?"

Alexa stared at him a moment, chewing slowly, contemplating his question as if she hadn't a notion of whom he was speaking. And then, with a mere shifting of her eyes to the canapés once again, she dismissed him.

"Darling girl." With one finger beneath her chin, he lifted her face to his. "Didn't you eat today?"

She shook her head. "I forgot. I was busy weeding."

"Weeding." A frown descended over his features. "Let the servants do the weeding, Alexa."

Her eyes flashed a soft emerald fire. "I'm not above that sort of work, Oliver. Indeed, I find I enjoy it immensely. You know, the feel of the dirt, the smell of newly turned earth, the innocence of a first blossom." She flashed a satisfied smile. "I'm quite a gardener. Now let me eat."

He grasped her fingers just as she reached for another canapé, and studied the delicate fingertips and sensibly short nails, some cracked from misuse. "You've got beautiful hands, Alexa. You should have long, lovely nails and twice-a-week manicures for the rest of your life." He glowered at her. "Garden if you must, but no more weeding."

She grimaced and slipped her hand free. "One cannot properly play the piano with long fingernails. Good grief, what the devil would I do with them?"

He grunted and gave voice to but an inkling of his thoughts. "Scratch my back, of course. Now, I'll ask you again, who was that dark-haired woman?"

She paused, the canapé lifted halfway to her mouth, her gaze drifting over the crowd for several moments. "Oh, that's Penelope Alleyne . . . or rather *Lady* Alleyne. She was Mother's dearest friend. The poor woman is in mourning. Her second husband died not six months past."

Oliver's eyes darted over the crowd. "She doesn't look like she's mourning to me. Tell me about the dead husband."

Alexa examined her canapé after taking a bite. "He was Sir Reynold Alleyne, one of the wealthiest plantation owners on the island, or so everyone thought. He owned Alleyndale Hall. Actually, he inherited it through a chain of sudden deaths. Odd, that, for he died in a fire that devastated one entire wing of his plantation. The mountain of debt he left behind had poor Lady Penelope in a dither, until Pomeroy settled the entire sum and bought Alleyndale Hall for a fraction of its true worth." Alexa heaved a knowing sigh. "Took advantage of the poor woman he did, solely to line his own pockets and turn Alleyndale Hall into a hotel. Sir Reynold would never have sold out to the man."

"Indeed." Oliver pondered this. "And the nature of the fire at Alleyndale Hall?"

"Mysterious, of course. Even the governor himself believes the place haunted."

"Haunted. Or perhaps simply more bad luck." Oliver drained his champagne and set the glass aside. "So how is it that Lady Alleyne came to know your mother?"

"Her first husband was my father's first lieutenant commander. A titled lord he was, though little good that did him. He died alongside my father at the hands of that hurricane. You can well imagine the bond between Lady Penelope and Mother as a result of such a tragedy."

"She was from London, as well?"

The entire canapé disappeared into Alexa's mouth and she nodded vigorously, already seeking another tidbit from the plate.

"Did they know each other in London?"

A swift shake of her head amidst all that chewing.

"Odd," he muttered, spotting Penelope Alleyne through the crush. Tall and willowy, she floated through the crowd like a sylph in her shimmery ivory taffeta, her every movement a study in graceful elegance, her winsome smile aimed with ruthless precision at the more unsuspecting of the gentlemen, particularly those in uniform. She was a beauty, offered forth like a rare delicacy, and Oliver knew her type well. Women like Penelope Alleyne abounded in Chicago, where they honed their particular form of seduction so skillfully upon only the more wealthy and guileless. Even Oliver had been duped once. Only once. After that, he'd learned to spot them from miles away. Especially the eager ones. And judging by the manner in which she fluttered like an agitated firefly on the arm of a handsome, gray-haired British officer, Penelope Alleyne was certainly one of the more ardent of her kind. Desperate, to Oliver's eye.

"I know what you're thinking, Oliver, and I won't have of it."

With little hesitation, he brushed a tiny crumb from the corner of Alexa's mouth and controlled a smirk. "What am I thinking, Alexa?"

She all but shook a finger directly beneath his nose. "The way you said, 'Odd.' You suspect Lady Penelope of Mother's murder, that's what you were thinking."

"No, I merely think it strange that they didn't know each other in England. Their husbands obviously did, very well."

Alexa waved a dismissive hand. "One can readily assume they moved in different circles, Oliver. As much as my mother loved the Barbadian plantation set, she eschewed the London social scene Lady Penelope embraced so fervently."

"And why was that?"

Alexa shrugged, bending over the canapés again. "She spoke so very little of her life before she came here. One can only suppose she simply didn't care for it. Why do you seem so surprised? I would think you would feel much the same."

"I do. But I wonder why a woman so obviously attuned to the social graces would shun the whole scene in London and not here. Unless, of course, she had good reason."

Alexa's eyes shot to his, her lips pursed with unspoken defiance. "Such as?"

"Perhaps your mother had something to hide there in London, Alexa. Perhaps she grasped the first opportunity to *flee* from England with her baby for reasons having little to do with her husband. She *did* remain here, even though your father had tragically perished, perhaps because she was far more welcome here as his widow, a woman nobody knew. It would be like acquiring a new identity. Now, don't get all puffed up and angry at me. You'll spill your champagne... and you've still half the canapés left."

Her cheeks bloomed with color. "You're accusing—"

"No, I'm simply conjecturing." He flashed a wicked grin. "We sleuths do an awful lot of that sort of thing, you know."

She gave him an exasperated look. "You're *contriving,* Oliver. Do it at someone else's expense, if you could."

He cocked an eyebrow, noting well her deep sipping of her champagne. "You can't deny it's within reason."

"Pure poppycock," she replied into her glass, her gaze refusing to meet his.

He leaned closer to her, his voice dropping. "Haven't you ever wondered why your mother spoke so very little of her life in England? Don't squirm, Alexa. You know, your blush gives you away every time." His fingers wrapped about her upper arm, resisting the instinctive urge to caress that slender length of linen. "I believe our Lady Penelope may know a little more than you about all that history, even something that may have occurred twenty years ago. Perhaps they weren't as best of friends as they would have liked you to believe. You know, the more impassioned of enemies have been known to commit a crime to avenge something that happened decades before." He removed Alexa's champagne glass and the canapés to a nearby table. With a wicked curve of his lips, he drawled, "Why, that sounds suspiciously like a viable lead, wouldn't you say? The second in as many minutes, in fact. Worthy of a dance or two, at least. Or perhaps a stroll upon the terrace. I would imagine the view from there would be quite lovely."

She pursed her lips and looked at him quizzically. "You're inventing all of this, Oliver, merely for a dance and a view you care nothing for." She lifted her prim nose and looked away. "I won't have any of it."

Oliver sighed heavily and directed his scowl toward the ballroom before settling it upon the saucy fall of her hair, tumbling halfway down her back. "Alexa, consider this. Suppose my father was killed for reasons having something to do with ownership or control of Bellefontaine. After all, look what happened to Sir Reynold Alleyne. Yet another mysterious death the British government refuses to investigate."

Sparkling emerald eyes and a brilliant smile set the blood churning all the more furiously in his veins. "There you go, Oliver!" She gave his arm a sisterly pat. "*Now* you're on to something. Why, I can give you at least a dozen reasons that—"

"Good." His hand engulfed hers before she could snatch it away. "I don't mind talking while we dance." Grasping her elbow, he moved her rather firmly toward the center of the room where couples breezed past in the throes of a waltz. "Don't deny me this," he said, sweeping her into his arms, hard against his chest, his grip far too unyielding for a mere waltz. "Besides . . ." He peered down at her all flushed and suddenly flustered, looking entirely too ravishable and innocent in all that white. "Some show of unity on our parts would be prudent, especially at such a function."

She rolled her eyes and sighed with supreme annoyance, yet somehow managed to feel weightless in his arms as he spun her about the room. "You must think me awfully gullible, Oliver. The only soul on this entire island who cares one whit whether we dance is *you*."

He bent nearer, his breath stirring the curls at her temple, her elusive scent momentarily clouding his mind. "I'll wager you a kiss that within five minutes after this dance we're approached by at least one person who asks about the state of the plantation."

"So very certain, are you?"

"I am about wanting to kiss you."

Her eyes flickered over the crowd gathered close around the dance floor, as if she suddenly couldn't bear to look at him.

"See any suspicious-looking persons, Alexa?"

"They're all familiar faces," she replied. "People my mother and Gabriel knew well." That dubious look again slanted up from beneath the brim of her hat. "So someone asks about the plantation. A reasonable question given the circumstances and the guests. What the devil would that prove to you?"

"If you're so certain it won't prove anything, make the wager with me. You've nothing to lose."

She glowered at him, then seemed to force a shrug. "Fine. But only if it proves useful to our case."

"A kiss," he reminded her.

"One."

"Openmouthed, of course."

Fire bloomed in her cheeks. "*Oliver.* You're hateful."

He laughed softly and settled her closer against him. "Never that, sweet Alexa. Never that."

The dance couldn't end soon enough for Alexa. Not that she had any desire to find herself upon that shadowy terrace with Oliver as he claimed his due from their wager. Indeed, she didn't truly believe his five-minute theory held any merit. But the mere thought of owing Oliver *anything* in the way of a kiss nearly sent her crumpling to the floor. God alone knew how very torturous the feel of a man's arms could be around a girl, especially if it drove sense from the mind, filled one's belly with a gaggle of twittering butterflies, made one conscious only of all that supreme masculinity towering above her...and stirred deeply disturbing doubts about the wisdom employed, or remarkable lack thereof, when entering into this agreement with the man. He'd built an empire out of business deals, outwitted many an able businessman, skirted the issues, twisted the facts, all to benefit his own cause.

She slanted an annoyed glance at that arrogant chin. Sly, clever and ruthless he was, employing neatly disguised theories as viable leads simply for her favors. Indeed! Yet...some part of her yearned to avenge her mother's death so passionately, she would blindly follow any lead he could possibly concoct at the moment, even if it held but a glimmer of hope. And Oliver, no doubt, had already homed in on this weakness, seen it for what it was and intended to exploit it to his full advantage. This would not do. Somehow, in some way, she had to regain control over the situation . . . over *him*. She wondered if anyone ever had.

"The dance is over, Oliver." Tapping a finger against his shoulder, she frowned up at him when his arms seemed only to tighten around her. "Oliver, the music has stopped."

Distracted, he asked, "So who taught you to dance?"

She pursed her lips. "Your father, if you must know. You waltz very much like him."

This prompted that characteristic shadow to descend over his features. "All men waltz alike, Alexa."

"On the contrary. Some men move effortlessly, whether or not they're on a dance floor, seemingly born with an instinctive inner rhythm. Others appear incapable of walking with any sort of grace, much less waltzing."

"We bumbling buffoon types require much practice." His fingers threaded through hers, sending a pulsing heat along her arm. "Ah, music. Shall we?"

The words trembled upon Alexa's lips . . . her soft denial . . . her plea that he, more than any man, required little practice. That he moved with a fluid, pantherlike grace that drew the eye and roused a woman's senses. That his simple moving about proved as potent an aphrodisiac as any known to man.

"I say! If I could cut in, what?"

Oliver tossed a suddenly hovering Stuart Jeffcoat a bored look. "Go away, Jeffcoat. The lady has been claimed."

Color flooded Stuart's cheeks and air rushed from his flaring nostrils. "I say, Keane. The lady looks as if she direly needs some air." He cocked his head, his lips peeling back over bared teeth. "Perhaps if you didn't find it necessary to hold her so bloody close. Isn't it enough that you're detested by nearly all in attendance? Must you cause a scene with Miss Fairfield on the bloody dance floor?"

Oliver's eyes glittered like diamonds. "We Yanks have always improved upon your British version of doing things, Jeffcoat. Waltzing is merely one of them."

Alexa glanced between the two, noting the challenge in their locked gazes, particularly the predatory twist to Oliver's mouth. "Please," she whispered, laying her palm upon Oliver's chest, an overt gesture, to be sure, but one she instinctively knew would divert him. This indeed drew his rapt attention, and more. Their eyes locked. His hand covered hers and his eyes flamed over her with something far more potent than challenge.

"What is it?" he asked softly.

"I—" she licked her lips and summoned a quivering smile "—I'd like some champagne, Oliver."

"Of course." His hand upon the small of her back guided her from the dance floor.

"Stuart, please join us."

What response this drew from Oliver, Alexa would never know, though Stuart seemed aglow with supreme smugness and all but clicked his heels before following in their wake.

"To the Princes Albert Victor and George of Wales," Stuart bellowed when they'd retrieved fresh champagne. Hoisting his glass, he threw Oliver a challenging look. "What's the matter, Keane? Won't you drink to Mother England? After all, that plantation of yours rests upon British soil. Ah, but you don't care, do you, or perhaps you've merely forgotten? You're sailing for the States rather soon, I hear. Back to your shipping empire. Have a good trip, I say."

"You heard wrong," Oliver replied in that ominous growl Alexa knew boded trouble. Glittering cobalt eyes found her above the rim of his glass. "I've extended my stay indefinitely. Miss Fairfield and I have a plantation to run."

"You *what?*" Stuart choked, half into his champagne. His eyes darted to Alexa, who had trouble concealing her own surprise at Oliver's revelation. "But he cannot stay... with you... *in the same house!*" he sputtered. "Why, that's... it's... I say, quite out of the ordinary. It's not done. Simply not done. As the executor of your father's will, I simply won't allow this, Keane."

"Stuart," Alexa interrupted with a soft laugh she hoped would dispel some of the almost palpable tension. "I appreciate your concern, but I'm quite capable of taking care of myself. Besides, Bellefontaine is immense." She suddenly found herself the object of Oliver's penetrating stare. "Why, Mr. Keane and I could wander about the place for months and not even see each other."

"Don't count on it," Oliver muttered, but his words were lost as he downed another glass of champagne in one ferocious gulp.

Stuart's gaze narrowed suspiciously upon Oliver, then swept over Alexa. "You look ravishing, Miss Fairfield. Unduly so. But this business of running the plantation . . ." He glared at Oliver. "Keane, here, notwithstanding. It disturbs me. Greatly."

"Get over it, Jeffcoat," Oliver growled with a disarming smile. "I'll watch over her."

"The hell you will," Stuart snapped. "Sugarcane is dangerous business these days, Keane. Some plantation owners have fled for their lives after their entire crop of cane was maliciously burned. You should be advising Miss Fairfield to sell her ownership in Bellefontaine, as should you, as quickly as possible. One would think you'd literally jump at the chance. You could sail away from here with a small fortune in your pocket. For years, your father and Sir Reynold Alleyne both refused to do so and look what happened to them."

Alexa stared at Stuart.

"Are you threatening me, Jeffcoat?" Oliver asked with deceptive softness.

Stuart flushed clear to the tips of his ears, his fists clenching at his sides. "I say, Keane, I'm no murderer, if that's what you're implying."

Oliver's lips curved in a blithe smile. "A simple question, Jeffcoat."

"Many men have found themselves in jail for attempting far less with a commanding officer, Keane," Stuart snarled.

"Another threat, Jeffcoat? Watch your tongue. One could almost infer that you believe Gabriel Keane was murdered because he refused to sell out. Don't tell me the government believes Lily Fairfield was behind all that?"

"You're twisting my words, Keane," Stuart retorted hotly.

"A simple enough task," Oliver replied, his manner beguilingly casual yet simmering with dire undertones. "So tell me, Stu, why all the interest?"

Stuart's eyes nearly bulged from his head, and his hand moved over his scabbard, rousing a warning clank from his sheathed sword. "Don't call me that, you bloody bastard!"

"Enough," Alexa interjected, forcing an airy little laugh as she insinuated herself between the two men. Oliver's heat penetrated into her back, his chest expanding and contracting against her. And then his hand, warm, possessive, upon her waist, moved slowly just to her ribs, then down, pausing at the curve of her hip. Her words seemed forced, breathless. "Stuart, your concern is well taken. Truly. But just as Gabriel refused to be intimidated into selling Bellefontaine, so shall I."

"What's this? *Not sell?* Balderdash, I say!" A ruddy-faced, bald-headed chap, grinning from ear to ear, peeked over Stuart's shoulder, then wedged his bulbous form around a rather plump older lady blocking his path. Shouldering a sputtering Stuart out of his way, the newcomer thrust a pudgy hand at Oliver and grinned jovially, his fat cheeks shiny with sweat, his tiny eyes flickering with keen interest over Alexa. "Pinkus Pomeroy, my good man. And you must be Keane. The one everyone's talking about. Nothing hateful and sinister about you as far as I can see. And the pretty little lady, here. Miss Fairfield, I presume." He patted her hand, ogled her bosom and winked conspiratorially. "My dear, we must talk. Dispel some of these ludicrous notions about not selling that plantation of yours." He rubbed his hands together and bobbed up and down on his toes. "But for now, Keane, tell me of *your* plans for Bellefontaine. First, some bubbly, eh?" Retrieving champagne for each of them, he again winked at Alexa and gave a deep-throated chortle. "You're actually smiling, Keane. Odd chap, you are. Enjoying yourself, eh?"

With a subtlety not beyond Alexa, Oliver glanced meaningfully at his watch, then hooded a smoldering gaze upon Alexa that set her insides to trembling. "The night just took a remarkable turn for the better, Pomeroy. You see, I'm a man who enjoys winning a wager."

Chapter Nine

"Not a darkie to be seen within a half-mile radius of here, and all's the better for it, I say, eh, Keane?" Pinkus Pomeroy carelessly gulped at his champagne, wiped his red satin sleeve over his slack mouth and erupted with a guttural belch.

Oliver glanced at Alexa. She wore her revulsion well for a woman unaccustomed to these sorts of affairs. Though she seemed preoccupied with the goings-on around them, he knew Pinkus Pomeroy had captured her full attention, that the telltale pinkening of her cheeks with rage had been prompted by Pomeroy's contemptible remark. Then again, perhaps her thoughts were upon the paying up of their wager, something he himself couldn't seem to keep his mind off of, in spite of Pomeroy.

"Ruined the plantation owner, the darkies did," Pomeroy remarked, frowning into his glass.

"And here I'd thought it was fellows like you, Pomeroy, who claimed that honor."

Pomeroy's enormous belly jiggled with his chuckle. "Come now, Keane, we're both businessmen. From Boston, are you?"

"Chicago," Oliver corrected him, shooting Alexa a sideways glance.

"Some sort of powerful shipping magnate, or so I hear."

"That depends on who you talk to."

"Bought out many a struggling little company along the way to the top, eh? You didn't get there by being kind and friendly now, did you, Keane?"

Oliver's smile never reached his eyes. "I don't have many friends."

"Ha! You see there. We both know I wouldn't be enjoying such success with my hotels and resorts down here were it not financially reasonable for me to do so. Indeed, I find myself in the midst of a tremendous pecuniary flush at the moment." He smiled a yellowed, vile, little smile. "Thanks to those darkies. You see, Keane, they've put such a financial burden upon plantations, operating a profitable sugar operation since the abolition of slavery has become all but impossible. Those darkies demand high wages for lazy work and bleed plantation owners dry. One poor season of weather and *poof!* I can tell you, more than a few of those same plantation owners have come *begging* me to buy them out."

"Only a limited number of people can exploit sugarcane profitably on an island of this size, Pomeroy."

Pomeroy nodded vigorously. "My thoughts precisely. Yet I can't convince some of them." Pomeroy snorted into his champagne, then drained it. "Stubborn, confused lot they are, and your father was one of them. As stubborn as they come. Hell-bent on preservation of the land and the people and some such balderdash. Gives me a bellyache, it does, all their useless defending of the darkies." Pomeroy pursed his puffy lips with obvious annoyance. "Damned Bims and their smug self-satisfaction. Stout and clumsy they are, yet no people ever praise themselves so constantly, no set of men have ever been so assured that their occupations are the main pegs on which the world hangs. I'll bloody show them, eh, Keane?"

"By putting them to work on your resorts?"

Pomeroy gave an eager little smile. "Indeed I shall. Whip them into shape I will. I tell you, Keane, there are titled Englishmen in London who import these male Bims for employment as footmen. A bloody competition it is in some of the more fashionable districts to see whose darkie looks best in his white silk stockings and blue satin breeches." Pomeroy leaned closer, assailing Oliver with the stench of stale breath, his tiny eyes agleam with something devilish. "'Tis their calves, Keane. Long and superbly muscled, they are. Near perfection in white silk stockings. Come have a look-see for yourself. My latest undertaking at Alleyndale Hall shall be open to the public in less than a month, and I've imported a hundred pair of those silk stockings all the way from the Orient. Worth a look, I tell you."

"It seems to me, Pomeroy, that you're asking for the same fate as the plantation owner."

"By depending on the Bims?" Pomeroy snorted and waved a pudgy hand. "Rubbish, I tell you, they'll work for me, no matter what I pay them. They'll have no other choice, Keane. The day of the plantation is over. Tourism is the business of today and tomorrow. The British populace is bloody good and tired of traveling to the continent. By Jove, everyone's seen Paris twenty times over. They want something tropical and lush. Something heathen and untouched and they'll pay plenty for it. Ha! That Alleyndale Hall is supposedly haunted. What do you wager a Brit will pay for that, eh? I tell you, there's money in tourism on this island, far more than in sugar. Why, just yesterday I was in Bridgetown, at that Beefstake and Tripe Club. I overheard that several export shipping lines have been discontinued to your New England. A devastating blow to sugar prices come harvest time." Pomeroy cocked an eyebrow. "Something to consider, Keane. A man like you in an operation like mine?"

Oliver hardened his stare. "Are you talking partnership?"

Pomeroy closed his beady eyes and shrugged. "Of course, once you sell out to me. Your plantation sits on prime property, Keane. That District of Scotland has never been good for sugar growing. Soil's too erosion prone. Too hilly. Too much deforestation and overgrazing of those low pasture areas. But the views..." Pomeroy all but smacked his lips and cast his lascivious leer at Alexa for several moments too long to suit Oliver. "I could even find something for our little lady here to do, eh, Miss Fairfield?"

Alexa swung a look of such fierce loathing upon the man, Pomeroy retreated a step. "I own half of Bellefontaine, Mr. Pomeroy. I suggest you keep that in mind." She turned to Oliver, her lovely jaw tense, her emerald gaze liquid fire. "I'm going to take some air, Oliver." She barely nodded at Pinkus Pomeroy, then turned and was instantly swallowed by the crowd.

Oliver started after her, pausing only when Pomeroy's chubby arm blocked his path. "A fiery little thing, isn't she?" Pomeroy chortled. "Talk some sense into her, Keane. A woman like that—" Pomeroy licked the spittle from the corners of his mouth and looked as if he yearned to devour something almost as much as Oliver yearned to smash a fist into that jellylike girth. "Indeed, a woman like that should be kept flat on her back and breeding for the rest of her life. She has no business running a plantation." Again, that conspiratorial wink, the wicked insinuating grin. "Go and convince her. A little more of what went on on that dance floor."

"If you'll excuse me." Oliver forced a nod and shouldered past the offensive little man.

Pomeroy, however, refused to be put off, his squeaky voice trailing in Oliver's wake. "I shall call on you soon, Keane. Tomorrow, perhaps. We can discuss the particulars then. Eh, Keane, what was that you said?"

But Oliver merely growled the same livid curse beneath his breath and hastened after Alexa.

The crowd bulged around her, suffocating her with its heat, thick with the stench of perfumed flesh gone stale after hours of profuse sweating in heavy satin and taffeta. Alexa gulped for air and jammed an elbow into the beefy side of a gentleman who trod all over her foot. Gritting her teeth, she forced a smile for several who greeted her and noted the disdainful looks from those who obviously knew she'd come with the notorious Oliver Keane. Up above and ahead of her she could see the open terrace doors... freedom from all this... and surged toward that opening. Freedom from vile men like Pinkus Pomeroy and all they represented. From the overt glances, the suspicious looks.

Clutching skirts in hand, she hurried through the doors and across the flagstone terrace, pausing only when she'd reached the farthest shadowed corner. She leaned her hips against the ivy-covered stone wall and filled her lungs with warm night air. Like a peaceful rain, tranquility seeped into her, banishing the sounds of revelry to a distant dull drone, banishing, as well, the echo of Pinkus Pomeroy's loathsome voice. Beneath her sloped towering cabbage palm trees and the sleeping gardens of the spacious governmental villas that dotted the hills surrounding Government House. All was bathed in milky moonlight and enshrouded in the rising mists. Over one hill in the distance, a full blue moon inched into the night sky, and below it the ocean glistened like a priceless jewel.

And then warm hands caressed her upper arms, his touch so very gentle and coaxing, rousing slumbering passions deep inside her. For a moment, she luxuriated in the heat of him pressed against her back, felt the warmth of his breath close to her ear, thought perhaps she felt his lips brushing against the side of her neck. Or perhaps she merely wished it so, so desperately did she need a soothing touch.

Her eyes swept closed and she swayed back against him, reveling in the sensations for the one fleeting moment she allowed herself to do so. And then she drew a deep breath, her gaze upon the moon.

"Have you come to tell me you're casting your lot with Pinkus Pomeroy?"

His deep chuckle reverberated against her back. "Alexa, you've so very much to learn about me." Those large hands moved with infinite leisure down her arms to entrap her hands. "Come. I'll take you home."

Without a word, she followed him across the terrace and down a wide set of stone steps. Her feet moved twice as fast as his along a cobblestone path that led to the front of the manse. He paused to summon his coachman, drawing her close beside him and tucking her hand beneath his arm. How very natural it suddenly felt to linger with him thus in the stillness of the night with naught but the dim flickering shadows cast by sputtering gas lamps surrounding them. So much to say, so much to discuss... a wager to be paid... yet silence seemed oddly soothing, his imposing presence and stoic demeanor at once arousing yet strangely comforting. Indeed, as she stared at the impeccable expanse of white cotton covering his chest, she was assailed by traitorous thoughts of curling up against all that fine white cotton, of nestling within his embrace, of enjoying *hours* of silence from that vantage.

She almost didn't dare breathe, so precarious did the moment seem, so poised were they just a hair's breadth from each other. She stared at the buttons of his shirt, knowing he stared off into the distance, wondering if he, too, was as besotted by that champagne as she...for surely it was that. Strange that he, too, didn't speak. Stranger still that he had yet to remind her of the debt to be paid...and that some part of her direly wished he would.

He handed her into the landaulet and settled close beside her. And the silence endured as they proceeded down Constitution Road beneath a canopy of towering Spanish oak, then onward along a beaten dirt road that led toward the coast, the starlit sky sweeping endlessly above them. The evening breeze cooled Alexa's heated cheeks and plucked like insistent fingers at the wayward strands escaping her hat. At length, she drew the hat from her head, scattering gardenia petals all over Oliver's lap and drawing his silent regard. For some time he watched her, and she the back of the driver's head until they suddenly emerged upon a coastal road flanked by thick jungle on one side and an infinite span of ocean on the other. With little thought and not even a glance at Oliver, she tugged at the driver's coattails and requested he stop. The landaulet hadn't even completely halted when Alexa leaped from it. With skirts hoisted, she clambered down a steep embankment, leaving her shoes and hat in her wake, and shoving the pins from her hair. Her toes dug into the cool sand, propelling her onward. Her fingers plucked at the hook at the back of her dress, her eyes fixed upon the foaming surf not twenty yards farther along. Beyond that, the ocean lay inky black and fathomless, yet prompted not one whit of fear in her. Like a narcotic it was, this sea with its almost mystical power over her, something she craved, something for which her soul yearned.

"Alexa, you're not going in there."

From somewhere behind her, rising above the roar of the surf came Oliver's deep voice, edged with concern. Then his fingers firmly wrapped around her arm and spun her.

He caught her hard against him. "Alexa—no!"

In the brilliant moonlight, his eyes glittered dangerously. "Oliver..." With both hands she pressed against his chest, her eyes seeking his. "It's wonderful." Her palms moved slowly over the heated muscled plains beneath that shirt. "Come with me."

"No." He stared at her even as she eased away from him. "Alexa, don't do this."

A smile crossed her lips, a decided impishness rising within her. "Oliver, you look positively morbid. And you needn't be. I do this sort of thing all the time."

"I knew you were a damned foolish woman," he growled, advancing upon her, one hand reaching for her. "But not this foolish."

With a yelp, she spun about, nearly tripping on her gown, felt his fingers slipping through her hair, clutching at what little excess fabric there was about her waist and then . . . a rending tear. But Alexa didn't look back. Instead, she plunged into the surf, her legs cleaving through the powerful tides, before she dived into a wave that crashed over her head. Only when she surfaced did she look toward shore. Oliver stood at the edge of the water, what looked to be the very bottom ruffled portion of her dress clenched in his fist.

"Hullo, Oliver," she called out with a dramatic wave of her hand before the surf crashed unexpectedly over her and sent her tumbling nearly head over heels beneath the surface. When she emerged, sputtering saltwater and sand, she peeled her hair from her eyes and saw Oliver standing knee-deep in the water. A murderous fear had carved itself into his hawk-like features.

"Get the hell out of there!" Taking what looked to be one hesitant step, he stopped and snarled, "Damnation, woman!"

A husky laugh escaped Alexa's parted lips as she swam even farther from shore, beyond the breaking waves. At length, she paused and floated on her back, blinking at the stars above, reveling in the feel of her gown floating about her.

"I would have never thought you possessed one prudish bone in your body, Oliver Keane," she called cheerily at the moon. "Never thought you'd let a little water stop you. Come join me!"

No reply. She glanced toward shore. He stood bathed in moonlight upon the sand, clutching her ruffle, glowering at her. Very silent. Very ominous. He remained there for the duration of her swim, silent and unmoving, his stance daring her to come ashore. Which she did, eventually, wringing seawater from her sodden half-gown and boasting a satisfied smile.

"Nothing like a late-night swim to invigorate a person," she chirped, reaching for the remnants of her dress. Her fingers had but brushed the linen when Oliver pulled her so roughly against him all breath was driven from her lungs.

"What the hell were you trying to do?" His eyes spat blue fire into the darkness. "Do you direly wish to become a late-night snack for some carnivorous fish?" His fingers dug into her arms, hauling her against him. "Or did you think I'd simply rescue you?"

Alexa grimaced at him. "Good grief, quit growling at me, Oliver. You're making no sense. Loosen up a bit, will you? I've never once required anyone's aid—"

"You've never been in the ocean half-drunk before, either."

Alexa sucked in her cheeks and attempted to force the faint haze from her mind, the traces of slurring from her speech. "I am not drunk," she retorted hotly. "And as for carnivorous fish—"

"They exist."

"Perhaps miles offshore, but—"

"They've been known to attack not twenty yards offshore, my dear," he rasped through gritted teeth. Her parted lips drew a caustic grunt. "Surprised, are you? I told you, sweetheart, know your enemy."

In spite of herself, Alexa found her gaze drifting toward the foaming surf, which not moments past had seemed so much a part of her. "I wouldn't think carnivorous fish abound in Boston, Oliver."

"I wouldn't know," he muttered wryly before glowering fiercely at her. "*But that's because I'm from Chicago.* Hell, I've only been to Boston twice." And then suddenly, he was frowning at her, his change in manner disturbingly abrupt, his eyes full of suspicion. "Who the hell do you know in Boston?"

"Nobody. But all those investors aiding Pomeroy are from Boston."

"Well, I'm not one of them." He stared at her for several long moments, his grip upon her arms easing, almost gentle.

"Don't go in the water alone—at night—hell, alone *at any time,* do you hear me? Stay in the freshwater ponds or swim in the damned fountain."

Alexa slanted her eyes at him. "Why, Oliver, is that *concern* I hear in your voice?" she asked saucily. "Or could it be you've developed some fondness for me, hmm?"

He shook her so hard her head almost snapped. "Listen to me, woman," he snarled. "I watched a man die like no man was ever meant to perish. Here, not twenty yards from this very shore. Limb from limb he was ripped apart, by a fish. Yes, a fish. And I stood upon this shore, helpless, a lad of but six, unable to do anything but watch because I hadn't yet learned to swim. I stood there until the blood washed over my feet, and then shredded flesh, *his* flesh, as if he'd been shoved into a meat grinder."

"Stop—" Alexa whispered, sagging in his arms.

"And I wouldn't be able to save you, Alexa," he rasped. "No matter how much I would want to... because I can't swim. I haven't been able to set foot in the water since that day."

"Oliver..." Her nails dug into his chest, her eyes meeting his, still smoldering with his torment. Suddenly, all revulsion and shock was banished beneath an unconscionable desire to clutch him close against her breast, to ease the anguish, and all else that tortured him. She swallowed deeply and instead stared at his shirt, aware of a faint trembling that had besieged her... perhaps at her realization that this man was capable of feeling fear. "Oliver, I'm sorry. I didn't mean to scare you... to rouse unpleasant memories."

"Then don't do it again." He caught her head between his hands, smoothed the tangles from her face and drew her close until her forehead rested against his chest. Muttering something unintelligible into her hair, he shed his topcoat and swung it about her shoulders, anchoring her against him with the pressure of his hand upon the small of her back. Alexa wrapped her arms about his waist. She listened to the vibrant beating of his heart and stared at the moon hanging low over the sea.

"It's so beautiful," she said softly.

"The most dangerous things usually are."

Her eyes slid to his. "Is that why you seem to hate this island so much?"

"I've many reasons to hate it . . . too many." He traced a finger over her cheek, beneath her jaw, cupped her face and lowered his mouth to hover but a breath from hers. "Any reasonable man would have to wonder why the hell I can't seem to leave." His words were a mere whisper, his lips brushing like thistledown over hers. "Then again, if he had any reason at all, he'd know why."

"Why?" Alexa whispered, womanly instinct and, yes, perhaps too much champagne, prompting her to arch up against him, to mold herself to those muscles straining against his shirt.

And then his hand caught deep in her hair, yanking her head back. His other hand grasped beneath her hips, lifting her high against rock-hard thighs. "Don't flirt with me," he breathed against her mouth, his eyes glittering with a savage light. With a boldness that sent a shiver through her, he caressed her hips, her buttocks, his touch like forbidden fire through a wet tangle of linen. "If you want to know why I can't leave, Alexa, ask me to show you. Because I will. . . ." His mouth was a hot flame against her throat. "Again and again, I'll show you—"

"Oliver—"

"A kiss, Alexa." This time he snatched her breath with a devilish grin. "You promised, remember?"

"I—" She drew deep gulps of air, hoping to still the world from careening about her. Oliver helped little, occupied as he was with nibbling along her neck. "Oliver—"

"Anxious, are you?"

"Hardly."

"Good." His hands spanned her waist and moved torturously over her ribs, his fingers memorizing every curve and hollow. "Because I'm enjoying the wait."

Alexa stilled those long fingers not a moment before they reached the tender undersides of her breasts. "You're taking advantage," she said meaningfully. "Please, Oliver, we've an agreement."

"Really?" He raised his lips to her temple, his hands attempting to sweep hers aside to resume their trek up her bodice. "I can't seem to remember the particulars of that contract at the moment. Too much champagne and moonlight." A husky groan escaped his lips when his gaze lowered to her breasts. "Or maybe it's just you in a wet, clingy dress. You wouldn't happen to be as forgiving of agreements as I am at the moment, would you, Alexa?"

A hint of a smile teased her lips when a shiver chased up her spine. Born of this odd power she wielded over him, perhaps. "I'm unreasonably unforgiving at the moment, Oliver."

"You're torturing me. Banking on my being noble and forthright about our little contract. Quite a risk, wouldn't you say, being that I'm known as a despicable rakehell?"

Alexa lifted a shoulder. "Possibly, though you seem the type to stand by your word."

His teeth gleamed in the moonlight, his voice laced with a seductive drawl that sent heat coursing through Alexa's veins. "I've never been tempted by the most beautiful breasts known to man. So full, so taut, so supple, they fill my hands perfectly, make me want to—"

"Oliver."

He laughed huskily and nuzzled her neck. "Surely you didn't expect me to forget? You're causing me to have sleepless nights, you know, all this remembering. Give me something else to help while away the hours, will you?"

An unexpected self-confidence swept through Alexa, urging her to slip her arms about his neck. She returned the sultry look he gave her with a saucy curve of her lips and snuggled her breasts against him. "Open your mouth, Oliver."

"I think I like this agreement," he murmured, looking as if he ached to devour her lips.

"Quit talking, Oliver."

Their eyes locked, his full of potent, raw passion as yet unleashed, hers sparkling with the awareness of the power of her newfound womanly wiles. His lips compressed and she brushed her thumb over them, the full lower lip curved with promise, and his teeth captured her thumb. An odd sensation tremored through her, igniting some primal need, drawing a husky groan from deep in her throat...or perhaps it was he... And then he crushed her to him in a savage kiss. Soft whimpers sputtered and died and she surrendered entirely to him...how could she not...he would allow her nothing else. Her fingers sank into his hair and clung as he arched her against him, yet she yearned to be closer. His hands branded her everywhere...beneath her hips, her buttocks, her thighs...molding, grasping as if they would savagely shred the damp linen. And he ravaged her as she'd never dreamed of being ravaged by a single kiss, his tongue plundering, retreating, his lips demanding, then taking the response he alone could stoke within her.

In a rush of air, their mouths parted and they stared at each other, their harsh, swift breaths mingling, their chests surging against each other. It took a strength of will Alexa didn't realize she possessed to push against his shoulders and avoid being consumed by the fire smoldering deep in his eyes.

"I believe the wager had been paid," she said softly, and slipped from his arms before he could reply, before he laid claim to her very soul...and ran for the landaulet, never once looking back.

Oliver stood in the dimly lit foyer, staring at the second-floor balcony, listening to the steady drumming of his heart. He could almost imagine the dying echo of Alexa's bare feet flying over this marble as she fled from him. Yes, she'd fled from him, the moment the landaulet pulled to a stop, just as she'd sat beside him the entire trip home, wrapped in his topcoat and a cocoon of silence, and worse yet, coolly detached. He hadn't attempted conversation, of course. Hell, a man never had to worry over such matters with a woman. At least, not with a typical woman, one who babbled incessant nonsense with such dull regularity a man could depend upon it as he did the very rising of the sun. So much so that the art of conversation had become a one-sided female diatribe, without so much as a pause for an obligatory "Is that so, my dear?" Indeed, Oliver had almost come to rely upon that drone of chatter, so conducive was it to deep, inner thought. In fact, he'd found the mere mention of some society gossip by his mother or Daphne to be the perfect prelude to an inner debate of the merits of iron-hulled ships over wooden-hulled ships.

A frown troubled his features. Not so with Alexa. Island goddess. With her, he couldn't even compose a logical thought. He stared at the remnants of her gown still clenched in his fist, and with not the slightest hesitation pressed it to his face, inhaling deeply. His eyes swept closed as the scent of gardenia tumbled over him like falling petals, filling his mind with tantalizing images, forcing the breath from his lungs.

"Oliver."

His head snapped up, his teeth gritting against the heat rising from his collar when he encountered his mother standing in the darkened hallway, just at the shadowed edge of the foyer.

"You're back," she said, stepping into the dim light that shimmered over her rich burgundy dressing gown. She sipped from a glass of amber liquid and paused directly before him, her eyes flickering over him. "Had enough of all the hobnobbing already, I see. You'll never change, will you, Oliver? So determined not to be one of *them*." Again she tipped the glass to her lips and seemed to sway on her feet, her voice slightly slurred. "Well?"

Oliver cast her an admonishing look, then brushed past her into the darkened hallway. "It's late, Mother. Go to sleep."

"I already tried," she called after him, her slippered footfalls echoing behind him. "I've been soothing my bruised ego with brandy half the night. Wouldn't you, if you hadn't been invited to the event of the season? But then again, these British Barbadians never could recognize quality in a person. Oliver, don't ignore me."

Oliver's jaw worked against his mounting irritation as he swung toward Eleanor. He knew damned well what she wanted from him, something he'd rather not discuss at the moment. "It's late. I'm tired. Good night, Mother."

Eleanor erupted with a husky laugh. "Come now, Oliver, you're holding what looks to me suspiciously like part of a woman's gown. Your shirt is nearly soaked. And yet you've that caged-lion look about you...as if you're intent on a kill. If my life depended upon it, I wouldn't be able to tell if the evening went as planned or not."

"With regard to what specifically?"

"With regard to your seducing that Fairfield chit," Eleanor hissed. "Good grief, what the devil else would matter to me?"

Oliver tugged at the knotted cravat high under his chin. "Not the solving of Father's murder, I wouldn't guess."

Eleanor shuddered and momentarily closed her eyes. "Dear God, don't tell me you've been entertaining ridiculous thoughts like that. It's the girl, isn't it? She's put these delusions in your head."

"Hardly delusions." Oliver loosened his black cravat and the top few buttons of his shirt. Folding his arms over his chest, he leaned a shoulder against a doorjamb. "Care to hear my theories on the matter?"

Eleanor advanced toward him. "If I didn't know any better, I would say the girl is seducing *you,* or at the very least, robbing you of your senses. What the devil is going on?"

"If you thought I could coerce the plantation out from under Alexa in one evening, you were sadly mistaken. With some women, one night would be plenty. With Alexa, however—"

"*Alexa,* is it?" Eleanor stared at him, at the dress bunched in his fist, then seemed to shrink back a pace, her fingers clutching at her breast. "*No,*" she breathed. "You cannot even think of jeopardizing our plans by...by...*falling in love with that... that...*"

"Calm yourself," Oliver said. "Perhaps you would be content to allow me to proceed at my own leisure with this if I told you a little about my friend Pinkus Pomeroy."

Eleanor's lip curled with distaste, Oliver's sarcasm obviously lost upon her. "Who the devil is that?"

"An English investor. He seems to think Bellefontaine would make a prime tourist hotel. I'd wager he'd be willing to pay handsomely for the opportunity to develop it."

Eleanor's eyes glittered, her teeth baring in a smile. "And the longer you hold out, the more desperate he will become, and the higher your price. Oh, Oliver, you're brilliant. Yes, yes, take your time with the girl, if you feel you must to succeed with her. I've infinite confidence in your abilities." She stared meaningfully at him. "I've never known you to possess one weak, emotional bone in your body, especially regarding women. Forgive me, will you? Falling in love is something reserved for the commonfolk, is it not? Men with far less substance than you. But remember Daphne. Before we left, she started making all sorts of noise about that English lord who fancies her. We don't need that sort of problem, Oliver. Both she and her father's company shan't wait forever for you, you know."

"They'll wait." Oliver turned on his heel and proceeded down the hall toward the study. "They'll have no choice."

Chapter Ten

Oliver jarred awake, his head snapping up and banging against the back of his chair just as his booted right foot slammed into the solid mahogany underside of the desk. It took only a moment to realize his other foot, as well as the entire left side of his body, was asleep. He blinked, attempted to unfold his stiff limbs and rubbed his bleary eyes, squinting at the mantel clock through the blinding rays of sunlight that streamed through the study windows.

"Eight," he growled, frowning at the empty glass upon the desk. Beside that glass rested an empty crystal decanter that had contained, at some point during the night, and judging by the bone-dry taste in his mouth, very mellow whiskey. Beside the decanter lay his father's journal. Beneath that lay the plantation's ledgers, and surrounding those, pile upon pile of untended correspondence. He glanced at the clock again, scowled and rubbed a hand over his stubbled jaw. He needed coffee, *real* coffee, the kind old Hedda Berghoff brewed at her coffeehouse on the corner of State and Adams, right around the corner from his office. He'd patronized the place on many a late night, specifically for Hedda's coffee, the gut-warming, strong black stuff that had seen him through reams of contracts and ships' manifests, sometimes well past three in the morning. A not untypical habit of his. Indeed, he knew Hedda and her husband, Otto, well. They were, perhaps, his only true friends. After all, even he'd found the quiet of a coffeehouse at three in the morning surprisingly conducive to conversation. His gaze shifted to the decanter. When the hell had he developed such a passion for liquor?

With a grunt, he rose to his feet, his body unfolding like brittle tree limbs, refusing, then resisting, aching from a night spent in an office chair. Or possibly it was simply age insinuating itself upon him. That thought set his teeth to grinding and he shoved a hand through his hair, slinging his discarded topcoat over one shoulder. He left the sun-dappled study, intent upon the dim warmth of the kitchen and Cook's version of Hedda Berghoff's coffee, only to stop short just as he reached the hallway. As if incapable of anything else, he simply stood there and stared at her.

The same sunlight poured through the tall foyer windows, yet somehow the effect was not some brilliant assault upon sleep-addled senses, something he yearned to flee. No, this sunlight bore an altogether different aura, a golden-hued softness, like the tender caress of a woman's hand sweeping the fuzziness from his brain. Then again, maybe it was simply that which it caressed which claimed his breath for several long moments.

Looking like she had been kissed by angels, Alexa stood there in that golden light, the very essence of serenity, her profile like that of a porcelain doll. She was dressed all in white, her blouse resting just off her shoulders, her skirt brushing the tops of her bare feet. She radiated health and youth, as if she'd enjoyed a splendid night's sleep and had just leaped from a refreshing bath. So completely did she hold him captive, so entirely did he devour her with his eyes, that for several long moments he did not realize that Stuart Jeffcoat stood quite close before her, hat in hand pressed nobly against his chest, glove upon sword. They faced each other, heads bent low in a shared soft exchange, entirely unaware that Oliver loomed, the intruder, just down the hall, suddenly consumed with the precise manner in which he would dismember Stuart Jeffcoat.

It was then, when Alexa laid a hand upon Jeffcoat's arm, when she seemed to peer up at the officer with eyes that said she thought him man of all men . . . and Jeffcoat seemed to grow three inches . . . yes, it was then that Oliver was besieged by a most disturbing thought. A thought which, given but several more moments of witnessing their display of affection—and one could hardly label it anything but—would burgeon into a full-blown theory, one he would be hard-pressed to abandon without ample proof to the contrary. After all, it made sense. Indeed, it made far too much sense, and, if nothing else, justified his immediate and supreme despising of Stuart Jeffcoat, a despising that heretofore he could only lay to some sort of... dammit, jealousy. Until now, admitting this had caused him supreme aggravation. Him, *jealous?* Of anyone, much less a man like Jeffcoat? Hell, no. Instinct had prevailed over that weakness. He all but snorted, yet his eyes narrowed even more when Alexa's laughter bubbled forth, a soft seductive laugh to his jaded ear *and* to Jeffcoat's, judging by the flush in the officer's ruddy cheeks. She'd never laughed like that before....

Oliver's fist clenched, his gaze skewering Jeffcoat, then sliding to Alexa. For such a prize, what man wouldn't even for a moment consider murder? Especially a trigger-happy oaf like Jeffcoat intent upon proving himself a man. A man quite capable of taking the matter much further than mere fleeting consideration. A man perhaps capable of acting upon such thoughts, consumed with having the prize...especially knowing what the prize would inherit. After all, even the most noble of British officers had a price...and Jeffcoat could have easily discovered the contents of the will before Gabriel's untimely demise.

Jeffcoat was the murderer.

Oliver could hear his pulse thundering in his ears, felt the tightening deep in his chest—not the ill effects of an overindulgence in spirits but the impatience of knowing what others did not. Tact. He would need to employ this now more than he had at any other time over a bargaining table. Yes, tact...and infinite patience while he gently nudged Alexa into his way of thinking, and devised a scheme to ensnare Jeffcoat.

And then Stuart Jeffcoat lifted Alexa's hand to his lips. Before Oliver could give tact and gentle nudging even a moment's consideration, he advanced upon them, his gravelly snarl spilling from his twisted lips, to put a swift end to whatever Jeffcoat had in mind.

"Get the hell out," he growled at Jeffcoat, duly registering Alexa's gasp of outrage, yet supremely uncaring. He stood nose to nose with Jeffcoat, aware that his unshaven, rumpled appearance lent him an appropriate air of savage intensity. He gritted his teeth into a sneer. "Now, Jeffcoat."

"I say!" Stuart huffed, his insignificant chin jutting forward.

"Then say it elsewhere." The twitching of Jeffcoat's upper lip proved adequate testament to the man's distress, though something flared deep in his dark eyes.

"I could call you out," Jeffcoat sneered.

"Go ahead," Oliver drawled, his lips curving. "I'll look forward to it."

"No!" Like a sylph, Alexa slipped between them, shoving a tiny hand into Oliver's chest and glaring at him.

His gaze drifted over her and he summoned a lopsided smile. "Good morning, my dear. You're looking well."

Her breath spilled from her parted lips. "Good grief, Oliver, what's the matter with you? This talk of duels, it's barbaric. How could you?"

Oliver's eyes flickered to Jeffcoat and back. "It was his idea."

"I say, Keane!"

"Enough!" Alexa glanced between them, her forehead knitted with agitation. "The male animal, forever needing to prove something. Stuart, for what, pray, would you call him out?"

Jeffcoat's eyes widened with obvious disbelief. "Why, for remaining in this house with you, of course. For neglecting to return to wherever it is he came from. Posthaste. He has all but compromised you."

"Stuart, I have not been compromised."

This surprised Oliver, being that he knew she truly believed herself to have been stripped of her virtue not two evenings past in the garden. Then again, perhaps her fervor to find her mother's killer far outweighed her grievance with him. The scowl hovered, the rage igniting in his chest. He opened his mouth and—

"I say, the way the man looks at you is quite more than enough," Jeffcoat declared with righteous indignation, looking as if he were about to sweep Alexa safely behind him.

"And to think I allowed this...even lent my hand, so to speak."

Alexa laughed and patted Oliver upon the chest as she would a bothersome pet. "Don't mind him, Stuart. Oliver is a grump until well past noon. He simply needs more sleep, a better diet and some exercise." She cocked her head and gave Oliver an assessing sweep of her eyes. "Indeed, even *he* could be quite likable I would think."

"I'd rather you not like him," Jeffcoat sneered before again jutting his chin forward and leveling Oliver with a confident look. "You see, my dear Miss Fairfield, I would rather our courtship was conducted in more, shall I say, private circumstances."

Alexa clucked her tongue with a breeziness of manner that set Oliver's vitals to churning. "Oh, he shan't be any bother, Stuart, I assure you. Will you, Oliver?"

Oliver stared at her, the words falling like lead from his lips. "He's courting you."

Alexa's smile wavered. "Actually, Oliver, he simply—"

"Not in my house."

"Oliver."

Oliver glared at the pinch-faced officer. "Goodbye, Jeffcoat."

Alexa's fingers plucked at his sleeve, her voice laced with a supreme agitation he knew well. "Oliver, we were simply going to Bridgetown for the day."

"I'll take you wherever you need to go," he said. He grasped her elbow and attempted to guide her down the hall, but she planted her feet and twisted from his grasp.

"Unhand me," she breathed, practically trembling with anger. Oliver could only stare at her, the words aching in his bone-dry throat, begging to be spewed forth in a stream of bellowing and raging. Why? Why Jeffcoat? Why—when all he yearned to do was take her in his arms and kiss her until she couldn't bear it...and then he'd simply take her to his bed. And all she wanted was to spend an entire day in Bridgetown with another man. The man who murdered her own mother.

"We may jointly hold this plantation, Oliver," she said through clenched teeth, "but you have no hold over me. No man does or ever will."

Oliver looked mockingly at Jeffcoat, ignoring the fiery rage burning in his chest. "Did you hear that, Stu? Kind of puts a damper on all your noble plans for Miss Fairfield, doesn't it?"

Stuart bristled anew. "What the devil are you implying, Keane? As if you've a notion of honorable intentions—"

But Oliver barely heard the other man's blustering, so intent was he upon Alexa. She stood proud and defiant, yet small and fragile in her beauty, cloaked in all that ability to render him senseless. Coffee...no, another whiskey to sweep this fog from his mind. He nodded briefly and swept a hand to the door, his lip curling with only a whit of his anger. "Far be it from me to stand in the path of true love," he mocked. "My dear Alexa, enjoy your day." And with that, he turned on his heel and strode down the hall.

"He's known as the preserver of the West Indies."

"Indeed." Alexa cast Stuart a quick glance before fixing her attention once more upon the enormous bronze statue before them. Horatio Nelson, hero of Trafalgar, grandly commemorated in all his bronzed glory, the monument erected here, precisely in the center of Bridgetown's Trafalgar Square. "Imposing, isn't he?"

"I should say, and rightly so. The father of the British Royal Navy he was."

Something in Stuart's tone drew her attention to the marked puffing up of his chest, yet his manner seemed vaguely wistful. The clattering of coach wheels upon cobblestones all around them suddenly grated upon Alexa's nerves like a dull knife, prompting her to seek the curricle. Yet Stuart seemed wont to linger, gazing at the statue as if seeking answers from that unforgiving countenance. If statues of heroes could speak, Alexa would have thrown herself at those bronze feet.

Yet, even a man like Nelson couldn't possibly have known of the unfathomable workings of her own mind, couldn't possibly have explained to her why she couldn't seem to ask the appropriate questions of Stuart, questions that needed asking. Questions regarding her mother's death and the government's refusal to investigate the matter. Questions regarding Pinkus Pomeroy. Indeed, these questions were the very reason she had agreed to accompany Stuart today. But even Nelson couldn't have told her why she couldn't keep her mind upon anything but the image of Oliver Keane, wild-haired and wild-eyed, smelling faintly of whiskey and looking too darkly forbidding for words, yet vulnerable in his own peculiar manner, as he sought to throw Stuart from the house. The memory was enough to make the blood flow like warm honey through her limbs...certainly enough to make her rue her decision to accompany Stuart Jeffcoat on this outing, a decision made solely to seek answers from him and, yes, to keep herself from Oliver's path for the better part of the day. God knew, she needed time away from the man... if only to recoup her wits, left scattered on that beach yesterday evening.

She tapped an impatient toe and cast unseeing eyes about the bustling thoroughfare, upon the coral stone building that was the House of Assembly, particularly upon the stained-glass panes depicting all the royal British sovereigns who had ruled over England from James until Victoria.

The air hissed from between her teeth. No, this simply wasn't working. "Stuart," she called from beside the curricle. He barely glanced at her, so deep in thought was he, no doubt. Her toe resumed its tapping and she heaved a sigh. He'd been awash in pompous self-confidence ever since they'd departed Bellefontaine, a self-confidence prompted by what he believed a victory over Oliver, and that had lent him an uncharacteristic boldness of manner. Something she'd found as disturbing as she did offensive. Evading his sly innuendo, his brief yet lingering touches upon her arm, seemed an easy enough task compared to dealing with this...this... She frowned at him from beneath the brim of her hat. Why, the man looked positively morose, and worse yet, she cared little for the reasons, and wanted only to return forthwith to Bellefontaine. With Oliver Keane's dark moods and fierce passions she felt far more inclined to deal, perhaps because she'd glimpsed more of the man beneath the myth last evening upon that beach, something that intrigued her far more than it should have. Perhaps because some unseen force seemed to lure her to him.

"I say, it's the heat, what?"

Alexa almost jumped from her skin at Stuart's slight touch upon her arm. "The heat," she repeated dumbly, allowing him to hand her into the curricle.

"Indeed." Stuart clicked the reins. "I should say, I couldn't be more pleased that you joined me. You see—" Stuart paused to tip his hat at a passing battalion of British officers on horseback "—nothing like a bloody good show of naval strength to keep the blacks in order."

Alexa cast a perplexed look about the bustling thoroughfare surrounding Trafalgar Square. The passing carriages were those of the well-to-do British Barbadians, their crests boldly emblazoned upon their sparkling equipage. The sidewalks bulged with their brightly colored parasols and highbrow bowlers as they browsed through the shops. Of the blacks, Alexa spied only the typical hawkers huddled beneath the shade of awnings, peddling their wares of fresh fruit and vegetables and handwoven baskets. Their laughter tickled the senses from time to time, a deep-throated explosion of great guffaws so symptomatic of their zest for life.

"They hardly warrant any show of military strength, Stuart," she responded with a marked coolness of tone. At his distinct grunt in reply, she continued, "You would be hard-pressed to find a more optimistic or carefree people in all of the West Indies. Hardly a threat to the British Royal Navy, wouldn't you agree?"

"A threat nonetheless," Stuart replied stiffly, maneuvering the curricle through a tangle of coaches. He sneered a curse beneath his breath when an unfortunate hawker's mule and wagon somehow managed to find themselves blocking the curricle's path. "Move your bloody wagon before I put a lead ball through your mangy mule's heart!" Stuart roared, half out of his seat with rage.

"Stuart!" Alexa grabbed his arm, attempting to jar some sense into him. But he shrugged off her hand and leapt from the curricle, his eyes bulging from his head as he advanced upon the young black lad struggling for control over his wayward mule. Noting well Stuart's fondling of his sheathed pistol, Alexa wasted not a moment. She jumped from the buggy and lunged for the mule's tether. The wide-eyed lad she recognized immediately as one of her piano students, and with a quick smile, shoved him behind her before Stuart could lay one hand upon him.

"There now, Stuart," she crooned through clenched teeth, murmuring softly to the crazed mule. "Control yourself, eh? That is indeed the governor himself passing by, is it not?"

"What?" Stuart skidded to a halt, visibly blanched, then spun about, one hand upon the hilt of his sword, the other jerking into an awkward version of a salute. Capitalizing on Stuart's distraction, Alexa coaxed the frightened mule away from the curricle and whispered hasty instructions to the lad, which sent him swiftly on his way. When Stuart ceased craning his neck for some view of the governor and had turned about, the wagon had long since clattered off down the cobblestone street.

"Didn't you see him?" Alexa asked airily as she climbed into the curricle.

"No, I did not," Stuart replied crisply. "A breech of protocol, I tell you. I wasn't informed the man would be anywhere near Bridgetown today. Odd, that." With a frown troubling his ruddy features, Stuart again clicked the reins and guided the curricle away from town.

Alexa concentrated on sucking in her cheeks and avoiding eye contact with the man lest she double over in a fit of laughter. Indeed, the mere grim set of his jaw nearly sent her into giggles, though his next comment swept any hint of amusement from her mind.

"This talk of murder..." he began, his gaze directly before him. "Could it be our Oliver Keane has remained at Bellefontaine for reasons having nothing to do with operating the plantation?"

"Such as?"

"Come now, Miss Fairfield. Everyone including Keane knows well the day of the plantation is gone. In fact, he and Pinkus Pomeroy discussed the matter at great length last evening. And though he may be the most pompous and unlikable of men, Keane is no fool. Especially when it comes to business."

"Indeed. Knowing this of him, one would then have reason to wonder if the day of the plantation is truly over, Stuart. Perhaps Oliver Keane knows something the others do not."

Stuart lifted a meaningful eyebrow. "Precisely my point. And it has nothing to do with the making of sugar, my dear Miss Fairfield."

"Then what, pray, does it have to do with, Stuart?"

"Murder."

Alexa felt the blood drain from her face. "What are you implying, sir?"

Stuart hauled up on the reins, halting the curricle beneath the shade of a huge cabbage tree. He turned to her, his expression grave, his tone deep with forewarning. "I have given this matter considerable thought... and, well, given the manner in which the governor has chosen to handle the matter of your mother's and Gabriel Keane's death—"

"Stuart, what the devil are you saying?"

Stuart swallowed deeply and cast a hasty glance about. "I'm saying that I have reason to believe your mother was not the killer. Meaning that the governor is merely seeking to avoid it being known that they both were quite possibly murdered... by another's hand."

Alexa stared at him, her breath coming swift and deep. "Stuart, dear God, why didn't you tell me sooner?"

"Miss Fairfield..." He grasped her hands and bowed his head, his whispers urgent and filled with emotion. "I fear for your very life. Every waking moment of every day. The murderer..." His eyes lifted to hers, his grip upon her hands almost painful. "You're living beneath his very roof."

Alexa blinked several times, then erupted with heartfelt laughter. "Surely you don't mean *Oliver?* Oh, Stuart, be reasonable."

"I am stretching reasonable to its very limits by allowing you to remain in the same room with the man, much less in the same house."

Alexa shook her head, then paused at an awful thought. "Surely the governor doesn't share your suspicions regarding Oliver?"

"No, I alone harbor this theory, but I intend to prove it, forthwith, to the governor himself or die trying, by God."

"Oliver hasn't set foot on this island in over fifteen years."

"According to him, perhaps. His presence could go relatively unnoticed were he to mingle with the shipping merchants forever clogging the harbor and frequenting that nasty Beefstake and Tripe Club. The man owns a bloody fleet of ships. He could easily come and go from this island at whim." Stuart's reddish eyebrows puckered. "Then again, the man has enough money to hire thugs to carry out his schemes. The murderer *in absentia*. Dear heaven, I hadn't thought of that. An interesting possibility, indeed."

Alexa resisted the urge to roll her eyes heavenward. "Stuart, Oliver is not a murderer."

"He despised his father."

"True, but—"

"And he stood to inherit the plantation, a plantation which upon sale could bring him a fortune, perhaps even see him into an inordinately profitable partnership with Pomeroy."

"Oliver has no need for any partnerships with Pomeroy. Good heavens, the man owns a shipping empire."

"Then why, Miss Fairfield, does he remain here, if not to gain complete control over the plantation and to ensure that someone else is convicted of his heinous crime?"

"Stuart..." Alexa paused, her gaze sweeping the lush countryside where tall cane rippled in the warm, golden breeze. Why *had* Oliver remained in a place he professed to despise? Even *she* had assumed his purpose in remaining had been to claim complete control over the plantation solely for the purpose of selling it. Precisely in keeping with Stuart's theory, though Alexa somehow could envision his motive having more to do with revenge upon his father than any fortunes he could amass. This notwithstanding and callous as he may have been toward all his father had cherished, Alexa refused to believe this made Oliver a murderer.

"Anyone with eyes in his head can see the way the man looks at you," Stuart gently urged. "It is only a matter of time before he compromises you... before he coerces your share of the plantation from you."

"No," Alexa breathed with firm conviction. "Never."

"Then he will kill you."

Alexa glanced sharply at Stuart, willing the hammering of her pulse from her ears. "I refuse to believe this. It's ludicrous. And I shan't stand for any more of it."

"You're in love with the man."

"I am not!" she retorted hotly, too hotly, judging by the wistfulness in Stuart's gaze. Alexa forced a swallow and directed her eyes elsewhere lest guilt find itself emblazoned upon her face. "Take me home, Stuart."

"As you wish" came his reply, punctuated by the slapping of the reins upon horseflesh. "I want you to know I have every intention of looking after you, of being your champion, by God, even if you choose to disregard my concerns and remain at Bellefontaine. I shall bring this criminal to a due justice, Miss Fairfield, a power as is granted me by the queen herself."

"I shall keep that in mind," Alexa said.

"I pray that you do, Miss Fairfield. Indeed, I pray that you do."

Oliver shaded his eyes against a relentless midday sun and squinted up at the massive windmill adjoining a conglomeration of rough-hewn buildings. "What do you call this, Luke?"

The man at his side grunted. "Ingenio."

"Ingenio." The word caught on Oliver's tongue.

"Sugar works," Luke offered.

"I like that better." Oliver looked over the entire works, noting the crumbling chimneys, the sagging roof line, the entire deserted, dinge-covered countenance, so entirely not in keeping with the tangle of bougainvillea struggling up one whole wall of the place. "I don't suppose the interior looks any better, eh?"

"Worse," Luke replied. "Boiling house coppers and furnaces need regular care."

"How long has it been this way?"

"Three, maybe four months," Luke replied.

"What the hell was the man thinking?" With a grunt, he set out around the perimeter of the sugar works, his boots swishing through knee-high grasses, Luke following close behind. Perspiration dripped from his lashes, onto his lips, trickled down his neck, his chest, into his waistband. Myriad gnats and bothersome pests stirred by his boots swarmed about his head, and he swatted ineffectually at them, then paused and contemplated a tear in one of the windmill's sail-cloth vanes.

"No electricity here yet, eh?" he asked, his hands on his hips.

Luke stared at him.

Oliver offered a twisted smile and thrust a hand at the unmoving vanes. "Electricity, my friend. Even on a day like today, when there's not a breeze to be found, you could operate your sugar works on electricity. Or steam, for that matter." He shoved a hand through his hair and kneaded the muscles bunched at the base of his neck. "Ah, hell, you say harvest time is November. Enough time to get the place in some kind of shape, at least to fix the damn vane?"

"Enough time," Luke replied, flashing a huge white-toothed grin.

"I'm putting you in charge, Luke, to handle this and the tending of the fields before planting and harvesting season sets in. You can be the—" Oliver frowned, vainly seeking his word, and waved a hand.

"The overseer."

Oliver pointed at Luke and grinned. "That's it. I'm appointing you overseer."

"Miss Alexa's already done that, sir."

Oliver's grin faded slightly. "You don't say. One step ahead of me, isn't she?" This he muttered, half to himself, his thoughts straying, as they had been wont to do since Alexa had departed with Jeffcoat that morning. The now-familiar tightening filled his chest like tinder igniting.

"Excuse me, Mr. Keane, sir?"

The red haze parted and Oliver glanced about to find a white-faced Cyril poised not ten paces from him.

"An unexpected visitor to see you, sir," Cyril intoned, clasping his hands behind him. "Lady Penelope Alleyne."

Oliver couldn't temper the lift of his eyebrow, or the hearty slap upon the shoulder he dealt Luke. "Come to the house later today, Luke. We'll discuss the particulars of getting the plantation back in shape."

And with that, he turned and strode briskly past Cyril, his gaze intent upon Bellefontaine, nestled upon a distant rise, his thoughts upon all the favors Alexa would owe him...once he learned all he could from the ardent Lady Alleyne.

Chapter Eleven

Without pausing for anything but a cool rag and a clipped order for lemonade, Oliver entered the parlor. At the untempered scrape of his heels upon polished wood, Penelope Alleyne turned from the windows in a rustle of pale lemon-yellow taffeta. She stood thus for a moment, studied, cool, pristine elegance amidst all that dark-haired, ivory-skinned beauty. Her perfectly painted lips parted rather obviously when Oliver paused not two paces from her to rub the cloth vigorously over his face, his neck, clear to the middle of his chest, which was exposed by the parted buttons of his damp linen shirt. The honorable Lady Alleyne seemed inordinately fascinated by all this for several long moments, allowing Oliver to wonder if she'd planned this response as precisely as she'd positioned herself in the room. The proper midday lighting. The perfect backdrop of a garden in full bloom, all chosen with infinite care to aid her in her game. Just as she had to know this scoop-necked lemon-yellow taffeta seemed to offer her forth like a precious jewel.

Oliver carelessly tossed the cloth aside and grasped Penelope's extended hand, bending low over the white-gloved fingers. "Lady Alleyne."

She seemed to struggle for composure for several moments, her breasts heaving above the low neckline like plump luminescent balls, so very white, yet shot through with blue veins.

"Sir," she breathed, her fan flapping agitatedly at her breasts, her lashes fluttering in the manner of one about to swoon. A studied art, that. "I simply had to come."

"Is that so?" Oliver replied, turning as Cyril placed a tray upon a low table. "Lemonade?" he offered over his shoulder as he retrieved a cool glass.

"Uh . . . no . . . I . . . don't believe I shall."

Without hesitation, Oliver lifted the glass to his lips and drank deeply, robustly, until he'd drained the glass. "God," he breathed hoarsely, setting the glass aside and glancing at Penelope. She simply stared, fan flapping, breasts heaving. Oliver indicated the settee opposite him. "Would you care to sit?"

A hesitant smile. A batting of her lashes. "Why, of course." The sensual glide across the room. The perfect pose upon the very edge of the settee. How utterly predictable women such as she had come to be for Oliver, whether they be money-hungry widows like Penelope or repressed little virgins like Daphne. As if all their studied perfection could ever lay claim to a man's soul. Most men he knew would be afraid to touch them.

Oliver sprawled opposite her, slouching low in his seat, legs thrust before him beneath the table, his boots just brushing the lace hem at the bottom of Lady Penelope's skirts.

"I came to pay my respects, of course," she said in that smooth, lilting, oh-so-British manner.

"You knew my father well." It was purposefully neither a statement nor a question.

"Very well," Penelope answered easily. "Being that Lily Fairfield and I were the very best of friends."

"She and my father were lovers."

A brief widening of those dark eyes, then a furious blush invaded Penelope's powdered cheeks. "Lily would never have consented to such a thing. She was . . ." Her eyes seemed to linger yet again upon his chest and her tongue flicked out over her parted lips. "She was not of that persuasion, you see. Even though one would have expected it of her, of course."

"How so?" He leaned forward, his elbows on his knees, hands clasped such that his shirt stretched taut over his arms. This drew the expected shimmying in her seat from Penelope. Oliver had to wonder how long the woman had been without a man. Hopefully long enough to prevent her from growing too curious about his questions.

"My," she breathed, peering at him through her lashes. He well imagined she'd done that very thing at least a hundred times before. "You're quite something, Mr. Keane. Not at all like what we're used to around here. A scoundrel in every sense of the word."

Oliver gave her a predatory look, one that Penelope gobbled right up. "Tell me about Lily Fairfield."

"Lily—yes, of course." She made a slight adjustment to herself upon her perch, seemingly unaware that her movement was just enough to set her breasts to quivering upon the very edge of her neckline. Oh, but the practice that must have required, endless hours before a mirror to get it just right. Again the slant of her dark eyes as they traveled ever so slowly, ever so obviously over him. Hopefully, she thought he was interested in Lily Fairfield simply as a mutual topic of conversation they'd stumbled upon, a vehicle for them to get to know each other, a facade concealing the conversation Penelope was orchestrating with every sensuous movement, every increasingly bold flicker of her gaze over him.

"You've good reason to despise the woman," she observed softly.

"I do. I was told she murdered my father. Did she?"

Penelope shrugged and laughed deeply, huskily, sending a warning through Oliver. "She could have, I suppose, if one were inclined to believe in fantasy. Far too many here would never believe it. One of this island's mysteries, or so they'll say. You see, Lily was—how shall I say—aptly named if anything. Some called her a beauty. I suppose she could have been, in a fragile, almost fairylike way. Her hair was this—this cloud of white, her skin like downy snow, her voice like an angel's. She was very slender, tiny. So fragile, the next wind could sweep her away. Yet she had this manner about her, an almost childlike innocence that made men want to protect her, I suppose. And, oh yes, she had these large bosoms." Then Penelope's tone sank flat. "All the men here were in love with her from the moment she set foot upon the island. Even the bloody governor, if you can believe that. You see, they had had their fill of us dark-haired beauties, no matter that we sprang from the most envied of British bloodlines, that Lily Fairfield was but a tavern wench who slithered her way into our fold by seducing Brighton Fairfield—" Penelope paused, her eyes widening slightly as if she were suddenly far too aware of the echo of her voice drifting through the room. "Well, that was only one version of the story." She snatched the full glass of lemonade from the table and raised it to her pursed lips.

"You knew her husband," Oliver said.

Penelope clucked her tongue. "Knew him? I was engaged to the man for nearly six months, and then..." Penelope's lips spread over her teeth. "He was the most revered of Her Majesty's naval captains. And the wealthiest. Contrary to my wishes, he found it necessary to move from time to time in seamen's circles. This meant frequenting the dockside taverns. One in particular. The tavern where our Lily worked as a barmaid. She stole him from me."

"A most annoying habit," Oliver muttered. "My mother would claim the very same of the woman. So, she plotted to ensnare a man betrothed to another."

"Oh, no! Lily never *schemed,* at least in any conscious manner, you see. She simply never had to. That was, without question, the most hateful thing about the woman." Penelope sucked in her cheeks and lifted her nose. "Other than her looks, of course. A true ingenue with regard to men. Brighton and, no doubt, your very own father simply fell hopelessly in love with her. I don't know if you can understand this, but she had this *power* over men—"

"Power."

"Something quite intangible and elusive, you see. Something quite maddening to the rest of us women here."

"Like witchcraft. As if she robs a man of his mind."

"Precisely." Penelope plucked at her skirt. "Even so, once she and Brighton had married and he'd set her up in a posh town house and all but abandoned her there for his naval career, she was never admitted into the social circle in London. You can understand, of course. Why, the upper crust cannot be expected to forgive a person of laboring in a dockside tavern, now, can they?"

"I can understand why she chose to stay here rather than return to all her well-wishers in England," Oliver said with a sarcasm Penelope seemed to miss. "But that could hardly be just retribution for you, now, could it?"

Penelope laughed harshly. "Me? Why, I consoled myself with Brighton's best friend and first lieutenant, of course. We married precisely one week *before* Brighton and Lily. It was all carefully arranged, you know. My reputation simply wouldn't have stood for the gossip if Brighton had married first. As it was, half of London thought *I* was the one who had called it off."

"And the other half?"

Penelope gave a wistful sigh and forced a smile. "Timing, Mr. Keane, is fundamentally important...but, of course, you must already know that."

"I do. I'm merely wondering why you chose to remain here, Lady Penelope, when all of London awaited you."

Penelope skewered him with a glittering gaze. "Mr. Keane, men like you can't be found within a hundred-mile radius of London. Why the devil would I have returned?"

Oliver studied her closely, ignoring her innuendo. "You and Lily even managed to become best friends."

Penelope all but snorted, delicately, yet laced with sarcastic bite. "I would never have believed it—seeing as how the woman almost ruined my life. But there was something about her, something wonderful that made me forgive her, that made me understand how men would happily die for this woman." Again, the haughty sucking in of her cheeks. "Besides, she was society's darling here, and I didn't exactly want to be left out of all the fun. A woman has to concern herself with such things, Mr. Keane, if she intends to live well."

"And you didn't envy her."

"Mr. Keane, I wouldn't be much of a woman if I said I didn't. Tell me what quality a woman must possess to keep a man like your father, a man quite virile and handsome, wealthy—" Those gleaming dark eyes drifted over the parlor as if registering the net worth of this room alone. "Gabriel Keane could have had his pick of paramours, me included. Yet the fragile, white Lily managed to keep him coming to her house *daily,* sometimes twice a day to perch upon her settee and drink tepid tea and simply talk. Nothing more."

"He *was* married."

Penelope scoffed delicately. "Don't tell me that sort of thing matters to you?"

"Perhaps he loved her," Oliver countered.

"Of course he did. But at some point, the man must have gone out of his mind with wanting her. And he had ample opportunity to—shall I say—*appease* himself elsewhere."

"I didn't know my father well," Oliver replied, decidedly uncomfortable with the notion that his father had managed to exercise tremendous self-control where Oliver could not. Indeed, the picture Lady Penelope was painting of his father was decidedly opposite to the one his mother had sought to impress upon him all these years, and one he couldn't quite bring himself to accept. "I can't imagine your average man standing for it," he said with a frown.

"No," Penelope breathed, seductively lowering her lids over her eyes. "I wouldn't think *you* would, Mr. Keane. And you're far from average." In one fluid motion, she slithered out of her chair and slinked around the table to insinuate herself between his knees. She stood poised there before him, lids heavy, lips parted, nearly trembling with her passion and offering herself so brazenly, even Oliver was momentarily taken aback. And when he simply stared at her with his cool, even gaze, registering nothing even as his eyes drifted over her swelling bosom, she took it upon herself to grasp his forearms and lean perilously close to him.

"Tell me, Mr. Keane," she whispered huskily, her tongue darting over her lips. "Or shall I call you Oliver?"

Odd how he could manage to remain so detached with such an abundance of meticulously powdered bosom not two inches from his nose. He forced a soft laugh. "Lady Penelope—"

"Tell me you don't want me." She smiled with sublime confidence. "Tell me you haven't been thinking about it."

He caught her wrist when a razor-sharp red fingernail began a torturous trek down his chest. "Listen, you're a beautiful woman—"

That husky laugh erupted and she threw back her head. "We could make quite a pair, you and I, Oliver. I've always been drawn to bad boys like you. I hear you're planning to stay on . . . indefinitely." She smiled at him seductively and in one movement straddled his lap, a feat indeed for a woman encumbered by such narrow skirts. Those talons threaded through his hair, her lips brushing over his cheek, her breasts rubbing provocatively against his chest. "We could make it a permanent arrangement, you know," she whispered hotly against his ear. "Anything you like."

For a brief moment, Oliver envisioned such an arrangement with this desirable, overly eager woman, a woman he could see himself using ruthlessly, simply because he knew her game. He knew instinctively that she would do anything to achieve an end he had no intention of granting her, knew, even more, that he would never care for her beyond the basest of needs. And he was indeed a man of base needs, a man of fierce passions, whether they be work or pleasure. Yet a man who had somehow agreed to content himself with whatever favors Alexa deigned to bestow upon him.

With a scowl, he placed his hands about Penelope's waist and sought to ease her from him. "This isn't a good idea."

Not to be denied, Penelope wriggled against him with a laugh. "Come now, Oliver, there's peculiar talk circulating about you." Like tiny vises, her fingers wrapped about his biceps, then moved reverently over the length of his arms. "I, for one, however, simply cannot imagine a beast of a man like you preferring—"

"I don't prefer men," he growled, employing tremendous strength of will to keep himself from shoving her from his lap.

"I didn't think so," Penelope purred, arching up against him, her palms delving within his parted shirt. "There's something in your eyes when you look at me. Oh, how I want you to touch me, Oliver."

And then, just when he'd decided force was definitely the prudent thing to exert, something drew his attention, a sound like a swift intake of breath that seemed to echo through his mind. He turned his head, felt Penelope's lips upon his cheek and his eyes locked with Alexa's.

Perhaps his blood running instantly cold roused Penelope from her passion. She, too, glanced into the foyer and murmured huskily as from the very heights of sensuality, "Oh, my. *Well,* hullo, Alexa."

What Oliver expected, he didn't know. He knew only that he'd never quite experienced such a powerful surge of guilt, no matter his intentions with Penelope. Never quite felt like such an abysmal fool. Never before ached to take a woman into his arms and beg her forgiveness—for something he hadn't even done. Never before felt his pulse threaten to burn through his cheeks.

Alexa walked slowly into the parlor, and time seemed suspended for Oliver. To her credit, Penelope had the wherewithal to leap from his lap and commence with a show of poking and tucking at herself to make it seem she'd been duly ravished. She even managed a silly little giggle that grated upon Oliver's tightly drawn nerves like a dull knife.

He rose to his feet, completely consumed by Alexa. In her cloud of white, she stood a good six paces from him, as if she'd rather not venture too close for fear of being bitten. Or perhaps revulsion and disgust prompted both this and the peculiar glittering deep in her eyes.

She didn't speak, perhaps because her words clogged like mire in her throat, just as Oliver's did. Penelope, however, experienced no such difficulty. Amidst a giddy cooing and bubbling, she chattered on like a babbling bird, about what, Oliver did not know nor did he care. And Alexa seemed as oblivious to Penelope as he, her gaze fixed with resolute coolness upon him.

For the first time in his life, Oliver Keane didn't know what the hell to do... the humiliating calling card of many a besotted man, something he had thought himself far above... until he'd met Alexa and all reason had abandoned him. Just as it did at this moment. Thus, like any bumbling oaf, he moved toward her, one hand reaching for hers, her name the only hoarsely emitted sound escaping his lips. Possibly he retained some vestige of logic, as he instinctively knew the entire scene smacked of impropriety and seduction, that at this moment Alexa would never believe otherwise, no matter what he said in his own defense. Yes, her chin had assumed that stubborn perch, her lips a barely perceptible compression. Yet she stood her ground without flinching, even when he grasped her ice-cold fingers.

"Cyril," Oliver heard himself say when the servant made a timely appearance at the parlor doors.

"A telegram has arrived for you, sir," Cyril intoned, indicating the missive within his white-gloved fingers.

Oliver waved a hand to the sideboard, his eyes never once releasing Alexa. "Put it there, Cyril. And then you may show Lady Alleyne out."

"Excuse me?" Penelope erupted with a lighthearted chuckle and plucked at Oliver's sleeve like a scavenging vulture. "What's this? No late luncheon invitation, Oliver? Oliver? *Oliver,* look at me...."

Oliver gave the strident tones but half an ear, tucking Alexa's resisting hand beneath his arm and jutting his chin toward the door. "Shall we?" Without the favor of a response, he led her from the room.

"Get your filthy paws from my person! You're nothing but a servant!" Penelope railed from behind them. "I can see myself out, thank you." And in a furious rustle of taffeta, Penelope scurried around them to block their path. Her dark eyes spewed venom as she glanced from Oliver to Alexa and back again. "I see," she sneered. "So this is to be the way of things, Oliver. Funny, but I find it strange that you seem to be following precisely in your father's footsteps, an obliging victim of a mere wisp of a woman." She arched a knowing eyebrow that roused some sixth sense in Oliver. "No doubt you shall make the same mistakes as he—and perhaps find as just a destiny." Cold eyes raked over Alexa. "As will you, my dear. Consider yourselves duly forewarned." Lifting her skirts with dramatic flourish, she stalked from the room and seconds later punctuated her departure with a floor-shaking slamming of the front door.

Oliver glanced at Cyril. "We'll take lemonade in the study. Now."

The servant nodded. "Very good, sir."

"I don't care for lemonade." Alexa's voice stilled both men midstride.

"Fine," Oliver said. "Make it tea."

Again, both men had but taken a step when Alexa's husky voice brought them to a perplexed halt. "I never drink tea before three."

She gave him a smug smile that never quite reached her eyes and clasped her hands primly before her. Oliver filled his lungs near to bursting, then exhaled slowly. "Make it one very tall whiskey, Cyril."

"You'd best make it two," Alexa said, and again Cyril paused, this time to glance with stupefaction at her. She merely waved a hand. "Go on, Cyril. Mr. Keane will grow inordinately grumpy if he's kept waiting."

"I didn't know you drank whiskey," Oliver drawled, folding his arms over his chest when Cyril shuffled from the room.

"I don't," Alexa replied blithely. She breezed past him and left him no choice but to follow her from the parlor and through the foyer. "They're both for you. For so disciplined a man you're developing quite a habit."

"I'm being driven to it," he growled, his gaze sweeping from her smoothly undulating hips to the hypnotic sway of her hair.

"Ah, all this sleuthing has taken its toll." She paused, as did he, her eyes tilting to his. "Isn't that what you would call what you were doing in that parlor with Lady Alleyne?"

"Yes. Of course."

"Just as I thought." Her full lips twisted snidely. "You insult me, Oliver." With that, she took off at full stride down the hall.

"Hey! What the hell?"

"I'm not some obtuse little ninny you can manipulate at whim, Oliver. Some fool who will believe your every word."

He marched alongside her. "You *should* believe my every word. I've never lied to you, nor *will* I."

With eyes fixed forward, she huffed, "I suppose you would have me believe you had nothing to do with that display? That *you* harbored a most noble plan. That Lady Alleyne took it upon herself to leap onto your lap with absolutely no encouragement from you."

"That's precisely what she did."

Alexa skidded to a halt and swung blazing eyes upon him. "You—" with one finger, she jabbed him in the chest, harder and harder with each word she spoke "—are... *the*... most... insufferably... loathsome... man—"

Again, she took off down the hall.

Gritting his teeth with frustration, Oliver once again stalked after her. "Need I remind you that you just spent an entire day with Stuart Jeffcoat dressed in that—that—" His eyes raked her slender form, his scowl descending. "Dammit, you encouraged a man who needs absolutely *no* encouragement, on the pretext of courting, when I hope to God you were sleuthing, as well. Alexa—"

"Don't talk to me, Oliver."

"You're being remarkably unreasonable."

"Get used to it."

"I am used to it," he growled, lunging for her and capturing her about the waist. He spun her, lifted her around a corner, through an open set of double doors and into a dimly lit room. Shoving her against the damask-covered wall, he held her there, his hands upon her shoulders. "In fact, I'm finding that I like it too damned much."

Faintly, she shook her head, her voice deceptively soft. "I'm not speaking to you, Oliver."

"Fine, then I'll talk."

She looked over his shoulder, all cool detachment. "I won't listen."

With his fingers upon her jaw, he turned her face to his. "Why? Dammit, Alexa, look at me. Because you don't want to hear what I learned today?"

"Even Lady Alleyne would have nothing to teach you, Oliver," she said disdainfully.

His grip upon her shoulders tightened with the clenching of his jaw. Against his entire heated length she was supple and yielding, no matter the words spilling from her tongue, no matter her feigned preoccupation with whatever loomed beyond them. No matter that until her dying day she would deny her body ached hot and yearning for him. Forcing a steadiness to his voice, Oliver said, "She talked quite a lot. Enough to grant me a slew of favors from you, my dear. Care to pay up?"

Again she looked away. "Our deal is off."

"The hell it is." The frustration exploded in his chest, frustration, yes, and a passion so tightly held, so stoked to its limits by her ignoring of him, by the sheer feel of her against him, he paused, however momentarily, to rein it in a notch.

And then he shoved a knee between her legs and surged up against her. His gaze penetrated hers, daring her to stop him before his mouth claimed her neck. Like a starved man, he inhaled her scent, her flesh, his lips devouring her, then tugging the banded neckline low until he'd bared both her shoulders. His fingers hooked in that neckline and tugged farther, exposing the high curves of her breasts, lower and lower until the blouse slipped over her swollen nipples and her breasts spilled free.

"Alexa, sweet Alexa," he breathed against her skin, his mouth upon the fragrant swells of her breasts, then closing over the engorged peaks. He felt the weight of her breasts in his hands and his passion raged unleashed, his tumescent manhood straining his trousers to the seams and pressing brazenly against the soft curve of her belly. In the moment he thought he imagined her fingers threading through his hair, clutching him nearer, a strained "Excuse me, sir," echoed through the room.

"Ah, hell," Oliver snarled, glancing up in what he knew was a remarkably cavalier manner, given that Cyril stood just outside in the hall. The servant's gaze was everywhere but upon Oliver and Alexa, his cheeks uncharacteristically rosy.

"A gentleman to see you, sir," Cyril said flatly, as if his attention were captured by something far in the distance down the hall. "In the parlor, sir. A Mr. Pinkus Pomeroy, sir."

"Fine," Oliver muttered, and sent the servant shuffling down the hall. He glanced at Alexa and she simply stared at him, clutching her blouse high over her shoulders. "Sweetness..." He brushed his thumb over her full lower lip, his chest tightening. "I'm a man insane because of you." He cupped her face and vainly searched for the proper words. "Listen, we have to talk. Later... of course. Pomeroy—"

"No," she whispered. "You talk to him, Oliver. I..." She slipped from his arms and backed slowly away from him. He could almost imagine her mouth trembling, her fingers faltering at her neck. "I need—" And then she was gone in a sweep of sheer linen, though her scent lingered upon Oliver, haunting him throughout the remainder of the day and well into the evening.

Chapter Twelve

Alexa stood upon the beach, watching the inky black clouds gather violently upon the horizon. Like the pall that had settled about her heart, the storm began its descent upon the island, gobbling up a dusky, cloudless sky as if gathering sustenance from it . . . then growing, bulging, stirring the waters below into a foamy gray. An unforgiving wind pulled her hair flat against her head, plastered white linen against her breasts and belly, tangled it between her legs, and yet she remained unmoving upon those deserted shores. The surf foamed over her feet, swirled about her ankles, then retreated only to venture higher seconds later, nearly to her knees. The first splash of rain fell upon her cheeks like tears, and then, above the roar of the tide, the whistling of the wind, the hammering of her pulse, his voice . . .

"Dammit, Alexa—"

It was him, all right, leaping from his steed's back even before his horse skidded to a halt in the sand. He strode toward her, the devil himself. The wind ravaged him, as well, snaking within his shirt to set it billowing about him like sails unfurled, recklessly tossing his blue-black hair. Yet, for all his posturing as a man entirely out of sorts with the island, a man better suited and bred for plushy offices and stately promenades through well-tended parks, walking stick in hand, of course, he and the storm seemed peculiarly attuned, making it seem that one didn't quite belong without the other. Or perhaps they simply complemented each other, the thunder of his voice matching the ominous rumbling in the distance.

His boots splashed through the surf, stopping a hand's breadth from her. He loomed, eyes blazing, yet with an odd concern furrowing his thick eyebrows. "For the past two hours, I've combed the damned island looking for you," he bellowed above the roar of the wind.

"I went to the cottage," she replied, focusing upon the advancing storm. She felt his bold assessment over every inch of her, heating her from within like a flame that refused dousing, and her nipples swelled and thrust outward. With a helplessness she had never before known, she closed her eyes and wished for the hundredth time that day that it all didn't feel so predestined, so wondrously right that this man she had avowed her greatest foe, that this man's touch, his very essence fulfilled a part of her she'd never before known had been desperately yearning and void. Indeed, his laying bare her bosom and ravishing her in Bellefontaine that afternoon somehow had seemed the natural thing to do; servants and guests seemed to have mattered very little. Nothing mattered, save for this incessant flame burning between them.

Could fate be more cruel?

His fingers entwined with hers and he murmured something deep and husky, far more threatening than the storm, though unintelligible, and then the rain began to fall.

Alexa resisted the gentle pull upon her hand, lifting her face heavenward until the water ran in thick rivulets down her neck. He tugged again, then with a growl, hoisted her over his shoulder like a sack of wheat flour. With remarkable agility, he sprinted across the sand and thrust her upon the horse's broad, bare back. Before she could swing her leg over to straddle the stallion, Oliver mounted behind her. Managing the reins with one hand, he slid one very large hand about her waist and anchored her against him with an unyielding pressure upon her belly.

The rain fell in torrents, and the horse struggled through a sea of sand, urged on by Oliver's commands. They reached the road, which was fringed by thick, low-hanging palms that served as a patchy roof, and Oliver reined the horse up.

"Which way?" he asked, his breath playing against her ear.

"The cottage is closer than Bellefontaine," she replied, all too aware that the fullness of her breast rested against his arm.

His hand seemed to burn through damp linen, and his thumb moved between her ribs. "We can wait there until the storm subsides." She pointed to the right and attempted to ease away from him slightly. Yet he seemed to move with her, his damp chest and her back somehow irreparably joined. He reined the stallion about, yet kept him at a slow walk. Only a scattering of huge raindrops penetrated the curtain of palms overhead despite the deluge pounding the thick jungle on either side of them. Above the din, Alexa heard only the clopping of the horse's hooves, and a peculiar sense of peace invaded her. Perhaps Oliver felt it, as well. He retained a firm hold upon the reins, he, too, apparently in no great hurry.

How easy to relax against the man, to fill one's senses with his scent, a supremely male, potent scent stoked by midsummer heat and warm rain. The slow undulation of the animal beneath them rocked their hips together. That muscled wall of his chest pressed against her back and then his mouth was warm upon the tender side of her neck.

"Oliver..." she whispered, capturing his hand in both of hers just as it slid possessively over her ribs to cup one breast. She flattened that palm against her belly and wondered if he could feel her pulse there.

"You smell like the rain," he breathed against her neck. "So beautiful..."

Tiny shivers of delight danced through Alexa and she arched her back. "Odd that you would notice the smell of the rain when you seem so oblivious to the beauty of this island."

For a moment, his chin rested upon her shoulder as he guided the horse through a tangle of brush and then his lips brushed over her ear. "I notice everything about you."

Alexa's belly flipped and slammed into her ribs. "Then you should be very aware that I'm chilled. Could we please... hurry just a bit?"

His husky laugh set the blood coursing like wild heat through her veins and before she could stop him, his long fingers brushed over one very taut nipple straining against transparent linen. "Are you sure it's a chill you've got? Or are you as consumed with heat as I—filled with these flames that torture and consume..."

A shudder rippled through her and settled low and writhing between her thighs. "Oliver, stop talking."

"Do you have any idea how much I want you?"

The palms above her seemed to sway and she closed her eyes against the sensual tide lapping at her will. "We've a bargain, Oliver."

"How convenient of you to remember."

"Solve my mother's and Gabriel's murder—"

"And then?"

Alexa swallowed deeply, suddenly beset by the image of lying with Oliver upon a downy soft bed, of allowing him to do all that his sensuous voice promised, all that she wanted, and so very much more. She felt the untested power in the arm encircling her, in his hand beneath hers, knew those long fingers were capable of stroking her will from her, of evoking passions—

"Sweet, tortured Alexa, will you then come willingly to my bed? Will you then allow me to take what I want? Tell me, love." He tugged on the reins, stilling the horse, and then his hand was beneath the linen bunched about her thighs, his fingers sweeping over her inner thigh, pausing only when they ventured deep into the tangle of blond curls between her thighs, seeking the heated pulse that beat there. And his voice swirled about her, husky and deep with raw passion. "So hot—you're like heated honey. Tell me, Alexa, can you wait until then? Or do you want it now?"

Before those fingers could stroke once more, before another word could snatch the very last of her resistance, she grasped his wrist and sucked in a huge breath. "You're a man of your word, Oliver. Solve the murder."

He seemed to hesitate, and the world ceased to spin. Then he withdrew his hand and grasped the reins, digging his heels into the horse's flanks. "As you wish, my dear," he said close above her, and she could imagine the tight line of his mouth now, the narrowed eyes, all so very familiar. All so very much easier to deal with than his passion.

Oliver was indeed a man of his word. But Alexa couldn't help but wonder if even he had his limits.

* * *

Oliver left the horse tethered to a tree and ran for the cottage through the blinding rain, hurdling the steps in one leap and bursting through the front door directly behind Alexa. He slammed the door behind them, then skidded to a halt, one hand instinctively wrapping about Alexa's arm. Over the top of her head he saw the black woman walk slowly from the kitchen toward them. With a face devoid of expression, she paused before Alexa, those unfathomable coffee-brown eyes drifting over her, missing nothing, Oliver was suddenly certain.

"Shura," Alexa breathed before she turned. "Oliver, this is Shura."

Oliver nodded, stiffening when the woman merely grunted, then swung that mysterious gaze back to Alexa. For some unconscious reason, Oliver was beset by the most peculiar feeling that the woman could with one glance delve into a person's innermost thoughts, could indeed probe to the soul. As if aware of this, Alexa gave the woman a lingering hug and hurried from the room, obviously with little intention of allowing Oliver the merest glimpse of her in all that thin, wet linen. Imagination and their torturous ride here had done enough. It was all he could do to simply follow her with his eyes, to content himself with the knowledge that soon, very soon, she would be his.

With clenched teeth, he turned his gaze back to Shura and almost retreated a step. He obviously wore his hunger for Alexa like a gaudy, crimson cape, for all the world to see, such did the venom spill from this woman's eyes. And Oliver returned her stare, as if daring her to deny him that which he would kill for, by God, if it came to that.

What the hell had he become? Precise logic, a keen, sharp mind, a schedule both rigorous and precisely kept, the managing of his business empire—*all* had been carelessly shoved aside in favor of a mindless, irrational, entirely consuming quest for Alexa's virginity. Not because he simply could not stand to lose a wager or because he sought to seduce the plantation out from under her. No, the reasons ran deeper, the passion far too consuming, far more consuming than any task he'd ever undertaken.

The woman had laid claim to his very soul.

He gave this Shura one last meaningful and dismissive glare, then directed his efforts to stoking a fire in the shadowy front parlor. Feeling rather bulky and a trifle too broad-shouldered for such a tiny cottage, he moved with infinite care around the delicate furniture, his boots squishing with every step, water dripping from his cuffs and his hair onto the whitewashed floors.

Once the fire surged to life, he remained kneeling before the hearth, warming himself beside the low flames, his gaze drifting over the parlor. A woman's house it was, draped in soft white lace at the windows, the furniture, walls, floors, even the pictures on the walls and the flowers in the vases, all white and hazy gold in the firelight. A faint lemony scent tickled his nostrils, beckoning him to breathe deeply of the very essence of the place and his thoughts strayed....

It had been here, upon this very settee, before a fire much like this one, that his father had sat, day after day, contenting himself with whatever Lily Fairfield chose to give him, be it tea, conversation, a light touch upon the arm, a winsome smile. Perhaps his father had also stoked a fire in this hearth and lingered, feeling too big and clumsy for such a place, awaiting Lily as anxiously as Oliver now awaited Alexa. He had to wonder if his father had also lusted after Lily Fairfield, just as he, Oliver, ached to simply touch Alexa's smooth, golden skin—and wondered, too, how the man had managed to retain his sanity through it all. Little wonder the plantation records had been kept, if kept at all, in such thorough disarray. The poor man probably hadn't been able to keep his mind on anything but Lily Fairfield. Oliver knew the feeling well.

With a scowl, he rose to his feet and stared into the flames. "You're humanizing him," Oliver muttered half-aloud, and shifted his shoulders as if to ward off the ghosts that seemed to linger in this house. Or perhaps he'd been reading his father's journal far too much, learning far too much about a man he'd once despised and now with whom he had somehow, against his will and better judgment, formed a camaraderie of sorts. "You're as weak as he was," he said wryly, leaning his head against his forearm braced upon the mantel.

"What did you say, Oliver?"

He lifted his head, allowing himself a good long look as Alexa moved silently into the room, and curled into a corner of the settee nearest the fire. She looked fragile and tiny, swathed in white linen, of course, her hair a damp cascade of honey-gold ringlets that all but engulfed her. The fire's soft light only enhanced the rosy splashes high upon her cheekbones, the tempting fullness of her lips, the warm emerald glow deep in her eyes as she gazed up at him. Oliver ached all over to take her in his arms and kiss her, softly. Instead, full of noble intent, or perhaps so very certain of his abilities to ensnare a murderer and capture the prize, he directed his eyes once more into the fire and sought logical thought. How many times had his father done the very same?

"Are you going to tell me about your visit with Pomeroy?" she asked.

He stared at the flames. "Are you going to tell me about your day with Jeffcoat?"

"He thinks you're the killer."

His head snapped up.

"I told him you weren't, of course."

"Of course." They stared at each other, and the fire popped, the only sound save for the soft drumming of the rain upon the roof. Oliver worked a muscle in his jaw, then turned back to the flames. "Odd that Jeffcoat is seeking a perpetrator. Or perhaps not so odd."

"He's not overly fond of you."

"All the more reason to point the gloved finger at me."

"I'm not following you, Oliver."

"What better way to avoid suspicion than by casting it upon someone else? Especially someone intent upon making himself a hell of a thorn in Jeffcoat's side."

Alexa scoffed and snuggled deeper into the settee. "Stuart is not under any suspicion."

"Oh, yes, he is."

Their eyes locked. "Oliver—"

He turned from the fire and took several steps toward her, his hands upon his hips. "It makes a hell of a lot of sense."

Alexa shook her head as if dismissing the idea entirely. "He had nothing to gain by killing Gabriel . . . or my mother."

"The hell he didn't. There's the plantation, which, thanks to men like Pomeroy, the entire island knows sits on highly desired real estate, worth a small fortune, by Jeffcoat's own account. As for your mother, Jeffcoat, by virtue of his position, knew the government would cover up a particularly ugly murder, one that cast a gruesome light on the British populace. What could be worse than a lover's tryst gone awry? Not a soul in the Governor's House would want to touch that one, and Jeffcoat knew it. And then, of course, there's you."

Alexa seemed to weigh his words, then shook her head. "No. I can't believe it."

Oliver's eyes narrowed. "Odd that you defend the man. Can you deny his interest in you has piqued considerably since your mother's death and the reading of the will? The shoulder to lean on in times of need and all that drivel?" Her emerald eyes lifted to his and he pressed his case, hunkering down on one knee before her. "He could easily have known precisely the contents of the will *before* my father died. Furthermore, anyone acquainted with my reputation on this island would also assume I would hastily relieve myself of my share in Bellefontaine simply because my father had given it to me."

"And why didn't you?"

His gaze drifted over her lips, so full and inviting. "No one can meet my price . . . and I don't think Jeffcoat counted on that. Hence his need to dispose of me in some efficient manner. What better way than to paint me the killer?"

Again she shook her head. "But Stuart isn't in need of a plantation or a fortune. He's devoted to his brilliant naval career."

Oliver snorted. "Doing what? Parading his mock authority for all these restless workers lest they find themselves in the throes of revolt? Alexa, Jeffcoat is like a badly broken horse, temperamental, skittish and cocky, straining at the bit to prove himself in an arena that will never allow him that. Envision how frustrating it must be for the man to have to *imagine* a threat from the blacks in order to have a purpose to suit up each and every day. Give the man enough brains to realize his quandary. I would imagine the thought of year upon year of this sort of noble servitude would sicken him.

Even the pay wouldn't be enough recompense after a time. And if presented with an opportunity to become part of the Barbadian aristocracy for whom he's sacrificed so much, a landowner, if not a wealthy businessman, husband to the most beautiful creature on this island . . . ?"

Rosy pink flamed high in her cheeks and her eyes darted to the fire. "If what you say is true, Oliver, the man assumed an awful lot, thinking I would readily become his wife."

"Indeed, he did." Oliver's thumb stroked over her hand. "He doesn't yet realize he's no match for you, Alexa."

"And who might better suit?"

He grinned. "Me, of course. Surely you knew that."

Alexa paused for a moment, oddly distracted by her fingers fiddling in her lap until his one hand enveloped both of hers. "Oliver..." She inclined her head and stared at the fire. "At times I do believe you forget you've a fiancée awaiting your return." Her luminous eyes captured him. "*She* is the one to whom you should be best suited. Not me."

Oliver felt his lips tighten just as the muscles in his belly constricted. Daphne. The merger. He hadn't given any of it, including his White Star shipping line a scant moment's thought since the second Alexa had breezed into his life. Two weeks ago, he'd been consumed by his business, every waking moment. Now . . . now, it all seemed a world away.

He shoved a hand through his damp hair and jerked rather abruptly to his feet, for now finding the fire far more forgiving than Alexa. "My marriage—Daphne—hell, it's got nothing to do with who we are as people, how we suit each other. I don't even know the girl. Courtship these days is just a ritualized formality. You know that. For me, marrying her is purely—"

"Business."

"Precisely." He spread his arms, his fists balling with the powerful rush of emotion tightening his chest. "Alexa, you've got to understand an international shipping line has been a dream of mine, *the* dream, something I've worked toward . . . it's all I've been for years."

"And for Daphne?"

He paused and found himself glowering into the flames as images of plump, pink, dimpled Daphne invaded his mind.

He waved his arm and grunted. "I don't know. I suppose she thinks she's marrying well. You know, the kinds of things that matter to women like her. Making her father happy and all her friends jealous with the money, the clothes, frequent travel abroad, invitations to the right parties. Class-conscious snobbery. That sort of thing."

"Children?"

Oliver had to snort. "Yes, I suppose she would think we would have to have a few."

"And a home?"

"At least two. Women like Daphne and my mother have to surround themselves with things, Alexa. And the more the better. To their way of thinking, if one object of art enhances a room, another five hundred will surely make it better."

"That doesn't sound the least bit comfortable."

Oliver's fists clenched against his thighs and his scowl descended lower over his forehead as he envisioned his mother and Daphne set loose to decorate his home. "I call it an uncontrollable mania for the absolutely useless. And they love their little decorator fellows, especially if they're imported. These fellows have perfected the art of finding ways to adorn the most mundane objects with manifest opulence." He glared at her. "That, my dear, is what Daphne seeks from marriage."

"Oliver, I wonder if perhaps she might love you."

"I believe she thinks she loves some foppish English lord. But love me?" He laughed harshly, then as he looked at her, his heartbeat quickened. His voice seemed to catch in his throat. "You believe me deserving of such a thing?"

She shrugged, her slender fingers plucking at her skirts, unfathomable eyes lifting to his. "I believe we all deserve it, Oliver."

"Even we coldhearted bastards?"

"Especially you coldhearted bastards."

He could only stare at her and ponder the frantic thumping of his heart against his damp shirt. With but a few words, she'd probed so very deep, with a deftness of touch that filled him with some sweet agony nearly as overwhelming as his desire to escape it. Vulnerability... at the hands of an island nymph. *No.*

"You look so very much like your father."

He gritted his teeth and turned hastily to ponder the darkness beyond the cottage windows. "I'm nothing like him."

"No..." Her heat, her sweet warm-rain scent swirled around him as she rose from the settee and stood at his side. "You're so very wrong about him," she said softly, her voice barely audible above the rain. "Like you, he was consumed by his dream, a dream for Bellefontaine."

Oliver ground his teeth. Yes, the journal was full of that—full of prose that seemed to bellow and bark with a life all its own, impassioned words that drove straight to Oliver's core like a meaty fist. "The plantation records and sugar works are in a hell of a sorry state for a man who sought to preserve them."

"Gabriel was full of misplaced intentions, I agree. Perhaps he should have tended the plantation better, but he thought he was doing himself more good by daily beseeching the governor and the House of Assembly on behalf of the plight of the plantation owner."

"Little good it did him." For a moment Oliver stared into the fire. "And what of his gambling? His drinking? His infatuation with your mother? Did he speak to you of that and what it did to his wife?"

"No, he never spoke of her or the circumstances surrounding all that. Not even one unkind word. He simply wasn't like that."

"No? Perhaps he realized his mistake. He was a man of little or no willpower, Alexa."

"He had a huge appetite for life, Oliver, and was beloved by all. His dream . . . why, he spoke of it as you do. With passion, as if it claimed his very soul. He ached with a passion for life, and would have done *anything* to achieve his dream, just as you will when you marry Daphne. And, just like you, he was abominably stubborn."

"I call it being of singular purpose."

"You see? Gabriel would have said something just like that."

He glanced sharply at her. "You're inventing this. You've nothing to gain by attempting to reconcile me with a dead man."

"Perhaps. But I cannot passively suffer your contempt for him."

He moved to the window and stared out into the night, unaware that she'd left the room until she returned bearing a tray laden with tea and sugar cakes. He watched her curl up again on the settee, teacup balanced in hand, her eyes on the fire. She was so achingly beautiful, so fragile yet so powerful, a raw ache welled in his chest and lodged somewhere in the region of his heart.

"I don't know," she ventured finally. "Call it intuition. I truly don't believe Stuart capable of murder." Delicately, she sipped her tea, then swung blazing eyes upon him. "Penelope Alleyne, however, rouses all sorts of murderous thoughts."

"Hell hath no fury..." he muttered wryly, settling himself on the floor before the fire, one knee drawn up. "Lady Alleyne had about a half-dozen reasons for hating your mother. The least of which were jealousy, revenge for stealing her fiancé, making a social laughingstock out of her. You know, the typical sort of thing that drives a female to murder."

"She told you all that in one afternoon?"

He gave her a wicked smile. "You forget, my dear Alexa, I'm a man of singular purpose."

Although she still obviously doubted his motives, she chose to ignore her uncertainty. "So you consider her a viable suspect."

"My money is still on the bumbling British commander. When I was in Bridgetown yesterday, I spoke with the physician who attended my father and Lily after their deaths. We talked about the murder weapon. Those stab wounds could easily have been made by a sword, just like the one Jeffcoat carries."

"He and two dozen other officers. The wounds could also have been made by an ordinary knife like those in Bellefontaine's very kitchen," Alexa scoffed. "Oliver, you're being unreasonable about Stuart."

"I have *never* been unreasonable."

"You're jealous."

He stared at her, at the delicious curve of her lips, wondering if this alleged jealousy brought her some perverse delight. "Jealous? *Of Jeffcoat?*"

Alexa tilted her head in that supremely self-righteous and confident manner that females alone possess. "He threatens you."

Oliver's jaw sagged, then his teeth slammed together. "The hell he does. You honestly believe a man like me would feel *threatened* by the likes of him? That you would even choose that word to describe me—"

"Sobering, isn't it?" A genuine smile parted her lips and brought him to his knees, his thighs straining angrily against his damp breeches. "You *are* allowed to be human now and then." She leaned closer to him, her words barely above a whisper, her eyes dancing with mischief. "I promise I won't tell a soul."

"Put your tea down, Alexa."

"No." She wriggled deeper into the settee and sipped slowly. "See? I'm not yet finished. Have some, won't you?"

"Put it down."

"Stop growling at me, Oliver. That sort of manner may have served you well in boardrooms, but—"

Before she could even draw another breath, he snatched the cup from her fingers, slipped his arm about her waist and yanked her out of her seat. In one movement, he rolled and pinned her beneath him upon the whitewashed floor. Firelight danced in her wide eyes, played softly over her golden skin, over lush lips still parted with unspoken gasps. Oliver managed to set the teacup somewhere on the floor beside him. "You're wrong about my father," he rasped. Some part of him relished her sudden squirming against him, and he captured both her hands in one of his and pinned them over her head. "And you're wrong about me." Every lush curve and hollow tempted his sanity, burned like hundreds of tiny flames into his skin.

"Oliver," she whispered.

"Alexa." He stared deep into her wide eyes and sensed something he couldn't bear to allow. "Don't ever fear me, love." He caressed the silken curve of her cheek. And then his hand captured one full breast, his breath catching when through the linen the nipple pushed into his palm. "My noble father was able to content himself with far less than I shall with you. Remember that when you choose to taunt me, Alexa. The only thing keeping you from my bed is my good faith in honoring our flimsy little bargain. And as for my being threatened by any man—including your Jeffcoat..." He shifted his weight such that all that pulsed hot and heavy and supremely male pressed brazenly between her thighs. She sucked in a deep breath, trembling slightly, and he brushed his lips over her breast, his tongue wetting the linen transparent. "No man could make love to you as I do...*as I will*...and we both know it."

"Oliver—please—"

With whisper-soft strokes, he suckled her breast, a confident rumble filling his chest when she arched against him. He released her hands and something powerful surged through him when her fingers sank deep into his hair, cradling him nearer. "Alexa, you torture me more than I ever could you."

Her husky laugh drew him from his task, and he poised above her, every fiber of his being screaming for release.

She stared up at him with innocent eyes. "You mean to say I wield some power over you, Oliver?"

"Don't abuse it." He brushed his lips over hers. "My desires have never been so at war with my reason. There's little telling what might happen."

"Are you trying to tempt me?" she whispered.

"Tempt *me,* witch," he rasped against her mouth. "See which of us has the stronger will. Trust me, there will be no losers."

He kissed her, fleetingly, all but out of his mind when her lips melted soft and pliable beneath his. Then he grasped her hand and pulled her to her feet beside him. "When I take you," he said softly, brushing the curls from her cheek and cupping her chin such that her eyes lifted to his, "it won't be here. It will be in a very private, carefully chosen place."

Color flooded her cheeks and she turned away, despite her hand still trapped in his. She took a step. "Oliver—"

He drew her fingers to his lips and gently kissed the trembling tips. "And there will be enough light so that I can see every inch of your beautiful body."

"Stop talking, Oliver."
"The bed will be extremely large—"
"Look. The rain has stopped."
"Because we'll be there for days—"
"Perhaps we should get back to Bellefontaine."
"Devouring each other's flesh—"
"They'll be worried, you know."
"I'm going to taste you everywhere—"
"We must go, Oliver."

He smiled and followed her out into the night. "As you wish, my dear."

Oliver rapped twice upon the chamber door, then swung it wide. His mother stood at her dressing table, draped in an emerald silk robe, her gilt hairbrush pausing midstroke. Cyril stood at her side. A peculiar expression passed swiftly over his pale face before it disappeared.

"You wished to see me?" Oliver asked, noting that his mother dismissed the servant with a wave of her bejeweled hand.

"Where have you been?" Eleanor asked a trifle too breezily. She busied herself with her reflection for several moments, and Oliver crossed his arms impatiently over his chest, his gaze following Cyril as the servant padded silently from the room. "I've been out."

"With her?"

"Yes."

"And?"

He felt himself stiffen with irritation. "I would think you'd be far more interested in what Pinkus Pomeroy had to say this afternoon."

"I am." Eleanor patted her neck, her cheeks, paused, then stared at Oliver in the mirror. "You don't think I'm looking old, do you? The sun here—it's doing awful things to my skin."

Oliver's mind swam with images of Alexa's smooth golden skin, taut yet silken . . . begging for a man's touch. "No." He cleared his throat. "No, Mother, you don't look any older."

"Even so . . ." In a sweep of silk, Eleanor glided from her chair and gazed into the darkness from the floor-to-ceiling window, liberally draped in burgundy velvet. "When are we leaving, Oliver? Cyril tells me you've allowed that Fairfield chit to appoint one of those Bims as overseer."

"And did he also tell you that I agreed with her decision? Cyril isn't shirking his responsibilities now, is he, Mother?"

No doubt due to the sarcasm dripping from his words, Eleanor spun about. "Cyril has always proven a most faithful servant to me."

"Odd that you should say that, Mother. He was, after all, Father's servant for fifteen years after you left."

"Even so, he remained true to me." She advanced upon him, taking his hands into hers, a desperate gleam in her eyes. "Tell me, Oliver, you don't intend to linger here overly long, do you? This talk of reviving the plantation... Surely you've far more pressing matters to attend to back in Chicago."

"I told you not to question my tactics."

"But, Oliver. Surely you can negotiate the plantation from the girl without becoming a damned sugar farmer in the process!"

"This has nothing to do with her." He moved past her to the windows. He stared into the night, seeing nothing but his mother's reflection in the glass. "From what I could gather from Pomeroy today, for the next several months at least, he'll be far too busy making his Alleyndale Hall venture a success to fret over acquiring Bellefontaine. He mentioned something about hurricane season and its effect upon the tourist trade. I think he'll wait."

"He doesn't want Bellefontaine?" Eleanor asked in an unusually tight voice.

"He wants it," Oliver replied. "But not enough. Yet."

"What was his mood when he left?"

"He was angry. Not outwardly so, of course." Oliver's eyes narrowed, his voice dropping to a soft mutter. "At least not angry enough to kill, I wouldn't think. Not yet."

"What was that you said? Oliver, don't even speak of that murder rubbish. I refuse to listen to any of it. Now, surely you're not suggesting we stay here for *months?*"

"You can leave anytime you wish."

"I'd rather not."

Oliver continued to peer through the window. "Don't you trust me, Mother?"

"I do...yes, of course, I do, Oliver. I've entrusted you with my life for the past fifteen years. Yes, of course, I trust you."

"Have you enough money?"

"Enough...? Why, yes, of course, I suppose. What an odd question."

"Perhaps. Your expenses have remained consistent yet you're forever asking for advances on your monthly stipend. Is there a problem I should know about, Mother?"

"What are you suggesting, Oliver?" Eleanor railed, her voice suddenly strident. "Surely you don't believe I'm one of those women who *gambles?*"

"Just manage your money well, Mother. I won't tolerate your squandering of it."

"Oliver, you've millions."

"And I intend to keep them." He released his breath, fogging the pane. "It's settled then. We'll stay until I say it's time to leave." He turned and stalked past her to the open door. "And yes," he said, pausing momentarily in the doorway, "that may very well be months from now."

Chapter Thirteen

Alexa spent the next four days at the cottage, weeding and gardening lest the place become helplessly overgrown. When the rains came in the afternoons, she returned indoors where she set about cleaning the place from floorboards to rafters. She applied herself to the task with fervor, bleaching and boiling bed linens, scrubbing and polishing with lemon oil until her fingers cramped and her wrists refused command. Her muscles ached in every spot imaginable. But she welcomed the pain—indeed, relished it for it was scant penance to pay to escape Oliver Keane. No, she simply needed her own air to breathe without the fear of him stealing it from her lungs . . . needed a welcome return of some sort of normalcy, needed to feel close to her mother.

She hadn't fled Bellefontaine, of course, and late in the evenings returned to her elegant chamber there with its goose-down pillows and comforters. Each night, she couldn't fail to notice the lamp burning low in Oliver's study, well into the deepest hours of the night, and thus she slipped soundlessly through the darkened halls lest she disturb him. That he hadn't sought her out over the course of these four days attested to his attending to some matter of importance. The plantation, perhaps. She knew the records were in a disastrous state, and could well imagine Oliver not standing for it. She ignored the niggling deep in her belly, a bothersome, fleeting feeling that perhaps he had no desire to seek her out, that perhaps that was the only reason she hadn't seen him.

In the evenings, she ventured with Shura to the workers' quarters, situated well behind and below Bellefontaine on a gently sloping rise that swept clear to the beach and the ocean beyond. As she'd often done before her mother had died, she lingered among them late into the night, enjoying their evening rituals of food and drink, their nightly round of music and song around a fire. They embraced Alexa, flooding her with a sense of peace and happiness amidst all her turmoil.

In spite of herself, she sought out Luke on several of these nights on the pretext of inquiring about the plantation. From him she learned that Oliver rose before dawn each day, to inspect their progress on the sugar works, and more often than not to lend a hand. Luke remarked on the man's quickness of mind, his thorough understanding of the sugar-making process in but a few days' time. And the man was strong, Luke told her. Strong enough to cut five tons of cane a day, just like Luke, well above the average man's production of only three tons.

Oliver had even asked Luke to show him how to cut cane. Bare-chested, with machete in hand, he'd cut a respectably wide and smooth path, chopping the cane stalks neatly at the base, precisely trimming the leafy tops, then cutting the stalks into convenient lengths for loading. Almost as quickly as Luke. The overseer thought perhaps Oliver enjoyed it too much. What other reason would a man of his position have to come daily to the fields and labor for hours beneath the sun?

Alexa chose not to contemplate the reasons.

Stuart Jeffcoat called upon her in the mornings at the cottage, perching upon the settee opposite her, and shamelessly pressed his case that Oliver had indeed murdered her mother and Gabriel Keane. She didn't tell him Oliver thought the very same of him. Didn't tell him that she had lain upon that very floor before the hearth, beneath Oliver the "murderer," and had all but begged him to make love to her.

Alexa sucked in her breath and pressed a hand to her belly, her gaze upon Bellefontaine, just visible through the foliage upon a distant hill. She had somehow found herself out on the cottage porch, amidst the dense, afternoon heat. An unforgivable heat on this particular afternoon, a heat left unassuaged by any afternoon rains. The sun hung like a doubloon in the sky, baking skin and earth, stoking yearnings and rousing memories of several days past. Damp tendrils clung to her forehead and cheeks, lay like a blanket upon the back of her neck, and perspiration trickled between her breasts and over the curve of her belly. A pulse throbbed low and hot between her thighs and her breathing became labored, falling in soft gasps from her lips. Four days keeping herself from the man and she had become a woman possessed, her body a traitorous tool molded by his very hand. The mere thought of him looming before the parlor fire, his damp shirt plastered like a second skin to his muscled chest . . . the heavy bulge of his sex boldly displayed by his trousers . . .

Alexa's breasts ached, the peaks swelling against her blouse, and the pulse grew hotter, more insistent—

"You coming?"

She glanced sharply at Shura standing in the cottage doorway and felt the flames lapping at her cheeks. Shura knew, indeed, knew so much more than Alexa at this moment.

"Yes," Alexa managed to say, avoiding Shura's gaze. "I'm coming with you. But I must bathe first . . . and change. You go on ahead. I'm certain Luke is eagerly awaiting you."

Shura merely grunted, her fathomless brown eyes delving into Alexa's very soul. "Hurry" was all the woman said before she ambled slowly down the steps.

"A moment of your time, if I may, Keane."

Oliver glanced up from his work, then frowned. "I wasn't expecting you, Jeffcoat. As you can see, I'm inordinately busy." He focused on his work once more. "Cyril will show you the way out."

"I think not." The British commander closed the study door behind him. He clasped one hand over the hilt of his sword and stalked with confident strides toward Oliver, his eyes flashing beneath the low brim of his plumed hat. "This is a matter of immediate importance."

"To whom?" Oliver growled, rising to his towering height, a good head above Jeffcoat even without his boots.

Jeffcoat looked supremely smug, jutting his insignificant chin at Oliver. "To both of us, actually. It's regarding Alexa."

Oliver stiffened and gripped the edge of his desk. The pup had to but mention her name, with that sly gleam in his eye, his mind very likely swarming with debauched thoughts, and all Oliver could imagine was the satisfaction he would gain from throttling the man. "What about her?"

Jeffcoat puffed up his chest. "I intend to ask for her hand this very night."

Oliver broke into a feral grin. "Sorry, Jeffcoat, she doesn't want you."

"Ah, but she does," Jeffcoat gloated, and the red haze of rage swam before Oliver's eyes. "The girl is quite ardent in her displays of affection, you see..."

Oliver heard only a furious drumming in his ears and stared at Jeffcoat's gloved hands, hands no doubt soft and white, small and almost feminine...and the image of those hands moving over Alexa's flesh brought a strangled growl to catch in his throat.

Jeffcoat seemed unaware of his tenuous circumstances, his confidence brimming. "I merely thought it prudent to mention this to you, seeing as how this will affect the living arrangements."

"Get out."

Jeffcoat cocked a belligerent red eyebrow. "She will be my wife, Keane, mark my words. I suggest you get used to the idea and perhaps remove yourself from this house and this island, forthwith. I hear tell you've a fiancée back in Chicago awaiting you. And of course your White Star Line shipping empire. No need to linger here unnecessarily, is there?"

"Go to hell." It was all Oliver could do to reseat himself at the desk. Focusing upon whatever lay before him proved an impossible task, as was ignoring Jeffcoat.

"She loves me, Keane," Jeffcoat boasted, and Oliver started to count to ten...slowly. "I say, she'll be a handful to be sure, but hell, I'm feet over the mark for her. And who could blame me. Man to man, eh, Keane? What man wouldn't want as his wife a woman who looks like Alexa? Every man on this island will wish it were he riding between her lovely thighs each night—!"

In one motion, Oliver lunged from his chair and smashed his fist into Jeffcoat's nose. Blood spurted everywhere and the commanding officer swayed on his feet, then toppled to the floor with a mighty thud and a clank of his sword.

"I say, you bloody well hit me!" he gurgled, eyes blinking wildly. "I'll have your head on a stick for this, Keane!"

Oliver towered over the man and flashed a contemptuous sneer. "Quit making promises you can't keep, Stu. Listen well." Oliver planted his heel in the middle of Jeffcoat's chest, stilling the officer's attempt to rise. "Alexa will be my wife before she is to any other man, least of all to you." With a snort of disgust, he removed his foot and gestured toward the door. "Now take yourself from my house. You're bleeding all over the damned carpet."

Jeffcoat stumbled to his feet, one bloodied glove pressed over his nose. With jaw trembling and eyes blazing with loathing, he snapped, "Damn you and your carpets to hell, Keane! You'll pay handsomely for this! You bastard!"

With a growl, Oliver twisted his fist into Jeffcoat's white-and-gold jacket and hauled him from the room. The halls echoed with Jeffcoat's curses and the scraping of his boots against the polished floors. With resolute purpose and tightly clenched jaw, Oliver stopped only to fling the front portal wide and shove Jeffcoat onto the porch.

He gave Jeffcoat one last look. "If you come near her again, Jeffcoat, I'll kill you." Before Jeffcoat could do more than sputter, Oliver slammed the door. He turned and strode down the hall, past the study, past the library, through another long hall and out into the white rose garden. He paused in the very center of all those blooms and lifted his face skyward, filling his lungs with thick, fragrant air. Above him, lush, warm apricot hues streaked the sky, boding well for a clear, peaceful evening. Yet in his head the blood still hammered the same angry, relentless beat. He flexed his fingers, relishing the pain along his knuckles as he did the ache in every muscle from days spent ruthlessly cutting sugarcane.

"Alexa, what have you done to me?" he whispered into the early-evening sky. Just then, in the distance, he heard a soft thumping, a muffled sound carried on the breeze from a faraway hilltop. Drawn by that haunting beat, he followed a narrow path through the garden that spilled out onto Bellefontaine's sweeping lawns. Onward he moved, toward the setting sun, closer to that incessant pulsing beat, through gardens, tangled brush...and then he stopped. There, ahead of him upon a soft rise was the glow of a dozen small fires amongst the workers' quarters...and the drums beat louder, and voices lured him onward.

Down in the workers' quarters, Alexa gingerly lifted two baked coconuts from the edge of the fire and settled back upon her heels, handing the coconuts to Shura beside her. A knife's thick blade flashed in the firelight as Shura cleaved a coconut in half and handed one to Alexa. Licking her lips with impatience, Alexa lifted the coconut to her mouth and tasted the warm, sweet milk. Some dribbled down her chin and she laughed, caught it with her fingertip and sucked her finger clean.

"Better to drink kill-devil," Shura muttered without looking up from her task.

Alexa frowned slightly and tipped the coconut again to her lips, her gaze drifting toward the group of black workers clustered about the fire. Some beat their palms softly on drums cradled between their thighs. Others hummed low and lilting tunes, their dark eyes upon the western sky. Still others filled their bellies with baked conch and coconut, and drank deeply of their kill-devil. From their laughter and the rising of their voices above the beat of the drums, Alexa could well imagine they'd been drinking the fiery rum drink since early afternoon. The brew was widely known to induce all-night frolicking amongst the workers who favored it. Alexa shook her head. "I prefer warm coconut milk, thank you, Shura. One taste of kill-devil and I would sleep for a week. There would be no waking me."

"Good," Shura mumbled, never once glancing up from her task. "Then drink. Man-beast comes."

The coconut paused at Alexa's lips. A weakness stole like quicksilver through her limbs, and her fingers went momentarily limp, spilling warm coconut milk over her chest and between her breasts. With a gasp, she pressed one trembling hand there, as much to catch the liquid as to still the sudden fluttering beneath her skin. She felt Shura's lingering stare, felt, too, the heat climbing high into her cheeks, heat that had nothing to do with the warmth of the fire. She said something indistinctly and glanced away, and God help her but he stood there, at the very edge of the clearing, bathed in firelight and the setting sun, simply staring at her.

Time hung suspended for Alexa and all else ceased to matter but this man. With a boldness never before so profound, her eyes drifted over him, over the foamy white linen shirt that bared a darkly furred and muscled chest, over the narrow, jutting hips, the skintight breeches with their careless display of his masculinity, the muscled lengths of his thighs. His hair was an untamed mane of blue-black, his face sun-darkened and stubbled. The face of seduction incarnate. His eyes reflected wild flame, as savage and untamed as he this night. He seemed somehow borne of the lushness of the jungle... all potent male, emanating heat and sex and danger.

Alexa licked her lips and rose slowly to her feet, as if silently commanded by him to do so. Some primitive instinct bade her to stand thus before him, her shoulders squared, bosom upthrust, lips parted with her swift breathing even though the palms pressing against her thighs were damp and trembling. And the firelight danced in his eyes, moving with slow deliberation over her. The air between them crackled with far more than the embers dancing skyward from the fire that separated them... the fire and, yes, the workers, though Alexa was barely aware of them. He advanced toward her and she ached as never before to feel hot, male skin beneath her palms, to know again the sweet agony of his touch upon her.

She watched him approaching as one facing one's doom, knowing, despite every vow she'd made to the contrary, despite reason and logic, that she would follow him wherever he chose to take her this night, clear to the heavens and back... and that there would be no stopping him this time. Her tongue felt thick, her mouth gone dry long ago, and she took a step toward him... and then Luke materialized, blocking Oliver's path, slapping him upon the shoulder as one would a friend. Their shared laughter rang deep and hearty, Oliver's so mellow and rich, Alexa trembled anew at the mere sound of him so very close. Without hesitation, he took a slice of *sangfrit* from Luke and slowly slid it into his mouth. *Sangfrit*—made of the fresh blood of a steer, boiled by the workers until it congealed, then seasoned with pepper and fried in thin slices. Its taste was like that of delicate liver, and one that Oliver seemed to savor.

His eyes met hers over Luke's shoulder as he tipped a crudely fashioned cup to his lips and drank deeply. Kill-devil. Alexa sucked in a slow breath.

"You think he was beast before *sangfrit* and kill-devil?" Shura uttered low and husky. "Go home."

"No, Shura," Alexa replied, her eyes still locked with Oliver's. "I cannot."

"You love him," Shura whispered, now close to her ear.

"Is that what this is?" Alexa pressed one hand to her bosom to assuage the ache deep in her soul. "God help me, but I do."

Like a vise, Shura's fingers wrapped about Alexa's wrist. "He will leave you. He has another woman. He will leave."

"Perhaps." The ache burgeoned and melded with the one mounting low and deep between her thighs. "But I shall face that when it happens, Shura. If it happens."

"It will happen."

Alexa didn't reply. With something akin to frustration, she watched as Luke and Oliver, along with a dozen of the black men, moved away from the fire and took to a path which led to the cane fields.

"Don't," Shura warned, tugging one last time upon Alexa's wrist.

"I must." Wrenching her arm free, she hastened after the men. She found them gathered in a wide semicircle on the very edge of a field of ripe cane, shouting and wagering against one another. In the center of the semicircle Oliver and Luke stood, an impenetrable wall of ten-foot rows of thick cane before them. Alexa paused at the front of those watching, her gaze riveted upon Oliver as he stripped his shirt from his back and flung it carelessly aside. The fiery rays of the setting sun played upon his sunbaked skin, upon bronzed shoulders as wide as Luke's if not wider. Sleek muscle rippled and flexed when someone tossed him a machete, and he hefted the blade as if he had been born to the task.

The wagering took on a new dimension.

Alexa itched to spread her hands over the sculpted planes of his chest, yearned to sink her fingers into the dark fur covering that expanse. His ribs were sleekly muscled, his abdomen like the washboard Alexa had used that very morning. He stalked about like a panther intent upon a kill, his buttocks flexing, thighs tight and unyielding against his breeches as he surveyed the area he was to cut. Alexa knew a raw hunger so mindless and consuming she nearly cried out when he stopped directly before her, eyes hooded, his sensuous lips curved slightly.

"I've missed you," he murmured, his voice husky.

Alexa's lips parted. "And I you."

"Would you care to make a wager?"

Alexa allowed her eyes a bold raking of his splendid form, as if she were assessing him. "And what would I win, were I to place my confidence in a novice?"

One dark eyebrow lifted wickedly as he tested the tip of the machete with his finger. "Me."

"To do with as I wish this night?"

The flames leaped in his eyes as they moved with brazen intent over her. "Anything you wish, my lady."

"And if I lose?"

His teeth flashed in a smile that set Alexa's blood churning, and he reached out to capture a curl nestled upon her breast. "If you lose, beauty, you will be mine, to do with as *I* please until dawn. And it will be a very long night, I promise you."

Alexa could scarcely draw sufficient breath. "If I agree, you might be tempted to swing that machete with a bit less fervor."

"Sorely tempted," he corrected her with a devilish smile. "Take your chances." His eyes bore into hers. "A wager, my lady?"

"Yes, a wager," she whispered, her knees almost buckling when he drew the blond ringlet to his lips, then turned about to meet his opponent, Luke. From his pocket Oliver withdrew a round gold watch and tossed it to a black nearby. For several moments, Oliver, Luke and several of the workers gathered in earnest discussion.

"Twenty minutes," the black with Oliver's watch called out when they dispersed, and a new round of wagering commenced, most of it in favor of Luke. After several moments, the wagering subsided and Oliver and Luke positioned themselves, legs braced wide, machetes raised high overhead. A shout rang out and the shiny blades flashed in the sunlight.

Around her, the men's shouts rose skyward, intensifying with each stalk neatly cut and stacked. The crowd rushed forward, encircling the two men like the dust stirred by their blades, and Alexa was swept along with them. With hands clutching at her skirts and her eyes darting from Luke to Oliver, to the piles accumulating behind them, Alexa found herself whooping whenever Oliver's machete sliced precisely through the cane. To her mind, his heavy knife seemed to emit a clearer, sharper whack than Luke's, the blade flashing that much more brilliantly in the sun, his strokes just a hint more assured and powerful. That Luke was perhaps the most formidable slayer of cane on the entire island caused her little pause. This was Oliver, the man who never lost, the man she believed capable of conquering the world. The thought of his losing simply didn't cross her mind.

Fifteen minutes into the battle, the score was tied. Alexa labored with each stroke of Oliver's blade, as if she, too, hefted that machete. His hair clung to his forehead and sweat dripped into his eyes and into his mouth parted with his breathing. With each swipe of his blade, a groan escaped his lips and the sweat dripped from his chin and ran in rivulets down his chest, his belly, and into his waistband. Yet he didn't pause to wipe his eyes, or even to glance at his opponent. Another stalk was hefted onto the pile and he advanced upon another, his jaw set, eyes blazing. He lifted that blade and a shout rang out above the din, stilling his machete midair.

Oliver lost by one stalk of cane.

The crowd let up a tremendous roar and coins changed hands. Oliver and Luke were momentarily mobbed by the group and Alexa took full advantage, slipping through the men to the rear of the crowd . . . and onward. Her bare feet swished through the grass as she headed back for the fires and whatever awaited her this night.

Oliver immersed his fine linen shirt yet again in the barrel of fresh water and, without wringing one cool drop from it, slung it over his face and chest, then lower over his belly. A satisfied groan filled his chest and he absently worked the shirt over the muscles still burning in his arms. His gaze roamed about the clearing, seeking. Several women gathered close to the fires to tend to the evening meal, their children playing about them. One tiny tot even ran smack into Oliver's leg to escape a game of chase. Oliver ruffled the child's dark curls and found himself smiling into the enormous black pools staring up at him. Again, his eyes strayed about the clearing, over the clusters of workers moving about in the fires' soft light. Alexa was not among them.

Squeezing the water from his shirt, he stuffed one corner into the back of his trousers and nodded his thanks when a young woman with liquid black eyes pressed a large cup into his hand. She lingered before him, a soft smile playing upon her lips seeming to invite appraisal of her full breasts and generous hips displayed by her thin batiste dress. She tossed her head, ruffling the black curls that hung to her hips.

She reached for his hand. "Come."

"I seek Alexa," he replied, avoiding her reach and drinking deeply of the rum.

She simply smiled and nodded and started across the clearing. Something prompted Oliver to follow, the distant beat of drums, perhaps, drifting over the surrounding hills. The woman climbed a smooth rise and paused, until he stood beside her.

She pointed out over a sweeping plain of sand that stretched below them toward the foamy surf and the inky black of ocean beyond. "There. She dances *biguine*."

The drumbeats reverberated through Oliver's chest, as if born of the blazing fire in the distance. In that firelight, sensuous shadows moved in time with the drumbeats and the pounding of the surf. Draining the last of the rum, Oliver handed the cup to the woman and started off across the sand. Like liquid fire the rum filled his chest and seeped through his limbs, igniting flames in his loins and passions not easily caged this eve. The pulse of the drums matched that in his veins, a sensuous, primitive beat that lengthened his stride and brought a hot sheen to his skin. His pace slowed when he reached the very edge of the group, his gaze flickering over each of the women swaying before those flames . . . and then he saw her . . . dancing nearest the ocean.

Biguine. It must have been the Creole word for seduction. Alexa's slender arms moved like sapling willows over her head, her fingers tracing over her wrists to her elbows, then drifting high overhead once again. Her eyes were half-closed, her full lips parted as she swayed. Her feet barely moved in the sand beneath her, yet a fine sheen bathed her skin, borne by some inner heat. The tempo increased and she flung her head back, that cascade of honeyed blond ringlets swirling about the slender curve of her hips. Her movements were hypnotic, a supple undulation of her spine and hips that set Oliver ablaze. He paused not a hand's breadth from her and a seductress's smile curved her lips. Again, she flung her head back and spun about, allowing him to feast upon the lush fullness of her buttocks slowly rolling in an age old rhythm, a rhythm that would have tempted a eunuch. Like a man possessed, he clenched his fists and devoured the hypnotic sway of her hair just brushing the high curve of her buttocks. She spun toward him, cat's eyes reflecting flame and passions ignited. Her fingers splayed over her taut belly, massaging the rhythm deep within her. The pounding of the drums increased as did her rhythm, and her blouse slid from her shoulders, sagging low to perch upon the thrusting peaks of her breasts. Oliver's eyes flamed over the lushness of her breasts swaying full and heavy with her every movement, over the pale pink nipples pushing against damp linen, tempting him . . . just as she tempted him beyond his endurance when her palm slid low over her belly, her fingers inching lower still into the linen trapped high between her thighs.

With a groan of the purest agony, Oliver swept her off her feet and into his arms. Without pause, he turned and carried her away from the fire, across the sand, consumed with his purpose. He felt the sureness of her arms wrapped about his neck, reveled in the feel of her head nestled against his chest, and his strides lengthened. Only once did he pause, at the top of a soft rise, to place her feet on the ground and pull her close against him. In the pale moonlight she looked up at him, all liquid eyes and soft lips. A groan again escaped his parched throat and he bent to taste of her. A sweet, agonizing kiss it was, her lips pliant and yielding beneath his. It was all too new, too sweet and irresistible. His tongue plunged deep into her warmth and he slid her entire supple length against him, grasping her full buttocks and pressing her softness against his throbbing sex.

"Not here," he rasped, resting his forehead against hers and clenching his teeth against a desire that threatened his sanity. He grasped her hand and tugged her along behind him.

Through the moonlit darkness she followed him around the workers' quarters, down a gentle hill and up again through Bellefontaine's quiet gardens. He led her through the white rose garden and into the silent, dark halls of Bellefontaine. He paused to retrieve a decanter full of pale liquid and two lead crystal glasses from the study before drawing her behind him up the sweeping stairs. Her step seemed to falter slightly, and he rubbed his thumb over her fingers, drawing her deep into his chamber. A lone candle burned beside the bed, a huge mahogany four-poster lushly draped in midnight-blue velvet.

Oliver poured a liberal draft of the wine for her and handed her the glass, noting well the slight trembling of her fingers, the lowered gaze even as she sipped. His thumb brushed lingeringly over her cheek, then he turned and set about lighting at least a dozen tapers throughout the massive chamber. Only when the room was bathed in a soft golden light did he pause before her, feeling massive and beastly, and far too potent for an unwilling girl. Taking the glass from her fingers, he cupped her chin and lifted that fathomless gaze to his.

"Forget the wagers," he said softly. "If this is not what you wish, tell me, and you're free to go. You know what I want, Alexa, and I will gladly take it if you stay. But I want you willing."

His eyes searched hers, but found nothing in those emerald pools. Then she placed a tiny hand on his chest and her lips parted.

Chapter Fourteen

A tremor passed through Alexa when her fingers splayed across the dense fur covering his chest. A heady, heated scent emanated from him, chased like wildfire through her and branded her soul as his for a lifetime.

"At this moment, you are all that I want, Oliver," she whispered, her eyes fluttering closed. "All that I need. . . ."

She expected a savage onslaught, the beast uncaged and untamed, set loose upon her. She did not expect the silken murmuring of her name, the gentleness of callused palms moving almost reverently over her bare shoulders, easing her to him until her breasts brushed softly against his chest. His fingers tangled in her hair and he buried his face in the tumbled curls, drawing her arms about his neck. She tasted salt and smoke upon his skin as her lips brushed over his throat. Her fingers sunk into the blue-black curls falling nearly to his shoulders and she trembled anew, sensing a deep trembling within him, as well. Kisses fell like a soft summer rain upon her cheeks, over her jaw, until at last his mouth claimed hers in a long, leisurely tasting that robbed the very air from her lungs. His velvety tongue encircled hers, parried and plunged deep, and he crushed her against him hungrily. Their mouths parted with a rush of air and Alexa's world spun when he bent to ravish her breasts. Linen seemed to dissolve beneath his hands and in moments she stood before him, her clothes pooled at her feet. Warm night air and his heated gaze caressed her, and she shuddered, reaching for him.

"You're more beautiful than I imagined," he murmured, his hands cupping her breasts, then caressing the sweep of her ribs and spanning her waist. "More delicate than an island flower." His mouth captured one thrusting nipple and suckled in long, smooth pulls. "You taste like coconut milk."

Alexa shuddered as pleasure rippled through her and she cradled his head close. Those warm fingers caressed the curve of her belly, then delved deep between her trembling thighs, parting, seeking, and he dropped to his knees. His mouth was aflame upon her thighs, his tongue seeking and finding.

Her legs buckled. In one motion, he caught her in his arms and bore her to the bed. Downy softness enveloped her and then he loomed in the soft light, so magnificent and savage in his nakedness, she struggled for breath. He seemed sculpted of the finest bronze, his body sleek, finely muscled, his sex thick and heavy. His mouth slanted over hers and he crushed her into the down, flattening her breasts and drawing soft whimpers from deep in her throat. That sensual tide lapped at her in smooth, sweeping strokes, just as his fingers moved between her thighs and inside her, stoking a need so very deep she cried out, arching against him when he stopped.

"You're so hot," he rasped against her throat. "So wet... you want me inside you, Alexa. So very deep inside."

She offered scant resistance when he kneed her legs apart, even less when that thick, male muscle pressed intimately against her. Oliver kissed her softly, then surged into her so powerfully she felt impaled by pain and an anguished yearning. A cry escaped her lips and then another when he retreated slowly and surged even deeper within her.

"I cannot—" she breathed against his shoulder.

His hips stilled against hers and he cupped her face, brushing his lips over hers. "Yes, my love, you can. You were made for this... for me... so small and tight you are."

"B-but it hurts, Oliver."

He nibbled at her neck, then cupped her breast and sucked her nipple deep into his mouth. Delight danced along Alexa's spine and she arched her back with a soft moan. "Do you want me to make it stop hurting?" He caught her nipple between his teeth and tugged gently.

"Yes," she whispered, clutching at his shoulders when his hips moved against hers in a gentle rhythm. A gasp escaped Alexa's lips. A yearning mounted so very deep now, dispelling the last traces of pain. Her body throbbed with pleasure as Oliver penetrated her again, his arms braced on either side of her. And she met him, thrust for thrust, her soft belly pushing into his, her arms encircling his neck until he lifted her with one flex of his arm about her waist. And she clung to him as the waves built to an anguish inside of her and she cried out, again and again, as he plunged deeper . . . deeper, and then a pleasure so poignant with sweet agony lifted her and set her tumbling into a starry void. She heard her own soft cry, felt Oliver's last deep thrust and the shudders wracking his body, and the tears slipped silently from her eyes.

With infinite tenderness, he laid her gently back upon the bed and pressed his lips to her cheeks. "I suppose even a beast should apologize," he said softly.

She could only shake her head. She caressed his heavily stubbled cheek, the cheek that had branded her soft inner thighs and the tender undersides of her breasts. This man, who knew her so intimately, who had given her such pleasure . . . this man she loved.

"I don't suppose I am a virgin any longer," she whispered, willing her tears to subside.

He laughed softly and rolled to his back, sweeping her close against him. "No. You have been duly compromised, Miss Fairfield. And before the night is out, I promise you will be again and again . . . and even again."

By morning, Alexa was forever convinced that Oliver always kept his word.

Oliver awoke to a peculiar soft drone. It drew him from the depths of as peaceful a slumber as he could ever have imagined. With eyes still refusing to open, he listened to that strange rhythmic drone above the stillness of the morning, until his palm moved over a warm, lush, feminine curve and his nostrils filled with the scent of crushed gardenias. His eyes snapped open.

Beside him, lying upon her belly, Alexa slept, her head buried beneath a pillow. The drone coming from beneath that pillow ebbed and flowed with the shallow rising and falling of her ribs. A smile crept across his lips and he passed his palm across her buttocks.

His island flower snored.

Sweeping the tangled sheets aside, Oliver half rose in the bed and pressed kisses in a long, leisurely trail down her spine. She smelled of sleep, felt like warm silk, looked like a golden angel in the morning light. His mind flooded with the memory of the hours he had just spent with her. Some spent sleeping, most making sweet, passionate love to her. They hadn't spoken much. It hadn't been a night for talk. Oliver cupped the fullness of her buttocks rising high and round from the gentle sweep of her back. No, this morning wasn't shaping up for talking, either.

She mumbled something, a sleepy, half-roused mumble, turned her head beneath the pillow and in moments the snoring once again commenced. With one pressing purpose, Oliver shoved the pillow aside and pressed his mouth to the exposed nape of her neck, his fingers tracing over the full sides of her breasts.

"Good morning, lover," he murmured against her ear.

The snoring ceased and she mewled like a kitten stretching, arching her back in a supremely provocative manner, then shoving an elbow right into his ribs. She mumbled something that sounded suspiciously like a man's name. Not his.

With one sweep of his arm, he turned her on her back, slipped potently between her thighs and eased his swollen manhood into her, into a sheath so very tight, so very wet for a still-sleeping woman, all reason momentarily fled him.

"Now do you know who I am?" he breathed against her lips, claiming them in a hungry kiss that left him only hungering for more.

Her slender arms slipped about his neck. Roused yet or not, she snuggled her breasts against his chest and wrapped her legs around his hips, one foot tracing up and down his calf. "Oliver—"

"Who else?" he growled, thrusting deep and spreading kisses over her breasts. "Are you awake yet?"

"No." She arched her back, offering herself to him. "Perhaps if you try harder."

"This is as hard as it gets." With torturous deliberation, he filled her, then retreated, again and again, until her eyes fluttered open and her fingernails dug into his back. They moved as one, higher and farther, until their surcease was a shared one of soft cries mixed with deep-throated groans, and whispered love words.

Oliver chose to await the return of normal breathing nuzzled against her breasts. He listened to her heartbeat and wallowed in the sensation of it all . . . the slender fingers tracing endless circles over his shoulders, the heavy fullness of her breast filling his hand . . . the simple manner in which their bodies seemed to fit together so precisely. A supreme sense of peace enveloped him like a dusky cocoon one would never wish to leave, filling a part of his soul he hadn't before known he possessed. He lifted his head and leisurely laved one nipple with his tongue, intent upon doing this and so very much more all damn day and to hell with the rest of the world.

And then the very rafters reverberated with a sudden banging upon the chamber door. Alexa jerked beneath him, and Oliver snarled and pressed a kiss to her rosy, passion-swollen lips before slipping from the bed. He yanked on his knee breeches and, without buttoning them, strode to the door. Again, the fierce banging and Cyril's thin voice penetrated the thick wood.

"Sir, a telegram—"

Oliver yanked open the door, all too aware that Cyril paused midsentence to openly gape at him, an uncommon feat for a man like Cyril, so typically stone-faced. The servant's wide eyes flickered past Oliver in the direction of the bed, then swiftly darted back. Color flooded his cheeks.

Oliver snatched the envelope from Cyril's hand, his thoughts upon another telegram, one delivered—when had it been?—some four, no five days past. One he had forgotten about entirely. Still unopened, it awaited his attention in the parlor. A cold, cruel dread crept through him as he muttered his thanks to Cyril and slowly closed the door.

"What is it?" Alexa asked. She sat in the center of the bed, the white sheet drawn clear to her neck, looking as beautiful as a woman could. Tumbling golden curls, luminous emerald eyes . . . all entirely not in keeping with the ominous chill that stole through his veins.

He took two steps toward her before tearing the telegram open. He read it once, twice, even a third time, then sank upon the bed and rested his forearms on his thighs, hanging his head.

"Oliver..."

He studied the polished mahogany floor between his bare feet, unaware that he crushed the telegram in his fist until Alexa's fingers wrapped about his hand and eased his grip. She moved to his side, swathed in her sheet, her voice coaxing.

"Oliver, good grief, what is it?"

"It's from my chief counsel." His mind was numb, refusing. "Apparently, my company has fallen into serious financial jeopardy."

"How can that be? Surely there's some mistake."

His laugh rang harsh and cold through the morning stillness. "It can happen, my dear, very easily in this business. A string of bad luck in the form of foul weather, ships lost full of cargo worth a small fortune...even the insurance won't be able to cover it all...." He forced himself to swallow and lifted his head to feast upon her lush beauty. A hint of warmth seeped into his belly. He brushed his thumb over her lips, recognizing the concern deep in her eyes. "I have to go back. As soon as possible. If I don't, I could lose everything. As it is, I still could."

She simply stared at him, unaware of the torture she inflicted upon him just sitting there with her sheet slipping from her shoulders to expose the ripe curves of her bosom. "Of course. But I don't understand. You've been gone only—"

"I've been gone for over a month. And that's an unconscionable amount of time to be away. Every year at this time, the Association of Great Lakes Merchants convenes in Chicago to determine tonnage commitments and to charter cargoes. It's like an auction of sorts, and one's success depends entirely upon who you know and how well you take care of them. Success in this business isn't simply a matter of being the most efficient or the safest shipping line offering the most competitive prices. Anyone with brains can do that. To make a fortune in this business, it takes cleverness and skill and making certain you're in the right place, with the right people, at the right time. Shipping is very fraternal, Alexa, and success depends upon establishing a sort of charmed entrée into the most elite circles. Ties have to be maintained with the people controlling the manufacturing industries, and I mean daily ties, if need be, to assuage their fears, however unfounded they may be. The proper lunches and dinner parties have to be attended where the suitable amount of groundwork can be laid with those manufacturers seeking to ship their goods. One may be in Buffalo. Another in Detroit. Yet another in Cleveland. That's a hell of a lot of ties to keep strong and healthy with men who believe the industrialized world cannot survive without them. But one contract with a giant steel or iron ore manufacturer has made me a fortune in a single year."

"So what's stopping you this year?"

"For more than a month, I've been entirely out of touch with these people when I should have been cabling them *daily*. And according to this telegram, we lost five ships in one week alone to bad weather. Three of them full of grain...now resting at the bottom of Lake Michigan. A sure sign of bad luck, and that's like a death knell in this business. Damn." He rubbed the dull ache between his eyes. "I knew it was a risk. Why the hell did I have to do it?"

"Do what?"

"Grain. Give me steel, iron ore, lumber, and I'll haul that anywhere. But grain? Alexa, a wise shipper treats grain with the courtesy he would accord a wealthy maiden aunt with rheumatism. An even wiser shipper refuses to ship it." At the fine knitting of her eyebrows, he explained, "Grain shifts in the bottom of a boat very easily. Especially in heavy seas. All stability can be lost. A relatively small storm could capsize a huge sailed vessel very easily. Even an iron-hulled steamer."

"But that wasn't your fault. You've no control over the weather."

He grunted. "Tell that to my fat merchant in Buffalo who only cares about when his grain will arrive. Solely by virtue of his shrewdness and business acumen alone, he firmly believes his fleet will have smooth, uncomplicated passages with fast turnarounds, and will return fair and just profits. This particular fellow also owns one of the largest iron ore holdings in all of Pennsylvania."

"So you agreed to ship his grain against your better judgment solely to secure contracts to ship all that ore."

Oliver's eyes moved appreciatively over her. "You'd make a shrewd businessman, Alexa. Yes, that's it precisely. Iron ore is the single largest tonnage factor in Great Lakes shipping and I have every intention of monopolizing it."

"So talk to this fellow at the convention, Oliver. Surely your reputation alone will reassure him in the meantime."

"If only it were that easy. The association convenes tomorrow... and I'll be on a ship in the middle of the damned Atlantic... losing every last one of my contracts. Dammit, I knew when the association was due to meet. How the hell could I have forgotten—" The air hissed between his teeth and then, God help him, he had to touch her, simply couldn't sit this close to her and remain unaffected by her. His fingers slipped around her neck and drew her mouth to his. "See? Since the moment I saw you, I can't think clearly."

Her eyes flashed and she shoved a hand into his chest. "You're blaming me for this?"

"Hardly." He thrust a hand through his hair, then kneaded the muscles bunched at the base of his neck. "It's entirely my fault. Consumed I am, by this—" He shot her a hooded glance. "You've bewitched me. Robbed me of sense and logic when I most need it. Just look at me."

She arched a saucy eyebrow and her eyes flickered over the expanse of his chest, then lower to his parted breeches. "Indeed."

"I should be stomping around here packing."

"You should."

"I should be summoning Cyril and booking passage on the first damned boat out of here."

Her bare legs slipped over the side of the bed. "Yes, you've much to do—"

"Stay where you are, woman," he growled, his fingers wrapping about her leg just above her knee. He moved his hand slowly over that slender length of thigh, shoving tangled sheets aside as he went. "I should be shaving—"

"Yes, you should," she said a trifle breathlessly, her hand stilling his just as his fingers drifted over her inner thigh. Emerald met cobalt. "Shall I help you?"

"Alexa..." Her name was a soft groan as he swept her into his arms, cradling her in his lap. His lips found hers in a long, slow kiss and he crushed her against his chest. "Yes," he breathed. "Help me. Tell me why all I can think of is making love to you again, even as my shipping empire crumbles."

She looked up at him, her fingers caressing his jaw and sweeping a tousled fall of hair from his forehead. "I don't know why, Oliver."

"Come with me." The words escaped before he could think.

Something peculiar flickered across her features and was gone, yet her cheeks remained unusually pale. "Oliver—"

The air seemed to compress in his chest, preventing him from snatching his words back. "I've a town house on the Gold Coast. You'd be comfortable there. I'll buy you anything you want...clothes...hats with fresh gardenias daily...tickets to the opera. Anything. I work extremely long hours...and I'll be traveling, of course. Extensively. Meeting with all those manufacturers. Hell, I don't know how I'm going to recoup all those lost contracts, but..." He stared at the pulse beating at the base of her neck, feeling clumsy and tongue-tied. "I want to wake up with you in my bed, Alexa. I want to sleep next to you when it's frigid and snowy and I want to make love to you endlessly." He pressed his lips to her forehead and willed the faint trembling from his limbs. "I've never wanted a woman more, Alexa. Will you come with me?"

For one blissful moment, she seemed to melt against him, and God help him, his heart soared. Then her voice, soft yet filled with some deep conviction, swirled about him. "And what of Daphne?"

Oliver closed his eyes and worked a muscle in his jaw. "What about her?"

"She'll be your wife."

"I don't want to talk about that, Alexa."

"And I'll be your mistress."

"Most women would prefer to be— *Hey!*" Like a sylph, she slipped from his arms and swept her clothes from the floor, presenting him with an unimpeded view of her, naked and glorious, willowy yet sensuously lush in the morning sunlight. His breath caught in his throat at the sight of her and his mouth went bone-dry. He lunged for her but she easily sidestepped him, her slender legs flashing through the rays of sun, her full breasts swaying with every movement.

"Is that a yes or a no?" he growled, his hands finding his hips.

She scoffed and looked at him as if she thought him profoundly addled. She slipped into her white linen like one who had done so hurriedly many a time. She fluffed her hair, an innocent fluff it was, though those golden curls fell in a thoroughly wanton yet studied disarray that would have been the envy of every last woman in Chicago. And the undoing of any full-blooded man.

"Yes," she snapped. "I mean, no. I mean, yes, that was a no. I can't possibly go with you."

"And why not? I offer you much."

"Perhaps."

He frowned at her, something tightening deep in his belly. "Do you seek marriage? Is that it?"

"Marriage?" She blinked several times, then erupted with a disbelieving laugh. "To who, pray? *You?* Ha!"

"And what the hell would be so wrong with that?" he asked, his scowl ferocious.

She tossed her head and peered down her upturned nose at him. "Other than your being married to another...why, Oliver, losing your shipping empire would leave you quite desperate, I would think. The fortune you could make from selling this plantation would be all but irresistible to you. Why the devil would I marry you and hand it all over to you?"

His fingers wrapped about her upper arm and squeezed beneath the frustration balling like a fist in his chest. "If I asked you to be my wife, it would be for one reason alone, Alexa."

"No one's arguing that point with you, Oliver. That reason is business. It's your sole motivator. Just ask poor Daphne."

He yanked her against him and she merely glared at him with eyes spitting fire. "Listen to me," he growled, his mind seeking logical thought, but refusing to give voice to the words that welled from his soul. *The way I feel about you...I would sacrifice everything...*

Just like his father had done.

"No!" With a snarl of self-disgust, he released her and turned brusquely about, seeking some distraction. Packing...yes.

"I'll have Luke move into the east wing," he muttered, yanking a mahogany armoire wide and staring unseeing at his clothes.

"Why the devil would you do that?" she asked from somewhere near the windows.

Oliver turned toward her, resting one hand on the armoire handle. "You'll feel safer with him here at the house...and I will certainly rest easier. If our murderer was someone intent upon frightening plantation owners into selling, Luke may prove ample discouragement."

She stared from the window, her hands clasped demurely behind her back. "You mean to Pinkus Pomeroy."

"Yes, Alexa, we both know he's a suspect. But he's not the sort to view a female as a threat in any way. As long as I'm in Chicago, he'll leave you alone, I'm rather certain of it. Besides, he'll be far too consumed with making a go of his Alleyndale Hall venture to fret over Bellefontaine...at least until I return."

Her lips parted and that fathomless emerald gaze all but swallowed him whole. For several moments, he was a man drowning. "You're coming back," she said softly.

"You can count on it." And then, before he could sweep her into his arms and bear her to the bed, he forced himself back to contemplating the dark depths of the armoire.

Words . . . words . . . He stared at his clothes and sought the proper words. When he finally thought he'd found them, he turned about but she was gone.

His mother soundly in tow, Oliver boarded a merchant ship later that day without seeing Alexa even once more.

Chapter Fifteen

Chicago, February 1891

"The news isn't good, Oliver."

Oliver stared from his ten-story window through fog and mist at Grant Park, its barren trees colorless and devoid of life. *Tap-tap-tap.* His gold quill met with the arm of his chair.

"Oliver? Did you hear me?"

No, he really didn't want to hear this. His chief counsel visited so very rarely, and only bore bad news, or so it seemed. On this particular afternoon, he perched somewhere at Oliver's back upon an overstuffed chair, rustling mounds of paper piled on the floor, in his lap, and scattered all over Oliver's mahogany desk. Without turning from the rain-splattered windows, Oliver knew the man squinted at him with profound confusion from behind his wire-rimmed spectacles, that he'd been doing an awful lot of that each and every time Oliver had met with him over the course of the last seven months. Since the very day he'd set foot back in Chicago.

God, it seemed only yesterday.

He shifted lower in his chair and scowled at nothing in particular, just the gloom. *Tap-tap-tap.*

More rustling of paper. "Oliver, I know you're tired. You've been keeping a schedule that would kill any normal man, traveling to and from New York, and all over the Midwest, meeting with financiers, the backers and all those manufacturers. Hell, you've only been in the state three days out of every month and I doubt even then you've slept in your bed. That settee over there doesn't look too damned comfortable. Listen, Oliver, speaking solely as your advisor and one who owes his success to you, I'm inclined to think you're working yourself into an early grave."

"What's the news?" Oliver muttered, peering through the fog to seek the gray mass that was Lake Michigan.

"Fine. Ignore me, if you wish. The news is regarding your wheat futures."

Oliver closed his eyes and took an invisible blow to his midsection. Yes, he'd cornered the market on wheat, a risky investment to be sure, and one he'd only dabbled at in the past. But days after his return to Chicago seven months ago, a market analyst he'd long trusted predicted skimpy harvests for wheat and thus extremely high prices if one had wheat to sell come harvest time. Thus, it made good sense, if one had the money and chose to risk it, to buy up wheat futures at a relatively low price. When the predicted shortage came, he would simply sell his interests at an inflated price and reap tremendous profit. But the reason he'd chosen to invest his entire fortune in buying up *all* the wheat expected to be harvested, and thus cornering the market, eluded him at the moment. He'd never taken such a risk before, a much-publicized risk, at that, at such a threat to his financial stability. It had been a tremendous gamble. Then again, he'd never before been so damned . . . *desperate* . . . never before had envisioned losing all that he had worked so very hard to achieve. Never before had been ruled by such an inner recklessness . . . a fever, like the gambling fever that had possessed his father. As if he were daring himself to lose everything—as if some part of him wished he would.

He opened his eyes. "And?"

"The harvest reports are in. It was an extremely bad year, as anticipated. But there's one problem." His counsel's gulp was profoundly audible. "A group of investors on the West Coast have imported an exorbitant amount of wheat from overseas. They're flooding the market. As we speak, wheat prices are plummeting, Oliver. Your—your entire fortune is lost."

Yes, Oliver could almost hear a great sucking sound, as if his coffers were being bled dry.

"I don't know what to say, Oliver."

Neither did Oliver. Words seemed somehow inappropriate when one was facing financial collapse . . . the loss of everything he'd ever worked for. He watched a lone figure moving briskly through Grant Park ten stories below and wondered where the fellow was going.

"Oliver, I don't suppose I need to add that you should seriously reconsider Theodore MacAdoo's offer for your company. It's a fair offer, complete with a wife, if I remember correctly. I know from the start you've been dead set against seeking help from anyone, especially MacAdoo, and I understand, truly, I do. But this isn't simply a momentary setback. My God, you're poised on the brink of financial disaster. And MacAdoo's providing you with a way out, a means to avoid the inevitable headlines in all the papers, the bankruptcy proceedings. Messy stuff, I tell you." A forced laugh rent the air.

The fellow below in Grant Park disappeared into the mist. Oliver rose slowly to his feet, his limbs stiff, his body numb and tired. His fingers clenched around his gold quill.

"I can draw up the papers, Oliver. It shouldn't take me more than an evening. We'll contact MacAdoo and the whole thing can be settled by morning. Even the wedding date, eh?"

Gray . . . the entire world outside of this room was a cold, lifeless gray. Just as Oliver was, deep in his soul. "That seems to be the only course," he said.

A rush of air was released behind him as if tightly held and then papers rustled frantically. "You're a brilliant man, Oliver. Just need to get yourself out of this string of bad luck, is all. I would wager MacAdoo will appoint you head of all his domestic shipping and pay you a small fortune in salary. Not to mention the house you'll receive upon marrying his daughter, Daphne. A man could do worse. Indeed, far worse. I'll meet you here tomorrow morning. Seven sharp. I'll take care of contacting MacAdoo this evening. You need only sign on the dotted line. Now go home, Oliver."

"Good night," Oliver said stiffly. The office door closed behind him.

How long he stood staring into the gathering dusk, merely a deepening of the gray, he didn't know. At some length, he turned and retrieved his heavy wool greatcoat, then doused the lamp and left his office.

Outside, the world was indeed cold and bleak. Any snow that had fallen had long since been blanketed by a film of soot that crunched beneath his boots. He stuffed his hands deep into his pockets and drifted into the late-day crowd bustling along the downtown streets. A frigid wind robbed him of breath and snuck deep into his belly, prompting him to alter his course, if one could call a mindless wandering that. He followed State Street south, then turned east onto Adams and was met with a wall of wind. Bending his head into the onslaught, he blinked through the tears blinding his vision, glanced quickly right and left, then darted across the street and surged through the double doors into Berghoff's Coffeehouse.

The place was like an overhot oven and bulged with patrons seeking something to chase away the chill. Most gathered around the tables that filled the great room, hoisting their beer steins. Their boisterous voices echoed off the high-beamed ceilings. Oliver filled his lungs with the familiar scents and chose a seat at the bar, some distance from the hooting and howling. His high-backed stool scraped hollowly against the hardwood floor as he settled himself and ordered coffee from a ruddy-faced, mustached barkeep he'd never seen before. When it arrived, he curled his fingers around the coffee mug, stared into the inky black liquid, and listened to the sound of failure thumping through his veins.

Tomorrow he would do what he had vowed never to do. He would take his sorry state of affairs to Theodore MacAdoo and allow himself to be rescued. He would nod and smile graciously, agree to set a wedding date as soon as was practicable, and conduct himself like any prospective bridegroom and future son-in-law.

He'd spoken with MacAdoo only once since his return from Barbados and that had been on Christmas Eve when he and his mother had joined the MacAdoos and their daughter at their palatial North Shore home. At that time, it had been mutually agreed upon that the wedding should be postponed until Oliver had concluded his nonstop traveling and could take at least a two-week wedding holiday. Daphne had only stared solemnly at him with her enormous brown eyes, then at the chunky emerald-and-diamond ring weighting her left ring finger. A bauble to placate her while she waited, one Oliver had presented to her that night along with a chaste brushing of his lips over her powdered cheek. She'd blushed profusely and skittered away to fawn over the ring with her mother, leaving Oliver with cigars and brandy and Theodore MacAdoo in the parlor. All ritualized formality it was, the posturing, the saying of the proper thing. Oliver hadn't been able to leave soon enough.

Since then, he hadn't seen his fiancée even once, and had spoken with his mother only briefly, whenever he was in town. She'd looked pale and wan, obviously distraught over his endless traveling and results that couldn't happen fast enough to please her. He'd advised her to stop fretting over his bank balance and find herself a companion, or better yet, a husband. She'd gaped at him, aghast, and launched herself into yet another diatribe on the hardships of married life for women. Ah, yes, the bride's enduring of the groom's exercising his conjugal rights. She didn't come right out and say it, of course, but Oliver knew what prompted the vicious curve of her lips. Indeed, endless nights spent aboard trains crisscrossing the nation had provided him with ample opportunity to read and gain further insight into his mother.

His fingers wrapped about the worn, leather-bound journal stuffed deep in his pocket. A familiar spot, that, for his father's journal. He worked a muscle in his jaw and gulped his coffee, relishing the burn that filled his chest and belly. Shoving the cup aside, he glanced up when a door to the kitchen banged open and lodged against the doorjamb. Unaware that Oliver looked on, plump, gray-haired Hedda Berghoff stood at the stove not ten paces inside the kitchen, bent over an enormous steaming pot. She stirred slowly, her plump cheeks red and shiny like small apples, a satisfied smile lighting her eyes. Oliver's gaze flickered to her husband, Otto, a suitably burly, bald-headed fellow possessing of a full-bellied laugh and deep-set twinkling eyes. He had turned from his task, his hands covered with flour, his chef's cap slightly askew upon his head. With a grin, he ambled toward his wife and stopped directly behind her, one beefy hand moving possessively over the generous curve of her hip and belly, then cupping one of her breasts. Her smile deepened and she lifted a steaming ladle for him to sample. Otto bent near her shoulder to taste the soup and nuzzled his wife's neck even when she shoved an ineffectual elbow into his side. His rumbling chuckle echoed through the kitchen, and with a lingering fondle of her breast, he ambled back to his task. The flush staining Hedda's cheeks clear to her gray hair was unmistakable, as was the loving smile on her lips.

Oliver watched the pair and felt anguish like a knife plunge deep into his vitals and twist. A despair he'd never before imagined rose in his chest, forcing a haggard breath from his lips. It filled him with a sorrow for all that he would never know, even if he owned every shipping company there was to own...even if he were the most powerful, the most successful businessman in the nation.

And then she blossomed in his mind's eye like a single, fragile white rose. Seven months had passed, the different atmosphere, the simple passing of time somehow dimming all memory of Barbados...somehow casting it all in a dreamy haze. Yet Alexa remained a vivid and tormenting memory. Yes, he remembered everything about her...how could he not when every time he closed his eyes she was there, haunting his troubled dreams nightly, her voice drifting through his mind almost continuously, those emerald eyes blazing through his consciousness even as he sat through countless meetings with prospective financiers. How many times during one of these high-level meetings had he caught himself staring from a window into the bleakness of the winter landscape, trying to remember the way the beach looked that night under the moon and the heavens, the night Alexa had danced the *biguine* by firelight...the night he had taken her to his bed, just as the memory tormented him every night since? How many times had he sat amidst a group of businessmen bellowing with laughter at some ribald joke, their cigars clamped between yellowed teeth, their bulbous girths quivering as he'd yearned to hear the Bim's deep-throated standpipe laugh echoing through fragrant night air...just as he longed to feel the tropical sun slapping at his skull like a callused palm strikes the head of a drum?

That many times he'd shoved those thoughts to some distant corner of his mind and forced himself back to the task at hand. The task...the task...his company, his fortune, proving he was a better man than his father, again and again, dammit. It was all he'd ever cared about.

He need but show up at his office tomorrow, sign the papers, marry Daphne MacAdoo...swallow a good bit of his pride...and eventually all would be his once again. Hell, the wedding presents alone would provide enough capital to set his ships afloat. And with one good weather season, he would be well on his way...add a few children, perhaps, a full social calendar for years to come, and sweet Daphne growing plumper and softer and more dimpled as the years passed...a certain affection for him in her smile.

He stared at Hedda Berghoff again, at the peaceful smile on her lips. At Otto Berghoff as he bellowed a German folk melody and glanced from time to time at his wife, something fiery and passionate in the depths of his dark eyes, even from Oliver's vantage. That wasn't a "certain" affection. That was something far more powerful, something deep and lasting, something found once in a lifetime if one were lucky. And it was worth far more than any commodity, any company, worth more than any man's pride, even his.

Something snapped in Oliver, like a brittle, tired twig.

Realization washed over him like a tropical rain soothing baked earth, and a huge breath escaped his lips. With a supreme sense of purpose, he thrust his hand into one coat pocket, then the other, then frantically searched his topcoat pockets until his fingers closed about his pocket watch. He snapped it open, grunted and then shoved it back into a pocket and drained his coffee in one giant gulp. He grabbed his greatcoat in one fist, tossed several coins upon the counter and darted out the double doors.

Outside, the wind still raged and ice pellets descended from hovering skies. Yet Oliver was barely aware of this as he shoved his way through the crowded streets. Several passersby glowered at him as he jostled past. Others merely glanced at him, their bland expressions suggesting it was normal that a man would run bareheaded through the streets of Chicago with greatcoat clenched in hand as an ice storm engulfed the city. Even so, these people knew nothing of the joy heating Oliver from within like a tropical sun.

He made a swift calculation of blocks as he darted through a tangle of coaches and wagons clogging one intersection. Three blocks to the bank; four more to Union Station. With a little luck he would make the five-ten train bound for New York. From there, if his luck held, another two weeks to Bridgetown aboard any ship that would take him. Of course they would take him, even if he hadn't the money for passage. After all, dammit, he was a man in love. Who could possibly deny him?

He stopped short in the middle of the intersection as a coach careened past, and found himself staring up into the sky. An el train clattered past on its suspended tracks, sending sparks showering to the street below. The ice prickled like tiny needles against his face and swirled in crazy patterns in the glow cast by the sputtering gas lamps. It was several moments before he realized the peculiar sensation upon his face had little to do with the ice and cold. He was smiling, for the first time in nearly seven months. And then he laughed, huge and robust, his head thrown back, smack in the middle of one of Chicago's busiest intersections, until a kindly passerby nudged him in the back. With a whoop of thanks, he darted across the street and into the crowd.

The hansom cab pulled to a stop along Bellefontaine's circular cobblestone driveway. Oliver paid the driver and without waiting for assistance, hefted his one bag and stepped to the ground. He listened to the retreating clatter of wheels upon cobblestones for several moments and stared at the imposing double doors before him. Somewhere in the distance thunder grumbled. A fine mist fell around him, dampening his shirt and further mussing his hair, which fell in too-long waves to his shoulders. His beard-shadowed face felt drawn, his body tired and misused. He hadn't shaved in three days. For an unconscionable fee, he'd bribed one of the fishermen with whom he'd shared a berth to fill a barrel with fresh water just before they'd docked in Bridgetown. It had been his first full bath in nearly six weeks, since the day he'd left New York on that fishing trawler.

Six weeks...far too long to spend aboard any ship. But the burly captain had assured him that the journey would take no more than three weeks—and the ship was a fast one, he'd boasted, a sleek three-masted clipper. As no other ship had been bound for anywhere near Barbados, Oliver had secured passage immediately, never once imagining the grueling six-week trip awaiting him. Uncomfortable with idleness and in exchange for cheap passage, Oliver had labored alongside the fishermen, casting and hauling enormous nets and reeling in lines as thick as a man's thigh. He grew accustomed to the foul smells and the bloody gore after several days of swallowing thick bile, and learned to sing along with the fishermen as they toiled elbow to elbow. In the evenings, he gathered with them around heavy tables, laughing as they shared stories and swigged rum in huge mugs. The work filled his days, tested the very limits of his endurance and thus drove impatience from his mind. Every night, he fell into an exhausted slumber, his muscles screaming for some surcease, his mind finding the comfort only his dreams could bring him.

Two weeks into the trip, a savage storm blew the ship off course and badly damaged the mainmast and foresails. For ten days, the ship labored against heavy seas and strong winds. Then, not a breeze could be had even to ruffle the sails hanging listlessly from the masts. After yet another ten days, the ship finally limped into Nassau's harbor for repairs and restocking. This took an inordinate amount of time, compounded by what Oliver soon discovered to be the captain's penchant for Bahamian women, something the crew, but not Oliver, shared. Bristling with impatience, Oliver had rejoined the crew when they again set out for Barbados, only to experience new heights of frustration when again the ship was besieged by a furious storm.

Luck. God knew, his had indeed run out. There had been times over the past few weeks when he'd doubted if he'd ever set foot upon Bellefontaine again.

His eyes drifted over the manse, over the luxuriant foliage that draped itself about the stucco. All was well tended, meticulously so, by a kind hand, yet it somehow seemed more lush than he remembered, the fragrances that much thicker, the colors more vibrant. A sensual assault, and one he'd waited for far too long.

He entered Bellefontaine without knocking. Even here, the place had changed somehow, though it looked the same. The familiar scents stirred memories that brought an ache to his soul, and his strides gobbled up the hall. He threw wide the doors on either side, finding the rooms deserted, and marched on. His footsteps echoed through the manse as did the banging of the doors as he flung them open, one after another. And then Cyril materialized before him in the shadowed hall, his dark eyes wide, his jaw sagging.

"Where is she?" Oliver barked, his hands upon his lean hips.

Cyril seemed to swallow with some difficulty, and squeaked, "Sir?"

"Alexa," Oliver boomed. "Where is she?"

Cyril blinked, opened and closed his mouth three times, and Oliver knew so all-encompassing a dread he nearly throttled the man before he could reply. No…he hadn't come all this way, prepared to say the things he should have said before he'd left, wearing his fool's heart on his sleeve . . . no . . . she had to be here. He hadn't even considered the possibility that perhaps she wouldn't be.

Finally, Cyril replied, "Why, I believe she's in the garden, sir."

"The garden," Oliver repeated dumbly, his gaze upon the tall windows at the end of the hall and the gardens beyond.

"Welcome back, sir," Cyril intoned. "Will you be staying long, sir?"

"You could say that." Oliver shouldered past the servant. His strides matched the thundering of his pulse in his ears as he made his way through the white rose garden and out onto the lawns. He didn't contemplate the dryness in his throat or the rain now falling softly from the heavens. Onward he proceeded, around the perimeter of the house until the gardens lay like lush carpet before him. And then he saw her, beneath a low-hanging cabbage tree not twenty paces from him.

With leaden limbs, he moved slowly toward her, drinking her in from head to toe. His heart threatened to burst from his chest. She stood with her back toward him, obviously talking to someone . . . but he didn't care. Her hair fell in a lustrous torrent of curls to her waist, liberally shot through with white-blond and deep honey as if sun-kissed. It seemed thicker than he remembered, and longer, hanging lushly past the full curve of her buttocks. She wore her characteristic wide-brimmed hat and a loose sheath of soft white linen that fell just to her ankles . . . and she was barefoot.

He paused not five paces behind her and struggled for breath even as he inhaled deeply of the scent that was hers alone. Gardenia . . . invading his mind and setting his world careening about him. Then she seemed to stiffen, her shoulders inching almost imperceptibly upward, and her head turned slightly, affording him a glimpse of her upturned nose. With a wave of one hand, she dismissed the young servant girl she had been talking to, and time hung suspended. One arm moved as if she massaged a fluttering somewhere deep in her belly . . . and she turned slowly about and faced him.

He took one step toward her and froze. The words clogged in his throat. Cold sweat popped out on his forehead even as the rain began to fall in torrents. His palms pressed against the muscles bunched in his thighs and his breath caught so fiercely in his lungs, a burning ache filled his chest.

His eyes drifted yet again over the face that had haunted his dreams for months . . . a face even more beautiful than he'd ever imagined, if that were possible, the face of the woman he loved beyond reason. And then his gaze fastened upon the enormous swell of her belly.

Chapter Sixteen

Again, Alexa pressed her hand to her belly, quite certain that this time it was the child within her that stirred, sending a sharp, familiar pain stabbing against her ribs. She barely flinched, so accustomed to it was she. Or perhaps seeing Oliver standing in the pouring rain before her drove all sense from her beneath the onslaught of an uncontrollable inner trembling. She had believed she'd never see him again. Yet, seemingly conjured forth by the jungle itself, here he loomed, looking far more savage and untamed than memories had served her over the past eight months. His hair was a wild cloud of blue-black, the same blue-black as that revealed by the thin linen shirt now plastered to his chest. He seemed massive, his every muscle sculpted brawn that tested the limits of his clothing. A fire smoldered in the depths of his eyes as they possessed every inch of her and lingered upon her swollen belly. His mouth parted and a look of anguish flickered across his face and was gone. Alexa felt as if a blade had plunged to her heart.

He took one step toward her and Alexa could barely breathe. "Alexa," he whispered.

A lump welled up and lodged in Alexa's throat, yet she forced her chin up a notch. "You're back," she said. *Without a word... after eight months with but one or two hastily penned missives that oozed stilted formality and said nothing....*

Another step toward her and she drew a step back, struggling with a traitorous desire to feel those arms tightening around her... wishing to God she didn't yearn so desperately to throw herself against his chest and weep uncontrollably. Yet the familiar bitterness and an acute sense of betrayal had both found too comfortable a home within her to allow for any hint of weakening now that he was here... the embodiment of her every wish for months. It seemed like years... a very long time for all that to stew. At her withdrawal, he paused, his eyes narrowing, those sensuous lips compressing. His hand reached out to touch her belly. "My God, Alexa," he rasped. Again, she took a step back and their gazes locked, his like a storm-tossed sea, eyes full of unspoken questions.

She drew her resolve about her like a velvet cloak and summoned a steady voice. "Why have you come, Oliver?"

"The babe is mine."

She bit her lip to keep it from trembling. "Are you asking me, Oliver?"

A muscle worked in his jaw. "I know it's mine."

He claimed her with his eyes as if it were his birthright to do so at will. Heat crept to her cheeks and she averted her gaze, feeling entirely too self-conscious all of a sudden and hating herself for it. Of late, she'd found simply moving about to be an exercise in frustration. She waddled, that was the only way to put it, her belly so distended and low, she had to thrust her hips forward and lean back simply to bear the weight. Her breasts had swelled like overgrown melons, her legs and ankles filled with fluid and her back ached incessantly. She wept almost daily, and she knew not why. Had she not been so entirely filled with joy over the impending birth of the baby, she would have been utterly miserable.

"You look beautiful."

She closed her eyes upon the resonant reverberation of his voice above the softly falling rain. "I'm fat as a house," she grumbled, her hand moving by rote over the low-slung curve of her belly. "I can barely move about. I—"

His hand covered hers upon her belly and liquid flames shot through her. "You've never been more lovely," he murmured from very close above her, yet she didn't raise her eyes. She couldn't. Instead, she stared at the chest just inches from her nose, allowing his hand, so very large and warm, to slide slowly over her belly. "When?" he asked.

"The doctor says the babe could come any day." Her eyes fluttered closed and she swayed when he placed both his hands upon her belly, caressing, molding...and God help her but she couldn't have stopped him, even though her conscience bade her to flee from him. How many nights had she lain awake aching to feel his hands upon her just like this? How very natural it was to allow him this.

"Alexa..." His breath stirred her hair. "My God, you're so warm...so very smooth and round. Are you...has it been difficult?"

She released a slow breath. Difficult? Enduring months of waiting for word from him, contenting herself with the two letters he'd sent, more months of waking each morning from dreams that set her aflame with a yearning so great she wept, growing more assured with each passing day that he would never return...that he had, as Cyril informed her, married. And all the while the seed he had planted deep within her blossomed and wrought such havoc within her even while it filled her with a poignant joy. "Difficult?" She could barely temper her sarcasm. "At first, I suppose." She grasped his hands just as his fingers brushed the heavy undersides of her breasts. "Oliver, please—"

"Alexa, God, don't deny me this." His breathing was hoarse and ragged against her temple and a masculine heat emanated from him, threatening her will. "You're mine...the babe you carry is mine...I want—"

"No." Garnering her resolve, she clasped his hands in hers and stepped a pace back. She blinked through threatening tears and drew upon that well of strength she'd tapped incessantly these last months. "Oliver, listen to me."

"No." He drew both her hands to his lips, his eyes capturing her. Soft kisses pressed against each of her fingers. "You're going to listen to me because I've a hell of a lot to say to you. Things I should have said before I left, but I..." A boyish smile curved his lips and Alexa's heart plunged to her toes. "Ah, hell, I was every kind of fool, saying things I shouldn't have said and—"

His words hung in the thick air, catching in his throat when his eyes fell upon the ruby ring weighting her left hand. A scowl descended over his features and he glowered at her, imprisoning her hand in a death grip.

"What the hell is this?" he growled.

Alexa swallowed and thrust out her chin. "It's a ring, Oliver."

"Dammit, Alexa, don't play coy with me. Where did you get it?"

She sniffed and lowered her eyes, a mistake, as all she could seem to stare at was the heavy bulge filling his skintight trousers. Memory flooded through her, so very torturous now, and she closed her eyes. "I... Stuart presented it to me."

"No—"

"We're betrothed."

"You're not."

"Oliver—"

"I won't allow it, dammit!"

She winced at the ferocity of his bellow and tugged upon her hand, vainly, as he refused to release her. Indeed, his fingers curled possessively around hers. She glared up at him. "I'm marrying him, Oliver."

"You're carrying my child," he said through his teeth. "Surely Jeffcoat knows that."

"He does. Indeed, he's known since the very start."

"And what of me, I ask you? Did I not promise you that I would return? Did you bother to tell your Jeffcoat that?"

"You never spoke of returning in your letters, Oliver. You spoke only of the plantation and your business schedule. Besides, Stuart considered your leaving here after you had... I mean, after we had..." She had to avert her gaze, knowing that Oliver, too, remembered well the night they had shared in his bed. "Stuart called it abandonment and offered for my hand that very night I told him of the babe."

"Abandonment...." A strange light glimmered in Oliver's eyes. "So he wished to pass the baby off as his, damn his—"

"No, Oliver. He simply sought to ease the burden for me. Had I allowed it, yes, I believe he would have claimed the child as his. We agreed to wait until after the babe was born to avoid the talk. We thought it best...."

"*We?* All this damned 'we.'" His chest expanded and he shoved a hand through his unruly hair, giving a disbelieving shake of his head. He gazed deep into her eyes. "Are you in love with him?"

"You more than anyone know that love is certainly no reason to marry."

He seemed to stare right through her. "Give me a better reason."

She blinked at him, somewhat confused. "Mutual respect."

"The man is a buffoon and you know it."

"Indeed? I believe it was *you* who lost his temper and bloodied Stuart's nose, then threatened his very life."

Oliver smiled grimly. "And I'll do it again if he steps foot near you."

"You'll get yourself thrown from the house and put in jail."

"Don't count on it." His eyes moved slowly over her breasts. A tingling pulsed through her and settled in the swollen peaks pushing against linen. Oliver's mouth parted with his breathing. "By God, if he's touched you, I'll—"

Without thinking, she pressed her hand against his chest, then nearly snatched it to her when his heat branded her fingertips. "No, he . . . has not. N-nobody has since you—"

"Don't do this."

She stared up at him and forced the words from her lips. Lies . . . half lies . . . to soothe a broken heart. "It's what I want."

His lips tightened into a thin, unforgiving line and he released her hand as if it were suddenly aflame. His hands found his hips and he swung his gaze past her, seeking something in the gardens and the rain that fell beyond the overhanging cover of the tree. "Have you forgotten that the man quite possibly murdered your own mother? That by marrying him, you'll be playing into his hands, handing him your share of the damned plantation?"

Alexa shook her head with conviction. "No, Oliver, you couldn't be more wrong about him. Over the course of these last months, Stuart has shown himself to be of the finest character—"

Oliver snorted. "Of course he has. Any man would put his best foot forward if he's desperate for a woman."

And what of you? she longed to cry out. "He has proven himself a true and loyal friend as well as a trusted and constant companion." Her gaze caressed the stubbled jawline jutting so very stubbornly, the deep creases around those cobalt eyes, as if he hadn't slept in weeks, the predatory hook to his nose...that cold gleam in his eye. She swallowed and ventured into uncharted waters. "He has promised to cherish me. I truly believe he loves me, Oliver."

Nothing. He simply stared into the rain, his rugged face devoid of expression. Alexa battled a dozen conflicting emotions, and then...

"Why didn't you contact me about the babe?"

Why didn't you come sooner? her mind cried out. *Why did you have to come back at all?* "It wouldn't have mattered, Oliver."

"I would have come."

"And done the proper thing? Somehow, I think not." Her soul filled with an anguished conviction. "Besides, my child and I shall be no man's forced responsibility."

Heavy-lidded eyes flickered to her. "You must indeed believe the very worst of me to prefer a lifetime spent with Jeffcoat."

Alexa forced aside the images that sprang to her mind. Images that had haunted her for months, images of waking each morning in Oliver's bed... of bearing an entire brood of his children to fill every last one of Bellefontaine's eight bedrooms. Her teeth tugged at her lip and she shrugged off her thoughts. "You're speaking in what-ifs, Oliver. It simply wasn't meant to be. Besides, you've your Daphne."

"I'm not marrying Daphne."

Her heart lurched. "I see. And what of your dream of an international shipping conglomerate?"

His cobalt eyes penetrated to her very soul. "I guess that, too, simply wasn't meant to be."

"But what of your company?"

"I no longer have a company, Alexa. Or a fortune, for that matter. All I have in this world is on my back and, of course, I own half of this plantation."

An angry trembling seized Alexa in its talons and prompted the snide curve of her lips. Indeed, her greatest fear had come to pass. Oliver had returned for one reason alone: to gain his share of the plantation from her. Nothing had changed, after all. "Ah, now I see. You've returned to lay claim to Bellefontaine once more...and perhaps your child now that you've nothing left. Indeed, after months of near silence, months allowing me to believe the very worst of you, you now reappear with no warning whatsoever and expect me to play into your hands, the willing woman."

His drawl was wicked and laced with innuendo. "You were more than willing at one time, my dear. You've a babe in your belly to prove it."

Her cheeks flamed and she clenched tiny fists against her skirts to keep from pummeling him. "You've no purpose here, Oliver. I suggest you take your arrogance and duplicity and sail back to wherever you came from."

"Sorry," he drawled. "I intend to stay. I own half, remember?"

"Odd, that," Alexa sniffed. "I've managed quite swimmingly without you."

He flashed a smile that weakened Alexa's legs in spite of herself. "Imagine what the place could accomplish with me here."

"I rather don't like the sound of that, and neither will Stuart." She relished the murderous look that passed over his features at the mere mention of Stuart's name. Revenge could indeed be very sweet...and might have been were it not for the deep ache in her soul. With a lift of her nose, she said, "If you think I intend to remove myself to the cottage, you're sorely mistaken."

"I wouldn't hear of it."

"Then you must find someplace else to stay."

Again, his eyes moved possessively over her. "And relinquish my claim? I thought you knew me better than that."

"Indeed, I do. But you're underestimating Stuart."

"Not half as much as you're underestimating me, Alexa. Your Jeffcoat has no claim here."

"Yet."

He stared at her, a long, brutal stare that tore through months of resolve. "That, my dear, I would wager against."

"And you would lose."

He inclined his head, his words cold and clipped. "Meet me in the study in one hour. All else aside, we've the plantation business to conduct."

"As you wish," she replied, lifting her chin and brushing past him only to pause midstride when a sharp pain sliced through her leg. A soft cry escaped her lips before she could snatch it back, then a muscular arm slipped about her waist and caught her against his side.

"What is it?" he asked, his voice laced with a soft concern.

"N-nothing," she stammered self-consciously, shoving an elbow into pure sinew that didn't give an inch. "I-it happens fairly frequently. The babe... he's very large and he rests low—"

"He?" The word swirled above her head, low and seductive.

"She, he...whatever." Her eyes darted to his, then quickly darted away. "I can manage now."

"It's raining," he said. "You'll catch a chill."

"Oliver, I've never caught a chill in my life."

"Then you're sure to slip and fall. And we can't have that." Before she could voice any protest, he bent, and with one arm beneath her knees and the other around her back, lifted her from her feet and snuggled her obscenely close against his chest. He frowned and shifted her in his arms as if testing her weight. "You *are* heavy," he observed too casually.

She huffed and sputtered and flushed clear to her toes. "Oliver, you're hateful."

He took one step and stopped. "No, Alexa," he murmured, his eyes full of a raw intensity, "I'm not the least bit hateful. And that's something I will take great pleasure in proving to you." With that, he took off with long, sure strides across the lawns, through the pouring rain and into the house. When he finally set her down, she mumbled something about getting into dry clothes and waddled off down the hall toward the stairs. She had but reached the first step when he materialized before her, one brawny thigh blocking her path and that same strange concern on his face.

"What the hell is this?" He glowered at her as if he thought her half-mad. "Your things will be moved to one of the chambers on this floor. I'll have none of this up-and-down stairs." He sent her a wicked look. "I'm surprised your noble champion Jeffcoat didn't recommend this earlier. Rather lacking in concern, isn't he? Cyril!" The very rafters shook with his bellow. "Have you no sense, woman?"

Alexa scoffed and attempted to swat him from her path. "Your concern is touching but I've been up and down these stairs countless times daily and I find I enjoy the exercise. And, I'll have you know, Stuart respects my wishes. Now move aside."

"The hell I will." Again he scowled at her and bellowed, "Cyril, dammit, man, where the hell are you?"

The servant's head appeared above the upstairs balcony. "Sir?"

"From now on, Miss Fairfield will be occupying the west-wing chamber," Oliver instructed in clipped tones. "See that she is comfortable there." The servant disappeared and Oliver frowned at her. "How the hell do you dress?"

Alexa released an exasperated sigh. "You are simply too much, Oliver. I manage to dress myself."

"You should have a lady's maid."

She smiled primly. "I don't require a maid. I'm entirely self-sufficient."

"Indeed." He rubbed his bearded jaw, clearly contemplating something. "What else should I know about? You aren't still swimming in the damned ocean, are you?"

"No, I swim in a freshwater pond near the cottage."

"Not anymore, you don't."

Alexa planted her hands on her hips and glared at him. "You obtuse man. I'm not some mindless employee you can order about. Who the devil do you think you are?"

"The father of your child, of course," he asserted, and folded his arms over his massive chest. "And the man who will soon be your husband."

Alexa felt the blood drain from her face. It was several moments before she could salvage her voice. "Stuart Jeffcoat will be my husband, Oliver. No one else."

He leaned close to her and brushed a damp tendril from her forehead. "Keep saying it, Alexa, over and over, and I'm liable to start thinking you're trying to convince yourself." He cupped her chin and lifted her gaze to his. "One hour. In the study." He left her then and strode down the hall. Several moments passed before Alexa realized the sound echoing about her was Oliver's cheery whistling.

At the sound of the study door swinging open, Oliver glanced up from his work. Without hesitation, he all but bounded out of his chair and around the desk to assist Alexa into a cushiony chair. She drifted past him in a cloud of heady gardenia, casting him an appropriately puzzled look when he produced a footstool and positioned it beneath her feet.

"This is highly out of character for you," she said as he settled himself once again behind the desk.

"Perhaps you don't know me as well as you think you do, my dear." He found himself staring at her and wondering how the hell he could have ever left her eight months ago. She looked like a golden gem nestled in folds of creamy white, her cheeks unusually flushed, her lips full and rosy, her body soft and round, tempting the sanity from him. Dusk had fallen over the island, necessitating the lighting of a fire in the hearth and tapers in every corner of the room. Yet Alexa seemed to radiate a light and a heat all her own; for him, she alone occupied the very center of his universe. Her hands rested demurely upon the high curve of her belly and he lost himself in the liquid emerald pools gazing upon him with such unabashed innocence.

He didn't even pause to contemplate the myriad reasons that this woman would agree to marry Stuart Jeffcoat. He had learned long ago that the workings of the female mind were beyond a man's complete comprehension. Yet, somehow, even this typically exasperating quality rendered her that much more intriguing to him. That she still believed him motivated solely by all the demons that had possessed him for years...yes, this was all too obvious. And worse yet, he couldn't deny that he had been driven, ruthlessly, without compassion or regard, *obsessed* for many years in pursuit of his dreams. No matter what he had sought, he had made it his. A man did not cultivate a beastly and notorious reputation on idle gossip alone. And his reputation was decades old . . . and so firmly ingrained in Alexa, he knew well the simple speaking of the words *I love you* would be lost in what she viewed as a muddle of twisted motivations and cunning duplicity. No, he knew well his efforts would be wasted on words. Yet how did a man direct himself entirely to claiming her soul, to winning her heart, to proving to her that she couldn't possibly live another day on this earth if she wasn't his wife, when he didn't know how the hell to start?

Like nothing he'd ever known before, his passion for her and their child filled his soul with an anguished joy, and it was all he could do to refocus his attention upon the ledgers spread upon the desk before him. His vision blurred at the thought of losing all that had come to mean everything to him. Patience . . . a gentle hand . . . that had to be the way of things. Leaping over the desk and crushing her in his arms, as much as he ached to do so, might not be the best course. She had to come to him . . . with a little urging, of course.

"The ledgers have been meticulously kept," he observed, scanning the neat columns where her fine, feminine scroll recorded the daily receipts and disbursements for the plantation. "You've obviously been frugal yet extremely fair, especially regarding wages."

"The workers deserve it," she replied softly, her cheeks just a hint more rosy. "They've been working from sunup until sundown since the harvest began in November."

Again, his eyes swept over the ledgers. "Production figures look good. We can only hope that exports are up and prices remain steady. If not—" his gaze focused upon the balance in plantation reserves "—I don't believe we'll be able to remain in operation through the summer. The cost of supplies and upkeep on the sugar works alone, not to mention the wages, will drain us of all cash." He massaged his stubbled jaw and leaned back in his chair, his eyes drifting over her.

"Exports are expected to be drastically reduced, Oliver."

"Who told you that? Don't believe Pinkus Pomeroy, Alexa. The man has every reason to make us believe the very worst." He glanced sharply at her. "He hasn't been causing trouble for you, has he? Throwing his weight around to get you to sell out?"

Her delicate features quivered with agitation. "No. He seems far too preoccupied with making a success of Alleyndale Hall and drumming up interest at all the governor's dinners. Nevertheless, I'm well aware that he shall inevitably set his sights upon Bellefontaine."

He smiled. "I know you are, Alexa. You're a remarkably intelligent woman." He indicated the desk before him, a desk that had been swept clean of all those piles of correspondence he'd left behind. "And you make a hell of a businesswoman. Efficient. Well-organized. Uncommonly beautiful."

She pursed her lips and lowered her eyes, and he watched one slender hand moving slowly, lovingly, over her belly. A fierce possessiveness swept through him and muddled his brain until she said softly, "I've been to the Beefstake and Tripe Club on several occasions—"

"You *what?*" Oliver half rose from his chair and a brawny fist met with the desk. "Dammit, Alexa, that's a men's club and no place—"

"For a woman?" She met his glower with a finely arched eyebrow. "How the devil am I to compete in this business if practically all of it is conducted in a men's club?"

Oliver rubbed his jaw. "Enough is discussed at those blasted dinner parties the governor throws from time to time."

"And I've been to those, of course, though there's something in the atmosphere that isn't quite as conducive to discussing business as at a men's club, I must say. Of course, once I... that is..." She flushed like a wild rose despite the slight curve of her lips. "Once I'd grown too big, of course, I had to decline all invitations and keep myself here. But that was just in the past month or so."

Oliver stared at her. "You mean you've been all over the blasted island, for all to see...?"

"Precisely. Surely you didn't expect me to sequester myself in this house for nine months? Good grief, Oliver, pregnancy is not an ailment, or something to be embarrassed about."

"Of course," he muttered with a frown, again rubbing his jaw. He pondered this. "You weren't the least bit uncomfortable with the circumstances?"

"Not in the least, once everyone grew accustomed to the notion of an unwed woman with child. That took some time, of course—but I am, after all, the owner of the largest plantation on the island. That carries quite a bit of clout, and as I said, things are going rather swimmingly. People tend to gravitate toward those who succeed and even find it within themselves to forgive a slight transgression. Some have even gone so far as to consider me unduly victimized."

"By me." Oliver gritted his teeth and moved to the hearth to punch a poker into a fire that required little stoking. He glanced at her. "You, of course, set them straight regarding that."

She stared at him with disbelief. "A lady doesn't speak of such things, Oliver. Besides..." A smug little smile teased her lips and she smoothed the linen over her belly. "A woman must learn to capitalize on certain things if she is to achieve what she wants. Your notorious reputation has only helped to elicit sympathetic reactions. You can't imagine the enormous amounts of fatherly advice I've gleaned from various shipping merchants who regularly visit the Beefstake and Tripe Club. They've even been so generous as to invite me to join them there. And, of course, that's where I've learned of the atrocious state of the islands' exports."

Oliver could only shake his head, his hands upon his hips as he gazed down at her. "You're more shrewd than half the men I know. How the hell you developed such an instinct for the business—"

"I simply listened to everything your father said. He was a brilliant man."

Oliver grunted. Yes, he knew that. Indeed, he'd come to know so very much over the last eight months...and it weighed upon his shoulders oppressively all of a sudden. He hunkered down and took one of her swollen feet into his hands. At first, she seemed to stiffen and he half expected her to sputter and resist. It never came. He caressed the tiny foot, so very white beneath his long, brown fingers, so very fragile, just as she herself was somewhere beneath all that fierce determination. Like a fine white rose.

A soft breath escaped her lips as he worked her foot in his hand, gently massaging it, then sweeping his fingers up over her swollen ankle and back again over the arched instep. He shoved the footstool aside and settled her feet in his lap, his hands massaging both, then venturing beneath that flowy linen over the slender turn of her calves. At some point, he glanced up at her, a grievous error that, for he was suddenly lost...and powerless to stop himself. How she beckoned to him....

Her name escaped on a groan and he rose on his knees, easing her legs apart with the gentle pressure of his hands upon the silken flesh of her calves. His hands rested there and he pressed his mouth to her belly, filling his lungs with her warm, womanly scent. Desire raged like a tempest through him yet he remained unmoving, his cheek pressed to her belly, willing her to allow him this...aching for some response from her and then, from beneath his cheek, came a sharp jab.

His head snapped up and he stared at the swollen belly, his hands slipping from beneath her skirt to cradle her stomach through one thin layer of linen. Words caught in his throat when again, directly into his palm, came another jab. "Ah, God," he rasped. "He moves."

"He's kicking," Alexa replied softly. Her hand slid over his and moved it to the side of her belly. "Here...I think this is an elbow."

Oliver waited, his entire body tensing, his senses alive with wonder. Several minutes passed and nothing. He glanced up at her, his voice thick. "What's wrong?"

She smiled, a wondrous, enchanting smile that touched his heart, and her fingers brushed a wayward lock of his hair from his face. "Nothing is wrong. The babe sleeps, is all."

He caught her hand and pressed it to his lips. "Alexa, listen—"

"Oliver, please." Like a wisp, her fingers slipped from his and she shoved her hands against the arms of the chair in an attempt to rise. "I have to...that is...I drank three glasses of lemonade this afternoon and I have to—"

"Of course." Feeling too big and incredibly dumb, Oliver lurched to his feet and bumbled his way through helping her from her chair and to the door. "Do you need . . . ?"

"No," she whispered, staring down at the door handle.

He ached to nestle her in his arms and soothe her every discomfort. Instead, he simply stared at her like a fool and allowed the silence to well about them.

"Stuart is coming by this evening, as he does every evening," she said without looking at him. "Please...in the best interests of all involved . . . I would hope that you would find yourself elsewhere . . . or at the very least control your temper."

"You ask too much of me."

Her hand pressed against her belly as her eyes lifted to his. "If for no one else, do it for the babe."

"If you're implying that I don't know what's best for my own child, Alexa, you're wrong, I do. And Jeffcoat isn't it." She shook her head and opened the door three inches before Oliver pounded it shut with his fist. "Dammit, woman! What do you want of me?"

She swung upon him, fury and fire, her face contorted with pain. "Haven't you already given me more than enough? This child...who shall now become yet another pawn in your game of power and control?" Her chest heaved with every breath. "More than anything, Oliver, I want you to realize this child and I shall never succumb to you. Oh, the flesh may be weak and willing...and God knows I rue that day and no doubt will many more to come . . . but heed me well, the spirit is not."

This time when she yanked open the door, he let her. And when it closed behind her, he released his pent-up frustration with a bellow of pure rage...and shoved his fist into the solid mahogany, again and again, until a new pain replaced that in his heart.

Chapter Seventeen

The mists had just begun to dissipate, the skies to relinquish a hint of darkness to welcome the morning when Alexa pulled the door closed behind her and set out across Bellefontaine's lawns. Dew-laden grass cooled her swollen feet and dampened the hem billowing about her legs. She breathed deeply of early morning as she passed through the gardens heavy with scent even now, and in the shadowed darkness found a path she used each and every morning. Into the thick jungle it led her, a jungle now alive with the sounds of birds, monkeys and any number of wild creatures. Were it not for the streaks of molten gold and pink in the skies overhead, the gloom would have been impenetrable and far too imposing to one not so familiar with this trail and where it led. Then again, perhaps even Alexa, heavy with child, slow-footed, and weary from lack of sleep, yes, even she would have had cause to hesitate before venturing through the jungle alone at such an hour, were it not for the havoc occupying her mind.

Four days had passed since Oliver's return, each one plunging Alexa deeper into her quandary and another day nearer to the birth of her child. The babe had settled even lower within her, pressing against her back such that sleep proved impossible. During the days she snatched naps, her chin falling onto the ledger as she worked. At night, however, she tossed fitfully and more often than not padded through Bellefontaine's dark halls seeking the library and awaiting the dawn if only to escape, just as she did now.

Escape. An odd choice of words being that Oliver had been nothing short of gracious since his return. Whenever they happened to encounter each other, he was exceedingly formal and polite, forever mindful of her comfort, yet he remained aloof, and took himself from the house very early each morning, returning only after dinner had been served. From Luke she learned that he spent his days in the fields and tending to the sugar works, and had traveled once or twice to Bridgetown to the Beefstake and Tripe Club. Whether to keep himself from her or to devote himself to the survival of the plantation, Alexa knew not.

That he seemed determined to run the plantation to the very best of his ability filled Alexa with nagging doubts even as it stoked her deepest convictions. Perhaps Oliver obsessed himself with the plantation business simply to bide his time while he plotted to ensnare her as soundly as he had plotted to ensnare Daphne and an international shipping line. Just as he had plotted and schemed his entire life to get whatever he wanted. A chilling ruthlessness had filled his eyes each time he had spoken of marrying Daphne and achieving his dream, one that had lent his voice a deep passion she had never believed he possessed. Dreams, she had come to realize, were not easily forsaken, especially for a man like Oliver who had little or no regard for the dream his own father had probably died protecting. Indeed, why on earth would Oliver seek to nurture something his hated father had cared about so profoundly? He simply had to harbor deeper motives. A man, after all, could not change so entirely in eight months, could he?

These thoughts she could not banish from her mind, even as she'd listened to Luke recount with a certain admiration the hours Oliver devoted to the business, to negotiating with the merchants in the hopes of opening export channels to the States and elsewhere. A cold, cruel dread filled her whenever she thought of her unborn child and the rights she knew a man like Oliver would wish to exercise over the baby. Coercion, seduction, and if that didn't gain complete ownership of the plantation for him, as she had vowed it wouldn't, what then? To what depths was Oliver capable of plunging to achieve his ends?

And yet . . .

Her heart dictated an altogether different set of circumstances. Their eyes would meet across the room, or perhaps she sensed him staring at her, and an anguish so deep and palpable would emblazon itself upon his rugged features, albeit fleetingly and swiftly masked beneath that hardened visage, she all but flung herself into his arms and begged his forgiveness for believing the very worst of him. Even as she dreaded his nearness, she craved his touch. Even as she nursed her doubts, her pulse quickened whenever he spoke confidently of the plantation . . . and her heart ached at the unmistakable pride in his voice as he echoed his father's sentiments, whether knowingly or not. Even as she vowed to uphold her promise to be a good wife to Stuart Jeffcoat, she realized, despite the dictates of her conscience, that it was Oliver, ruthless, notorious, calculating and arrogant, yes, Oliver who had laid claim to her soul and set the butterflies to fluttering in her belly whenever he but glanced her way.

With every glance, he made her betrothal to another man a travesty by shoving her lack of feeling for Stuart into her face.

The British officer visited twice daily, something Alexa had come to dread since Oliver's return for several reasons, the least of which was the inevitable confrontation certain to occur between Oliver and Stuart. So preoccupied was she, on more than one occasion she found herself staring directly over Stuart's head at the closed parlor door, in anticipation of Oliver storming into the parlor and pummeling an unsuspecting Stuart Jeffcoat into the Aubusson carpets. Her consternation knew no bounds when Stuart, obviously aware of her distraction, waved a hand over his head as if to smooth a wayward hair into place or, God forbid, to remove some foreign object that had found a home upon his head and was the cause of Alexa's wandering eye.

Were she not so entirely irritated by his presence, Alexa might have felt a tad sorry for Stuart. As it was, where Oliver's constant regard for her condition sparked a warmth in her heart and somehow made the man seem wondrously vulnerable, Stuart's very touch suddenly made her skin crawl. Of late, she craved the firmness of long fingers upon her, not the tentative, soft, rankling strokes Stuart only seemed capable of. Her ear suddenly longed for a deeply masculine voice offering comfort or simply relaying the news of the day, not Stuart's incessant mewling and high-pitched whining whenever he spoke of his situation in the Governor's House. Indeed, since Oliver's return to Bellefontaine, it seemed Stuart couldn't do anything quite right, and Alexa found herself wishing he'd simply not do anything at all.

And with each passing day, she knew the birth of the baby drew nearer, and with it, Stuart's demand that they set a date for the wedding.

Had a woman ever been so soundly ensnared by a set of tragic circumstances? Then again, her doctor had told her to expect all sorts of conflicting emotion during the pregnancy. Yet, somehow, the wee babe nestled in her womb seemed far too innocent to have contributed in any way.

Doubts…doubts… One night, almost nine months prior, she had been able to set those doubts aside…or perhaps passion had proven her weak enough that she had given her soul to Oliver. Would she indeed pay for that misdeed for the rest of her life?

Thrusting these thoughts aside, she parted the last of the brush and stepped from the jungle's cover into a small clearing. In the center of the clearing, a small pond awaited, its surface glassy smooth, reflecting the pinkening sky above. She slipped the drapey linen dress over her head and waded slowly into the warm pond entirely naked. The water lapped at her thighs, and she closed her eyes, willing all but peace from her mind and soul. Instinctively, her hands moved in circular strokes over her belly, and her thoughts drifted to the sweet child she would soon nestle to her breast.

And then a tremendous splash and what sounded like a huge gasp of air snapped her eyes open and brought a frightened shriek to catch in her throat. There, from the center of the pond, Oliver arose like a savage beast, shaking water from his hair. He froze when their gazes locked.

He, too, was entirely naked. This she realized with a sinking heart as he waded slowly toward her, his eyes blazing like hot coals. The water receded over his chest and arms, exposing sleekly muscled ribs, a corded belly and lower… and still he advanced upon her….

With a soft cry, she spun about, unable to move her leaden limbs for the trembling that had beset her. Her mind cried out even as her body tingled with wanton anticipation. She felt him behind her and her eyes fluttered closed when warm, wet hands encircled her waist and claimed her belly. Like a sapling willow, she swayed back against him, shuddering with pleasure when his mouth pressed against her throat, her shoulder, then nuzzled her ear.

"I—I thought you didn't swim," she said softly.

"It was time I learned, don't you think? Come..." He drew her with him, deeper into the water. All strength of will, all logical thought, seemed to have deserted her and she offered no resistance, even when he grasped her hand and turned her about to face him.

"Alexa," he breathed, his gaze moving so very slowly over her, she trembled anew. "My God, look at you. I've ached to see you this way...to touch you..."

"Oliver—" It was a plea, forced from a parched throat even as tears spilled from her lashes. He murmured her name again and again and drew her into his arms. Strength and heat enveloped her and she clung to him, it seemed, for a lifetime. He drew her deeper into the pond until the water lapped at the undersides of her breasts. Beneath the water, his hands moved over her belly with such tenderness a poignant joy filled her soul, and when his mouth hovered over hers, she could do naught but part her lips. He kissed her gently, almost reverently, as though she were made of the finest porcelain, his lips firm yet infinitely soft upon hers, asking nothing from her. Her breath caught when he bent to spread the same soft kisses over her throat and the high curves of her breasts. So very right this all felt, so very natural that when his mouth claimed one swollen nipple, she could only cradle his head nearer. He suckled her with deep, long strokes, as if he had an entire lifetime to while away in this pond. She pressed her face to his tousled hair and inhaled his masculine scent. Her palms moved over his muscled shoulders and arms, and her mind reeled when he cupped her breasts and gazed deep into her eyes.

"You belong to me," he rasped hoarsely, his breath falling fast and ragged. "No matter who you think you're going to marry. Know this well, Alexa." His thumbs brushed over the peaks of her breasts and a triumphant flame leaped in his eyes when her nails dug into his shoulders. "Yes, love, it hurts, doesn't it? To be so very near each other yet so very far. I shan't rest until these doubts that plague you are banished. I was once a man possessed by demons, a man who thought his greatest passion his work. I now know that you, my love, and our babe are alone what I live and breathe for."

"No," she whispered, the tears again spilling to her cheeks. "I cannot—"

He caught her hand beneath his and pressed it to the heated skin over his heart. "Feel me, Alexa. Ah, but you don't want to, just as you wish I wouldn't touch you as much as you crave that I do. You know what's between us is far more powerful than either of us... powerful enough to drive all doubt from your mind if you would but let it. I dare you to deny it."

"I will."

"You won't marry him."

She swallowed deeply and pushed against his chest, her heart aching. "Yes, Oliver, I gave him my word and I intend to stand by it—"

A savage snarl jumped from his throat and he crushed her against him. "And how will Jeffcoat feel when you flee his bed for mine... when every child you bear will be mine?"

Alexa's legs crumpled beneath her and she sagged in his arms with a soft cry. "You torture me," she sobbed brokenly, even as she luxuriated in the feel of his arms cradling her against him.

"Forgive me," he rasped into her hair. "But I can't let you condemn us both to that sort of life without one hell of a fight. Because, Alexa, trust me, I will never let you go, even if you legally belong to another."

"Oliver—" And then a sharp pain sliced through her belly and around her back, forcing a cry from her lips. She doubled over, clutching her belly, and felt a cold fear prickle through her.

"Alexa, what is it?" His face, deathly pale and drawn, appeared before her.

"I—I'm not quite sure," she replied truthfully.

She barely drew a breath when Oliver swept her from her feet and waded swiftly to shore. "Damn, damn, damn," he muttered over and over as he gently placed her onshore and swept her dress from the sand. With hands shaking visibly, he helped her into the dress, then plucked his dark trousers from a nearby bush.

"Are you all right?" he asked brusquely, tugging on his pants.

She nodded, aware that she feared simple movement even though the pain had subsided.

"Damn my fool's soul to hell," he growled. He lifted her into his arms and cradled her against his chest. "I upset you—"

"Oliver, stop it."

"No," he said, stalking into the jungle. "I'll be a man insane if something happens to you or the baby. I'll—I'll—" She slipped her arms around his neck and buried her face against his throat, if only to sweep the tortured look from his face, the clouding of those cobalt eyes, the trembling of his mouth.

She remained thus until he kicked open the door to her chamber and gently deposited her upon the bed. After a lingering look at her, he strode to the door and bellowed into the hall, "Cyril!"

Alexa lay upon her side upon the cream-colored damask coverlet, a pillow clutched to her belly, her gaze moving appreciatively over him. His bare shoulders seemed miles wide, tapering dramatically to an impossibly narrow waist and hips snugly encased by his damp trousers. His buttocks were high and superbly muscled, flexing as he shifted his weight and again bellowed into the hall.

"Dammit, what does a man have to do to—" And then a pale-faced Cyril skidded to a breathless halt just outside the door. "Fetch the doctor," Oliver instructed tersely, turning again to Alexa. "*Now,* Cyril. Send Luke. Anybody."

He knelt beside the bed and she reached for his hand, wishing she could as easily assuage the concern taking up permanent residence upon his face.

"I'll stay with you," he said, brushing her hair from her face. And that he did, talking incessantly, often rambling on about his plans for the plantation. He talked of his plans to increase the yield per acre of cane through improved cane-breeding and more modernized production methods. The first to go, he told her, would be the wind-powered mill, which he would replace with a steam-driven mill with more modern equipment like heavy rollers to squeeze more juice from the cane. He would begin to clear more of the plantation's timberland and plow it up for planting. Then the doctor arrived and banished him to the hall. He agreed but with much grumbling and scowling, his heavy footsteps as he paced the hall audible even to Alexa through a closed door. And he was there, filling the doorway with his bulk, when the doctor opened it several moments later and declared both Alexa and the baby fine.

"It shouldn't be more than a few more days," the doctor proclaimed as he shuffled down the hall.

Oliver stomped after the smaller man. "Then what the hell was that all about?" he barked. "She was in *pain,* dammit."

The doctor waved a hand and scoffed. "And she'll be in a lot more pain once the child decides to come." He gave Oliver a much unappreciated pat on the back that merely deepened his scowl. "Make sure she rests. She'll need her strength."

"You're not to move," Oliver ordered when he reentered her chamber and stalked immediately to the hearth to stoke the fire.

"Oliver, it's quite warm enough in here." Alexa pushed herself up on her elbows and couldn't contain the smile on her lips when he merely scowled at her and continued with his task. "One would think you've nothing better to do."

"It can wait." He stared at the sputtering fire, hands on his hips, allowing Alexa a long, leisurely perusal once again of his splendid form. A certain pride seeped into her soul at the thought of her babe looking very much like his father. He spun about and hovered beside the bed. "You don't look comfortable."

"Go to work, Oliver," she said with a sigh as he fluffed and refluffed the pillows behind her.

He stared at her, then placed his hand almost tentatively upon the highest curve of her belly. "Has he moved?" he whispered hoarsely.

"He hasn't stopped. He *is* your child, after all."

"How can I forget." He bent to press a kiss to her belly, then brushed his lips lingeringly over hers. "I'm going to get Shura to come stay with you. Don't move until I get back."

She watched him stride determinedly from the room, aware of a new and wondrous sense of peace and contentment enveloping her.

Oliver stood out on the loggia, watching nature's fury wreaking havoc. Lightning pierced the night sky almost incessantly. Thunder tested the very foundations of the house and the rain billowed past in horizontal waves, driven by gale-force winds that flattened Oliver's shirt to his chest and snatched at his breath. He leaned his forearms upon the iron railing, his gaze drifting over the low-hanging trees bending beneath the force of the wind. It was a hot night, even with the rain, and Oliver lingered, enjoying the blasts of wind, the frequent swells of rain washing over the loggia. He wondered if his father had also enjoyed watching the storms as much as he. Somehow the very smell of it stoked an age-old memory of him as a young boy standing thus upon this loggia beside his father, watching the rain, listening to the man talk of his dreams for the plantation, for his only son—

Just then, through the open door leading to his chamber came the chimes of a clock striking midnight, prompting him to abandon his post and venture from his room, as he had done hourly since he'd returned from the sugar works earlier that evening.

His well-worn path took him down the stairs and through darkened halls, brilliantly lit by intermittent flashes of lightning. He paused at her door and pushed it slightly open. There, where Alexa should have been resting as she had these five hours past, was nothing but rumpled sheets. A crash of thunder shuddered through the house as he shoved the chamber door wide. He took two steps into the room, his eyes darting about as lightning illuminated every dark and deserted corner. Even Shura had abandoned her post, it seemed.

With a growl tempered by a sudden urgency, he strode swiftly from the room and down the hall, not knowing where he was going. He thrust the doors open on either side of the hall as he proceeded, their fierce banging against the walls punctuated by snarls of thunder. A blue flash momentarily blinded him and a crash exploded through the house, robbing him of breath. Too close... the storm was too close....

With fists clenched and his shirttails billowing about him, he ran through the halls toward the back of the house... the kitchen...where was she? Her name echoed in his mind, over and over, and fell mindlessly from his lips, though he knew the pounding of the rain upon the roof and against the windows obliterated all sound.

Acutely aware of the acrid taste of fear on his tongue, he shoved the kitchen door wide, took three steps, then bumped smack into a heavy, rough-hewn table. It slid several feet and he grappled with it until the lightning flashed, illuminating a wraithlike form poised in the open back door.

"Alexa," he rasped.

"Oliver, good grief, you scared me."

Oliver swallowed heavily, aware that his heart hammered a staccato rhythm in his chest. "What the hell are you doing?"

"I'm watching the rain, of course." She turned, again filling the open doorway. Beyond her, the rain pummeled the earth with a dull roar. "I thought I was hungry, and then... well, I found I wasn't. I feel rather restless."

He moved behind her, his hands instinctively rubbing her upper arms through the soft cambric nightgown. "You should be in bed."

"My entire body aches from lying there all day."

"Where's Shura?"

"With Luke, I suppose."

"Luke."

"They're lovers."

She swayed back against him and he rested his chin on top of her head, gazing into the rain. "I didn't know."

"I don't believe she likes it here much."

"A sorry excuse to leave you untended."

She tilted her head and gazed up at him. "Untended? With you hovering over me every hour on the hour, Oliver? It's a wonder she could sneak away without your being aware of it." Her frown was barely visible in the shadows, her fingers tracing over his jaw, then beneath his eyes. "You're not quite used to all this, are you? You seem tired."

"Worried is all." He caught her hand and pressed it to his lips. "Come." His hand moved possessively over her belly. "You're getting wet."

She followed him from the kitchen and down the hall. "I'm not sleepy," she said as he pushed her chamber door open.

"Fine. Then you can talk to me." He lit a bedside candle and shed his boots, then sat on the bed, extending his legs before him and propping several pillows behind his head.

"Stop grinning like that, Oliver. You can't possibly stay here with me."

"No? It's the only way I know of to keep you where you belong."

She shook her head and folded her hands over her belly. "I'm not getting in that bed with you."

Oliver glowered at her. "Good God, woman, but you think me the devil himself. Surely you don't think I'm going to attempt to seduce you while you're…?" He waved a hand over her from head to toe and contemplated the shadowed ceiling above him. "Alexa, come lay beside me. Let me hold you."

She studied him in a manner that made him want to yank her into his arms. "You look a trifle dangerous, Oliver."

"Is that so?" In one swift motion, he rose and grasped her hand in his, tugging her nearer. "Keep looking at me like that or refuse me and see how dangerous I can be."

This time she allowed him to nestle her back against him, his one arm encircling her stomach. She shifted and resettled herself a half dozen times, repositioning pillows under her legs and behind her back. With a huge sigh, she finally peered up at him, her lips parting. He required no further invitation. As soft as thistledown, he brushed his lips over hers, tasting rain and warm woman, his arm tightening about her waist. With a patience he thought himself incapable of, he kissed her long and leisurely, his tongue parting her lips, and claiming unhurriedly, without demand. She murmured something and buried her head against his chest.

"This is madness," she whispered. "Please, go to sleep, Oliver."

"I can't." His hand moved to cup the heaviness of her breast. "How can I be a man at peace when the woman I love wishes to marry another?"

A broken sigh escaped her lips when his fingers captured one nipple. "Oliver, please, you're trying to seduce me—"

"No," he whispered into her hair. "I'm loving you. When are you going to realize that? Tell me which mountain to move and I'll gladly do it. Will that prove to you that I am a man insane for you?" He shifted her in his arms, drawing her into his lap, his hand moving boldly over her breasts. "You let me touch you, kiss you, you let me love you once very long ago... and still deep in your heart you cannot trust that what I feel for you is true? If you seek to torture me, you've done it, Alexa. Now, please, cease the madness."

She shook her head, her eyes shining with tears. "You are two entirely different men to me, Oliver. One man possesses no heart, no soul, just a consuming desire to conquer and control, no matter the price. The other—" A soft sob escaped her lips. "I pray that it is his child I carry. I—"

Gritting his teeth, he gathered her close. "Lord, don't cry. Please...you're so damned fragile, yet so strong...you're like no woman I've ever known, or man, for that matter. You've turned me inside out, shown me the man I truly am, taught me more about myself than—" His words caught in the great lump lodged in his chest. "Do you know the hell I went through to get back down here? Six weeks hauling fish on a damned trawler..." He paused and frowned. "You're laughing. What the hell is so damned funny?"

She glanced up at him. "Nothing, Oliver, truly. Continue. I'd love to hear about your fishing trawler."

He gave her a wicked look. "Laugh again, woman, and I *will* start seducing you."

Snuggling her deeper into his arms, he drew the coverlet over them and began his tale of six interminable weeks at sea. He told her of his reckless and foolish squandering of his entire fortune in wheat futures. He told her of the months he'd spent before crisscrossing the country by train, attempting to revitalize his company by garnering cargo contracts. He told her that he'd left Chicago on the eve of his signing on with MacAdoo.

"I have forsaken everything I've worked for these past fifteen years. Indeed, I have discovered that I am more my father's son than I could ever have imagined. I have become what I've despised and I couldn't be more pleased about it. Alexa . . . Alexa?"

In reply, he received only her soft snore. With a wistful smile, he doused the flame and closed his eyes.

Alexa was dreaming she floated in a warm pond. A stubbled jaw nuzzled her throat and a very large hand captured one breast. She opened her eyes upon the semidarkness of early dawn, aware that Oliver slumbered beside her, one long leg thrown over hers, anchoring her there. She smiled and eased from beneath him, pushing herself up to sit upon the very edge of the bed. Not a moment later, the sheets rustled behind her and Oliver's voice rumbled close against her ear, his chest pressing against her back.

"What is it?" he asked softly.

She bit her lip and pressed a hand to her taut belly. "I don't know, I—" Slowly, she eased to her feet, took one step, and a gush of warm fluid pooled at her feet. "Oh, Oliver."

"I'll get the doctor," he said as he lunged from the bed.

"No," she cried, sucking in her breath as a wave of tightness spread through her belly into her back. "Get Shura. She's at Luke's cottage in the workers' quarters."

Oliver yanked the door wide. "I'm getting the doctor."

"Oliver—"

In two strides, he was beside her, easily lifting her from her feet into his arms, then easing her back onto the bed. "Just this once, my dear, don't argue with me."

She clung to him, the tears spilling from her eyes as heedlessly as the trembling suddenly besetting her limbs. "I'm not ready to be a mother," she blubbered against his throat.

That deep rumbling filled his chest and he cradled her close against him. "I'm going to fetch the doctor, Alexa."

She swallowed deeply, aware of a pressure building between her thighs with each successive tightening of her belly. "I don't think there will be time for that."

He stared at her, then pressed his lips to her forehead. "Fine. This time you win. I'll get Shura." And he ran from the room as if his very shirttails were aflame.

Chapter Eighteen

Even through the heavy chamber door, Stuart Jeffcoat's strident tones were distinctly audible. "I say, Cyril, unhand me at once! I weathered a bloody hurricane to get here, and by God, I intend to see my betrothed in her hour of need, I say, I—"

The chamber door slammed against the wall beneath the force of one of Jeffcoat's heavy black boots. The British officer took two steps into the room and froze, his eyes blinking rapidly. All color drained from his face and his Adam's apple bobbed furiously before he pressed a gloved hand to his mouth, then all but tripped over his sword to flee the room. With the only deeply felt satisfaction he'd experienced all day, Oliver closed the door behind Jeffcoat and returned to Alexa's side. Grasping her hand close, he ignored the sideways glance Shura shot at him, just as he'd ignored her seeking to banish him from the room since the moment she had arrived. Never could he be kept from witnessing his child's birth, by her or anyone else.

Unlike Jeffcoat, who had obviously been unable to stomach the sight he beheld, Oliver had, for the past two hours, endured Alexa's writhing upon those sweat-soaked sheets and her screams that had pierced his heart and chilled his blood. It was small penance to pay when her nails bit into his palms and raked over his arms as he watched her toes curl and her entire body arch beneath the agony she suffered. With eyes glazed, she'd lashed out at him, lunging to clutch at his shirt so violently she tore it, only moments later to collapse upon the sheets and softly murmur his name.

He remained beside her, feeling entirely useless and consumed with a maddening guilt for being the cause of all this. He obeyed Shura's clipped commands, fetching this or that, turning Alexa to one side or the other, lifting her, dribbling cool water into her mouth. And when Shura glared at him and mumbled something about the babe being too big . . . too big . . . his own bellow raged above all else when Shura produced a small knife and swiftly cut Alexa before he could stop her. Moments later, through a haze of disbelief, of frustration and anger, and above Alexa's mind-numbing scream, a baby's solitary cry pierced the air.

Her name tumbled from his lips, over and over . . . a mindless ramble as he enveloped both her and the babe in his embrace. Alexa spoke, something about the child looking just like his father . . . and he tasted tears somewhere through the enormous lump lodged between his throat and chest. He stared at the tiny form swathed in a white blanket, nestled in his mother's arms and tentatively reached what seemed an atrociously huge finger into his son's tiny hand. Almost instantly, those small red fingers curled about his own and clung. That enormous lump in his chest swelled to near bursting.

"Oliver, good grief, look at you," Alexa said softly, her hand venturing over the tattered remains of his linen shirt and the thick stubble shadowing his face. A flush stained her cheeks and she averted her gaze to the baby. "Was I horrible?"

He smoothed the damp strands from her forehead, then pressed his lips there. "You were magnificent."

Some time later, he took himself from the room, mostly at Alexa's urging, to fill his belly and rest. He, however, was more of a mind to hoist a few glasses of whiskey and bellow a round of fishermen's tunes from the second-floor loggia. Thus, when Stuart Jeffcoat extricated himself from the shadows and hastened after him the moment he stepped from Alexa's chamber, Oliver barely favored the British officer with a glance and continued toward the stairs with little break in his jaunty stride.

Above the furious clanking of his sword came Jeffcoat's snarl. "Where the hell do you think you're going, Keane?

Keane? I say, don't you ignore me, Keane. We've a score to settle once and for all!"

Oliver paused at that, one booted foot poised upon the first step. Jeffcoat skidded to a halt not a nose from him, his face mottled with a rage that set his limbs to trembling. Oliver shot the officer a pointed look. "Had a rough morning, Stu?"

Oliver saw the punch coming long before it met its mark. With jaw set against an overwhelming urge to pummel Jeffcoat into the marble, Oliver caught the other man's raised fist in one hand and shoved Jeffcoat back against the damask-covered wall. "Have you some problem, Jeffcoat?" he asked through clenched teeth.

Jeffcoat's chest heaved with his every breath. "That was my future wife in there with you, Keane!" Jeffcoat shrieked. "The level of impropriety alone *demands* my calling you out!"

Oliver bared his teeth. "I'd rather not kill you, Jeffcoat."

An atrociously confident gleam shimmered in Jeffcoat's eyes. "Just like you killed your father and Lily Fairfield, eh, Keane? Alexa believes it to be true, as does the entire plantation community. Indeed, my future wife thinks you no better than a monster, and well you know it. She abhors you so much she can barely stand to whelp your demon's seed."

Before he could think, Oliver balled one mighty fist and shoved it dangerously high beneath Jeffcoat's weak chin, relishing the bulge of Jeffcoat's eyes, the draining of all blood from his pompous countenance. "Say one more word, Jeffcoat," Oliver snarled, the muscles in his entire body taut and straining. "Give me one more reason."

The words were barely audible, a squeak emitted through a windpipe moments from being crushed. "I'll see you hanged and shot thrice over, Keane, for the murders, or I shall die trying."

"And you surely will," Oliver sneered silkily. And then from somewhere down the hall came the muted sound of a baby's cry. His son. Like a cool rain dousing a smoldering fire, his anger seeped out of him, leaving him momentarily shaken. He frowned at Jeffcoat, easing his fist from beneath the officer's chin, and muttered, "You're lucky my son was born today. I've some celebrating to do. It's not every day a man becomes a father." Releasing Jeffcoat with a snarl of disgust, he turned on his heel and slowly climbed the stairs.

Amidst a great clanging and clamoring, Jeffcoat shoved himself from the wall to stand in all his pompous supremacy at the foot of the stairs. His high-pitched laugh rent the air. "Enjoy it while you can, Keane. Even as we speak, the governor is reviewing my preliminary account of your involvement in the murders. Your days here are numbered, Keane. Your every movement will be watched, and you can bet I shall present the governor with a full accounting of your behavior this very day. Soon, it will all be mine, this house, Alexa, even your own flesh and blood. Do you hear me, Keane? *Keane?*"

Only the sound slamming of Oliver's chamber door finally obliterated the last echoes of Stuart Jeffcoat's voice.

At the soft knock upon the chamber door, Alexa nodded at Shura and draped the blanket over her shoulder, concealing entirely the babe nursing at her breast. She noted well Shura's disapproving glare as Oliver's bulk filled the doorway and set her heart fluttering in her breast. He lingered there, half in, half out of the room, soundly ignoring Shura even when he shouldered past her finally, and strode into the room. Alexa dismissed the servant with a nod, and the door closed behind the woman with a sound "Harrumph!"

He paused at the foot of the four-poster and stared at her, his eyes startlingly clear and blue, his hollowed cheeks freshly shaven, his hair slightly damp and still looking in dire need of a good shearing. He'd dressed in his typical white shirt, black knee breeches and boots, and he radiated a clean masculine scent entirely too unsettling to Alexa. Despite his immense stature, the arrogant thrust of his jaw, all she knew to be so much a part of him, his fingers moved self-consciously over the bedpost. He jutted his chin toward the door. "She doesn't particularly like me," he remarked.

"I think she's trying very hard," Alexa replied truthfully.

He gazed at her intently. "Are you?"

A heat suffused her entire being and she averted her eyes to the babe nestled against her. "I— Stuart paid a brief visit." No reply. "He—lingered outside of the door, of course."

"Of course."

She tucked the blanket closer about the babe. "He wished to set a date for the wedding. He seemed a trifle upset."

"Isn't he always?"

Her head snapped up. "Oliver, what did you do?"

He seemed to ponder that, looking at his fingers encircling the thick bedpost. "I don't think I have to do much to upset the man, Alexa. He's relatively bent upon proving me a murderer." He looked at her quizzically. "Funny, that."

"Indeed." Again, she focused upon the babe, easing him from her breast and gently nestling him against her shoulder. Her eyes met Oliver's and a new pain sliced through her heart.

"Tell me you're not going to marry that fool."

She swallowed back hot tears. "Would you like to hold your son?"

He hesitated a moment, his lips parting, and then he moved slowly toward her.

"Sit here upon the bed," she said, patting the coverlet beside her. The bed dipped beneath his weight and he stared at her, at the babe, his fists clenching in his lap. "Relax your arms, Oliver, or you're likely to break him." Oliver shifted and frowned at her, only to dissolve like melting sugar when she placed the infant in his arms. The child was but a fraction of the length of Oliver's forearm, all but disappearing within his embrace.

"Alexa," he breathed huskily.

She leaned closer against his side, peering over his shoulder at the tiny face in repose. "He looks like your father. And you."

No reply, yet one long finger brushed over the thick tufts of black hair crowning the tiny head, hair as dark and thick as Oliver's, and Gabriel's before him. "We have to name him, you know," she murmured, sensing the stiffening in him.

He turned to her, his gaze searching hers yet beseeching all the same. "Alexa—"

"I want to name him after your father," she whispered, then a sudden yearning enveloped her, a yearning to fling her arms about him and drive all the cynicism from his heart, if only she could. Gingerly, she stroked the chiseled jawline, then parted her lips and drew his mouth to hers. It was a tentative kiss at first, soft, then sweetly poignant, until she felt the heat of his hand upon her breast through the thin batiste of her nightgown and his thumb brushing over one nipple.

"Marry me," he breathed against her lips, setting the world spinning about her. "Marry me this very night, Alexa."

Dear God, how she had yearned to hear those words from him even as she dreaded the tragic rending of her heart when he did at last utter them. Yet how did one reconcile so deep a division of her mind and soul? How did one cast all finely honed and deeply ingrained suspicion and doubt to the four winds solely because one wished so desperately to believe it the right course? How did one love a man, yet still nurture doubt in him? She ached to find the proper words, to grasp at that which would banish all uncertainty from her mind.

"Time," she whispered, averting her face only to feel his mouth branding the length of her throat just as his hand flamed over her breasts. She stilled his hand beneath hers and shuddered when, even now, her nipple pushed into his palm. "Please, Oliver, give me time."

"Fine. You've got all the time you want. Tell Jeffcoat you won't marry him."

"I—I feel rather badly for him."

"A sorry reason for marrying the man," he muttered, nuzzling her throat. "I give you my word I won't pressure you, but set the poor man straight, Alexa."

"Fine," she whispered, and reveled in the feel of his hand moving over her once again.

"Tonight."

"Tonight," she repeated softly. Her soul swelled near to bursting when a triumphant rumbling filled his chest and his mouth claimed hers again in a passionate, savage kiss that threatened to snatch her sanity from her. And then a tiny wail thrust them apart with mutual laughter.

Taking the child from Oliver, she nestled him against her other breast and glanced up to find Oliver watching her with deeply smoldering eyes.

"I never thought I'd be jealous of my own son," he said wryly and bent to press soft kisses over her shoulder and her throat. "You smell like baby. . . ." He nibbled at the pearl buttons adorning the gown, then bent lower and his mouth seared the fabric covering her other breast.

"Oliver," she breathed. "No— It's not right...you shouldn't, I mean—"

"Who says?" His lips brushed over one thrusting nipple. "Don't tell me you're going to start adhering to convention after all this time? Don't you know that's one of the things I love most about you?"

Alexa shuddered with a strange pleasure and clutched at his shoulder. "You'll disturb the baby and you're...I mean, I'm—"

"You're lovely. You're wonderful. You're all I could ever want in a woman." He raised his head and gazed deeply into her eyes. "I love you desperately."

Her breath released in a soft rush. "Oh, Oliver—"

A resounding bang reverberated through the house. In one swift motion, Oliver leaped from the bed and in three strides, thrust the chamber door open. There, standing with mouth agape and eyes wide, stood a pinched and pale Eleanor Keane. A sickening dread seeped into Alexa's bones, sending a sudden chill through her. Instinctively, she drew her son closer.

"Good God," Eleanor kept repeating over and over as her eyes darted from Oliver to Alexa, the infant, and back again. "It's true. Dear God, it's true."

Oliver said something indecipherable, grasped his mother's elbow, closed the door behind him and led her down the hall. He didn't pause until he'd reached the relative privacy of his study.

"Sit down, Mother," he said as he moved behind his desk and found himself staring into the glory of the day from the windows. He felt he was seeing it all for the first time. This day his son was born. An elation even his mother couldn't squelch drifted through him.

"I most certainly will *not* sit down!" Eleanor railed. "Good God, Oliver, have you taken leave of your senses?"

A smile crossed Oliver's lips as he focused upon a gloriously colored macaw perched in a tree in the distance. "Now, why would you think such a thing, Mother?"

Eleanor grappled with her words. "Dear God in heaven, the entire financial world is reeling from the news that you disappeared without a word to anyone! Poor Daphne has been sedated for the past two months. Her father—well, God knows what the man truly thinks, he's so blasted busy. Your lawyers knew nothing. Indeed, they all looked as ill as I've felt since you left. Thank heaven Cyril cabled me the moment you arrived. I've been on a damn ship ever since. Oliver, blast you, *look* at me!"

With a certain calmness, Oliver turned about and settled himself in his chair. His eyes fell upon his father's journal sitting directly before him. Odd, though somehow fitting, that the journal should find itself here, between him and his mother. A coolness of manner proved easy to accomplish and he glanced up at his mother. And smiled, one which never reached his eyes.

Eleanor stared at him, then she, too, gave him a wavering smile and fumbled her way into a chair. "Oliver," she breathed, looking closely at him. "Ah, now I see it much more clearly. Well, let me just say I never had a doubt as to your abilities to seduce the girl, but to go so far as to get the chit with child—*well!*" A faint curl twisted her lips. "How very much like your father you are, in that regard only, of course."

"Of course," Oliver repeated with a deliberate sarcasm that was very likely lost upon his mother.

"He, too, was so very..." Her lips compressed as if she sucked on a lemon. "Potent."

"Odd, that." Oliver settled back in his chair. "You had only one child."

Eleanor fidgeted with her taffeta skirt. "Dear God, I couldn't bear the very thought of... that is... he was like an animal, incapable of controlling those appalling urges of his."

"He was your husband."

She glared at him. "And I was his wife, the woman he spurned, then shamed while he flouted his whore Lily Fairfield."

"You truly believe that, don't you? Over the course of fifteen years, you've been able to convince yourself of all that. I suppose you had to, seeing as how crucial it was that I readily believe you."

Eleanor swallowed with difficulty. "What the devil are you saying?"

"None of it is true, Mother. None of it."

Eleanor blinked rapidly, clutched a hand to her bosom, then seemed to force an airy laugh. "Oliver, come now, stop jabbering nonsense and let's get to the bottom of all this. You've obviously gone one step further in accomplishing our scheme to control the plantation, I see. It was a bit of a shock, of course, hearing about the baby, but now that the girl has been duly compromised and entirely humiliated as any woman would be, given these circumstances, I presume she will hand over her share of the plantation without much ado. Cyril tells me she's to marry that silly British officer. All well and good, I say. And she can keep the brat, as well. We don't need that sort of illegitimate-child scandal following us back to Chicago. That sort of peccadillo makes a man unfit to be mentioned in decent homes." She arched an eyebrow and smoothed her skirts with a trembling hand. "How very prudent of you to have returned to tidy all this up, Oliver, but I cannot help but wonder at your atrocious lack of *timing*. It will take *months* to dissipate the rumors once you return to Chicago, and God alone knows if poor Daphne will *ever* forgive you."

Oliver clenched and unclenched his fist around a solid gold letter opener while he counted to ten three times over. "I'm not returning to Chicago," he said with deceptive softness. "And I'm not going to marry Daphne MacAdoo."

Eleanor's eyes bulged. "But you *must!* You cannot expect to live forever off the relative pittance you'll receive once you sell this hellhole to that Pomeroy fellow. You *belong* in Chicago, Oliver, behind a desk, making loads and loads of money."

"I belong with Alexa and my son. Here."

"No—"

"Yes, Mother." Oliver gave his mother a hard look. "I'm going to marry her as soon as she decides she'll have me." His smile felt as if it stretched from ear to ear. "And I'm going to be a sugar farmer, just like my father. I'm going to feel that hot sun on my face every day and I'm going to sweat and toil alongside those workers, negotiating sugar from cane with all the fervor that my father did. And just like my father, I'm going to fight for the preservation of this land if it means waging war with men like Pomeroy and the damned governor himself until the day I die. Oh, and one more thing. I'm going to hunt down my father's murderer and see him hanged." He leaned his forearms on the desk and drawled, "Care for a drink, Mother? You look like you need one."

Eleanor visibly shook upon her chair, her feathered hat bobbing frantically over her head, her eyes wild and glazed. "N-no, I—I cannot believe this. Y-you—we had an agreement. We had a plan."

"*You* had a plan, Mother." Oliver moved to the sideboard and the brandy decanter awaiting him. "From the very start, mine was altogether different."

"B-but you agreed to it all—and all the while you—"

"I was in love with Alexa from the moment I saw her." He pressed a glass into Eleanor's hand and walked to the windows once more. "I wanted *her,* only her. You more than anyone know that when I go after something, I get it. Everything else became secondary to me. Yet, I refused to see it while I was here. Some part of me probably believed I was going along with your scheme, and some of that was all mixed up with a cynical revenge I sought against my father. And God knows I refused to believe I was a weaker man than I had forever believed him to be, erroneously so, as it turns out. Alexa Fairfield was the last woman I would have ever wished to fall in love with. But she has possessed me..." His words momentarily caught in his throat beneath a surge of emotion. "Fool that I was, I didn't realize it until I'd returned to Chicago. And there I was, hours from signing on with MacAdoo, attaining all I'd ever wanted, and then I knew. I loved her. It was that simple. All I ever *needed* was here, with her. I didn't even know about the baby until I returned." He turned from the windows and gazed long and hard at his mother, a peculiar chill chasing through him at the unnatural gleam in her eyes. "It's done, Mother. Indeed, I cabled Theodore MacAdoo the day after I returned. Daphne is now free to marry her English lord. Everyone, it seems, is happy."

"B-but your fortune—your dreams—you professed you'd never love any woman!"

"Perhaps because I didn't know what love was, thanks to—" His voice caught. "And as for those dreams, they were *your* dreams, Mother. I was but your vehicle to attaining those dreams." He moved around his desk, feeling a strange tightening deep in his belly. His fingers wrapped about his father's leather journal and he waved it before her. "It's all here. All the sordid details of your leaving here fifteen years ago. All his frustration of being married to a woman who despised the very sight of him, a woman who he came to realize had married him solely because of his standing in Chicago society."

Eleanor lunged from her chair, her teeth baring, her brandy glass spilling to the floor. "Yes, and what woman wouldn't, if she'd had as squalid a childhood as I? Why, fate alone decreed I meet him when I did, and of course I clutched at the opportunity! I was able to tolerate his exercising of his rights while we were in Chicago. But then we had to visit this horrible place... and then he met *her.*"

"He fell in love with the island, with being a plantation owner, and chose to remain here," Oliver countered through a tightening jaw. "An easy enough thing to do when one's soul yearns for such a passion in life."

"No!" Eleanor snapped. "*She* bewitched him from the moment he saw her. *She* made him buy this plantation, and he cast all thoughts of me aside, all that he had accomplished in Chicago. And she even visited here... until I saw the way he looked at her and banished her from the house. Good God, he was in love with her."

"He remained loyal to you, even after you left here. Something you couldn't even manage to do while you lived here."

Eleanor paled and sagged into her chair. "No—"

Oliver's rage ignited deep within his soul, a rage fostered by years of being deceived. The saying of it all somehow seemed easier than his reading of it had been. "For years, you banished your husband from your bed, yet you welcomed another man, isn't that what happened, Mother? Didn't Father discover you and one of his servants? Wasn't that the true reason for your *fleeing* here? Did he not vow to keep the incident secret, to protect you if you agreed to leave immediately? Was it then that you plotted to turn me against him, solely to use me for your own purposes? And how easy I made it for you, a lad young enough to be molded by your cynicism and governed by his own deep-seated revenge, a revenge and hatred you stoked almost daily."

She clutched at his arms, tears spilling from her eyes. "No, I—I loved you! Y-you were my only son!"

"A son you often spoke of as the mere sprouting of an animal's seed. Yes, he wrote of that, as well." Oliver grappled with the demon writhing in his soul. "I doubt you've ever loved anyone, Mother. Yet, some part of me refuses to believe a woman could be so harsh. I look at Alexa . . . I see the way she holds our child, the love in her eyes from the first moment he drew breath, and before, even when carrying him became torturous. A mother's instinct it is. I cannot imagine how deep your desire for vengeance must lie to deny me my own father—how twisted your very soul must be with greed—" He shoved a hand through his hair, then gripped her upper arms so tightly a cry escaped her lips. "God knows, I should forgive you this, but I cannot. Not when you speak so casually of forsaking my son, your own grandchild, solely to return to Chicago unscathed. It's all you've ever cared about, this accumulation of status. It means nothing to me. *Nothing*. I doubt it ever has."

His breath released in a rush and he thrust her from him, moving to the door. He paused, his hand upon the door handle. "I am wholly my father's son. I have come to realize his spirit lives and breathes in me with a ferocity I can deny no longer. Through his journal and because of Alexa, I have come to know him. He deserved my love, not my hatred, my admiration, not my contempt. His memory merits that I live as he would have wished me to. And I shall." He turned the door handle, and then she was clawing at his sleeve, her nails digging into his flesh.

"But what of me?" she wailed hysterically. "What am I to do now?"

He looked down at her, and saw a pitiful shell of what she had forever yearned to be. A fleeting sympathy drifted through him and was gone. "Go back to Chicago, Mother. Certainly you've enough money to live off of until you can find someone else to exploit. Some unsuspecting, wealthy older gentleman, perhaps?"

Frantically, she shook her head. "No, the money, it's gone. It's all gone. I—I—"

"You squandered it."

She nodded and all sympathy fled him. He strode to the desk, dug deep in one drawer and withdrew a heavy sack of coins. This he thrust into his mother's hands before he flung the door wide. "Spend that wisely," he intoned, noting well the sudden tightness of her jaw, the glittering deep in her eyes. "It's all you'll ever get from me again. Goodbye, Mother. I'm certain Cyril will show you the way out."

He had taken three strides down the hall when her voice rang shrilly after him. "You will regret this, Oliver. Trust me."

"I was foolish enough to trust you once," he muttered without turning around. "And I never will again."

Chapter Nineteen

Alexa grasped Oliver's extended hand and gingerly stepped from the landaulet. For what seemed the hundredth time since they'd departed Bellefontaine, she touched a gloved hand to her hair, then fidgeted with the low-scooped neckline of her gown. Oliver caught her hand, anchoring it beneath his upon his arm, and led her up the wide marble stairs that marked the entrance to Alleyndale Hall.

"Quit doing that or I'm going to ravish you right here, woman," he said when she again tugged upon her bodice.

Giving him a scathing, sideways glance, she allowed her gaze to linger momentarily upon the high curves of her bosom, then flushed and focused instead upon the marble steps. "Why the devil did I allow you to talk me into wearing this?"

"I thought you liked it," he replied softly, his hand upon the small of her back, guiding her through the columned entrance.

"I do...I mean, I did, but—" Of course she did. What woman wouldn't adore so elegant a gown, one highly fashioned of white silk taffeta overlaid with shimmering gold faille? The sleeves sat just at her shoulders and pouffed to her elbows. The beaded bodice was fitted to a point just below her waist and draped in a sweeping flared skirt with just a hint of bustle. Oliver had presented her with the gown on the very day the invitation had arrived from Pinkus Pomeroy announcing his Spring Festival Ball at Alleyndale Hall. He'd also bought her elbow-length white gloves, white silk two-inch-heeled shoes, lace garters, sheer silk stockings and a scandalous chemise that had stoked the ever-present flame in his eyes. A slow heat had filled her when her fingers drifted over the sheer chemise. Oliver's intent was all too clear. Shura, perhaps sensing this, warned Alexa against indulging in any sort of foolery until the babe was at least several months old. Oliver knew this. Yet, though the baby was but two weeks old, and Alexa still moved from time to time with a certain lingering stiffness, something told her that Oliver could content himself with whatever she chose to allow him. Odd, but as she glanced up at him, so very tall and darkly handsome, all she could envision was the joy to be found within his arms. Somehow, day by day, he'd managed to diffuse her doubts one by one, with such a deftness of touch even she had been unaware of it.

Indeed, he had done nothing extraordinary, or so one would think, looking back. He'd kept to his remarkably busy itinerary after the baby was born, rising well before dawn to peek in on her and baby Gabriel before closeting himself in his study to pore over the ledgers until the sun rose. His days he spent outdoors in the fields or at the *ingenio,* returning to the house for meals that he shared with Alexa, be it spread upon her coverlet while she rested or nursed the baby, or grandly laid out in the dining room. Evenings they spent together with the baby. It had been on one such occasion, on the floor in front of a fire, that he had told her of his last encounter with Eleanor...and all that he had learned from his father's journal. Since that fateful afternoon, they had not seen or heard from Eleanor and thus assumed she had returned to Chicago. Despite the bitterness lacing his voice and the harshness of his words, Alexa had glimpsed a sorrow deep in his eyes, and her heart swelled anew. So many questions answered...the demons of Oliver's deeply passionate hatred for his father finally put to rest.

Her fingers wrapped about his arm, feeling the strength beneath that fine wool. He looked so dashing and wonderful tonight. How very natural to imagine spending the rest of her life as she had these past two weeks...with this man.

He glanced down at her with that wicked gleam in his eye. "Yes, my dear, I believe there's much to like about your dress."

Alexa resisted the urge to fan herself. "Stop looking at me like that, Oliver."

"I can't help myself."

"I feel like I'm falling out of my bodice."

"You look like you are, too, my dear. That's why every man in this room is holding his breath."

Alexa glanced about the entry. Indeed, more than a few of the men in attendance seemed remarkably captivated by her bosom. "You're enjoying this, aren't you?" she asked archly.

"Immensely," he murmured. "You're the envy of every woman in this room. And the embodiment of every man's desires. Mine especially."

Alexa fidgeted and pasted on a deceptively serene smile. "I feel so...peculiar...and fat."

"Lush," Oliver corrected her, his hand slipping easily about her waist. "Just the way I like my woman."

My woman. The very sound of it set her aglow. With a sigh, she dismissed him and contemplated her discomfiture. "Perhaps I should have ventured from the house before tonight." Her gaze found his. "I haven't been away from him since the day he was born. Perhaps we should leave. Shura won't know what to do if Gabriel awakens. He'll cry because he's hungry and I won't be there for him. I'll be here, being selfish and frivolous and wallowing in all these stares."

He caught her hand in his just as she turned to flee, and drew her fingers to his lips. "Darling girl, Gabriel and Shura are fine. He was asleep before we left and he'll sleep until we return." Again, he drew her hand beneath his and his eyes drifted over the crowd, then focused upon her. "So when are you going to marry me?" he asked, his eyes gleaming with unspoken desires. "Could it be you've come to your senses? You do have a lovely flush to your cheeks this evening."

Alexa shot him a sideways glance. "You would, too, Oliver, if your bodice was too tight."

A wicked light flashed in his eyes as he led her into the sumptuous ballroom. "My trousers are too tight, my dear.

Have you a remedy? Cold swims in the pond are becoming rather tedious."

Alexa tried to look bored despite the heightening of her color. "Imagine that."

"Perhaps I haven't shown myself to be desperate enough for you. Shall I drop upon bended knee here?"

She clutched at his arm. "Good grief, don't do that."

"Why not? There isn't a man alive who would blame me." He retrieved two glasses of champagne from a passing servant splendidly outfitted in pale blue silk waistcoat and knee breeches. Pressing a glass into Alexa's fingers, Oliver took a long drink and said, "Ah, hell, here comes your pet Jeffcoat to spoil all the fun. And wearing his heart on his sleeve for all to see. Persistent little fellow, isn't he?"

Alexa's heart sank to her slippered toes when she, too, observed Stuart Jeffcoat all but shoving his way through the crush toward them. In as kind a manner as she was capable, she had informed Stuart nearly two weeks prior that she had reconsidered accepting his proposal of marriage. Circumstances being what they were, the birth of the baby...why, emotional havoc seemed as good a reason as any for her change of heart. She had confessed to not knowing at all how she felt from day to day and to suffering from recurring bouts of uncontrollable weeping. Thus, she hadn't thought it quite fair to imprison him in an engagement that was likely to become interminable. He had turned a most peculiar shade of green and had vehemently accused her of being in love with Oliver, the murderer. Despite his sputtering and frothing, she had done her very best to deny that this was indeed the reason without lying outright to the man, and had apparently failed miserably. Only after he had again proclaimed undying love and devotion for her, and had vowed to see Oliver hanged for murder, did he finally take himself from Bellefontaine. She remembered the look in his eyes before the door slammed behind him . . . a hint of sorrow amidst what looked to be a burning thirst for revenge.

He had the very same look about him this evening. Only tonight, Lady Penelope Alleyne was on his arm. They paused directly at Alexa's side, Stuart looking pained as he nodded a crisp greeting, and his gaze slid over Alexa. A polished Lady Penelope rose above all her reams of sumptuous emerald taffeta and devoured Oliver with one sweep of her luminous eyes.

"Who would have thought an unwed mother would be the belle of the ball?" Lady Penelope crooned at Alexa through a fake smile that set Alexa's own teeth on edge. "But you've somehow managed to set the place abuzz. Society's darling, aren't you, just like your mother was. Indeed, you're making motherhood fashionable." Penelope's smile wavered as it lingered upon Alexa's décolletage. "My, even *I* might consider it. It certainly seems to have its advantages." Punctuating her point, Lady Penelope again allowed herself a good long look at Oliver. "Mr. Keane, you're looking extremely well. All those long days beneath a tropical sun, eh?"

Oliver's hand moved slowly over Alexa's back, sending warm shivers tumbling through her, "No," he drawled with a dazzling smile. "I believe it's fatherhood. Does remarkable things for a man."

Lady Penelope arched a dangerous eyebrow, her lips curving seductively. "Is that so? Bold words for a scoundrel like yourself, Mr. Keane, a man who could have his pick of paramours. But then again, I suppose you've a score of illegitimate children littered throughout the world. That sort of thing can be habit."

"I've only one child," Oliver replied with an ominous softness. "My son, Gabriel."

Lady Penelope looked as though she shivered from the inside out. "Oooh, you've a possessive look about you. One cannot help but wonder then, as most of these gentlefolk will from time to time, why it is you don't make an honest woman out of your doxy here, hmm?"

Stuart Jeffcoat's jaw fell open with a decided *plop,* then quickly snapped closed beneath a look of bitter hatred he fixed upon Oliver. But it was the tensing of the muscles in the forearm beneath Alexa's fingers that brought the words tripping from her tongue. Anything to wipe that snide look from Penelope Alleyne's face, as the woman tried to make out that she knew and understood far more than Alexa ever would about Oliver, that this entire roomful of people had passed such a harsh judgment upon him. As if he were deserving of the very worst of reputations. Scoundrel... heartless beast devoid of feeling for his own family, notorious rakehell consumed with his pursuit of power and money...

No! How could she allow another moment to pass without rectifying their misconceptions? He was none of these! Indeed, she doubted whether he had ever been, even in his darkest hour. He was deeply caring, loving, compassionate to a fault, and dedicated to his work. He had laid bare his soul for her, had asked her in a dozen different ways to be his bride, had kept his passions at bay in deference to her wishes, had acted the part of gallant suitor so divinely...and still she had not found it within her to let go her reservations. All those doubts and fears long stoked by the same rumor and misconception held by these very people. Could she have been so blindly foolish?

Swallowing back the tears stinging the backs of her eyes, Alexa forced an airy laugh and leaned closer to Oliver such that his arm rested with bold familiarity against the underside of her breast. When Penelope Alleyne took obvious note of this, as did Oliver with a hooded glance, Alexa's heart soared and her voice rang with triumph. "My goodness, who's been spreading such rumors, Lady Penelope? Surely you've misunderstood. Why, I thought you were on the very forefront of all the gossip."

"I am." Lady Penelope bristled, her winged eyebrows puckering nonetheless. "Yes, indeed, of course, I am."

"Odd," Alexa mused, her gaze colliding with Oliver's. "Then you must have simply forgotten. You see, Oliver and I shall be married within the week."

"You what?"

Perhaps Lady Penelope and Stuart Jeffcoat shrieked in unison. Alexa would never know. She was joyously in love, rapturously so. Oliver stared at her as if dumbstruck for several moments, then swiftly drew her fingers to his lips. His breath was hot upon her skin even through her gloves, and he seemed to murmur unintelligibly against her fingertips. And then he was leading her through the crowd, mindless of the openmouthed stares they received. Alexa couldn't have tempered her smile if her very life had depended upon it, and the flush staining her cheeks and heating her bosom seemed to blossom with her every glance at Oliver's wonderfully tousled head and wide shoulders. Without pause, he led her through the entry and down a long hall lined with flickering sconces. At the end of the hall he hesitated, then forcefully opened a door, tugging her into the dimly lit room and slamming the door behind them.

His name fell from her lips in a gasp as he spun her and crushed her in his arms, filling her senses with the heady feel of impassioned male. His mouth claimed hers in a savage kiss, his tongue plundering, retreating, and plundering again. He crooned her name over and over and his hands claimed her waist, her hips, then pushed her breasts entirely from her bodice. Alexa nearly swooned at the force of his passions unleashed when he bent to spread kisses over her unbridled bosom. She gripped his shoulders trying to maintain her balance when he filled his hands with her breasts and brushed his thumbs again and again over the swollen peaks.

"Oliver, I love you so."

"Yes . . . Say it again, my love."

And she did say those once-elusive words, again and again, as a need so sweet filled her she nearly cried out.

"Tomorrow," he rasped against her breast. "You're marrying me tomorrow before you change your mind."

"Not tonight?" she whispered with a smile, sinking her fingers into the luxurious length of his hair.

"Give me a minute." He drew her nipple deep into his mouth . . . and then the door burst open and Pinkus Pomeroy's voice rang shrilly about them.

". . . will be just a matter of time before we may have to use force and— Oh, what have we here?"

Oliver had never moved so swiftly, spinning about and shielding Alexa behind him with one sweep of his arm. Her face flamed with embarrassment as she readjusted her bodice and pressed cool fingers against her swollen lips. She could almost feel Pomeroy's leering grin.

"Evening, Keane." Pomeroy's bulbous head appeared over Oliver's shoulder. "Miss Fairfield, of course." The sly cackle. "Well, Keane, need I say there isn't a man here tonight who wouldn't give his...er... A man after my own heart, and just the fellow I was looking for."

"Indeed," Oliver replied in that deeply resonant voice that sent a thrill through Alexa even now.

"My good friend Fitzhugh and I were discussing your plantation, Bellefontaine. Got a minute, Keane?"

"Of course he does," Alexa interjected, placing a hand upon Oliver's arm when he gave her a quizzical look. "Talk to them, Oliver," she whispered. "I'm in no condition—"

"Neither am I, my dear."

"I'm going to take some air."

"I'll find you."

With a cursory nod at the leering Pinkus Pomeroy and his companion Fitzhugh, Alexa lifted her skirts and with chin held high, left the room.

"So," Pomeroy said, releasing his breath as if he'd held it until Alexa had drifted from the room. "Enjoying yourself, I see, eh, Keane?"

Oliver clasped his hands behind his back. "Until a few minutes ago, yes, I was."

Pomeroy chuckled and indicated two chairs for Fitzhugh and Oliver. "Can I get you a cocktail, Keane? A green swizzle, perhaps? A wonderful concoction it is, made of white rum, falernum and a sprig of wild worm bush. Tasty stuff, I tell you. The established corrective of West Indian languor. I don't suppose you need that, eh? Ah, hell, consider it the solace of all who thirst." At Oliver's swift shake of his head, Pomeroy seemed to squat, then sank into his own deep chair with a great dispelling of air. "Had a tour of the place, Keane?" he asked, producing three fat cigars and offering one to Oliver. "No, eh? A disciplined man if there ever was one. Well, you must see the place, you know. We've done remarkable things here. It's become a showpiece for the island. Revenues are going up, up, up! And the footmen . . . did you see the footmen? Those darkies look divine in those silk stockings, don't they? I tell you I've had bona fide offers for several of them from British gentry." Pomeroy waved his cigar and cackled with glee. "Didn't I tell you, Keane?"

Oliver shifted his weight from one foot to the other. "State your business, Pomeroy."

"Ah, yes, you've your—" The cigar waved toward the door. "A surprising wench, that girl. Held her own with that plantation for going on ten months now."

"Miss Fairfield will be my wife before the week is out, Pomeroy. How fortunate that you have heeded her reminding you that she is indeed half owner of Bellefontaine. I trust you will accord her the same respect you do me?"

Pomeroy let out a huge guffaw. "Bristly fellow, aren't you, for a man who just lost his fortune. Still carrying your father's sputtering torch, I see, though I can't blame you for wanting to marry that girl. Maybe fooled with your head a bit, though. We should talk about it. Funny, but I thought a man like you would have decided it was high time to get your nose in politics. You know, take a senate seat now that the business challenges are gone."

"I believe my biggest challenge has yet to be met," Oliver said obliquely.

Pomeroy puffed on his cigar and grinned. "You're looking at him."

"We're not selling."

"So I've heard. Name your price."

"I don't believe you heard me."

"Life could get very difficult for you."

Oliver's gaze closed in on the other man somewhere amidst all that smoke. How very easy to believe the man capable of setting fire to cane fields, to entire wings of houses solely to scare plantation owners into selling. "Make my life difficult, Pomeroy, and I'll make yours a living hell," Oliver snarled.

Pomeroy stared at him, then jerked upright in his chair. "No need for theatrics now, is there, Keane?"

Oliver jutted his chin toward the sideboard. "Fix yourself a drink, Pomeroy. I've a proposition for you."

Alexa smiled and nodded her way through the ballroom, receiving a nonstop gush of congratulations on her upcoming nuptials. Lady Penelope had obviously wasted little time in reestablishing herself as the peg about which the gossip on the island turned. Alexa could only imagine the speed with which the woman had circumnavigated the ballroom spreading the latest news. Odd for a woman who seemed entirely distressed by the news, no doubt because she'd had her own plans for Oliver. Odder still that neither she nor Stuart Jeffcoat were anywhere to be seen since Alexa had returned to the ballroom.

She paused to nibble at a few canapés and glanced about for some sign of Oliver. Just then, a footman appeared at her elbow.

"Miss Fairfield?" he intoned, and at her nod, presented her with a folded slip of parchment. He then bowed and disappeared into the crowd. With a slight frown, Alexa unfolded the note.

Meet me in the gazebo near the back fountain.

O

With a smile curving her lips, Alexa read and reread the note before tucking it into her palm and hastening through the ballroom.

"Romantic man, where are you?" Alexa's voice drifted out over the moonlit lawns as she made her way from the manse. A delicious anticipation set her insides to trembling and her feet to moving swiftly over the flagstone path. The gardens here were much like those at Bellefontaine, sumptuous and heavy with fragrance, sweeping like a lush carpet along either side of the path. Up ahead, set high above the gardens surrounding it, was the gazebo.

She paused at the foot of the steep steps leading to the gazebo and glanced about, suddenly aware of the deep isolation here. Over her shoulder and through a tangle of brush, Alleyndale Hall loomed like a brilliantly lit jewel. The strains of the orchestra's melody wafted upon the slight breeze stirring Alexa's hair. The night was hot, yet she felt a shiver sneak through her when again she looked up those stairs at the dark gazebo. All was so very quiet . . . yet Oliver could be exceedingly quiet when he sought to be. Indeed, with Oliver near, this setting could be achingly romantic. . . the full yellow moon and fragrant garden, even the solitary stillness so very conducive to whatever he had in mind. No doubt he awaited her in the darkness, his arms ready to sweep about her.

With little hesitation, she lifted her skirts and swiftly mounted the steps. At the very top, she pushed the latticework door slightly open, listening to the lonely creaking of its hinges.

"Oliver?" she whispered into the darkness, taking several steps into the gazebo. "Oliver, if you don't cease this foolishness, I won't marry you. Please." Her voice echoed hollowly about her and she stared at the shadows cast by the moonlight streaming through the high latticed walls surrounding her. A peculiar scent tickled her nostrils, a scent not unlike that of the kerosene used in the boiling of sugarcane. "O-Oliver, you're frightening me."

Silence. And then the scream of some wild night creature in the jungle beyond pierced the air and caught Alexa's breath in her throat. Her heart pounded in her ears as she moved deeper into the shadows to peer from the lattice at the gardens below.

Something set the hairs upon the back of her neck standing on edge. A sound . . . like the creaking of those wooden steps beneath a man's foot. And then silence. It was he . . . it had to be, of course. Who else?

She spun about just as the lattice door creaked closed and a bolt was shoved in place. With mounting alarm, Alexa lunged for the door, her fingers grappling for the latch in the semidarkness. She gasped when her fingers closed about the handle, then tugged, again and again. The door refused to open.

"Locked in. . . ." Her mind refused to believe it. "Hullo!" she shouted through the lattice even as she heard the unmuffled sound of footsteps retreating down the stairs. She pounded on the door. "No, come back! You locked me in! Please, you—"

The cold sweat of terror engulfed her just as the scent of kerosene did, and the smell of smoke...and the flash of flame somewhere at the base of the gazebo. And then fire exploded around her.

Chapter Twenty

With a grin, Oliver turned at the soft touch upon his arm. "Alexa—" His grin collapsed when his eyes met with Lady Penelope Alleyne. He should have known by the touch. A trifle too clinging, too clawing it was, to have been Alexa's.

"Hullo," Penelope breathed, as if she melted into her word. Or perhaps the champagne sloshing in the glass dangling from her hand had proved the better of decorum this night. Her lips drifted apart as she traced a nail down the mother-of-pearl buttons of his shirt. "Looking for someone?"

He shoved her wrist aside. "Yes. Have you seen Alexa?"

The persistent Penelope cast a glance about the crowded ballroom. "And if I had, why would I tell you? Indeed, I'm wondering how the girl could have left your brawny side. Either she's supremely stupid or she has an inamorato, Oliver, someone you know nothing about. It's all too common. You *have* been gone for months, remember? A woman can get awfully lonely."

Oliver could only shake his head with disgust and seek to shoulder past her. Again, her claws dug into his hand as she clutched at his arm. "Oliver, I cannot help but wonder what could have been for us if Alexa Fairfield didn't exist." She licked her lips and slid his arm against her breasts. "You've thought about it . . . I know you have."

"To be perfectly honest, I haven't ever given you a second thought. Good evening." Despite the sagging of Penelope's jaw, he reclaimed his arm and shoved his way through the crowd. One swift glance about the ballroom told him Alexa wasn't there. As he made his way to the double doors leading to the rear terrace, many who had never once spoken to him blocked his path to offer hearty congratulations on the birth of his son and his upcoming nuptials. Dinner invitations were extended amidst much slapping upon the back. Many remarked on his resemblance to his father. Several even offered their quiet but fervent support for his struggle to retain control of Bellefontaine. Alexa's many virtues as a businesswoman were toasted and toasted again, and it was some time before Oliver finally made his way onto the back terrace. The place was all but deserted. Where the hell had she gone?

"Ah, Keane! I hear congratulations are in order!" Yet another of the Beefstake and Tripe Club crowd slapped him on the back and vigorously pumped his hand. "Looking for your bride, I'll wager," the fellow said with a grin and a wink. "I believe I saw her just a few minutes past taking the back path there...the one that leads to the gazebo. Have a right-o time, I say!"

Oliver muttered his thanks and looked out over the moonlit landscape at the dark gazebo. Why the hell would she venture all the way out there by herself? His lips curved at a delicious thought. Adjusting his cravat high under his chin, he set out with great loping strides across the terrace. What better spot for a romantic tryst than a dark and deserted gazebo?

He'd just reached the flagstone path when suddenly a fireball exploded before his eyes. A tremendous roar shook the ground beneath his feet. For what seemed an eternity he stared at the flaming gazebo... and then he ran, as hard and fast as a man could, on legs that seemed suddenly filled with lead. His lungs had been sapped of all air by a terror that engulfed him like a giant vulture's talons, clawing at his vitals.

"Alexa!" Her name seemed torn from his throat in great wheezes. He whipped his coat from his back as he ran, barely pausing when he reached the steep flight of wooden steps. Sparks whisked around him and sputtered into the sky. Smoke billowed in choking clouds. Yet he took those stairs three at a time, ignoring the flames licking at his legs. There was no other way to reach her if she was still in there . . . no way . . .

God . . . no . . . The flames had engulfed the base of the structure and shot upward as if propelled by some demon's hand. Moments . . . only moments from now the entire place would crumple in a heap of flaming timber. Steps collapsed beneath his feet. For one terrifying moment, the entire structure seemed to shudder. He reached the door, hauled once, twice upon it, then smashed his fist again and again into the lattice. Despite the flames lapping at him from all directions, he felt nothing but a mind-numbing terror as he drove his fist into the wood, shouting her name and tasting blood in his mouth. Beneath the force of one vicious kick, the door shattered and he lunged through a wall of flame into the gazebo. She was there . . . crumpled on the floor directly in the center of all that flame and blinding smoke . . . doubled over.

He swept her into his arms, and spun about only to pause beneath the chilling sound of timber succumbing to flame. With a bellow of raw fury, he plunged through the flaming doorway and down what remained of the stairs. One by one they splintered and dissolved. He was cast into flaming space . . . only to land half on his knees in a lush flowering bush. Instinct prevailed and he rolled as he landed, drawing Alexa on top of him as they fell. He lay there, staring at the sparks and flame billowing into the night sky. He finally became acutely aware of the scent of gardenia above the smoke...and then slender arms clutched at his shoulders and she was kissing him . . . on his chest, his neck, his face. Her tears spilled over his face, and he closed his eyes, crushing her against him. She wept uncontrollably, coughing and blubbering until he silenced her with the pressure of his lips on hers.

"Oliver—Oliver," she said over and over. "What would have happened . . . what if you hadn't come?"

"I came." He squeezed her near, refusing to ponder anything else. "I—" The words caught in his throat. "I couldn't live on this earth without you. I'd be a man lost."

"No." She pressed her fingers to his lips and trembled in his arms. "We're—good grief, we landed in a gardenia bush."

His hands swept over her back and ribs. "Are you hurt?"

"No, just the smoke. What of you? Dear God, look at your hands." She glanced up at him through a tangle of smoke-blackened hair, her cheeks smudged with soot and tears. An ache filled his very being and he cupped her face in his bloodied hands... hands that only now had begun to ache.

"Come, my treasure, let's get the hell out of this thing."

They had just extricated themselves from the bush when a panting Stuart Jeffcoat skidded to a halt beside them. He seemed momentarily dumbstruck, his jaw opening and closing, his eyes bulging from his head.

"I say, Alexa! My God, I—I—"

With a strangled curse, Oliver snatched the kerosene can from Jeffcoat's hand. "What the hell is this?"

"I was going to ask you the very same, Keane. I found it in the bushes over there."

"This is kerosene," Oliver said.

"Odd," Alexa murmured. "I thought I smelled kerosene when I first reached the gazebo but—"

Realization took hold in Oliver's mind. His eyes darted to the gazebo, now nothing but a heap of flaming timber. "Good God—"

"I say, Alexa, what were you doing out here?" Stuart asked.

"Oliver was to meet me at the gazebo."

Oliver's head snapped about. "Who told you that?"

She frowned at him. "Why, you did, of course. You sent the note requesting me to meet you here."

Oliver opened his mouth and stars exploded before his eyes beneath a slamming of pain into his jaw. His head snapped back yet he lunged for Jeffcoat, driving the smaller man flat on his back into the ground before the British officer could land another punch.

"You bloody tried to kill her!" Jeffcoat screamed, his fists glancing off of Oliver's chest and jaw as the two men rolled over and over across the flagstone path. "I knew it! You were going to kill her, too! I'll have you hanged for this!"

With one surge of strength, Oliver slung his leg across Jeffcoat's and pinned his arms to the ground. With chest heaving, Oliver sneered, "And what would the governor say if I told him it was *you* who appeared with a can of kerosene in your hands?" His fingers tightened about Jeffcoat's wrists until the other man growled with pain. "It was you who set the trap, Jeffcoat. You who wrote the damned note to lure her out here. It was you who wanted her dead so you could have your twisted revenge. You knew you'd lost her."

"No!" Jeffcoat wailed, his head shaking vigorously. "I couldn't kill her! I love her!"

"Never more than me." Oliver jerked Jeffcoat to his feet. "Tell it to the governor."

Alexa rushed toward them. "Oliver, no. Stuart could not—"

From out of the darkness came a high-pitched shout. "Keane! Keane! What the devil…my gazebo! Good God, my gazebo!"

Pinkus Pomeroy, waddling as fast as his pudgy legs could manage, skidded along the path to a breathless halt. Behind him pushed a crowd of elegantly garbed men alongside footmen carrying buckets of water. As they ran past shouting, Pomeroy doubled over, his hands braced against his knees as he fought to catch his breath. In the eerie shadows cast by the leaping flames, his face glowed with perspiration and disbelief. "How the hell—? Look at you, Keane! Miss Fairfield! It's this house, I tell you. At first I thought that talk about it being haunted was all mere rubbish. But we've a ghost, no doubt about it. Leaves doors open all over the house. Walks the upstairs halls at night. That sort of thing a Brit will pay for and enjoy. But this—and that fire that killed old Sir Reynold…" Pomeroy shook his head. "It *is* a damned ghost!"

"Not unless ghosts use kerosene." Oliver hoisted the kerosene can. "The fire was intentionally set."

Pomeroy blinked. "Good God, someone's after me."

"No, I believe Miss Fairfield was to be the victim."

Pomeroy's jaw sagged. "Miss Fairfield? Who the devil—?"

Oliver focused his eyes on Pomeroy. "Then again, I, too, could have been the prey. Or was it some scare tactic perhaps? Funny, but I'd thought we'd come to an agreement, Pomeroy."

Pomeroy gulped. With shaking hands, he snatched at a wrinkled handkerchief hanging from his pocket and dabbed his beaded upper lip. "Come now, Keane, I'm a businessman. True, I wanted your plantation. Hell, with a vengeance. But to stoop to this sort of thing—" He shook his head vigorously.

Oliver wasn't convinced. "And what of the cane fires that have driven other plantation owners from their land? What of those threats?"

"I tell you, it's not me! I'm not the only investor with stakes here. It could have been any of those fellows from Boston or London. I've even heard tell that some of those plantation owners purposefully set those fires on their own lands. Made it look like a scare tactic so their wives and families wouldn't give them hell for selling out." Again, he shook his head and stuffed his handkerchief into his pocket. He jerked his chin to the remains of the gazebo. "I had nothing to do with that. Hell, if I was going to try to scare you, Keane, I'd do it on *your* property, not my own, dammit."

Oliver was suddenly inclined to believe Pomeroy. Expelling a heavy breath, he turned again to a bristling Stuart Jeffcoat, then to Alexa. "What the hell is going on?" he muttered into her hair as he gathered her close. "Something—it's not right. I feel it."

"Keane! Pomeroy!" A shout rang out from across the clearing. "I think you'd better have a look at this."

Grasping Alexa's hand in his, Oliver advanced upon the small group of men clustered about something on the ground.

"What—?" The crowd parted and Oliver's gaze riveted upon the charred heap crumpled upon the grass. A chill crept into his heart even as that rage smoldering in his chest flamed out of control when one of the men turned the heap over with one shove of his boot, exposing a smoke-blackened face.

Alexa brushed past him, jerked to a stop and sagged against him. "My God, it's Cyril. Oliver, it's Cyril. He's—"

"Dead, miss," one of the men interrupted. "Far as we can tell, he went up in flames. Standing too close when the thing exploded. Did you know him?"

Alexa opened her mouth and then those emerald pools lifted to Oliver. "It was Cyril. Oliver, why would Cyril wish to kill me after all this time? I've lived beneath the same roof with him for months and now. . . ?"

A footman wedged his way through the group. He stared for several long moments at Cyril, then nodded and turned to Alexa. "That him. He gave me the note for you, Miss Fairfield. That man there."

The footman pointed at Cyril. Oliver's mind flew. "Jesus—" He grasped Alexa's shoulders. "Listen, stay here."

"Where are you going?"

"What's this? I say, Keane!" Stuart piped up, pressing a gloved hand over his mouth when his eye strayed to Cyril. "By God, is there something amiss? Perhaps I could be of some service."

A rush of gratitude and apology swept through Oliver as his gaze locked with Jeffcoat's and a host of unspoken words passed between them. He clapped the British officer on the shoulder. "Absolutely, Jeffcoat. You can make sure Alexa stays here."

"He will not!" Alexa huffed. "Stuart, do not allow him to bully you. It's a frightful habit of his." And with arms akimbo, she glared up at Oliver. "You would do well to remember that I have not yet married you, Oliver Keane. We have a partnership, do we not? Wherever it is you're off to, you're not going there without me."

Oliver could only shake his head and slip his arm about her waist. "You're a damned difficult woman, Alexa."

"Indeed. You wouldn't have me any other way."

He glowered at her, then glanced at Jeffcoat. "Come along, Jeffcoat, you take your horse. We've not a moment to spare. You can be my damned second."

"I say! Right-o!"

By the time the landaulet sped through Bellefontaine's wrought-iron gates, Alexa was in the throes of pure terror. Even before the carriage pulled to a stop, she leaped from the thing, Oliver close at her heels. A knot of bile wedged into her throat as she shoved the front portal wide. The solid door thudded against the opposite wall, its echo a low, ominous wail through the darkness. Alexa froze, consumed with dread, her voice trapped in her chest. Oliver managed to light a taper and grasped her elbow, propelling her down one strangely dark hall.

"Shura!" His shouts rang strong and true, yet carried more than a hint of his own panic. This house was their home...the home where they would live all their lives and raise all those children. Yet the closer they drew to Alexa's chamber, the more darkly foreboding the halls seemed to become. Eerie shadows leaped at her from the darkness. And the very silence itself was like that of a tomb.

They burst through the chamber door as one, and froze. There, bathed in the glow of the flickering taper, was Shura, lying on her side upon the floor. Alexa's scream exploded from her mind, her vision blurring when Oliver bent to Shura and slowly turned her on her back. Alexa's knees buckled and she sagged against the bedpost, staring at the ivory-handled kitchen knife protruding from Shura's stomach. The wound oozed a flow of dark liquid that had spread like a horribly disfigured hand over Shura's white blouse.

Oliver bent over Shura. His hand lingered over the knife as though he knew not what to do...even as Alexa flew to Shura's side, mumbling incoherently, her mind paralyzed.

"She lives." Oliver grasped Shura's shoulders. "Just barely."

"Eleanor—"

Like a rasping wind, Shura's deep-throated whisper pierced the air. Alexa's blood ran cold.

"Eleanor?" Oliver repeated, his voice cracking. "She did this. The baby—"

"Eleanor—"

Suddenly, Alexa couldn't get enough air. Her lungs compressed until pain exploded through her chest.

"Where?" Oliver seethed, his fingers wrapping around Alexa's, somehow giving her strength. "Where has she taken him?"

Shura stared with eyes wide and fathomless at Oliver. "The cottage."

At that moment, Stuart Jeffcoat skidded into the room. "Keane, I—! I'll fetch the doctor." Before he could turn about, Oliver's command stilled him midstride.

"No time." Gingerly, he scooped Shura into his arms and strode swiftly from the room and down the hall, his words flung over his shoulder. "Can you stomach this, Jeffcoat?"

With sword clanking at his side, Stuart hurried after Oliver. " 'Tis a matter of life and death. Indeed, I shall perform as is expected of me by the queen hers—"

"Good. Take her in the landaulet, straight to the Governor's House. It's closer than the damned doctor. I know the governor maintains a physician on the premises. If anyone can save her, he can."

With lead-filled limbs, Alexa followed Oliver to the landaulet where he gently laid Shura upon the tufted velvet seat. Alexa bent and pressed a kiss upon her forehead, the tears now flowing freely.

"Man-beast," Shura murmured.

"Yes," Alexa whispered, her breath catching when Shura's teeth parted in a tiny smile.

"Good man," Shura rasped.

Alexa choked on a sob, then squeezed Shura's hand one last time before Stuart Jeffcoat climbed aboard.

"We need your horse," Oliver said as he untethered Jeffcoat's gray stallion and in one swift motion loosened the saddle and tossed it to the cobblestones.

"However I can be of help," Stuart replied with a swift salute.

Oliver's eyes glittered like cold diamonds in the moonlight. "Give me your pistol, Jeffcoat."

Alexa barely contemplated the reasons for such a request even as the gun exchanged hands.

"Godspeed, Keane," Stuart said crisply as Oliver tucked the gun into the back of his waistband.

As the landaulet leaped forward, Oliver lifted Alexa onto the horse's back and swiftly mounted behind her.

"Our baby!" she cried as Oliver slipped his arm about her waist and spurred the animal into a furious gallop. "Oliver, she has our baby—"

"I know" was all he replied.

A lifetime of darkness passed before they thundered to a halt outside the cottage. Alexa slid from the horse's back and ran for the cottage, stumbling on the hem of her skirt and falling to her knees. Oliver caught her up in his arms and cradled her against his chest. All reason, all logic had fled her long ago, and she pummeled his chest and arms until the sobs wracked her body.

"My baby...my baby...she's killed my baby!"

"She hasn't," Oliver said gruffly, giving her a swift shake.

"You don't know that! She could have! She has!"

"Alexa, look at me. Listen to me. If she killed baby Gabriel, she'd have no bargaining power...no strength, nothing left to lose."

Wildly, she shook her head. "She's a demon! She has no reason to take an innocent babe! Please, let me go, Oliver. Let me—my baby...I want to hold my baby."

"Listen." Her head snapped beneath the force of his shake. He loomed beyond all the tears blurring her vision, his voice sounding as if she were in a drum. "Do what I tell you. No matter what. Just do what I tell you in there." He crushed her in his arms. "God...please...just do what I tell you. Trust me, my love, my heart...trust me."

He wrapped his hand around hers and led her slowly up the stairs. Silence descended about them, and darkness, a shadowy pitch that became even darker as they neared the front door. All the windows were dark, yet the cottage seemed to lurk there, harboring some deep secret.

The front door swung open easily beneath Oliver's hand, it's well-oiled hinges silent...and then a floorboard creaked and a match flared somewhere deep in the parlor.

There, in the glow cast by a lantern, Eleanor sat upon a high-backed rocker, slowly rocking, back and forth. A peculiar grin twisted her features. In one arm she nestled a tiny bundle that was baby Gabriel. Clenched in her other fist was a black-handled, ten-inch long butcher knife.

"We've been waiting for you," she said, her eyes glowing like smoldering coals. Her smile dissolved into a demon's sneer when her eyes found Alexa in the shadows. "Ah, I see poor Cyril failed me this time. You live, whore-child."

A wail escaped Alexa's bone-dry throat and she lunged toward her child, only to be entrapped by Oliver's arm about her waist.

"No," he muttered against her ear. "Please—"

"Let her come." Eleanor bared her teeth, stilling Alexa in her tracks. Her wrist flicked and candlelight flashed off the knife as she twisted it, as if taking full measure of the blade, before settling the hilt upon the infant's stomach. The tip of the blade seemed to rest against the child's chin.

Oliver shuddered against Alexa. "He lives."

Eleanor's head inclined slightly. "Why, yes, he sleeps."

Alexa knew a relief so intense all strength momentarily escaped her limbs.

"Then give him to Alexa," Oliver said with deceptive softness. "Your grievance is with me. Not the child."

"My grievance is with your slut, Oliver. If you want your child, give me the whore."

"No."

"Then the child dies." Eleanor smiled. "It's that simple."

"Oliver!" Alexa spun against him, her fingers twisting into his shirt. "Please...our baby. Let her give him to you, please. I couldn't live without him . . . but he could—"

"And risk your life?" His teeth flashed in a feral smile, then he said, "I have no intention of losing either one of you, my dear."

"I have a plan, Oliver," Eleanor said so conversationally Alexa could only turn and stare at her with horror.

"Could it possibly be better than your scheme to kill Father?" Oliver countered. Alexa could only gasp at this revelation.

"You were always far too clever for your own good, Oliver. I was coconspirator. But, of course, no one will ever be able to prove it. I was in Chicago at the time."

"But your lackey Cyril was here."

"Indeed." Eleanor sniffed with satisfaction. "He was in love with me. Painfully so, ever since he came to work here. He even forgave me my indiscretions with the other men,

Oliver, something your father was incapable of doing. For years after I left here, we maintained a regular correspondence. He kept me abreast of all the goings-on here. A pitiful chap he was, nevertheless. Frightfully inept at composing love letters. But he had a ruthless streak to him. Why, only one as coldly cunning as *he* could plot to kill a man he'd served for the better part of fifteen years and manage to dispose of that tramp Lily Fairfield in so convenient a manner. How very clever of him to think of killing her in that jungle, then carrying her all the way to Bellefontaine so that the whole thing would look like a love affair gone awry. Even the governor himself believed that to be the case. Lily Fairfield the murderess. He killed her and ruined her reputation in one fell swoop." Her cold laugh bounced off the walls. "Cyril actually thought he would win my hand by devising such a perfect scheme."

Alexa's mind reeled with the enormity of it all. She nearly cried out in desperation to tear her sleeping son from this madwoman's arms.

Oliver's hold tightened about her waist, knowing well her thoughts. "Why wait fifteen years to kill them both? Surely Cyril had ample opportunity to carry out such a scheme long before then."

"Of course he did, but for what? Revenge is only so sweet, Oliver. I wanted more," Eleanor scoffed. "You know yourself that Bellefontaine was all but worthless to anyone but your father for many years. Profits were steadily declining. What little Gabriel made he gambled away or squandered on lavish parties to impress the plantocracy. But then those foreign investors started swarming all over the island. And all of them wanted Bellefontaine, something Gabriel refused to give them. Suddenly, the plantation was highly desirable property, something those businessmen would pay plenty for. So, Cyril and I hatched our scheme to get control of the plantation."

Alexa shook her head with confusion, her word but a croak. "How?"

Eleanor's lip twitched. "So frightfully simple, aren't you? Oliver obviously wanted you for one pitiful reason alone."

Her glowing eyes raked with deprecation over Alexa. "Cyril knew long ago who would inherit the place. It's bred into British servants to linger outside of closed doors, you know, especially when someone is dictating a will." Her lips bared in a maniacal snarl. "But I thought I knew my son. I thought his hatred for his father would make it that much easier to guide him in the proper direction to selling the plantation. It was all supposed to be so very easy. He was a man with one weakness . . . just one . . . that seething hatred for his own father that I had planted in him. Who better than *me* to use that weakness against him?" Her glittering eyes fastened upon Oliver and potent venom seemed to spew from her tongue. "You were supposed to be above mere ordinary men. You weren't governed by that *thing* between your legs like those animals. You loved no one, only your work. You were to marry Daphne...to acquire all that power and influence. You wouldn't have had time to tarry with Bellefontaine. You hated it."

"So you thought I would simply gain control of Bellefontaine from Alexa, then leave it to you to do with as you wished," Oliver said with palpable bitterness.

"And you would have. I *know* you would have. You would have let me have my revenge on this island . . . on Gabriel . . . on Lily Fairfield. . . ." Her gaze fastened upon Alexa. "Even on *her.*"

"At one time, perhaps I would have let you," Oliver said wryly. "Revenge . . . by destroying Father and his dream for mere money, and all because you never quite fit in here. Isn't that it, Mother? You never cared to understand why my father loved Barbados enough to forsake everything he'd had in Chicago, and then you had to watch him fall in love with Lily Fairfield because you couldn't bear to be a wife to him. And she was the toast of society here, wasn't she? And you, the outcast. You could hardly bear it, could you?"

Eleanor visibly shook upon her chair. "He thought she was *better* than me. That's why he loved her. No, he *worshipped* her, yet somehow kept himself from her as if she were the Virgin Mother herself. With me . . . ha! With me he was but a rutting animal...full of those carnal, savage desires. And well

I know why! He knew where I came from...that slum in Chicago I once called home. He never forgot it. They made a fool of me here. A *fool!* That feeling never dies, Oliver, not even fifteen years later. I—"

Suddenly, a tiny cry rent the air, piercing Alexa's heart. One by one, long, slow wails cleaved the silence. Eleanor froze and stared at the bundle. The wails merged, closer and closer until they became one tortured shuddering cry, broken only by trembling breaths. A surge of fierce protectiveness swelled through Alexa and she struggled vainly against the force of Oliver's embrace.

"Stop," Eleanor snapped at the child, leaping from her chair, then backing toward a darkened corner. The knife she held outstretched, its long blade dancing with the candle's light. "Why, Oliver? Why did you have to *weaken* now and fail me? Why *her?* The more you saw of her, the more she turned you against me. She poisoned your mind just like Lily Fairfield did to your father, and seduced your very will from you."

"Give me the knife," Oliver said, sweeping Alexa behind him and advancing slowly upon his mother. "My God, you're the child's grandmother."

Eleanor blinked. "Yes, yes I am, but he has the blood of that whore. And your father's blood."

"So do I." Step by cautious step he moved closer. "I wonder, Mother, if you ever loved anyone, including me. This greed of yours, this thirst for status, you've loved only that, and somehow along the way you began to mold me in your likeness until even I seemed beyond hope of ever finding love and true happiness. I was consumed, just like you, with hatred and revenge and a thirst for power. I would have done anything to achieve what I wanted. Just like you. But somewhere...somehow...you drifted beyond the confines of normal thought."

"No—" The blade waved menacingly. "I haven't, I tell you. Just listen, Oliver. It's so very simple. We'll kill her. Everyone will believe it's suicide because you refused to marry her. We can even take the brat with us, if you wish. We'll send him away somewhere to be cared for."

Oliver stopped, not two paces from her. Behind him, Alexa stared at the gun stuffed in the back of his waistband and gripped a carved mahogany chair so fiercely her arms shook. Prayers spilled from her lips and ran incessantly through her mind. All she could think of was cradling her baby in her arms, of smelling the sweet scent that was his alone, of listening to his soft breathing as he slept at her side. An ache too painful to bear spread its talons through her and tears spilled to her cheeks. The thought of life without him— The gun seemed to burn into her mind, prompting her to lunge for it, to point that black muzzle at Eleanor and force her to give up the child. *Trust me,* Oliver had told her. Her nails dug uselessly into her palms.

"And the plantation, Mother?" Oliver said. "What of it?"

Eleanor seemed quite startled. Then her eyes narrowed. "Yes, well, we sell it, of course. We take the money and rebuild your empire in Chicago. You left me no choice but to follow you here, Oliver. When Cyril wrote that you'd gotten the chit with child, well, you can imagine my distress! But you seemed far too concerned with rebuilding your empire. I thought you'd *never* return here. After all, eight months had passed and you had all but set a date with Daphne. Had you even mentioned any plans to return here, why, of course, Cyril would have quickly disposed of the girl and the child in some wonderfully catastrophic manner. As it was, neither Cyril nor I thought she would survive as long as she did managing the place. Luck, I suppose. So, I followed you here. I thought I could convince you to return. I hoped . . . I hoped that it was all some horrible misunderstanding, your sudden disappearance. But then you—you *threw* me from the house with a pitiful sack of coins and I—I was left with no choice but to kill the girl. With her gone, you would have understood . . . you would have been the Oliver I know."

"I'm sorry, Mother."

Alexa's heart careened to a stop.

Eleanor blinked with confusion. "Y-you're sorry?"

"Yes. For all of it. You're right, you know. I suppose I didn't realize it all until now. Hearing you say these words. It's all making sense to me now. Yes . . ."

Eleanor's eyes bulged, her breathing coming in laboring gasps through her teeth. "Yes . . . yes, Oliver. I *am* right. You believe me?"

"Your plan . . . it *is* the only way, isn't it? This sugar plantation business is . . . well, it's a pitiful excuse for wasting a man's life. I—" His laugh rang softly and he kneaded the muscles at the base of his neck, then shook his head. "I can hardly believe I even considered it."

"And the weather, Oliver. The weather is horrid here."

"Ghastly." He took a step nearer. "Here, the child is crying, Mother." Slowly, his strong arms reached for Gabriel. "You know, I was wondering if Daphne will have me," he said rather breezily, even as Eleanor seemed to clutch the infant just a hint nearer . . . as if suddenly unsure of his motives. "I suppose the proper amount of flowers and chocolates and visits upon bended knee will have to be considered. It will take some doing, of course, seeing as she thinks she's in love with that fop from England, lord what's-his-name."

"His title is fake, Oliver."

"Imagine that. So, what do you think, Mother? You've always been right on the mark with that sort of thing. You know, winning a debutante's heart."

It was as though new life had been breathed into the woman. Eleanor seemed to square her shoulders and lift her chin, her nose assuming its once lofty perch, long ago lost. "Why, yes, of course, I am." The knife flashed again as her wrist seemed to relax slightly. The blade angled toward the floor. "How kind of you to remember, Oliver. I—"

He moved so swiftly he was but a blur. Eleanor's shrill cry pierced the air and she seemed frozen in space. The blade slashed downward and cleaved the darkness in a flash of flame. Oliver stumbled a pace back, then shoved a chair between him and his mother.

"Alexa!" he called, and she moved woodenly as he thrust the warm, squirming bundle that was their child into her arms. She clutched Gabriel against her, her sobs mingling with his waning cries. And then the candle's light illuminated the vicious bloody slashes across Oliver's arms and chest . . . and gleamed off the shiny black pistol he leveled upon Eleanor.

Eleanor stood transfixed, shaking from head to toe, staring at the gun. "Y-you tricked me," she said in a strangely high-pitched voice. "You *betrayed* me. For Lily Fairfield's daughter."

Oliver worked a muscle in his jaw. "You indeed trained me well. I still will do anything to get what I want. Mother, why... how has it come to this? Here I stand holding a pistol on my very mother, knowing that you would kill my child and the woman I love as easily as you plotted to kill my father and Lily Fairfield. You've left me no other choice. Don't you realize that I would die for Alexa and my son? That I love them more than... more than all the worldly goods money could buy?"

Slowly, Eleanor shook her head. "I cannot allow this. What is to become of me? I have nothing now—you've taken it all. Cyril—the plantation—my revenge. I suppose a sanitarium is all that's left for me." She lifted the bloody knife, stared at it as if seeing it for the first time and cocked her head at an odd angle. "There's nothing quite left to do, is there?"

The hairs on the back of Alexa's neck rose. Oliver growled something and shoved the chair aside even as Eleanor plunged the knife to the hilt into her chest. Alexa stumbled back against the wall and slid to the floor. Eleanor staggered, fell into her son's arms and crumpled in a lifeless heap.

Alexa buried her face in her son's blanket... and then she struggled to her feet and staggered to Oliver. He half rose to his knees, then swept her into his arms, and for some time only the sounds of their weeping mingled with the silence of the night.

Chapter Twenty-One

"*Coming!*"

The banging again echoed through the house as if delivered to the front door by a fist both brawny and impatient. After stuffing the last of his beef sandwich into his mouth, Oliver tossed his napkin atop a pile of ledgers and lunged from his chair, swinging around his desk with a purposeful stride.

He thrust the study door wide, grumbled a curse through his sandwich and marched down the hall toward the foyer. Again, the house shook beneath that fist upon the front door. With a certain agitation he'd grown accustomed to over the past several weeks, Oliver glanced about for some sign of their newly acquired steward. A man shouldn't have to answer his own damned door! Then again, Alexa no doubt had him, the ladies' maids, and even Cook, all out in the garden weeding or transplanting or trimming . . . leaving him to fend for himself. Fine. He'd made his own lunch. But answering his own door? His father had never answered *his* door, dammit.

Still chewing furiously, he swung the door open, intent upon scowling in a manner suitable to the king of a castle, only to find his jaw suddenly locked.

There, upon the front stoop, glowering from beneath the brim of a natty brown bowler was Theodore MacAdoo. "Oliver Keane," he boomed in a voice long misused by cigars and drink. "Well? Let me in, man. It's too damned hot." With a grunt, MacAdoo shouldered past Oliver into the foyer.

Oliver managed to close the door behind him and forced the rest of the sandwich down his throat where it managed to lodge. "MacAdoo," he said, shoving his hand at the other man.

"Had to come," MacAdoo muttered in his characteristic manner. "Not quite right, all this." His head swiveled about and he nodded. "Impressive. Damned impressive."

Oliver clasped his hands behind his back. What the hell was MacAdoo doing here, looking far larger, far more imposing, far more capable of tearing Oliver limb from limb for jilting his daughter Daphne, despite Oliver's carefully penned letter explaining why? "Yes," Oliver replied. "Thank you, sir."

MacAdoo's slate-gray eyes skewered Oliver. "Well, dammit, what's going on? I thought we had a deal."

Oliver blinked, then indicated the hall. "My study is far more comfortable, sir." MacAdoo mumbled something and ambled along behind Oliver in that rolling gait suitable to a man of his immense size.

Upon entering the study, Oliver found his eye immediately drawn beyond the wall of windows to his wife and baby picnicking beneath a cabbage tree. Picture perfect they were. His whole life was picture perfect. What man could ask for more?

MacAdoo had settled his bulk in a chair before the desk and studied Oliver from beneath bushy white eyebrows.

"I couldn't marry your daughter," Oliver said, jutting his chin forward. "I didn't love her."

MacAdoo's eyebrows dived low over his bulbous nose and Oliver tensed in anticipation of a good long bellow. Or would a man like MacAdoo resort to using his fists? *"What?"* MacAdoo roared. "Dammit, man, I don't want to talk about my daughter! Good God, the day after you disappeared, she eloped with that idiot from England, that phony lord something-or-other." MacAdoo shook his head and rubbed a meaty paw over his jaw. "Said she was in love with the man, God help us all. No, you did the right thing not marrying her. I suppose a man shouldn't say that about his own daughter, but hell. Maybe it was my fault..." Air hissed between his teeth and his eyes drifted toward the windows at Oliver's back. "Her mother still hasn't recovered, of course, but Daphne claims she's happy."

"That's all that matters, sir," Oliver replied, settling low in his chair behind the desk.

"The hell it is," MacAdoo growled. "For a woman like Daphne, perhaps, but for men like us, Keane? The challenges to be met in this world of industrialized change are what men like us are made for! We meet the daily risks head-on. We do anything to succeed...even agree to marry women we don't love. But that's all in the past and you're still the same brilliant man I would have made my damned partner. I heard about your financial collapse from your lawyer. The bad luck, hell, we all have that. But your investment in those futures...." MacAdoo shook his head. "That troubled me. It wasn't like you to risk everything like that. You were tempting fate there, Keane. I could almost believe you *wanted* to lose it all. As if you didn't care anymore."

"Perhaps I didn't."

"Ha!" MacAdoo's fist punched the air. "Dammit, I knew it. It was a woman, wasn't it? Nothing can turn a brilliant man into a reckless fool like a woman. So who the hell is she?"

"She's—" Oliver glanced out the windows, but Alexa and the baby were no longer beneath the tree. "She's—" A grin inched across his face and a warmth suffused his entire being. "She's my wife."

"Look at you." MacAdoo shook his head again. "By God, I can barely stomach it, though you're almost enough to make an old coot like me damned jealous. But that's fine, just fine. I'm certain she won't mind the weather in Chicago at this time of year."

"I'm not following you."

"Ah, hell, Keane, the reason I'm here is to offer you a job. I want you as my partner in my international shipping line."

"I have no capital."

MacAdoo snorted and shifted in the chair. "To hell with that. You will in time. Keane, I need a man with your Great Lakes experience and shipping brilliance in my organization. Do you want to know the damned truth of the matter? I've had my eye on you for quite some time. Wanted to merge our companies long ago. But how to do it? And then you started courting my daughter and it all fit neatly into place without any maneuvering necessary on my part. A family thing, you know." MacAdoo suddenly leaned forward and pounded his fist upon the desk. "Dammit, man, name your price. I'll pay you whatever you want. You can have a house, two houses, servants, the works. Memberships to the gentlemen's clubs and a share of the damned profits. Well?"

With a wistful smile, Oliver leaned back in his chair and feasted his eyes on the lush landscape spread like a brilliant carpet before him, a landscape as dazzling as the future MacAdoo had just spread out on the table. "Behold the Caribbean isle of Barbados, MacAdoo," Oliver said softly, his eyes drifting to the horizon where the ocean sparkled like a radiant jewel.

"What?"

"Here the pace is languid, the mood tranquil. Here the softness of the air induces the islanders to go unhurried and at once bids the stranger to relax. So fair, so verdant, with a perpetual warmth of springtime. Where blossoms follow blossoms. Where the brilliance of the stars at night is matched only by the clarity of the waters by day." His gaze swept to MacAdoo who simply stared at him.

"Hell, man, perhaps it's sleep you need. Lots of it."

"Sleep?" Oliver laughed deep and hearty. "Sleep is for people who live under gray skies and worry about life. A man wants to be awake in a place like this. My wife and I belong here, sir. Nowhere else."

And then, over MacAdoo's shoulder, he saw her, poised just inside the door holding Gabriel. In one swift motion, he leaped from his chair and scooted around his desk. "Alexa—"

She stared up at him with a peculiar sparkle in her eye. When he drew near, she placed a hand on his chest. "That was quite beautiful, Oliver. I—I never thought you felt that deeply about the island."

Oliver drew her fingers to his lips. "You don't know the half of what I feel deeply about, my love," he murmured, then drew her into the room. "Theodore MacAdoo, my wife, Alexa."

MacAdoo jerked to his feet with a grunt and clutched his bowler rather awkwardly to his chest. An appreciative twinkle lit his eyes as he nodded at Alexa, then winked at Oliver.

"I—I didn't realize we had guests," Alexa said with an apologetic smile. "I was going upstairs to tend to Shura."

"Of course," Oliver said, taking his son from her arms. "How is she today?"

"Better. Much better. In a few weeks' time she should be on her feet again." Again she smiled, and MacAdoo fussed with his bowler. Oliver suppressed a grin and slipped his arm about her waist, brushing his lips close to her ear. "Wait for me upstairs, wench." He watched the smooth undulation of her narrow hips as she left the room, knowing he would do the very same each and every day for the rest of his life. The thought made his chest swell with potent emotion.

MacAdoo scratched the back of his neck and studied his hat. "Well, Keane, I know when I'm in over my head. I don't think there would be any point in trying to change your mind."

"Not if you intend to try to get me to Chicago. But compromise holds tremendous opportunity, sir. That's a lesson worth learning."

MacAdoo seemed to study him closely, his gaze flickering over the baby cooing in Oliver's arms. "Compromise, eh? With a man holding a baby." With a shake of his head, he said, "Fine, I'll listen. You got any whiskey around here?"

"Sangaree," Oliver replied, moving to the sideboard. "It's a local drink. My father's favorite. And mine, too. Trust me, MacAdoo, you'll love it."

Alexa closed the chamber door behind her and moved slowly into the room. She paused in a ray of brilliant sunlight, closing her eyes and rubbing the ache that throbbed in her neck.

"What took you so long?"

She was smiling even before she opened her eyes and found Oliver seated in a chair deep in one corner of the room. Her lips parted and wild heat coursed through her. He was shirtless, wearing only those impossibly tight black knee breeches that hugged his narrow hips and bulging thighs and left bare the strong length of his calves. Like a fearsome lion he sat there, his eyes glowing with unspoken desires, his furred chest expanding to fill her vision with his every breath. That wild, savage heat emanated from him and she all but took a step back when he rose slowly to his feet and moved toward her. With every arrogant jut of his hips, every clenching and unclenching of his fists, Alexa's blood thundered all the more feverishly in her ears. He paused not a breath from her and she nearly cried out, so desperately did she want him to touch her.

"Wife," he whispered.

"Where's Gabriel?" she said breathlessly, even when his warm hands encircled her upper arms.

"Sleeping." His lips brushed over her temple. "And the servants are conspicuously absent, as usual. I think I could get used to that. We have, my dear, all the time in the world."

She spread her palms over his ridged belly, then threaded her fingers through the silky black hair covering his chest. "And Theodore MacAdoo?"

A deep rumbling filled Oliver's chest. "As we speak, he's frantically drawing up agreements to open shipping lanes between Bridgetown and Boston, not to mention Virginia, Bermuda, England and Tangier."

Her eyes lifted to his. "Oh, Oliver—"

A dazzling flash of white teeth amidst all that dark passion. "He's going to ship out all the sugar I can harvest. He'll receive a cut of the profits, of course. A fair percentage, I believe. *He* didn't buy into it at first."

"But you convinced him."

"I told him I would make him a millionaire yet again. How could the man resist?"

With a shuddering sigh, Alexa dissolved into his arms. "Have I told you that you're a wonderful businessman, Oliver?"

"At the moment, I'd rather be a wonderful lover," he said, his hands cupping her buttocks through the linen of her skirt.

Alexa inhaled of his heady scent, wallowing in the feel of powerful male against her. "No, you're a wonderful businessman. First, you convinced Pomeroy that his venture to turn all the plantations into resorts wouldn't work nearly as well if there wasn't at least one fully operating plantation left on the island. What better for tourism than an old-world sugar plantation? Pomeroy loved the idea! Even he wanted to make you a partner. How could he not? Oh, Oliver, you *are* brilliant."

"No, I'm not. I'm just a man who's half-mad with desire for his wife. I had to come up with something to get MacAdoo out of the house . . . and me up here . . . with you. My dear, I will lose my mind if I can't make love to you fully, as you were meant to be made love to, very soon."

"Soon, darling. I suppose Stuart is quite pleased with his new commission in Her Majesty's Navy, and I hear Lady Alleyne has captured the heart of a British general. We all seem to have found happiness."

"You're frustrating me, wife."

Alexa gasped when his hands slipped beneath her blouse, his long fingers caressing her back, her ribs, then claiming the full sides of her breasts. "I—I believe," she whispered as he brushed his lips over hers, "yes, I believe that enough time has passed since the baby was born."

"You're healed?"

"I am." She pressed a palm against his chest. "And you, my love? Are you yet healed?"

A fleeting pain glimmered in the smoldering depths of his eyes and was gone. "A man's soul can ache for what never was, for what could have been, only so long. I have searched my heart and blamed myself...and I have come to realize my mother's fate was in her control. Not mine. I couldn't have changed the course of her life without changing my own and losing all that I am now. All that I now live for. If my penance is living the rest of my days with you, my love, I will gladly bear that burden. Gladly."

He gathered her close, his arms tightening fiercely about her as a shudder passed through him. "I love you," she whispered.

"I love you. So easy those words are to say now...and yet—" His thumb brushed over her lower lip. "Somehow three simple words could never quite convey all that I feel for you...and our baby. I doubt any words could."

Her lips angled upward. "Then show me, Oliver. You *are* a brilliant man, are you not?"

Flames leaped in his eyes as he pressed her hips tight against his arousal. "Aren't you going to perform your fertility dance for me?"

Alexa arched an eyebrow and clasped her hands about his, slipping from his arms. "You mean the *biguine?*" She turned about and slipped her blouse over her head. She watched it float to the floor in a flimsy linen heap and began a smooth undulation of her hips. Closing her eyes, she flung her head back, feeling Oliver's heat behind her even though he didn't touch her. "This isn't a fertility dance, Oliver," she murmured, slipping her fingers into the knot at her waist.

"The hell it isn't." His growl was low, ominous and wonderfully arousing. "Alexa—"

With one tug upon that knot, her linen skirt pooled at her feet, leaving her clad in nothing but the sheerest of silk chemises. Licking her lips, she shrugged the tiny straps off her shoulders, and turned slowly about to face him. With an abandon stoked by the surge of emotion enveloping her, she moved in smooth, languid rhythms, her eyes fastened upon his. One tug upon the tiny ribbon and the chemise sagged from her breasts. With arms outstretched toward him, she swayed in time to some silent, haunting beat that thumped like hot liquid through her blood. And when she thought she couldn't bear it another moment, he swept her into his arms and bore her to the bed.

"You can tell me now," he rasped against her parted lips as he gently laid her upon the downy ticking.

"Tell you what?" Her pulse raced as he stripped off his breeches in one swift motion. All air fled her lungs for that one glorious moment when he stood magnificent and potent in the sunlight.

He nestled his hips intimately against hers and bent to spread impassioned kisses over her breasts. "Just tell me now . . . it won't matter . . ." His teeth caught one nipple and tugged gently, until a sigh escaped her. "You *are* a witch, aren't you?"

Her laugh was low and husky. Cradling his head against her, she reveled in the languid sensations coursing through her. "If it would make you feel better, Oliver—"

"Yes." He tore the chemise from her with one sweep of his hand. "Yes, I suppose it would."

Her hands slipped to his shoulders, kneading the rippling sinew beneath taut, sunbaked skin. With eyes closed, she arched her back, nearly crying out when he entered her with one sweet, long thrust.

"Tell me—" His breath was hot against her lips. "Nothing else will ever make sense to me—nothing else—is logical."

She opened her eyes and stared up at him. And then her arms slipped about his neck and a secretive smile curved her lips. "As you wish, my love. Whatever you wish, for all eternity."

* * * * *